PENGUIN BOOKS

That Green Eyed Girl

Julie Owen Moylan was born in Cardiff and has worked in a variety of jobs, from trainee hairdresser and chip shop attendant aged sixteen, to business management consultant and college lecturer in her thirties.

She then returned to education to complete her Master's degree in Film before going on to complete a further Master's degree in Creative Writing. Julie is an alumna of the Faber Academy's Writing a Novel course. She lives in Cardiff with her husband and two cats.

That Green Eyed Girl

JULIE OWEN MOYLAN

PENGUIN BOOKS

PENGUIN BOOKS

UK | USA | Canada | Ireland | Australia
India | New Zealand | South Africa

Penguin Books is part of the Penguin Random House group of companies
whose addresses can be found at global.penguinrandomhouse.com

First published by Penguin Michael Joseph 2022
Published in Penguin Books 2023

001

Typeset by Jouve (UK), Milton Keynes
Printed and bound in Great Britain by Clays Ltd, Elcograf S.p.A.

The authorized representative in the EEA is Penguin Random House Ireland,
Morrison Chambers, 32 Nassau Street, Dublin D02 YH68

A CIP catalogue record for this book is available from the British Library

ISBN: 978–1–405–94942–2

www.greenpenguin.co.uk

For Sean

Those cool and limpid green eyes
A pool wherein my love lies
So deep that in my searching for happiness
I fear that they will ever haunt me
All through my life they'll taunt me

Jimmy Dorsey

I

New York City, 1975

The day the box arrived, my mother thought she was Jesus.

She used to be so normal but then she wasn't and I don't know exactly when it started, but when I thought about it I couldn't remember the last time she wasn't missing in some way.

That day began as a soft blue morning yet the heat was already fierce and defiant, and my skin felt sticky with it. The air was filled with the tinny sound of sad songs blasting from the old transistor radio: Janis Ian singing about beauty queens and ugly-duckling girls.

Inside our cramped kitchen there was just me humming along to those sad songs and trying not to think too much. I was carefully covering my crackers with margarine, but smooth side not crevice side, because I had worries about the first pool party of the summer and a navy one-piece I hated. On the radio, the DJ insisted we buy a brand of cold cream for our skin and then shifted into 'I'm Not in Love' by 10cc. I couldn't tell whether I was in love either, but as I stood there that morning, I was considering the possibility with a boy that I had not yet spoken one word to.

I finished buttering my crackers, arranging them neatly on a blue plate before filling the coffee pot with water as the song faded to the part where the girl sings that 'big boys don't cry', and I wondered about that: about Cal, and whether he cried.

The sounds of my mother coughing interrupted my daydreaming, muffled at first and then louder as her bedroom door opened and closed, before her feet padded down the hallway and into the bathroom. My heart started to race a little and the familiar knot of worry clenched my stomach as I waited to see what mood she was in. Two black flies buzzed angrily while they tried to free themselves from an old strip of yellow flypaper that hung down from our kitchen window, the ends of it curling with age.

I grabbed her favourite cup, a brown-beige pottery mug with an orange band of sunshine wrapped around it and the word 'Morning' written in large white print on one side. It came with a matching saucer and as soon as I set it down on the kitchen table, I knew my mother would fill it with cigarette ash and coffee spill. I poured her coffee, black, no sugar, just the way she liked it, and waited.

The toilet flushed and I heard water running, then the bathroom door opened and there was more coughing. I swallowed hard, took a deep breath and then reached across and turned the radio down so low I could barely hear it, because she didn't like loud noises or sad songs. These days my mother preferred quiet at all times.

*

2

I could smell my mother before she set foot in the kitchen: the stale stench of cigarettes that clung to her and lingered in the rooms of our apartment even when she wasn't there; her unwashed skin and the sourness of her sweat, which was exactly four days old. I knew this because it was four days since my father last found a reason to return home to collect fresh clothing, before he disappeared again and she went back to avoiding people.

'Tell them I'm in the bathtub,' she would say and I would obey. I guess I didn't give it all that much thought to begin with. I was too busy thinking about school and Cal to really notice. But then it carried on, until the visitors just stopped calling.

Those days, that's just how it was. On the nights my father came home, my mother would be freshly bathed, but blank-faced and chain-smoking in her armchair. Occasionally there would be bursts of white-hot rage that exploded if she smelled perfume on my father's clothes. The scent of Charlie could set her off for hours, and then the silence would come again, brooding and bitter.

On nights when there were just the two of us, my mother would appear ghostlike at the end of my bed; childlike and whimpering, she'd plead to be allowed to stay because she couldn't stand her own company, although she never said so.

'OK,' I would mutter, but not one part of me wanted her there.

I should have told someone, I guess, but as time went

on it was like a broken bone that hadn't set properly. I had just learned to walk differently.

Finally, my mother appeared in the kitchen doorway, her face pale and her eyes puffy and ringed in red. She didn't speak. I tried to smile but my lips felt pinched and heavy. I hated the staleness of her, the strangeness of her. I wanted her to go back to how she used to be.

'I made you coffee. Do you feel like eating something?' I asked.

My mother didn't respond. She didn't even look at me.

She was smoking her usual Chesterfields, and a long grey chain of ash hovered dangerously close to her quilted pink robe as she wandered in and settled herself in her seat at our kitchen table. For a moment, the cigarette threatened to send her into a blaze of flames, but at the last minute she edged a shaky hand towards the saucer and the ash tumbled swiftly into a tiny pool of coffee spill. Her fingertips tried to scrub away an imaginary stain over the scratched corner of our kitchen set, reading it like Braille, back and forth. The clawing at the table edge continued for a few beats and then she paused and reached down for her coffee cup. She took a long gulp and rested the cigarette on the edge of the saucer.

Her hands began to tug at the neck of her robe, which was tightly buttoned up to her throat, even though it was already too hot to breathe in our kitchen and the cool-air system was making a strange rattling noise that didn't sound good. She pulled at her robe as if it was choking her, but then she stopped, distracted by an invisible something, and left her fingers hanging like little claws in mid-air.

The heat felt stifling and my mother's unwashed smell made me nauseous. I pulled the window latch up and opened it wide. The dusty air clung to my skin and I could smell the rotting garbage down below in the street. The city was going broke, they said on the news. Everything was crumbling and the air was filled with the stench of something dying.

As I snapped the window closed, I heard a strange hissing noise I couldn't place. I spun around to see what it was and then I realized: it was coming from my mother's lips.

'*Jessssssssusss,*' she said, but so quietly that the word was barely detectable. Then silence, not another sound.

I turned the radio off. Watching her out of the corner of my eye while I stirred creamer in my coffee and lifted a cracker to my mouth, chewing carefully. She was staring into the distance as if she was looking up at someone. Then the noise came again, only slightly louder this time.

My mother whispered through clenched teeth as though she were pushing the words out of her mouth against her will.

'. . . *me . . . Jesssusss . . .*'

This time I was sure that I'd heard her correctly.

'Mom, what's wrong?' I asked.

My mouth went dry and my throat felt tight. She didn't

seem to be able to hear me and the words grew louder and louder until she was shouting them at the wall.

Strange sounds fell from my mother's mouth, her lips moving quickly, stumbling to get the words out: odd pleadings; wild, rambling sentences. All the while she was holding her coffee cup just an inch or so away from her mouth, her eyes staring up wild and terrified, and her cigarette burning to grey in the saucer.

'MOM!' I yelled at her to make her stop.

At the sound of my voice, she froze and her eyes flickered, searching for where the voice had come from. She started to rock back and forth, her miserable shoulders hunched lower and lower over the table and then she screamed as loud as she could:

'...ME...JEEEESSSUUUSSSS!'

The rocking grew more violent and the coffee slopped out of the sides of her mug and splashed on to the kitchen table. Her hands were still clutching the cup, but her eyes were closed and her face twisted and contorted as if she was in pain.

Then a loud ringing noise split the air.

The sound of the telephone startled both of us and my mother scraped back her chair so violently that her coffee cup dropped to the table, smashing into several brown clay shards where there used to be orange sunshine and white words.

Pulling the kitchen door closed, I scooped up the telephone, muttering a non-committal 'Hello' down the line, my hands trembling, praying it was my dad, but of course it wasn't.

'Hello . . . Is that Mrs Winters?'

I recognized the woman's voice on the other end of the line and my heart sank.

'Yes, it is,' I offered, tentatively adopting my best impression of my mother's voice.

'Mrs Winters . . . this is Mrs Shaughnessy. I'm calling because Ava missed her exam last week and we don't appear to have an absence note on her file. I'm so sorry to bother you during the summer holidays but we do need a sickness note otherwise it will have to go down as a Fail.'

Suddenly, I heard a familiar scraping noise coming from behind the kitchen door and a wave of panic swept over me.

'I'll . . . send it right over . . . just as soon as I can. You'll have it by the end of the week.'

'Well, that's fine, Mrs Winters . . . Maybe you could come over in person? It might be good to talk to you – or Mr Winters – about Ava's progress lately. I have some concerns about—'

'I really have to go . . . but yes, I'll certainly take care of that. Thank you so much for calling.'

I was becoming a smooth liar these days but the school would have to wait. I hung up before Mrs Shaughnessy could say another word, my heart slamming against my chest as I ran to the kitchen door and pushed it wide open.

The window leading out to the fire escape yawned open; the kitchen door slapped back and forth in the breeze. My mother's pink quilted housecoat lay abandoned on the floor.

In the four or five steps it took me to run to the black metal staircase, I had a horrible vision of my mother's lifeless body spread-eagled across the sidewalk. Grabbing on to the iron railings, I began looking around at the buildings in my eyeline and all the time trying not to look down. Muttering to myself, '*It's OK . . . It's OK.*'

Gulping at a lungful of hot dusty air, I clenched my teeth and bent my head down towards the street. My hands gripped tightly on to the black metal rail and my fingers danced over deep familiar grooves where the paint had been carved away. The whole city smelled of hot asphalt and burning garbage. My breath caught at the back of my throat as I started to scour the street below. People were walking along the same as always. I figured they wouldn't be doing that if there was a woman lying dead on the ground, so I looked down properly.

Down in the street, two men were yelling at each other, their gruff voices competing with the background of a constant siren. I could see the faded red and white awning of Luca's, the old Hungarian bakery across the street. A couple of old ladies were waiting patiently to collect pastries for their morning coffee; a stray dog circled them, barking wildly.

I put my hands either side of my nose and exhaled like a prayer.

*

Making my way through the apartment, I picked up an old picture of my mother doing a funny little dance and smiling at the camera. I'd watched enough TV shows where hard-boiled detectives like Kojak went from coffee shop to coffee shop flashing a grainy picture of someone, and they usually found them.

Once I got to the bottom of the stairs, I raced past the line of neat green mailboxes on the wall that were as usual bursting with uncollected mail. Only ours seemed to get emptied regularly and that was just because I did it these days. Underneath the mailboxes, taking up most of the space on the hallway floor, was a large box covered in brown paper and brightly coloured stamps which I stumbled over, catching my shin on a sharp edge.

Rubbing at my leg and quietly cussing under my breath, I pulled open the front door with its peeling blue paint and stood there, staring up and down the street. Women in pastel dresses and white shoes walked by, trying to look ice-cream cool, while young men in faded T-shirts hung around on the street corner whistling at girls. The stray dog was still barking like crazy, while blasting guitar sounds from a tinny radio were drowned out by grumbling trucks and sirens. In the distance were smoke trails from yet another garbage fire weaving across the sky like patchwork.

There were so many people swarming in different directions. But none of them was my mother.

2

New York City, 1955

Gillian had left the photographs spread over our kitchen table. There were three of them, all taken on a sunny afternoon out on the fire escape in our apartment. In two of them my face was unaware and caught in shadows, but in the third photograph I was smiling without a care in the world, my hands resting gently on the black iron railings.

I bundled them up to stow safely in the drawer where we kept our private things. The drawer sat in a sideboard that was old and scratched, bought from Goodwill shortly after we moved in together. As I gathered up the photographs, I noticed Gillian had written my name on the back of them, along with the date and place, and it made me smile to see the way she catalogued everything about our lives, thorough and precise.

As I closed the drawer, I caught a glimpse of her pale green silk scarf abandoned over the back of our arm-chair. It was one of my favourite things to borrow and I tied it around my neck in a casual way, letting the soft edges trail down my blouse.

I dashed across the kitchen, gulping down some

coffee and nibbling at the toast that I'd spread with a little honey and a pinch of salt the way my grandmother used to like it. As I washed my breakfast dishes in the soapy water, singing along to the jazz on the radio, I noticed our whiskey glasses sitting on the coffee table, one of them still outlined with Gillian's lipstick. Collecting and rinsing out the glasses, I carefully dried them and placed them back on the shelf and took a final glance around, satisfying myself that everything was as it should be. Our two coffee cups, our whiskey glasses, our favourite china plates. The things we loved. I smiled at how perfect our life was together . . . behind closed doors.

As I ran down the hallway, stopping to grab my purse, I noticed to my horror that I'd spilled tiny drops of coffee on Gillian's beautiful scarf and a burst of irritation flooded through me. I was such a klutz sometimes. I dabbed at it with damp hands but it only made it worse and I didn't want to be late, so I slipped the scarf into my purse and vowed to clean it before Gillian realized it was gone.

Stopping briefly on my way out of the building to inspect my face in the dusty old mirror that hung over a neat line of small green mailboxes, I caught a glimpse of bright eyes, a layer of red lipstick and freshly permed curls that framed my face. I could hear the sound of show tunes coming from the downstairs apartment where our neighbour Mr Prince lived. I smiled at the thought of him singing along to 'Some Enchanted Evening' at the top of his voice alone in his rooms, before slamming the heavy blue front door shut behind me and stepping out into the world.

I was humming a song that I couldn't remember the words to as I arrived at the school gates, and the sun was shining. Small groups of girls had taken their revision into the park, and I could just make out the navy and gold of their uniforms as they sat around on the grass, lazily inspecting books that lay open and mostly unread. I had a free period, so I was later arriving than usual, and when I walked through the carved wooden doors the main lobby was empty, apart from Judith, our school secretary, who was fussing over some minor emergency as usual.

It was the first time I'd set eyes on Judith that week. She was standing in her usual spot, just outside her office, where she could see all the comings and goings of school life. It was her favourite place to trap people into conversation, and the teaching staff made jokes about it behind her back. I took three quick steps, hoping to get past her without an inquisition. But no such luck.

'Would you look at the state of these? I don't know why I waste my time.'

I tried to ignore her. Judith was an awful gossip and, as much as I didn't like the other teachers making jokes, I really didn't care for her much. She had the soft pouchy face of a busybody, sharp little eyes that inspected us whenever she was around, and there was not one conversation you could have with her that didn't involve her getting into somebody's business. I sighed softly and made a sympathetic noise in her direction but carried on walking.

'You would think by now they would be better than this,' she said.

My good mood was draining away and I could feel a slight headache beginning above my left eye; a dull thudding made worse by the knowledge that I was now trapped for several minutes whether I liked it or not.

I sighed and tried to focus on whatever it was that Judith was complaining about, nodding and smiling as she went on. I wanted to see Gillian before I headed to my classroom, but there was no stopping Judith. On and on she went without pause until eventually I couldn't stand it any more, and I made a weak excuse to get away.

'Where are you off to?' she said as I started to move towards the teachers' lounge.

'I . . . I've got Ninth Grade English now.'

'I thought this was your free period?' she said sharply.

'Err . . . yes . . .' I stuttered over my lies.

Judith typed out the entire school timetable, so she knew right away I was lying. I felt such a fool. She stopped talking, and I saw the glance of hurt across her face. She was upset with me and I couldn't take it back. I felt cruel, and I hated to feel cruel. I shuffled awkwardly from foot to foot and tried to think of something soothing to say.

'That's a pretty blouse,' I said, although it was her usual plain white shirt. Faded and slightly too tight under the arms. Judith stared at me for a moment as if she wanted to say something and then turned away.

I rubbed at my aching temples and made mental promises that next time I would be extra nice. Maybe I'd even sit and have coffee with her. She wasn't that bad.

Gillian was perched on top of her desk with a paintbrush in her mouth, turning a painting this way and that, as if she was looking for the right way to frame it. She smiled as she saw me approaching. I was still fretting over upsetting Judith but, as usual, one look at Gill's face cheered me up.

'Hey, you! Wanna go to the movies after work? There's a picture I'd really like to see,' I said.

Gillian took the paintbrush out of her mouth and frowned.

'I've got so much to do. You could go on your own, just this once, and I'll see you at home?'

'I hate going alone. There's plenty of time to do exam prep. *Please* say yes.' I grinned at her, making a pleading face that I knew she found hard to resist. She laughed.

'OK . . . but you're paying.'

'It's a date,' I whispered and blew her a silent kiss.

Just as I was about to walk away, who should be walking right by Gillian's classroom . . . but Judith. Her shoes clipping against the parquet floors, she gave us her usual inquisitive stare. I tried not to meet her eye.

'Good morning, Judith,' Gillian called out in a silly mocking voice, and then started giggling. I knew she didn't mean anything by it, but I could tell by the stubborn set of Judith's back as she disappeared down the corridor that she was hurt.

'Don't do that!' I hissed at Gillian, but she just laughed.

'That woman is always staring at people. Gives me the creeps,' she whispered to me in a low voice.

'Don't be cruel, Gill,' I replied but she pulled a funny face to make me laugh and I couldn't be cross with her.

As I left school that day to get the bus, I was mentally ticking off things I'd forgotten to do and made a note to call my sister, Franny, if we didn't get home too late that evening. I had some errands to run across town but by the time I got to the movie theatre, I still had twenty minutes to kill.

I decided to call into the diner across the street to get a cup of coffee and a piece of their peach cobbler, which was a particular favourite of mine. I slid on to a seat at the long grey counter as I didn't intend to stay long; the girl in her candy-striped uniform and white hat seemed glad of the company and started making conversation, mostly about the weather.

The diner was empty except for an old man reading a newspaper in one of the booths. Ordering my coffee and pie, I settled myself on the stool and checked the clock to make sure I wasn't running late for Gillian. The girl behind the counter drifted away to wipe up a spill and I sat there, eating my cobbler and staring at the people on the other side of the glass windows.

The door to the diner swung open behind me and, when I glanced over my shoulder, I saw to my horror it was Judith. I had no choice but to wave at her, but my smile felt rigid and forced. She didn't smile at all, just kind of squinted in a slight frown when she saw me, as if something was bothering her. I silently cursed Gillian for mocking Judith; I would have to pay the price for that. I sighed and chewed nervously at the inside of my cheek.

'Hello, Dovie,' she said without much enthusiasm, and I knew she was still upset. I felt an old familiar feeling of discomfort as my stomach clenched; the misery of someone being unhappy with me. I picked at a thread on the cuff of my blouse and tried to think of something to say.

'Judith! What a surprise to see you in this part of town. You're a long way from home?'

'I've been to look at a new apartment. You know my landlady is selling our building? Well, she had an offer . . . so I need to find somewhere quickly. It's so difficult to find a good place that I can afford.'

I made sympathetic noises and gave her a weak little smile, all the time watching the clock hands on the wall moving far too slowly. Judith was warming to her subject now, and our earlier upset appeared to be forgiven if not forgotten.

'I thought I'd found something the other day, over on 23rd. I mean, it's a nice place and all, but they want so much money up front and I need a few more paychecks before I'll have enough. It's not so easy on a secretary's pay but you think they care? Oh no . . . Well, not that you would know about that, being a teacher of course . . .'

She pinched her lips together and shook her head as if the thought of her salary was too much to bear and took a deep breath.

'So . . . how was it?' I asked.

'How was what?'

'The apartment?'

'Oh, that. It was just awful. A roach crawled across my shoe and I'm pretty sure there were mice.'

'It's tough to find a good place these days.'

'Tell me about it.'

I pulled as sympathetic a face as I could manage, desperate not to upset her again, and Judith acknowledged the gesture. She pulled her stout little frame on to the red stool beside me and leaned across to the girl behind the counter as though she was about to whisper some great secret to her.

'Can I get a soda . . . and I'll take a piece of that cobbler? It looks good.'

The girl scribbled on her notepad, stuck the pencil behind her ear in what she presumably thought was a jaunty fashion, and cut a hunk of peach cobbler which she slid on to a white plate.

'What are you doing here? Hot date?' Judith asked.

'No . . . I'm meeting Gillian. We're going to see a movie.'

'She's your lodger, isn't she?'

'Yes, although I don't really think of her that way. We just share the place.'

'I expect you have a lovely apartment. Must be so nice to be settled like that . . . just the two of you.'

Did it seem pointed the way she said that? I couldn't say. I don't think for one minute she gave much thought to us. We were just colleagues. But something about her made me uncomfortable, and I felt trapped, somehow.

Her voice droned on and on about apartment-hunting and how hard she was finding everything. I really wasn't taking too much notice, but then she leaned in close and said:

'I'd *love* to see your place . . . one of these days. Give me some idea of what's out there.'

She paused; her eyes filled with a desperate hopefulness. I said nothing and an awkward silence developed between us. I glanced up at the clock on the wall and swallowed hard, wanting to change the subject; then I filled the strained silence between us with a mouthful of pie, before pushing the plate to one side.

'Mmn,' I muttered with my mouth still full and giving a brief nod.

Judith kept on looking at me with those pleading eyes and I couldn't look away. I took a breath and my mouth felt dry. She kept right on staring at me until I couldn't stand it. I felt a deep sense of dread, but I managed a weak smile.

'We've been meaning to have some people over for

drinks, or even dinner, but it's been so busy at school with exams.' I was desperate to fill the silence.

'I think it's a shame the staff don't spend more time socializing. Us single girls need to stick together,' said Judith and she gave a silly little giggle that she hid behind her hand. Her laugh was strange, kind of alien, as if it wasn't connected to any particular event around her.

'Well, you must come over sometime.' A casual invitation designed to please and flatter but *never* to be accepted.

'I'm free on Friday as it happens. It's the only night I don't have apartments to view so I'm kind of at a loose end,' Judith said.

Her little busybody face lit up with anticipation. I felt a pang of guilt, then the words tumbled out before I could stop them.

'Well, why don't you come over for dinner?' I regretted the invitation the moment it left my lips, but it was too late. Before I knew it, I'd invited her and her cousin Peggy for drinks and dinner on Friday evening.

'Oh, really? Why I'd love to . . . Oh, that would be just lovely, Dovie . . .'

Judith's bottom lip seemed to quiver slightly and her eyes looked moist with tears. She seemed so peculiarly grateful that I had no idea what to say to her, but it was clear I couldn't put her off now.

'Well, I guess that's a date then. Is that the time? I have to go . . . I don't want to miss the start of the picture.' I forced myself to give Judith a bright smile as I picked up my purse from the counter.

'Enjoy your movie,' she said and I nodded in what I hoped was a friendly enough fashion.

'Goodnight, Judith.' My face felt rigid from the strain of talking to her and it was a relief when I could finally turn away. As I pushed open the glass door of the diner, I could see her sad little reflection smiling and watching me go. She looked so happy and I felt terrible for disliking her so much.

3

New York City, 1975

There is a kind of lonely sound that a telephone makes when it's ringing, and I listened to that sound for what felt like hours, before eventually a woman's voice said:

'Yeah, this is Candy.'

'Is my dad there?'

I'd rehearsed those words all the time that telephone was ringing away into nothing. Four little words, but the meaning was clear: I knew he was there. The hesitation lasted just a few seconds, but it was long enough for me to imagine her chewing on her bottom lip, wondering what to say that wouldn't land her in trouble. I heard a muffled sound, as though she'd placed her hand over the receiver, and then my father's voice, exasperated and slightly drunk.

'For Chrissakes, Candy . . .' The rest of the urgent, whispered words were not for me to hear, before—

'Ava, honey, is that you?' His casual voice, as if this was all perfectly normal.

'Dad . . . I can't find Mom.'

'Whadda ya mean you can't find her?'

'She was acting really strange . . . and then the phone

rang . . . so I left her alone. Just for a minute, I swear. Anyway . . . by the time I got back to the kitchen she was gone. I looked everywhere. I've been walking around for hours searching . . . I don't know where she is.'

I'd walked from downtown right up to Central Park, checking inside every church I could find along the way until my feet were sore. A small angry red blister throbbed on my left heel and I'd lost count of how many coffee shops I'd walked in and out of, flashing my mom's picture and getting the same response each time. Nobody had seen her. Eventually, after I'd lost all track of time, I headed home, knowing there was only one thing left to do. Calling my dad was definitely the last resort.

'Sweetie . . . slow down. You're not making any sense.' He was slurring slightly and trying hard not to, but I could hear the hours of drinks with Candy in his voice.

'She ran away . . . or something . . . I don't know.'

'What time was this?' He was angry now, as if I'd somehow caused my mother's disappearance.

'I don't know. We were having breakfast . . . but late because there's no school. Maybe nine?'

'NINE? Why am I only hearing about this now, for Chrissakes?'

My throat got tight and I couldn't get any more words out. Tears started to slide down my cheeks and it was all I could do to try and hold them back as my dad carried on yelling.

I tried to explain how I'd spent all day pounding the streets of the city showing people the grainy photograph of Mom, but I wasn't making any sense at all. Anyway, there was no denying that things were bad. By the time Candy Jackson answered the telephone, my mom had been missing for nearly ten hours.

I could hear Candy in the background asking what was happening and Dad hushing her, and then his voice back in control.

'OK, honey ... Ava ... don't get upset. Don't worry ... we're gonna find her. I'll be there as soon as I can, OK?'

I cradled the black receiver into my chin even after he hung up, listening to the purring noise on the line. It was comforting. My dad was coming home. Everything would be all right. I sank down on to the couch and put my head on the cushion. It was a mustard-yellow geometric pattern that my mother made from material she'd bought at the market before the sadness began. She sang as she sewed, but when the cushion was finished, she fussed over it and seemed disappointed. I traced the thick lines of shapes on the cloth with my finger and pressed my face into it. It smelled of stale cigarettes.

A loud buzzing noise filled the air.

Our doorbell was black metal, worn down from use, with a neat card and the word 'WINTERS' printed in thick black ink. It was a throwback to the days when we still cared what our neighbours from downstairs might think of us.

BUZZZZZZZZZZZZZZZZZ.

At this time of day, the finger stabbing at the buzzer could only belong to Miss Schnagl, who lived downstairs. And I knew that once she started, she wouldn't stop. After the buzzing was exhausted, her knuckles started rapping against the wood of our front door and she was calling out just loud enough for the entire building to hear her.

'Mrs Winters? Are you there, Mrs Winters?'

I cracked the front door open an inch. The familiar figure of Miss Schnagl stood there. She was looking vaguely irritated by something, and I guessed we were responsible for whatever it was.

'Ahh, so you are here. I thought I heard you come in.'

'Hi, Miss Schnagl.'

I offered nothing except my nose, which was occupying the small crack between us.

'This box has been sitting in the hallway all day long. You know people should come and collect their parcels, because it's not a very big hallway and you can't have people falling over boxes when they come in.'

Miss Schnagl looked at me, and then down at the floor, where the large box that I'd fallen over earlier lay at her feet. We both stared at it, but then she carried on talking.

'I carried it up all those stairs because I didn't see your father go past and I was waiting for someone to carry a heavy box because it's a lot of stairs . . .'

She was getting into her stride now, so I cracked open the door and offered out two hands.

'It's OK, I can take it.'

Miss Schnagl eyed me suspiciously, letting her gaze linger, but I just stared straight back and arranged my mouth into what I hoped was a pleasant enough smile.

'Everything all right, Ava?' she asked, scanning my tear-stained face.

'Oh, just fine, thanks. My dad had to work late. He'll be home any minute.'

Before she could say another word, I bent down and scooped the box into my arms, using my foot to jam the door so it couldn't fly open. The box really was quite heavy and I wouldn't be able to hold it for long, but we were approaching the point where Miss Schnagl might suggest the need to sit down for a minute before making her way back down the stairs, as was her habit. So I said:

'Well, if there's nothing else, it's getting late.' Same fixed pleasant smile.

'Your mother not here?'

'She's gone to bed. Migraine . . . It's a bad one.'

'You need a wet cloth and ice. Ice is good for that. You got ice? I can fetch you some if you need it.'

'We got ice, thanks, Miss Schnagl.'

That part wasn't a lie and it must have convinced her because she stepped far enough away from the door to allow me to push it shut with my foot while shouting:

'Thanks again, Miss Schnagl.'

I could still hear her muttering as she limped back down the stairs, pausing on every half turn to breathe hard and bemoan her inconsiderate neighbours, and their boxes.

Leaning back against the door, I dropped the box on to the floor, shaking my arms out with relief before squatting down beside it.

The box was around three feet wide and two feet high. It was addressed to Apartment 3B, which was us, but there was no name written on the outside of the box. In the top corner of the brown paper was a smudged black mark under the brightly coloured stamps, and I could just make out the word 'PARIS'. It gradually dawned on me that the box was from Paris in France – where we knew absolutely nobody, as far as I was aware.

The corner of the package was slightly torn and I pulled at the loose brown paper, curious as to what might be inside. Then suddenly, before I'd even thought about it, I was tearing off the wrapping and peeling back the thick brown parcel paper. Inside was a cardboard box that previously held farm vegetables, judging by the pictures on the lid of carrots and assorted salad produce. There was string thickly coiled around the cardboard box holding the lid in place. I tugged at it and gently lifted the box up to place it on the couch so I could get a good look at it.

As soon as I picked it up, the thin cardboard bottom collapsed under the weight and the contents of the box tumbled on to the floor. I scrambled about on the rug trying to repair the flaps of the box enough to stuff the contents back inside and started to inspect each item as I collected them.

There was a dark blue velvet bag lying at my feet. I picked it up, and inserted the tips of two fingers to pull the gathered top apart, before spilling the contents into the palm of my hand. It was a necklace of yellow enamel butterflies on a silver chain: two small butterflies on either side of one larger butterfly in the centre. It was the most beautiful thing I'd ever seen. The wings were delicate and you could run your fingers over the tiny wire tips. The yellow was like pale sunshine, and the backs were bronze and heavy. I spread it out across my palm and stared at it, before pouring it carefully back into its bag.

I tipped a plastic bag covered with what I presumed were French words on to the rug. It was filled with a bunch of crumpled old papers, with what looked like a whiskey tumbler set in the middle of them. The glass was old, and I couldn't tell what the papers were at first glance. It just seemed like the kind of junk you get from an overripe mailbox.

Next, out came a long delicate silk scarf, which I spread snake-like across our rug. It was whisper thin, and light as air, with strands of pale green gauze shot through with silver thread. I picked it up and wrapped it around my neck. It was soft and cool against my skin. There were some faded stains at one end but it was still beautiful. My mother didn't own anything as pretty as these things, and probably never would. Everything we bought seemed heavy and practical and made to last.

Underneath the scarf were some large green leather photograph albums containing a collection of black and white photographs of smiling young women. I picked one up and flipped open the cover. Scrawled in large curly letters in dark blue ink it read, 'To my Dovie, with all my love, G'.

I turned a few more pages, which were darkened with age. Some of the pictures had come unstuck and one floated face down on to my lap. On the back of the photograph was a date printed neatly in blue ink: 'Dovie, New York City, July 1955'.

I flipped the photograph over. A young woman smiled into the camera. She had dark hair with laughing eyes, and was leaning against a wall, holding on to some kind of iron railings. She was pretty. Not what you would call beautiful; but her smile was bright and full. None of that was what I noticed first, though. Because across her face, in deep veins of navy ink, someone had scrawled a single word:

'LIAR'.

4

New York City, 1955

The Roxy lights were glowing red and white, announcing the main feature, and I arrived at the box office just in time to see Gillian strolling around the corner in her khaki pants with hands shoved deep in her pockets. I loved to watch her for those few seconds before she could see me. Her face weary, her stride brisk and a half-whistle playing on her lips. Her face brightened when she saw me waiting. A familiar wave of the hand; that wide-open smile. I bought the tickets, just as I'd promised, and we went straight inside, sitting as far back as possible but right in the centre of the row, so we couldn't be spotted by anyone we knew.

The cinema wasn't that busy as it was an early showing; a few groups of girls and some singles dotted around the place, mostly middle-aged women trying to get some time for themselves. The back row was reserved for dating couples who clustered together waiting for darkness to cover them.

As soon as the theatre went dark and the big screen bustled with images, I reached my hand to the edge of the red velvet seat and felt for Gillian's fingers; I stroked her hand with mine and hooked my little finger around hers. She stroked my finger with her own and we settled down to watch the movie. It was the smallest gesture, but we sat like that: perfectly together, but invisible to everyone else. The movie was full of wise-cracking gals and men who liked wise-cracking gals, and we both found it disappointing. Gillian seemed restless and chain-smoked Pall Malls, nervously checking that people couldn't see us holding hands. Gillian was always worried about us being out in public and I wished she would just relax a little. I whispered to her that it was OK, but she was always tense, especially when the usherette was showing latecomers into their seats with her little torch, the firefly dancing too close to us for comfort.

Back in the safety of our apartment, Gillian made sure to pull the blinds down in every window before switching on the lamps in our living room. Then, and only then, did she finally relax.

'I'll get the whiskey,' I said as I headed into the kitchen, filling our glasses with a generous finger and a chunk of ice. Gillian put on a new record and the sound of jazz filled the room. As I handed her a glass, she pulled me close and we swayed back and forth in a slow dance for a few beats, her cheek resting against mine as the ice gently melted into our drinks. We giggled and collapsed on to our old couch, clinking our whiskey glasses together.

'To the road not taken,' Gillian offered in our usual toast.

'And all the roads ahead,' I finished off for her.

As we drank, I leaned against Gillian's shoulder and she kissed the top of my head and entwined her fingers in mine.

'What a day . . .' She sighed while kicking off her shoes and curling her legs up underneath her.

I sipped at my whiskey and hummed along to the song.

'I know. It's so busy, and way too hot for work.' I lifted my hair off the back of my neck with one hand and Gillian leaned across and placed a gentle kiss there. 'One day, we'll leave all this behind us . . .'

'. . . and live happily ever after in Paris . . . I know.' Gillian had heard this so many times before.

'We'll go to those little jazz clubs and dance cheek to cheek, and nobody will give a damn.' I loved to imagine a life for us together in Paris. Gillian could often be persuaded to join in if she was in the right mood.

'Oh, Dovie . . . until then . . .' Gillian raised her whiskey glass, clinked it gently against mine and pulled me closer.

'I love you, Gilly . . .'

'Love you right back, Dovie Carmichael. Hey, if you're good I might treat you to dinner out on Friday night.' She began to stroke my hair and gently tug the strands between her fingers.

At the mention of Friday night, my good mood evaporated. I'd forgotten all about Judith.

I was dreading what I had to say but there wasn't any

way to avoid telling Gillian. I took a deep breath and sent up a silent prayer that she wouldn't get mad at me.

'We can't on Friday . . . I've invited Judith to dinner.'

Gillian stopped stroking my hair and stared at me in shock.

'What? Why would you do that?'

'I *know* . . . and I'm sorry. I didn't mean to . . . it just kind of slipped out. Are you mad at me? Please don't be mad at me.' I gnawed at my fingernail nervously.

'You'll have to cancel,' Gillian snapped at me. She turned to face me, her face quite furious. 'We agreed we wouldn't have people over. It's too big a risk.'

Gillian's voice was sharp but I knew she was scared as much as anything. She got to her feet and headed to the kitchen as I scampered after her, desperate to make amends. I tried to explain about Judith, but nothing helped.

'Lots of women share apartments. She won't know,' I protested.

'Dovie, you're such a fool sometimes,' Gillian snapped. 'Why would you do this? And Judith of all people . . .'

I explained as best as I could but my excuses sounded hollow, even to me.

'I'm so sorry. It just came out . . . She was cross with me and I was trying to fix it . . . I messed up.'

'Oh, Dovie! How could you be so stupid? You know what will happen to us if people find out?' Gillian was biting down hard on her bottom lip and her eyes filled with tears. I was desperate to make her feel better.

'She won't find out. We'll be really careful,' I whispered. 'It will look worse if we cancel, like we have something to hide.'

'We *do* have something to hide!' Gillian hissed at me.

'It's just this once . . . I'll take care of everything. I *promise* it will all be fine. I'll make it OK. It's just dinner . . . Trust me . . .'

I meant every word, but I could tell Gillian was still mad at me. I hugged her as hard as I could, whispering, 'I'm sorry, Gilly. I know I'm an idiot sometimes,' and she hugged me back, which I took to mean that she knew, and she forgave me.

In the end, I made a potato salad and bought some cold cuts at the deli on the corner. It was a hot night and I thought that would be easy. I bought a tub of ice-cream from Zerilli's ice-cream parlour, and a freshly baked apple pie from the new Hungarian bakery that had opened across the street from us. As I set our tiny kitchen table for dinner, I was feeling quite relaxed about the coming evening. We had a fresh bottle of gin, another of vermouth and plenty of ice. It was just dinner and drinks. I was sure I could manage that, even for Judith.

The apartment looked nice; I'd taken great care with it. Our small kitchen was gleaming and our living room was warm and welcoming. Judith arrived a few minutes early with her cousin Peggy. Peggy seemed nice enough, but was so shy she barely spoke a word and flushed every time she was asked a question. I shoved two large gin cocktails into their hands, shuffling books and papers around so they could sit down on our old couch.

'What a lovely room. It's so . . . cosy,' Judith said, her beady little eyes darting around, taking it all in.

'Thank you. It's got great light,' Gillian said before lighting up her Pall Mall and giving me a look to show she was co-operating.

'Isn't it a big place for just the two of you?'

It was, truth be told. There were two bedrooms, a small room just off the kitchen that we called the nook and used for Gillian's art supplies, a bright and airy living room and tiny kitchen and bathroom; the rent stretched us every month, but the peace of mind it gave us to have a place to call our own was worth every penny.

I changed the subject and offered the cocktail sausages I'd made earlier to go with our drinks. They accepted them eagerly; the gin had made them hungry. But Judith was not to be put off so easily.

'I'd love to see the rest of the apartment, if you don't mind?'

I did mind. There was not a chance in hell that Judith would be getting a guided tour of our sleeping arrangements, even though I had the spare bedroom all set up, with a pile of half-read books on a bedside table.

I'd spent ages preparing the apartment for Judith's arrival. Every photograph had been removed before we opened the front door and I'd taken care to hide our green leather photograph albums under our bed in an old box. I'd thought of everything. I'd even separated our toothbrushes into different glasses. There was nothing to see. Just a couple of teachers with their books and papers. I put on my best forced smile.

'Maybe later – let's eat first. I'm starving.'

That part wasn't a lie, as my stomach was growling and I hadn't eaten since breakfast. Gillian was doing everything she could not to meet my eye and maintained a blank expression for most of the evening, except when she was forced to smile at some awful joke. Occasionally she rolled her eyes or pulled a face behind Judith's back and I bit down on my tongue to stop myself giggling. At other times she was charming and friendly, making polite conversation with poor shy Peggy, and I loved her for it.

At one point, Judith wandered off to the bathroom and I followed her out just to make sure that she wasn't snooping around. I caught her standing just inside our bedroom door as she made her way back to the living room. She had a strange way about her: her eyes rarely blinked. Her reaction to getting caught trespassing was laughter, but the kind that sounded like a wrong note on a piano. Everything about Judith was unnerving. I was quick to hurry her along, telling her dinner was almost ready and making sure to close the door after she moved away, but even as I did so, I could still feel her presence, like a shadow inside our bedroom.

The chitchat continued until the gin glasses were empty. Peggy was leaving the city in a few weeks to take up a job in Pittsburgh, so we made polite conversation around that while I laid out the cold meats and potato salad and called everyone to be seated. They shuffled in to take their places and scraped the chairs back on the hardwood floor. The small table was only really big enough to sit two people comfortably, but we all squeezed in and managed to get through the main course. Judith had brought a bottle of white wine for dinner that she insisted we open, which we did even though I was already feeling a little giddy from the generous amounts of gin I'd poured earlier in the evening.

The wine helped soothe the way, and Gillian was listening sweetly as Judith poured out her apartment problems, describing in tedious detail the place she'd fallen in love with on 23rd Street but wouldn't be able to afford for several weeks. Gillian sympathized just the right amount and was rewarded with a beaming, grateful smile from Judith.

I served the apple pie and Zerilli's ice-cream to everyone except Peggy, who was watching her figure. Somehow, we finished the whole bottle of wine and the evening wasn't going badly. I began to think that Judith was quite funny after a few drinks: she told little stories and was an excellent mimic. Her cousin Peggy started to open up a little about a man she was hoping to date; he worked in insurance and had 'prospects'.

The kitchen felt hot and sticky, overwhelmed by summer heat and too many people sitting in it, and so we moved back into the living room. I opened the window but the catch was broken and it kept sliding closed again until I propped it open with a library book. Judith and

Peggy slipped off their shoes, settling themselves with legs curled under them on the couch while I knelt on some old cushions on the floor, sorting through jazz records that we particularly liked: 'Chet Baker Sings', and a new record from Paris that was our current favourite. Dropping a record on to the turntable I let the needle fall and the melody started to play.

It must have been getting late, because Peggy at one point started to fall asleep, her little face flushed pink and dribbling a little as her mouth fell open. Judith got up to use the bathroom again and this time I couldn't be bothered to chase after her. I lit a couple of cigarettes and carried them into the kitchen. It was dark and all the windows were thrown open to let in some air. The hot air outside met the hot air inside and nothing much shifted.

Gillian was standing by the table lifting her fair hair off her neck and piling it on top of her head. I put the cigarette in Gillian's mouth and leaned in:

'See, it wasn't so bad?'

'I guess not.' She leaned back against me and I knew we were all right.

'So, I'm forgiven?'

'I haven't decided yet.'

Gillian moved towards the window in hope of a cooling breeze but there was none. She turned and smiled at me, tender and just a little forgiving. I was happy, slightly drunk, but I remember feeling that my life was just perfect right at that moment.

I leaned across and kissed Gillian softly on the lips as I often did when we were alone. She smiled and then I felt her stiffen and heard her voice, clipped and strange.

'Oh, Judith . . . I didn't see you there. Coffee's ready.'

I crushed my cigarette into a saucer and turned around with a stiff smile forced on to my face. Judith's mouth was upturned, but her eyes were glassy and gave nothing away.

'You go and sit down. I'll bring it through,' I said.

She paused for just a second; then she set her mouth into a strange little smile and walked back into the living room. I could feel my breath catching in my throat as I spoke but my face was a mask. The sounds of blood pulsed in my ears and my hands shook as I picked up the coffee cups.

Gillian shot me a look and I bit down on my lip.

'Do you think she saw?' Gillian whispered. I could see the panic starting to sober her up immediately. 'Christ, Dovie, what if she saw us? What will we do?'

'Let me think . . . Hush now.' I placed my hand gently on Gillian's mouth to silence her. She stared at me, her eyes desperate for some reassurance and I'd none to give her. My mind was racing but I picked up the coffee pot and nodded at Gillian to show her I would handle everything.

I carried the tray with the coffee and four cups set on their dainty saucers and put it down on a low table next to the couch. I poured, filling the tiny cups, and we sat in awkward silence sipping from them, with Peggy still asleep and oblivious. I changed the record, turning up the music a little and filling the air with Charlie Parker's 'Perdido'. I couldn't stop staring at Judith. I was willing her not to have seen us.

Gillian sat rigid, pale-faced and terrified. I plastered a smile to my aching face until Judith drained her coffee cup and shook Peggy awake and they both got to their feet to make their way to the front door.

'Thank you both for a lovely evening. I'll see you in school on Monday.'

Judith held my gaze for a moment too long. Her beady little eyes searched my face and then she smiled her sly little smile. My lips wouldn't move. I swallowed hard and managed a slight nod as I closed the front door on Judith and her cousin, listening to their feet clip down the stone steps of the building and then gradually fade away into the night.

5

New York City, 1975

The sound of a key in the door jolted me awake just as a crack of dawn light crept across the living-room floor. I must have drifted off on our old couch, curled up like a small animal and still clutching Dovie's photograph in my hands. The front door squeaked open and I heard the soft tread of my father's footsteps on the hall floor, a sound so familiar to me that I didn't even need to call out to check it was him. The sound of those footsteps made me realize just how much I missed hearing them. I slid the photograph back into the box and pushed it to one side so I could sit up. I heard his voice saying over and over, 'OK, Mary-Lyn, OK,' and I knew he'd brought my mother home.

As I sat up, smearing the sleep out of my eyes, my father appeared in the doorway. He was wearing a new shirt, a kind of pink nylon, and his hair had grown down over the collar at the back. He looked weary and older somehow than when he'd lived with us properly. My mother was tucked into the side of him, under his arm. She was wrapped in a coarse brown blanket that looked as if it had 'PROPERTY OF' stamped on it. I couldn't read the rest of it. Underneath the blanket I could see the dirty white edges of her nightgown. She was barefoot; her feet were black with dirt and one of her toes crusted with blood. She seemed calm but in a blank kind of a way, as though she was all cried out.

I leaped to my feet, but my dad gestured for me to go ahead and get the bedroom door. He started talking as though everything was normal and this was just what we did every morning before breakfast.

'Hey, sweetie, I'm sorry it took so long. Did you get any sleep?'

I nodded, unable to form sentences yet. My mother shuffled alongside him and between us we edged her gently into their bedroom.

I looked at my dad. 'Is she OK?'

'She's fine, honey. She got . . . a little confused, that's all. They found her wandering around Central Park. Lucky for us an old cop buddy of mine was on duty and here we are . . .'

'She got arrested?'

'It was nuthin'. She wasn't in the precinct more than an hour. I went right over there as soon as I got the call. No problem . . . Hey, kiddo? Hey . . . don't worry. Everything is gonna be just fine. Let's get her into bed.' Although he was telling me not to worry, I noticed that he hadn't stopped talking since he'd set foot inside our apartment.

I drew back the quilt on the bed and she sat gingerly on the edge of the clean sheet, staring straight ahead of her.

41

'Get a washcloth, Ava. Better clean these little feet up a bit, hey, Mary-Lyn?'

I ran to the bathroom and rinsed out a washcloth, dripping water all the way back to the bedroom but my dad didn't seem to mind. He was still whispering her name and that everything was going to be OK as he wiped her feet clean and laid her back in the bed. He drew the quilt up to her chin, fastening her arms by her side.

'OK . . . We're OK.' He kept repeating those words although we were anything but OK as far as I could see.

My mother lay there staring up at the ceiling. Her lips were moving slightly. From time to time her eyes flashed across to wherever my father was standing and then back again to the ceiling. I stood in the doorway, watching them and shuffling from foot to foot, wishing I was somewhere else. As my father backed away from the bed, I heard a soft tapping noise from the living room and I swung around expecting to see a doctor waiting in the hallway with his black bag of medicines to make us all better again.

A young woman stood in the doorway, smoking a cigarette she'd rolled herself and picking strands of loose tobacco off her bottom lip. She saw me standing there and her pretty face pulled into a smile that the rest of her didn't mean. Dark hair hung like two curtains either side of her face.

'Hi, Ava,' she said sulkily.

'Hi, Candy.'

'I knocked but I guess nobody heard me.'

That was it. Nothing else to say. We eyed each other and then stared at the floor in awkward silence. I fixed my eyes on a spot near the edge of the rug where a small insect was crawling across the wooden floor, scurrying to safety. It disappeared into a gap between the floorboards. I envied it.

My father closed the bedroom door quickly so my mother couldn't see Candy standing in her hallway. He was brusque with her and a little embarrassed, I thought.

'Did you get them?' he asked.

'Sure.' Candy opened the palm of her hand and held out a tiny bottle containing four blue pills. 'They're all I had left. They're good though . . . like eight hours good . . . maybe longer.'

I couldn't stop staring at them. Candy had brought my father sleeping pills and he took the bottle from her, shook one blue pill out into the palm of his hand, and then headed back into the bedroom. He left the door open a crack and I could see him lifting my mother's head, trying to get her to swallow it. She must have done so because a little while later my dad reappeared. He closed the bedroom door behind him and I noticed he'd taken the key from the lock and placed it on the outside of the door. Our doors all had old keys but we didn't use them, so they were rusted up and stiff. He jiggled it around in the lock for several seconds before it snapped shut, locking my mother on the other side of the door.

'Dad, what are you doing?'

'Your mom needs to get some rest, honey . . .'

He tousled my hair as he used to do when I was a kid and I knew it was pointless to say anything else. He always did that when he wanted me to quit asking questions.

Candy finished her cigarette, wet her thumb and fore-finger with her spit and snuffed it out. She gazed up at my dad and, after getting no reaction, she started to shuffle back towards the front door.

'I'll see you later then?' She seemed kind of unhappy with him and he knew it.

'I'll call you,' he said – conciliatory, I thought.

'I'm working the afternoon shift at Zerilli's.'

'I'll sort things out here and I'll call . . .'

Candy sighed and shuffled her feet as if she didn't want to leave him there.

'I said I'll call . . . and I'll call. Candy . . .'

My father nodded at her and she eyed him for a second; then, satisfied that he meant it, she left us stand-ing outside the locked bedroom door.

My dad slumped down next to me on the couch, leaning back into the cushions and rubbing his fists across his eyes. Outside, the city was bursting into life. Delivery trucks were backing up and their drivers calling out greetings to anyone they recognized. The rasping noise of metal as the back doors were flung open and crates unloaded. My mom had been sleeping for maybe an

44

hour and it was only now that my father decided it was time for us to have a talk.

'Honey, it might be best if you didn't mention this to anyone. We don't want people getting the wrong idea . . .'

'What do you mean *the wrong idea*?' I whispered, almost not wanting to hear the answer.

He was struggling for the right words.

'We just don't want people talking . . . that's all.'

'She's been this way for a long time . . . well, not this bad . . . but *bad*. It's a bit late for you to start worrying about what the neighbours think,' I snapped at him in a burst of anger.

'Hey, that's enough! Let's just keep it quiet for now. It's nobody's business.'

I nodded. I didn't have the energy to argue with him. I thought of all the times I'd heard my mother cry and how she would sit alone for hours with her lips forming silent conversations. I wondered what would happen if she kept running away and my dad wasn't around to bring her home again. I wasn't sure people *would* be getting the wrong idea exactly, but I was exhausted and glad to have him home. He wrapped his big arms around me, pulling me close, and for a heartbeat it was just as it used to be. I missed him being here. The sound of him whistling part of a tune or calling my name. All the times we would play fight and then I would curl up on his lap while he read his newspaper. We stayed like that for a few minutes and for a while it was just as it used to be when he was simply my dad and we had never set eyes on Candy Jackson.

'Dad . . . do we know anyone who lives in Paris?' I tried to keep my tone casual.

He stared at me, puzzled. 'Paris? Why would we know anyone who lived there?'

I shrugged. 'I just wondered if maybe we did.'

'No, honey . . . I don't think so.' As he shifted position his foot kicked against the box and he glanced at it for a second. 'What's all this?'

'Oh, it's nothing . . . just old stuff,' I said protectively. I kept wondering why somebody would write 'LIAR' across someone's face and what had happened to the woman in the picture, but I didn't want to show him what was inside the box until I could make sure it wasn't anything that might make things worse around here.

'You shouldn't leave stuff hanging around where people can fall over it. Keep your things in your room, Ava.'

'Yeah.'

He nodded and I leaned right into him, feeling safe and warm. He smelled of warm smoke and home. I decided to leave the mystery of the box for another day and just enjoy having my dad to myself, for a little while at least.

The feeling didn't last long, as after a few minutes he stood up and muttered something about needing to make a call. I watched him standing there with the tele-phone receiver to his ear, his back turned away and his hand flat against the wall as if he was trying to press it away from him. He lowered his voice as I walked by carrying the box to my room, but I knew who it was.

The apartment was already feeling the heat of the morning sun and the weird cool-air system my father had rigged up for us clanked and gurgled as it spat out warm air, which made everything worse. I tried opening the window but it kept sliding shut, and eventually I gave up. He didn't seem to notice, and when he was done with his phone call he turned to me, his voice unusually bright and forced.

'Whadda ya say we go get some breakfast? Your mom won't be awake for a while so how about we go to Benny's Luncheonette? Get pancakes and some coffee for your old man? Hey . . . whadda ya say?'

It didn't matter what I said, because even as he was talking, my father had already picked up his keys and wallet from the kitchen table and was waiting for me at the front door. I shoved my feet into my sneakers and followed him out of the apartment.

I went to close our front door, and as I did so I thought I heard a low moan coming from my mother's bedroom. But when I stopped and listened . . . there was only silence.

6

New York City, 1955

Gillian sat smoking her Pall Malls at the kitchen table, one hand on her forehead.

'What are we going to do?' she asked without looking up.

I shook my head.

'We don't know if she saw us. She didn't say anything.'

'What did you expect her to say? Of course she saw us.'

'Maybe she didn't. It was dark. How long was she standing there?'

'I don't know, but if she tells people we'll get fired. We'll lose everything ... What if it ends up in the newspapers?'

I'd heard Gillian panic over being found out many times before, but nothing like this. She was starting to rock slightly in her chair. She crushed out a cigarette and then straight away lit another one without thinking.

'They'll find out about us. I couldn't bear it ... You know what they do to women like us, Dovie?'

'We don't know if the stories are true. It's just rumours.'

Gillian's eyes filled with tears and she couldn't speak

for fear of what might happen to us. I didn't know what to say. I reached out a hand and tried to rub her back to comfort her but her shoulder blades lay rigid and sharp under my fingers.

'It's too late, it's done. We just have to wait for Monday and see what happens,' I soothed. 'I'll take the blame for everything, Gill. Please don't worry.' She shrugged my hand away and I knew it was pointless to try and reason with her. My words were brave, but inside I felt miserable.

I don't know if Gill slept at all, but she didn't come to bed. We didn't even have our traditional nightcap of whiskey, a tradition we'd started way back in college when we first met.

It was our thing. We would lie down on the floor of our dorm room, our heads resting against my bed and our feet touching, smoking cigarettes and playing jazz. I introduced her to Charlie, Billie and Ella. They were ours. She introduced me to whiskey. Gillian had a pair of old crystal whiskey tumblers that belonged to her grandmother, and we would each take one and make our regular toast to the road ahead of us and to all the silly things we loved about each other.

On freezing winter nights, the heating in our room was barely warm enough to stop our fingers becoming stiff with cold. It took an age to make the room warm enough to be comfortable, and while we waited, we would pour our whiskey, huddled up under my mother's patchwork quilt. We talked about going to Paris together, sitting in pavement cafés drinking small glasses of wine, and smoking those fancy black cigarettes we saw in movies. We would visit jazz clubs and see all the legends play. We would eat things we couldn't pronounce, and walk all over the city, tracing the houses where the great writers and artists lived. I built a whole pretend life for us in a city across the ocean.

In the winter gloom of our first semester, I watched Gillian's face as it glowed with promise and excitement. We became inseparable. From then on there wasn't a night that didn't end with Gillian's head on my shoulder and the clink of her grandmother's whiskey tumblers.

But tonight, I crept away into our bedroom alone.

Monday was grey and stormy wet, but the sticky heat of the uptown bus made small rivulets of sweat form on my forehead. It was crowded with people heading to work. Every seat was taken and people were leaning all over each other in the aisle.

I felt crushed into my seat and couldn't keep still for a second. My fussing bothered Gillian and she turned her face away, staring out of the window at the crowds of identically dressed men with their good suits and black umbrellas, all heading towards midtown to sit in identical offices and process pieces of paper.

An elderly man was patting the hand of his wife in one of the seats across the aisle. I wanted so badly to reach over and squeeze Gillian's arm – just for the reassurance of touching her. But I didn't dare. I stared at the small patch of freckled skin on Gillian's forearm.

The bus swayed from side to side and crawled to a halt, waiting for a light to change from red to green. A raindrop slid carelessly down the glass and Gillian traced its descent with her finger. Ours was the next stop, just by the park. We made this journey so often together, lost in silly gossip and plans for the future, but today we got out of our seats in silence. We made the short walk from the bus stop to the white stone entrance of the school with our chins raised and lips pursed, waiting for the blows to fall.

We parted without a word before we got to the teachers' lounge. My legs felt weak and my mouth tasted of metal. In the distance, I could see the back of Gillian walking towards her art room and I turned right and scraped the key in the heavy wooden door of the English room. We were supposed to be revising *The Adventures of Huckleberry Finn* that morning; I chose a short passage for reading aloud and then asked the girls to explain what it meant. Several offered shy explanations, some very good and some quite wrong, but I was happy to let them continue discussing it to let the time pass. Around thirty minutes had passed when there was a timid knock on the classroom door and the thin, sorrowful face of Mrs Potts came into view.

'Good morning, Miss Carmichael. Forgive the intrusion but Mrs Forrester would like to see you in her office.'

I felt the colour drain from my face. This was it.

'Now?' I whispered.

She nodded.

'I'll stay with your girls until you come back.'

Mrs Potts gestured to the door to hurry me along but my mouth was parched and my feet didn't want to move.

I laid my copy of *Huckleberry Finn* carefully on my desk and ran my hands over my skirt to smooth it down. The girls whispered to themselves, and the knowledge that they were watching me made the few steps to the door unbearable.

The corridor was empty and my heels clipped along the parquet, echoing all the way down the hall. I walked past the numerous photographs of class presidents long since gone, and school sporting victories, muscular girls holding silver cups, until eventually I arrived at the Head's office.

There was a small waiting area usually filled with disobedient schoolgirls about to be sanctioned in some way, but this morning it was just me. There was no sign of Gillian. The door was shut tight and I could hear the low hum of voices inside. I tried to listen, but the conversation was too quiet to make out the words.

My jaw ached from clenching it, and I rubbed two fingers into the hollows under my ears to ease the tension. I gently twisted my neck back and forth, trying to gain some release, but there was none to be had. Then the voices fell silent and the door opened and there was Mrs Forrester, smiling at Judith. The moment I saw her standing there I felt sick with nerves.

'Thank you, Judith.'

My legs felt heavy when I stood up and my heart was racing. Judith gave me a strange little smile as she passed me.

'Come in, Miss Carmichael.'

I obeyed and settled myself in the green leather seat on the opposite side of her desk. Mrs Forrester closed the door and took her usual place. She picked up a silver pen and then put it down again, her fingers gently tapping either end of it until she was ready to speak, at which time she leaned towards me.

'I'm afraid I've received some worrying news this morning and I wanted to talk to you straight away before the news travels. You know as well as I do how gossip spreads in this place.'

My breath came in jagged bursts and I clasped my hands together in my lap so Mrs Forrester couldn't see them shaking.

'Oh . . .'

'Jenny Atwood has left school with immediate effect. She's had some kind of nervous breakdown – or at least that's the story her family are telling – and they have decided to send her out of the city to recuperate.'

Relief flooded through me. I unclasped my hands. It was going to be all right. Judith hadn't seen anything and nobody knew about us. We were safe.

I mumbled some sympathetic words to Mrs Forrester about Jenny and excused myself. I intended to go immediately to let Gillian know we were safe, but as I started to walk up the hallway the adrenaline and my empty stomach collided and a wave of nausea swept over me. I pushed open the door to the staff bathrooms and locked myself in an empty stall, where I proceeded to vomit yellow bile into the toilet bowl.

Once I was finished, I washed my hands and splashed cold water on to my face before patting it dry with paper towels. My hands gripped hold of the sink and I stared at my face in the mirror. I could look attractive in the right light but not today; I looked white and exhausted under the harsh glare of the bathroom lights. I rummaged around in my pocket for a Life Saver mint but didn't find one, so I took a few deep breaths, and felt calmer. My lips even curled into a smile. And then the bathroom door opened.

Standing by the entrance was Judith. By her stance, I could tell that this was no coincidence; she was waiting for me. I knew the minute I saw her face that she *knew*, and all the relief I'd felt buoyant with just seconds before drained away, leaving a tight knot of fear in my throat.

'Did you think I'd tell?'

She didn't smile and her eyes fixed on my face, searching for my reaction.

'I . . . I don't know what you mean?' I could hear my lies like stones in my mouth.

'Don't make me say it, Dovie. You know what you did.'

I couldn't speak. There was no point anyway; the blow was surely about to be struck.

'You didn't tell?' I whispered.

'No.'

'Why not?'

Her mouth pursed as if she was thinking it over and then her lips curled into her sly little smile.

'Because there's something I want you to do for me.'

7

New York City, 1975

Benny's Luncheonette was the kind of place that always had two old men sitting at the back table shouting at each other because they were too deaf to hear what the other one was saying. The morning sun was beating on the windows and Candy was waiting for us in a corner booth. She looked exactly the same as before, except she had taken off her striped cheesecloth shirt and was wearing a vest with the thinnest spaghetti straps in the world and absolutely no bra. She wore a string of coloured love beads knotted around her neck. I tried not to stare but my dad made up for both of us. He kept stroking her arm and gazing at her, which was making me feel nauseous.

The two old men at the back of the diner were yelling at each other about the garbage strike.

'Garbage . . . and rats everywhere.'

'Cats?'

'Rats . . . not cats. Cats don't eat garbage.'

'Rats eat garbage, I'm telling you.'

My dad ordered blueberry pancakes for us, coffee for him and Candy, and a strawberry milkshake for me.

Candy's eyes were unfocused and sleepy but her bad mood was gone. She giggled as my father sat down next to her, pulling the love beads tight around her neck with her finger as she did so. My father leaned in and lit the cigarette which now replaced the love beads in her mouth, and that led to more giggling. I felt a wave of irritation bubble up inside me as I stared out of the window so I didn't have to look at them.

My dad and I had this thing when I was a kid. Every Sunday, come rain or shine, we would get up and walk down the block to Zerilli's ice-cream parlour, where we would slip into the soft red leatherette seats right across from each other and order two bowls of ice-cream. I can't even remember how old I was when we first started our Sunday routine, but we did it for the longest time. I must've been a very small child in the beginning because I remember the smoothness of holding my dad's hand, and the pale rose colour of his palm in mine. Some wintery Sundays there was more ice outside on the sidewalk than behind the counter, but without fail we were there: eating our ice-cream and feeding the jukebox, searching for Sinatra songs. Dad loved Sinatra songs and on good days he would sing along and we would laugh. With Frank singing about lost love and my dad's undivided attention, I would chatter away about my week in school, or try to put an early squeeze on him for Christmas.

The years passed, but two things in life remained constant: the fact that my mother never once came with us, and the ice-cream flavours we chose. We never changed, and I mean not once. It was our thing. Double chocolate chip for me and strawberry for him. Mrs Zerilli would look up from behind her counter and, as soon as she saw us coming, she'd place two glass bowls on the metal surface and reach for her scoop. Double chocolate chip and strawberry, every time. It never changed . . . until the day that it did.

In my mind, Mrs Zerilli was about a hundred years old. Her back was bent over and her hands shook a little and, more times than not those days, she missed the glass bowls and left a chocolate-stained dribble on the counter. It was getting harder for her to cope and finally she decided to bring in a young woman to help her out. That's when we first met Candy Jackson. Candy was tall and fine-boned like a teenage boy. Her dark hair was long and kind of wild, but she didn't seem to care.

At first, nothing much changed. Candy got to know us and our regular order and we would slide into our regular booth, get Frank warmed up and race to the bottom of our glass bowls, laughing all the way. Candy was all 'Hey there' and 'Bye now' but slowly she started hanging out a little at our table, just shooting the breeze. One day she mentioned the song that was playing and how much she liked it. My dad got his change from his jacket pocket and handed Candy some coins to play the songs she liked. Now, normally it was my job to feed the jukebox and choose the Frank songs. He loved Sinatra, I loved Sinatra, and Mrs Zerilli always liked Sinatra too, and so that's what we played. Now Candy started playing whatever she liked on the jukebox and before you knew it, she was playing the Rolling Stones and Carole King and Dad had started acting as if he liked this stuff. He was saying things like:

'Uh huh . . . yeah, cool.'

He sounded like someone I didn't know.

It was the beginning of Fall when I knew for sure that something was wrong. It was a beautiful Sunday, one of those days where the sun was warming the whole earth and you just wanted to soak it up before winter came. The sky was a deep blue, and we strolled along towards Zerilli's happy as clams. Dad was laughing at all my stupid stories about school and the gossip I loved to tell him, just regular stupid stuff.

We got to Zerilli's and I saw Candy behind the counter and I said:

'Hi.'

'Hi, yourself,' Candy said but she wasn't looking at me.

I slid right into our usual booth but Dad was kind of pulling back. He hesitated just for a second by the counter and started looking at the ice-cream. Eventually, after staring at the silver tubs of pastel cream for a few seconds, he headed over to join me.

Quick as a flash, Candy appeared next to our booth, a notepad in one hand and a pencil in the other.

'Hey, there. What can I get you guys?'

I was thinking this was a really dumb question and I

rolled my eyes at Dad, expecting him to say, 'Our usual,' and to roll his eyes back at me as if we're a team and she should know better, but he didn't.

He was looking right at Candy and she was looking right back at him and I wanted them to stop, because the way they were looking at each other was just not right.

'I'll try that new cherry vanilla you were telling me about the other day.'

'You like strawberry. You always have strawberry.' I was practically shouting at him as I said it and he gave me that look, the *that's quite enough of you, young lady* kind of a look.

'So one cherry vanilla and one double choc chip?' Candy said, and her smile felt like a wound.

'Sure,' said Dad and he grinned at her and she bit on her bottom lip and smiled back at him, and that's when I knew. The knowing landed right in my belly. Our Sunday routine was a lie; it was just to see Candy, and it had been for a long time.

The next Sunday I told Dad I felt sick and couldn't go to Zerilli's. We never went there together again, and the worst part was I don't think he even noticed that I stopped going with him. I never said a word to my mother or anyone, but that was the day he started coming home late. And I knew exactly where he was.

Benny shoved a bright pink milkshake in front of me, and I was so hot and thirsty that I gulped it down without drawing breath. I'd just got to the bottom, where I was making that awful slurping noise as I tried to suck up the last few pink bubbles, when I heard the door open behind me and three boys walked in. They were jostling each other out of the way to get to the counter and laughing as they did so. As my eyes lifted from the dregs of my milkshake, I recognized the back of Cal's head and his arms leaning across the counter.

Cal looked just like Robert Redford in *The Way We Were*, if Robert Redford had only been sixteen in that movie. He always seemed as if he'd been dipped in light gold. His hair was just that perfect shade of blond and his skin was always lightly tan, even in deepest winter. He was perfect and it wasn't just my opinion.

I was pretty sure that Cal would barely notice me as Candy was practically naked at our table, and I was kind of relieved as the humidity had caused my hair to frizz up into a kind of puffball and my face was pink and clammy. Candy was leaning back in her seat and sweeping her long dark hair on top of her head and then letting it loose. She was eyeing my father in a very off-putting way as I tried to nibble at tiny mouthfuls of pancake without being seen to eat. I once saw myself eat in a mirror and my mouth did that weird side-to-side thing when I chewed so I decided I would never allow anyone to watch me eat, and that especially applied to Cal.

It was hard to ignore my dad and Candy and keep watch to see what Cal ordered. This was new territory. I'd never been able to watch him eat before because my best friend Viola refused to eat in the school canteen, for reasons I wasn't entirely clear on. Cal ordered a grilled cheese sandwich and I found this satisfying. It was absolutely the kind of meal I could imagine myself cooking for him as we discussed his day.

The sound of metal clattering on to the tiled floor made Cal and his friends turn their heads to see what was going on. Candy had accidentally swept a knife off the table with her hand, and I ducked down to retrieve it as I didn't want Cal to see me in this state. As I reached towards the knife, I was greeted with an awful sight. Candy's skirt was hoisted up out of the way and my father's hand was proceeding up her right thigh. My head flew up and hit the edge of the table and I couldn't help but cry out:

'Ow, that hurt.'

As I rubbed the back of my head and tentatively felt around for any sign of blood, I caught Cal watching me. He took a mouthful of grilled cheese but was grinning as he wiped his mouth with the back of his hand. I couldn't believe what was happening because it looked for all the world as if he was smiling *at me*. He kind of nodded his head in recognition, but by the time I arranged my smile in what I was sure was friendly but not too friendly, he'd turned away and was deep in conversation with his friends again, and I felt like a fool. Sitting there with my dad . . . and Candy Jackson, of all people.

'Can we go now?' I stared at my father and tried to ignore Candy, who was leaning all over his shoulder.

'Candy hasn't finished her breakfast yet.'

'Dad, I don't feel so good.'

My dad was torn between me and Candy draped all over him. I wanted to pull her off him by her hair.

I sighed.

'Just give me the keys and I'll find my own way. It's OK.'

'Ava, can you just wait a few more minutes?'

His eyes met mine and I stared him out, noting that at least both his hands were back on the table. I shook my head and held my hand out. He passed the small brass keys across the table towards me and Candy giggled again. Cal was finishing off his sandwich and didn't turn around as I slid out of my seat and shut the door quietly on my way out.

The apartment felt strange, as though something was wrong with the air. I hesitated outside my mother's locked bedroom door, listening for signs of life, but there was just silence. Everything was just as we'd left it, except for a strange ripe smell which turned out to be a carton of milk that got left out in the heat by mistake. I emptied it down the sink and ran the water until the curdled liquid disappeared down the drain. Throwing open the windows, I tried to find some relief from the unbearable sticky heat. I couldn't stand the stale sweat on my skin for a minute longer. Eventually I headed to the shower, where I ran the water until it was ice-cold and let it wash the dust and sweat off my skin.

Wrapping myself in the bath towel, I flopped on to my bed, surrounding myself with the posters of people I loved and staring up at the ceiling. My walls used to be covered with David Cassidy posters showing his soft puppy-dog eyes and silky hair, but I removed him last summer and replaced him with Al Pacino and Robert Redford. I didn't yet love any of them the way I'd loved David, but I was hoping to develop more mature tastes. I figured if I tried to like cool people that I might become cool too, but so far it was a bust. I did my usual inspection of my flaws in the mirror, found they hadn't improved and mused on how it was possible for one person to be so below average, before pulling on my jeans and scraping my hair into a ponytail.

The low voice sounded strained and hurt but it carried right through our apartment. My mother was awake and my father, as usual, was nowhere to be found. Candy would be due at Zerilli's for her shift soon and I really hoped that my dad was on his way home, but I couldn't be sure.

The voice got louder and there were a series of small shrieks and then a scream. I stood outside my mother's bedroom door for several seconds just listening. She was muttering and moaning inside but I couldn't make out the words. I couldn't bear to listen to her for a minute longer and so I twisted the key in the lock and let myself in.

She was half in and half out of her bed and I could see that her nightdress was wet and clinging to the back of her thighs. My mom had wet herself and was now howling with fury and frustration. As soon as I entered the room her head twisted violently towards me and she made a low hissing sound.

'Mom . . . it's me, Ava.'

I stood just inside the bedroom door, too afraid to approach the bed and not sure what to do to help her.

I edged forward towards the bed, not wanting to get too close to her, but at the same time not wanting to leave her there in the hot stench of her own urine. My mother sank back against her pillows, closing her eyes while I tentatively reached out a hand but there was no response. She started to rock back and forth and then her eyes snapped open and she stared past me as if I wasn't there.

I patted her hand again and this time she did look at me. Her eyes were dull and sad and she started to cry. She'd stopped muttering and was furiously staring at me.

'You . . . you left me!' she yelled, her face so close I could smell her sour breath, her stale sweat and the stench rising from her nightdress. And then her eyes became unfocused again and she appeared to be shouting at somebody who wasn't there.

'Help me! Jesus, don't leave me!' Her voice cracked and the tears streamed down her face. Her hands clutched at thin air as if she was reaching for something. She kept repeating the same words over and over like a chant. *Help me. Jesus, don't leave me.* That's what she'd been saying.

'Mom, do you want to put a fresh nightdress on? Should I get you one?'

'Fuck you!' she screamed. 'Get your hands off me!'

She started to mutter obscenities at the top of her voice and then a howling scream that terrified me. Scrambling to my feet, I backed away from this mad, shrieking woman who used to be my mother. Running out of the room and locking the door behind me.

My dad had to come home soon and he would know what to do. My hands were shaking as I turned the radio up as loud as it would go, letting the sound of the Stylistics' 'Sing Baby Sing' drown out the awful screeching noises coming from my mother's bedroom.

Pulling warm air into my lungs, I started to calm myself down. I could still hear my mother yelling as I ran down the hallway into my bedroom and slammed the door shut behind me. Collapsing face down on to my bed, I put a pillow over the back of my head to muffle the things I didn't want to hear, but I couldn't catch my breath properly and eventually had to sit up on the edge of the bed with my knees clasped to my chest until I could focus. I was trying so hard not to think, but panic was flooding through me. A siren roared past in the street below and for a few seconds it drowned out the sound of my mother. I laid my chin on my knees and tried to blow air out of my lungs until I felt calmer. My mother eventually stopped screaming, and everything went quiet.

I slid off the bed and curled up into a ball in the

corner, wedging myself between the bed and the box that I'd abandoned on the floor. My hands were still trembling as I pulled things out of the box in a frenzy, laying them all out over my bedroom floor, pinning the butterfly necklace around my neck and looking at my reflection in the mirror before frantically flipping through the photograph albums without really looking at the pages.

In an effort to slow my breathing, I tried to focus on the pictures, scanning them one at a time and counting my breaths as I exhaled.

The photographs were mostly of the woman called Dovie and a second, fair-haired woman. Dovie had a kind face and dark wavy hair. She was shorter, kind of pretty, but not as pretty as the fair-haired woman. They were always smiling in the photographs, but their eyes seemed serious and I noticed that they never linked arms or messed around in silly poses as friends normally do in pictures. There was always a slight gap between them, as though they were soldiers standing to attention.

I took out the whiskey tumbler and held it up to look at it. There were at least thirty pieces of crumpled paper wrapped around it to keep it from breaking. They were letters – or at least somebody had intended them to be a letter. Some were screwed up into tight balls but most of them were abandoned as if the writer had just stepped out of the room. Pale blue sheets of writing paper and on each one was written 'Dear Gillian'.

'Dear Gillian, I will always love you' . . . 'Dear Gillian,

I am writing to say' . . . 'Dear Gillian, I don't know how' . . .

The letters all ended as if the writer had no idea what to put next. Some of them were crossed out but most of them just faded away.

I reached into the box and pulled out the photograph of Dovie. Whoever had scrawled 'LIAR' on her face had pressed down so hard that the pen had nearly gone through to the other side of the photograph.

8

New York City, 1955

It was a freakishly hot Saturday morning with air as thick as syrup and a laziness hanging over the city that dulled the senses, making us stupid and sleepy. Gillian and I sat in silence as the sounds of Chet Baker blew through our apartment, she with a dark look on her face and her arms folded against me. We had barely spoken all morning. Today was the day that Judith was due to move into our apartment.

Judith's condition for keeping quiet was to move into our spare bedroom and live rent free until such time as she managed to save up the key money for the apartment that she'd fallen in love with over on 23rd Street. She had it all figured out, the product of her busy little mind churning over how to gain advantage from my situation.

'It would only be until I could save enough. You know how expensive a lease can be, and you are so lucky to have that lovely place just for the two of you. I couldn't even imagine such a thing. I just want my own place, but how can I save on a secretary's pay? I wouldn't be any bother and it would only be for a few weeks . . .'

There was nothing else to say. I couldn't refuse, or else. Judith didn't specify and she didn't need to. I knew exactly what would happen if I refused to go along with her scheme. It wasn't me I was worried about though; Gillian knew nothing about this and I was determined that she never would. It took me a short time to recover from the shock of what it was that Judith wanted, but very quickly I could see no alternative, and I agreed.

It didn't stop the anger rolling through me like a river of hate. I was furious at myself for putting us in this position, but mostly I was furious at Judith. I wanted to slap Judith's face, to feel the skin of my palm sting the soft fleshy cheek right beneath her sly brown eyes, to shock her into understanding I was not going to take this from her. Instead, I did nothing but give a weak nod to show I understood and, worse, was about to comply. I stood there in the ladies' bathroom at school, leaning against the sink in case my feet gave way underneath me, listening to her ramble on and watching her mouth spill out tales of damp and roaches, the horrors of sharing with girls who are 'not my kind of people'. *We are not your kind of people*, I wanted to shout. My fingernails dug deep into the palms of my hands as I listened to her.

I thought about running down the corridor towards Gillian's classroom to find refuge there, to tell her the impossible situation we were now in. We could pack our bags and run away; go to Paris where we could teach English and spend our nights in jazz clubs watching

70

trails of blue cigarette smoke fade into music. But something stopped me. Maybe I was scared that Gillian would say no, or that her future plans wouldn't include me. I chewed it over for the rest of the day, miserable and distracted, so much so that even the class stopped gossiping and stared at me rather oddly.

I didn't see Gillian for most of the day, but when we met at the school gates to get the bus downtown to our apartment, she was tired and snappy. She rubbed at her temples and the back of her neck, trying to ease the tension that had seeped into her muscles. One look at the frown lines between her eyes and the slightly haunted look about her silenced me. When she asked about Judith, I lied.

Now, I sat in our apartment, watching the second hand on the clock work around to the time Judith was due to arrive, each tick reminding me that I was a liar. The lie was like a tiny spot of blood on a crisp white sheet, and it's all I could see. I had lied to Gillian and now I didn't know what to do to fix things. She was sure to find out. I justified it to myself, but liars do that anyway. It was the kinder thing to tell a white lie and so, when she asked me, I'd told Gillian that Judith hadn't seen us kiss, but she needed a favour from us and all things considered it was better to keep her onside.

Silently, I rationalized it to myself. Judith would stay for a short time so she could finally get together her key money for the apartment on 23rd Street. I would pay

Judith's share of expenses without telling Gill. It would stretch me financially, but I would manage somehow. I knew Gillian wouldn't be happy if she ever found out but it was a risk worth taking to keep us both safe.

I lied again and again, telling her that Judith had offered to sleep in the nook, but I'd insisted she take the spare room which I'd said was my bedroom. I hoped it might make it easier for Gillian and me to be together than if Judith was sleeping in the nook, which was right opposite our bedroom. I felt sick with every lie and the fact that Gillian believed me so easily made everything worse. Though it didn't stop her being furious.

'How long for?' Gillian glowered at me.

'A few weeks, that's all. By the time school starts again she'll be gone, I swear.'

'How could you agree to this? This is the only place in the world we can be safe and together . . . and now she'll be here? Are you out of your mind?'

'I panicked! Nothing will change. We can be careful for a few weeks.'

'Of course it will change; she'll be here watching us day and night.'

'I promise it will be fine. It's just for a few weeks, I swear . . . and in some ways it could be good to have her here. If we had something to hide, we wouldn't invite Judith to stay, would we?' I was babbling like a fool, and the fact that Judith could destroy us with one phone call gave me little choice but to keep on lying. I couldn't look at Gillian for fear she would find out.

'Trust me. I'll make it right.'

'You always say that.'

'I will look after you. I promise that nobody is going to hurt you, OK?'

Even as I spoke the words, I felt the emptiness of my promise. Gillian was so desperate to believe me that she didn't ask any more questions, but her fury at having to share her home with Judith was white hot.

Our days were silent, and our evenings spent mostly apart. I tried to make myself useful by getting on my hands and knees and scrubbing out the nook, but no matter what I did, Gillian remained angry. I played the music that we loved, Billie singing about 'Strange Fruit' or Chet crooning 'My Funny Valentine', but it just reminded us that something had changed, and we waited with a sense of dread for Judith to arrive.

The night before she came, we rolled back the rug and danced to our favourite songs, holding each other close and knowing it would be the last time for a while. Gillian was stiff with fury in my arms and everything felt wrong. Afterwards we sat out on the fire escape eating apples and drinking our usual whiskey nightcap and I felt sick with guilt. We made a half-hearted toast to a future I wasn't sure we believed in any more.

I ached to confess everything to Gillian but I couldn't bear the thought of what might happen if she found out. I sipped at my whiskey and gazed at her. Her face was a picture of misery and I so wanted to make things right again. I took my apple knife and started to carve our initials in the black metal rail.

'What are you doing?' Gillian asked.

'Only we will know it's here and we can come out here anytime . . .'

It was a small thing but I hoped it would be enough to keep us going for a while. Gillian drained her glass and laid back against the wall, staring up at the night sky.

When I reached for her, she turned away.

Three brown leather suitcases and four large cardboard boxes were hoisted up the stairs and into our spare bedroom by a gangly teenage boy with a pink rash on his cheeks and a habit of wiping his nose on his sleeve. As he piled the boxes into his arms, he bit down on his flaky lips with the effort even though none of Judith's possessions seemed particularly heavy. When he stowed the final box on top of my grandmother's wooden dresser, he hesitated in the doorway, shuffling his feet in an embarrassed way until Judith opened her large black purse and handed him a dollar for his trouble. He stared at it, unsure whether to be glad, and then as she snapped her purse shut with determination, he seemed startled and bolted out of the door.

The moment he disappeared the apartment became silent and awkward. It seemed too small for us, even though there was plenty of room. Gillian stayed in her armchair, arms still folded, chin raised, stubborn and unflinching. She stared half-heartedly out of the window and point blank refused to greet Judith; indeed, she was barely speaking to me.

None of this appeared to bother Judith, who unpacked slowly and precisely. She filled drawers with her belongings as I tried to make up for the lack of welcome from Gillian.

'I cleared out most of my things and moved them next door. Gillian won't mind sharing her closet,' I lied.

She opened the doors and saw our heavy winter coats still hanging there.

Judith tutted and fussed about not having enough space until I took the coats away and crushed them inside the only other closet. I bit my lip and carried on trying to make things right for everyone. Gillian sat there glowering at me while Judith was seemingly oblivious to the lack of welcome.

I helped Judith unpack the rest of her things and watched as she fussed around our spare bedroom, hanging up a pale pink summer frock and another pale blue one in identical style. She had two plain skirts in navy and grey, and a few good white blouses, some sturdy walking shoes and a pair of patent leather court shoes in black. There was in fact plenty of room for our winter coats, but I said nothing.

The other cases were filled with her woollens, underwear and mud-brown stockings balled up into little packages. We shoved the suitcases up on top of the closet out of the way and started on the boxes. Apart from a few books and a photo album, I was almost sorry for her having so few things. A few pieces of jewellery, mostly costume as far as I could see, and then in the final box some sheets, pillowcases and a small cream alarm clock that she set on the bedside table alongside her library book, which was a romance novel with one of those covers where the heroine is wearing a corseted dress and swooning across a dark-haired man. I took the cardboard boxes downstairs and stuffed them into the trash and then set about trying to keep the peace.

The minute Gillian got up to make us some coffee, albeit reluctantly, Judith settled herself into Gillian's favourite armchair nearest the window and tucked her legs up underneath her. Her little eyes flitted from corner to corner, taking everything in.

'You are so lucky to have such a lovely place,' she said.

I tried a weak smile but Gillian glared at her in such an obvious manner that I was immediately scared Judith would be offended.

'I thought it might be nice if we went out for dinner together this evening. We would usually make our separate arrangements for that,' I added hastily before Gillian lost her temper again. Judith's face lit up like a child looking forward to a treat and, for a split second, I felt guilty for disliking her so much.

Judith wanted to go to an Italian place just off Washington Square that was a favourite of hers and we didn't care enough to fight over it. We sat in a booth with a red-checked tablecloth and ordered plates of pasta and a bottle of red wine. Gillian sipped at hers, keeping her eyes lowered and only speaking in clipped sentences about the quality of the pasta (good), or the pianist (bad). I gulped at my glass of wine, feeling the warm relief flood through me. Judith told us long rambling stories about previous room-mates she'd had in the city: girls who scorched her clothes with their cigarettes by accident, and one who stole money out of her purse as she slept. She repeated over and over again how pleased she was to finally be staying in such a nice place with *good people* and, as Gillian's head snapped up so that she glared across the table, Judith added weakly, 'On a temporary basis.' Gillian lowered her gaze and went back to pushing ravioli around her plate with her fork. The evening ended with me offering to pay for dinner and both of them letting me, for very different reasons.

Once we climbed back up the stairs to our little front door it became clear very quickly how awkward these next few weeks would be. Judith liked to finish her evening with some warm milk and a sleeping pill. I felt a glimmer of hope at the news she took something to make her sleep.

We all seemed to want the bathroom at the exact same time and once that was all done, Judith still showed no signs of going to her room, leaving Gillian to appear with a pile of folded sheets in her arms which she dumped on to our pull-out in the nook along with a pillow.

'Here you are, Dovie. Sleep tight.' With that, she gave

me a look that would have soured milk and disappeared into our bedroom, shutting the door behind her with a contemptuous click. Judith chatted for a few more minutes but eventually started yawning loudly and wandered off to her own room. I watched until her light went out, waiting for the sounds of sleep before gently opening our bedroom door and creeping across the creaky floor to the bed where Gillian was lying with her back to me.

'It's better if you don't,' she hissed.

'But, Gill . . .'

She didn't turn over and I decided not to risk any further argument and crept back out to the nook where I sat miserably next to the pile of folded sheets and chain-smoked cigarettes until I felt too sleepy to think about the mess we were in.

I woke the next morning to find Gillian leaning over me with a hot cup of coffee and a morning kiss.

'She's in the shower,' Gillian whispered and I nodded, understanding we had just a few precious moments alone. We were still us as long as I could keep the peace for a little while longer. I held her tight before she pulled away from my grasp and disappeared out of the door. At least we'd broken the ice and I hoped I could finally begin to mend things between us, although the guilt gnawed at me.

I'm a liar. I'm a liar. It was all I could think about.

Sundays used to be our favourite day of the week. In the morning we lazed around tangled in warm sheets, only getting up to fetch the newspaper from the hallway and make coffee. We shared out pages of the paper and shook crumbs of cinnamon toast from our sheets. We played music and then took lazy baths together before heading off to a small jazz club in the Village. We were always careful where we went, making sure that it wasn't part of any 'scene', just somewhere that we could be two spinster teachers who liked jazz. Everything we did was careful, measured and precise (until I'd ruined it for us) and we guarded our Sundays fiercely, before getting ready to face the world again on Monday mornings. This particular Sunday, however, was rather different.

Gillian sat curled up in her usual armchair reading the newspaper while I tried to distract myself with a novel. Judith sat in between us, a cup of herbal tea in hand. At one point, she leaned across and took the crossword section before Gillian had got to it, smiling her strange little smile and saying, 'You don't mind, do you?' But Gillian did mind and glared at me while Judith just sat there chewing on her pencil.

I put a record on to hide the awkwardness between us. The sweet sounds of Ella soothed the room until Judith gazed up at me with a pained expression on her face and said:

'Oh, I hate to be a nuisance but would you mind turning it off? I've got the most awful headache this morning.'

'Maybe you should go and lie down, Judith,' Gillian said sharply but Judith just smiled her sly little smile.

'Oh no . . . if we just have some quiet for a while, I'm sure I'll feel better. Don't you worry about me. Maybe we could play cards later. I love a good card game, don't you?'

Without saying a word to each other, Gillian and I cancelled our plans to go to our little jazz club. We didn't want to take Judith with us and it was clear that there was no way to go without her. Gillian stared at her newspaper but I could tell she wasn't reading it. The tension felt unbearable and I was desperate to escape for a few moments of peace.

'Well, I think I'm going to take a nice cool shower.' I stood up, but nobody said anything. Judith was engrossed in her crossword and Gillian glanced up at me quickly and then looked away.

I escaped to the bathroom, locking the door behind me and exhaling with the sheer relief of being alone as I rested my head against the cool tiles and wondered how we could possibly manage this situation for weeks on end. I'd told so many lies that even I'd started to believe that Judith didn't know about us; but of course she did. I took a deep breath and turned to face the shower.

It was full of Judith's things. A rose-covered washbag hung from the hook that was meant for a hand towel. A blue washcloth was draped over our sink as if it belonged there. Her mud-brown stockings were rinsed out and hanging over the side of the bathtub while a freshly washed grey-white brassiere dangled from wooden pegs over the top of the shower. I couldn't bear the sight of her things sprawled across our private space but there wasn't a damn thing I could do about it. A wave of crushing despair swept over me and I sank down on to the bathroom floor and cried.

9

New York City, 1975

I must have fallen asleep right on my bedroom floor, because when I woke up the apartment was silent and my dad was standing over me, whispering, 'Ava, honey . . . wake up.' I was so relieved to see him that I wanted to cling to his legs, even managing a sleepy smile before I remembered my mother.

'Is Mom OK?' I panicked and tried to get to my feet, but my dad put his hand on my shoulder to comfort me.

'Everything's fine.' His face suggested otherwise.

He sat down on the edge of my single bed, smoothing down the covers with the palm of his hand, as he used to do when I was little.

'Is she going to get better?' My heart raced as I waited for him to answer but he just reached across and tousled my hair.

'Sure . . . she just needs some rest. She'll be—'

I guessed he was going to say that my mother would be fine, but he was interrupted by the sound of glass breaking and an angry howl of rage from the next room. We both leaped up and ran to the bedroom door. My dad twisted the key, unlocked the door with one hand and pushed me to one side with the other.

'Stay here, Ava.'

I stayed back and let him go into the room first, but I couldn't help trying to see past him.

The glass from the bedroom window lay shattered around her bare feet and she was bleeding quite heavily from her right hand, which was curled into a small bloody fist. She was screaming through the broken window, her bloodied hands reaching desperately upwards:

'Don't leave me! Jesus! Help me!' Her voice sounded hard and bitter. She couldn't see me because my dad was blocking the doorway to stop her getting past him. 'Don't leave me! Help me!' Her hands were clutching at something or somebody that none of us could see.

'Mom!' I couldn't help but call out to her, but she was fixated on the sight of my father going towards her and I didn't know what else to say.

'Mary-Lyn, stay right there! Don't move! You'll cut your feet. I'm coming to get you . . .'

My father's voice was soothing but I could hear the edge of fear and I knew that neither of us knew what we were doing. He walked steadily to where my mother was standing, stretching out one hand towards her and then gently leading her back towards the bed. She stared at him as if he was a stranger that she didn't quite recognize.

He put his arm around her, but lightly so as not to panic her; then he turned to face me and whispered softly:

'Ava, call Dr Cohen and tell him this is an emergency. He needs to come right away. Tell him I said that. Can you do that, honey?'

I nodded but for a split second I didn't move from my spot in the doorway. My mother was singing and crying. There was blood running down her arm and the room smelled so bad it made me retch, but still I couldn't move.

'Sweetie . . . you need to call now.'

At the sound of my father's voice, I stopped staring and backed into the hallway, heading towards the telephone and yellow pad we kept with all our emergency numbers listed on it. Dr Cohen was written on it in black ink, right between the all-night plumber and the number for my school. I dialled carefully, listened to it ring exactly three times before a woman answered and I was able to explain what we needed.

Dr Cohen arrived with his old brown medicine bag and gave my mother an injection that calmed her while he dealt with her wounds. There was silence and then they closed her bedroom door and sent me to my room so they could talk. The fact that they were standing right outside my door and hadn't gone to sit in the living room made it worse somehow.

Dr Cohen started to speak more loudly and I realized he was using our telephone to call someone. I cracked open my bedroom door an inch or two and saw my dad leaning against the wall in the hallway. He caught my eye and gave me a sad smile.

'The doc's calling the hospital. It's the best place for your mom.'

'How long will she be in the hospital?' I had a very bad feeling about how this was going to go.

He shrugged and looked away.

'Until they can make her better, I guess. I'm going with the ambulance and to take care of the paperwork. I'm coming straight back when I'm done. Can you stay here for me, sweetie?'

'Can't I come with you?'

'They need to get your mom settled and then we'll be able to visit. I can take you to see her in a day or so but for now it's best if you wait here.'

He leaned across to give me an awkward hug, which was interrupted by Dr Cohen appearing at my side and nodding at my dad that it was time to go.

I could hear her sobbing as they led her through the apartment and out of our front door and then I was all alone and it was strangely silent. I looked at the traces of my mother's blood on the floor and my legs buckled right from under me. I sat down on the kitchen floor under the poster of Coney Island that my mother pinned up there so she could look at the vivid blue of the ocean. It was faded now but she didn't care.

'One day we are gonna live right on the beach,' she would say.

On my last birthday, I turned fifteen years old and my mother and father took me to Coney Island for the day, just the three of us. I was supposed to invite my friend Viola, but she got sick and couldn't make it. We didn't really go on the rides; we just wandered around, watching other people screaming. Dad bought me a box of salt-water taffy with their pink and blue wrappers. I ate so many I got sick.

My mother was mostly silent that day and just stared out at the ocean with that strange blank look on her face and smoked her Chesterfields. I remember wondering if she was upset about something because all she did was stare and she barely said a word. When I offered her one of my candies, she didn't even look at me.

'People might be watching us too,' she said.

'What people?' my father asked.

'The people on the other side of the ocean.'

She wasn't making any sense and my dad pulled a face at me and ruffled my hair as if I was six years old. I didn't mind so much. I was drunk on salt-water taffy and birthday.

She looked so pretty that day. Her hair was curled in soft waves and she was wearing her best yellow summer dress with small white daisies on the straps. When she'd made me breakfast that morning, she pulled me out of bed and made me dance with her until we couldn't stop laughing. But now, just a few hours later, she seemed so quiet and sad, as though she'd never find anything to laugh about again.

As the sun began to set my father started packing up our beach things. My mother was still gazing out to sea as if she was hoping for something, and when she stood up to leave there was a large bloody stain on the back of her dress. It was dark red and shaped like a country that nobody visited. She didn't notice, but I saw people looking as we walked back to the car; a couple of girls giggled and pulled nasty faces to each other. I wanted to wrap something around her but there wasn't anything. We went home and nobody said a word about it. The dress was hanging on the fire escape with the washing the next morning, but she didn't wear it again.

My hands were trembling with the shock of everything that had happened and a couple of silent tears slid down my cheeks as I sat on the kitchen floor. I couldn't stop myself shaking and my legs felt as though they wouldn't hold my weight. The air seemed too heavy to breathe as the sun burned through the windows and I pushed one open and crawled outside on to the fire escape. The city was loud but comforting in a familiar way. I held on to the black metal rail and ran my hands along it, taking deep lungfuls of smoky garbage-ridden air to stop myself crying.

My fingers traced the outline of two deep grooves sliced into the metal and I ran my hands along the rough edges of them until I felt better. All I could do was wait for my dad to come home again and hope that everything would be OK. The silent tears were still falling on to my cheeks but at least I had stopped shaking.

I glanced down at the rail where my fingers had been

tracing outlines and saw something I'd never noticed before.

Carved into the black metal were two letters forming deep grooves: 'D & G'. I ran my fingers over the curled letters until a thought formed in my mind. D . . . for Dovie. The letters were made out to Gillian . . . G . . . for Gillian?

They were right here. Did they live here? Is that why the parcel had been sent to our apartment? Where were they now? Pressing my palm flat against the rail I felt the letters outlined against my skin and wondered about the women who had stood here before me.

I O

New York City, 1955

It had been exactly nineteen days since Judith moved in with us. Gillian and I were enjoying a peaceful day alone and for a few brief hours it was just like old times. I was sprawled across the couch with my head in Gillian's lap and just the feel of her cool palm stroking my hair made my eyelids close and my cares lift.

Gillian was still irritated by Judith, but at least she was less irritated by me, so I could breathe a little easier. Once she was sure Judith had taken her nightly sleeping pill, she even allowed me to creep into our bed for a few short hours. As we lay in the dark holding each other I started to hope for a future. I so wanted to confess everything to Gillian but I was too cowardly, and so at the first sign of light I would creep back down the hallway and into the nook, before Judith woke up. I was desperate for her to go, but every day brought another sign that she was making herself comfortable.

Everywhere I looked there was evidence of Judith: reading, eating, sleeping, showering. I could hear her bare feet padding along the landing to the bathroom, twisting the stiff brass faucet and then the gurgle of cold water until her teeth were scrubbed clean. A stray black hair in our sink and her toothbrush sitting in its little blue cup next to mine on our bathroom shelf. Her library book lay abandoned on the kitchen table and her unfamiliar perfume filled the air: lilacs and sweet talcum powder.

I came home from grocery shopping one day and found a brand-new blue lamp with a fringed shade in the living room, close to the armchair Gill liked to read in. Her usual armchair was now occupied by Judith because the shape of it was better for her back. There were unfamiliar cereals squashed into our kitchen cupboards and herbal teas that we didn't drink.

A fresh bottle of gin or whiskey appeared every time we looked like running short and two new summer skirts hung in her closet. It seemed to me that I was supporting a woman I didn't want in our apartment, while she was getting settled in, and not showing any sign of ever moving out.

As soon as we heard the front door slam and the rap of court heels on the stairs, I leaped up and was standing awkwardly in the middle of our living room with a guilty look on my face when Judith came in, looking very pleased with herself.

'I'm so glad you're here, Dovie. I practically ran all the way back because I couldn't wait to see your face when I told you the good news.'

'You've got the apartment? That's great news!'

'Well, no . . . it's not that.' Her face became crestfallen and the glee with which she held on to her news disappeared. 'Actually . . . I've had some bad news about the place on 23rd Street. I kept meaning to tell you about it.'

Gillian raised her eyebrows and stared at me.

'What kind of bad news?' I asked warily.

'Someone has only gone and offered the landlord more money and he's accepted their offer.'

'Wait a minute,' said Gillian abruptly. 'So there's no apartment now?'

I could tell by the tone of Gillian's voice that she was about to lose her temper and there wasn't much I could do to stop her.

'But there are other apartments out there?' I offered, trying in vain to keep the peace.

'Well, I'm looking. I hate to be a nuisance but it's just hard to find the right kind of place with the right kind of people. You know, I so appreciate how kind you've both been to take me in like this.'

Judith smiled her sly little smile but I could see the despair on Gillian's face.

'I'm sure we can help you find somewhere. So, don't keep us in suspense, Judith. What's this surprise?' I was desperate to change the subject. All I could think about was how much longer I could keep all of this a secret from Gillian.

Judith regained her composure and carefully opened her purse. She pulled out two tickets and offered them to me.

'I know how much you love jazz and I just thought this might be a way that I can pay you back because you've been so kind to me.'

I glanced down at the pieces of paper and was stunned to see that Judith had bought us tickets to see Chet Baker in concert that evening.

'You shouldn't have spent your money on this. I appreciate the gesture and all, but you really didn't need to . . .'

'It's no trouble at all. There's plenty of time for saving and I needed to show you how grateful I am. Not many people have friends as good and true as you've been to me.'

The sly little smile was back again and I could feel the sting of something nasty approaching.

'We'd better get ourselves ready, Dovie.'

I looked at the two tickets in my hand and then I stared at Judith with a puzzled expression on my face.

'Oh, I couldn't get a third ticket,' she trilled. 'I'm so sorry, Gillian, but you don't mind, do you? It's only that I know Dovie is the real jazz fan here, and she was the one who invited me to stay with you. I hope you're not offended. Please say you aren't. I'll take good care of her, I promise.'

I could see Gillian from the corner of my eye, lips tensed while exhaling a lungful of smoke, her eyebrows raised.

'Sure. You two girls have a wonderful time.' And with that she crushed out her cigarette in the ashtray and snapped open her library book, even though I could see she wasn't reading it.

I chewed at the inside of my cheek to stop myself saying anything that would make this worse. I just hoped that Gillian could see this wasn't my fault. Except that, of course, it was.

It was a thundery evening and a slash of lightning split the sky as we stepped out of doors. Large splashes of rain followed a deep growl of thunder and, before long, it was pouring into oily puddles that splashed at our stockings and left muddy stains on the backs of our legs. Judith stuck her hand out and flagged down a cab. I was glad to be out of the rain, but to watch her hand over dollar bills at a rate that I knew would keep her living with us until New Year made me feel quite sick. The cab crawled along the rainy avenues, came to the intersection and pulled in next to the club where a small crowd was already beginning to gather. Judith paid the driver, dismissing my offer to help, and we stumbled out on to the wet sidewalk. She slipped her arm through mine and pulled me in the direction of a cocktail bar next door.

'Let's get out of this rain. We've got time for drinks and maybe even a bite to eat before the show starts.'

The tuxedo-suited doorman greeted us with a 'Good evening, ladies' but I could feel him watching us and trying to work out what we wanted in his bar. We slipped into a booth and ordered a couple of vodka gimlets, which arrived promptly, along with the check that was tucked discreetly under a napkin. The message was clear: if we didn't have dates, then we were not expected to linger. Judith raised her glass and held it towards mine:

'Let's have a toast.'

'What shall we drink to?'

'How about to friendship?'

My smile grew brittle, but I held my glass steady and clinked it softly against hers.

The bar was quiet as it was that in-between stage between workers going home to the suburbs and the city drinker crowd turning up for their late night. In one corner, there were two middle-aged men, pot-bellied with slightly receding hair, obviously married but with the look of men away on some sales conference and enjoying their freedom. The taller of the two men had sandy hair and freckles all over his hands. I noticed him watching us as we came in, his eyes shifting up and down our bodies, appraising us and deciding our worth. I kept my back turned slightly so as not to encourage him, but it didn't matter because he decided to take his chances anyway.

The waiter appeared with a silver tray and two fresh vodka gimlets. Judith giggled and waved to the two men.

'Shouldn't we be going? We don't want to miss the show,' I said, trying to keep calm although my body was rigid with anger.

'Oh, there's plenty of time. Relax, Dovie, we're just being friendly and there's no harm in that.' Her voice was soft and girlish as if she found everything vaguely amusing.

The vodka gimlets were eventually followed by the men themselves, as I knew they would be. First the tall sandy-haired man and then, shuffling behind him, his shorter and timid friend. Judith giggled some more and squeezed over to the far side of the booth to let the sandy-haired man sit next to her, leaving me with no option but to do the same.

The sandy-haired guy was called Bob and his friend Mike. I wasn't even sure they were their real names, but Judith didn't seem to care. They were in sales right enough, but for dental equipment, and only in town overnight.

'Say, you two girls wouldn't like to do us a solid and have dinner with us, would ya?' asked Bob.

'We can't, I'm afraid,' I said quickly. 'We've got tickets for a show.'

'Oh, now that's a real shame. We hate eating alone, don't we, Mike? We've heard all our stories about a million times. I expect you two ladies are a lot more interesting.'

Judith looked up at them, widely. 'Aren't you sweet? We could have supper, couldn't we, Dovie? There's plenty of time.'

Judith leaned across the table and squeezed my hand. Her gimlet glass was empty and her face wore the flushed look of a woman who couldn't hold her liquor. Before I could say a word, Bob wrapped an arm casually around Judith's shoulders and said:

'Sure, that's the idea now. Whadda you girls like to eat? How about we get a nice steak somewhere?'

'It's a plan.' Judith slid closer to Bob so that she was practically folded under his arm. I tried to stand up, but I had to wait for Mike to get to his feet and move out of the booth to release me.

'We'll need to be quick if we're to catch the show.' I gathered my coat and purse and frowned at Judith.

Bob got to his feet reluctantly, without removing his hand from Judith's shoulder. She was flirting in a horrible way. I felt embarrassed for her and I reached for her arm to steady her and lead her to the door. She wasn't falling over, but she had certainly lost her good sense through drinking the second cocktail too quickly. Mine was still sitting on the table untouched. The doorman gave us the same unfriendly look as we left the bar, and as soon as the fresh air hit Judith, she steadied herself enough to walk to the restaurant.

'I thought this was a girl's night out?' I hissed quietly in her ear as we walked, the men following behind us. 'Are you sure you want to get supper with these guys?'

'Why on earth not? You need to have more fun in your life, Dovie. You're so serious. What's the harm in a little supper and some light flirting?'

I moved away from her then. 'I really don't want to go.'

'What's wrong? Not your type? But what am I saying? *Of course* he's not your type. Take no notice of me.' She started to laugh, a mean drunken cackle. She held her hands to her face to hide her mouth but still she giggled through her fingers.

As quickly as the laughter started it died away and

Judith folded her arms and tilted her head to one side. She held my gaze for a beat and then very slowly said:

'You're not going to disappoint me . . . are you, Dovie? I don't think you should upset me, do you?'

Her voice was suddenly icy cold and her eyes sharp and unblinking. She leaned in so close I could smell the staleness of her warm breath.

'It's important to be nice to people, don't you think?'

I swallowed hard. My throat felt tight with words I couldn't speak. She stared at me in a way that made me feel afraid of her, and then I thought how ridiculous that was, because it was only Judith. Yet I couldn't shake the awful cold feeling of fear in my bones. Finally, the bitter silence between us was broken by the sound of Bob and Mike exclaiming that they knew just the place to get a good steak.

My heart sank.

*

Judith stared into the powder-room mirror and unrolled her tube of crimson lipstick. She traced a slick around her mouth and smacked her lips together. She snapped open her compact to press the powder puff around her nose a couple of times; then she patted down a stray hair and smoothed down the skirt of her dress. Clicking her purse shut, she turned to me.

'I'm certainly ready for some supper now, aren't you?' Her manner was all sugary sweet again and I couldn't believe the change in her.

We walked back into the restaurant and made our way across to the table where we'd left Bob and Mike. The number of glasses on the table told me they had continued to drink in our absence. Bob spotted Judith and struggled to his feet.

'Hey, here they are.' His tone suggested we were their wives returned from a long shopping trip to the dressmakers and I bristled, but Judith didn't seem to mind at all. We slid back into another booth – this one decorated with pictures of movie stars, none of whom had ever eaten steak in this place – once again allowing Bob and Mike to sit on the outside, trapping us until they wanted to leave. At least Mike kept his hands to himself. The drink made him sleepy more than anything and from time to time his head fell back against the blue leatherette of the booth and the feeling of that woke him up again, and so it continued for several minutes until four steaks arrived on white plates with a mound of fried potatoes and buttered corn on the side.

I ignored the wine that arrived with the steak and sipped on a glass of iced water. Bob was telling some story about his army days and Judith was hanging on his words, egging him on. His war hadn't lasted that long. He'd enlisted and was shipped to England, where he was stationed in a small town about an hour from London. Before he could see any action, he'd broken his leg badly on a training exercise and had to be shipped back home. This didn't deter Bob from making his time in Europe sound as if he'd personally captured Berlin. It was just noise, though, and I was glad not to have to answer questions or offer any information about myself, so I nodded politely and sipped my iced water and ate my steak.

Once the bloody traces of meat were all that was left on the plates, and the wine was finished, Bob started to eye Judith as if she could be dessert. I glanced at my watch, but I knew without really checking that we weren't going to make the show and I was only focused on getting out of there as soon as I could.

'Hey, this fella looks like he needs his beauty sleep,' Bob said, nodding at Mike whose head was bobbing back against the blue leatherette again. 'But you are most welcome to join me for a nightcap at our hotel. It's just a couple of blocks away.'

'I think we all need our beauty sleep now but thank you for a lovely evening,' I said firmly. I wanted to get up but Mike was wedged between me and freedom. I tried to catch Judith's eye but she was gazing at Bob.

'We could go for one. No harm in one nightcap but then we really do need our beauty sleep.' She giggled.

'You girls do not need any beauty sleep . . . and that's a fact.'

Judith giggled again and patted at Bob's huge paw, which was moving from her shoulder to her neck.

I felt sick watching them. I couldn't understand why Judith was doing this. I wanted to get out of there, but I was crushed into the corner of the booth and unable to get free without making a scene. Mike was sound asleep now and starting to snore quietly. He slumped right over and I couldn't stand the weight of his body touching mine.

Bob kicked Mike under the table to wake him up. His job was to pay the bill apparently, which he duly did, and we all gathered our coats and started to walk towards their hotel. I was relieved to be out of the booth because at least I could move freely, and I kept trying to signal my disquiet at Judith every time she glanced over at me, but she would just look away.

Once we reached the entrance to the hotel Bob became suddenly coy and suggested some elaborate ruse whereby Mike asked for their key, while he distracted the receptionist long enough to smuggle us upstairs to their room. I took the opportunity to grab hold of Judith's arm and pull her to one side.

'Are you sure about this? We don't even know these guys.'

'One drink,' she said smoothly. And then, 'They seem like nice guys. Anyone would think you didn't like nice guys, Dovie!'

Her voice was sharp and she glared at me until I let go of her arm.

Bob got the receptionist to turn her back long enough for us to scuttle into the elevator, and after some fumbling around Mike eventually managed to turn the key and let us into a dingy little room with twin beds and a door leading off the far end, which presumably led to the bathroom. Bob reached for a bottle of Jack that was on a side table next to their luggage and filled some cups with a generous slug before patting the bed and indicating that Judith should sit by him.

Mike and I sat awkwardly: he on the bed and I on the only chair in the room, a small wooden hardback that was uncomfortable to sit in, but much better than the alternative as far as I was concerned. A lamp by the side of Bob's bed let out a dim orange glow that created eerie shadows of us on the walls, and I hugged the cup of whiskey between my palms and prayed for time to pass. Mike, true to form, lay back on his bed and started to snore softly, and Bob and Judith were seated so close it would have been difficult to get a cigarette paper between them. I excused myself to go to the bathroom and ran the cold water while I leaned against the sink and decided to count down ten minutes before I was absolutely leaving to go home.

When I opened the door a crack, I could see the dim orange lamp was switched off and two shadowy outlines of people were kissing on Bob's bed. I'd had enough, and if Judith was mad about it then so be it, because I couldn't stand being there one minute longer. I flung open the door letting the light from the bathroom flood the room, causing the kissing couple to break apart.

'I'm going home now. Are you coming, Judith?'

My coat was on and my purse under my arm before she'd even untangled herself from Bob. He seemed less than happy about it but she did eventually manage to get her coat on and within minutes we'd snuck past the receptionist and were sitting in a taxi in sleepy silence.

As we reached the front door and I slotted my key in the lock, Judith leaned over and patted my arm, whispering into my ear:

'That was fun, wasn't it? We must do it again soon.' She was back to using her soft, wheedling tone of voice, but I'd seen the flash of meanness and threat behind her act.

'Sure,' was all I could manage but every fibre of my being was screaming, *Over my dead body*. We said our goodnights and I waited until she'd gone through her routine, closed her bedroom door and was snoring soundly before slipping into our room where Gillian was sleeping. I could feel the Chet Baker ticket in my pocket under my fingers and I started to crumple it into a ball. I hung my dress carefully in the closet and tossed the unused ticket into my dresser drawer.

'How was it?' Gillian murmured from the depths of a tangled sheet.

I longed to curl myself into her warm body and confess everything. The secret weighed on me and I took a deep breath – it would be better to come clean. Gillian stroked my face with her fingers and kissed me so softly I didn't want anything to stop her.

'Great. It was great,' I replied.

I I

New York City, 1975

Someone was calling my name from down in the street. I ran to the window to see Viola standing on the sidewalk, peering up at our windows and hollering at the top of her voice. Viola was my oldest friend, and pretty much my only friend. We met by accident in an old junk store on East 13th Street, on a bitterly cold January day when I was in seventh grade.

Viola (which her mother loved to pronounce Vi-O-lah, as if she takes her time about even calling her daughter home), was pulling out 78s from a dusty box on the floor, while I was flicking through a pile of old movie-star magazines that were full of Rita Hayworth posing by swimming pools in the most beautiful costumes, all gingham checks and little bows. Rita was wearing cat's-eye sunglasses, a wide-brimmed sunhat that she held on to her head with one hand, and a smile that said, *Look how perfect I am*, but in a good way. I loved old movies and magazines about old movie stars.

From time to time you could find interesting stuff in the junk store, and it was a cheap place to hang out, especially on cold and rainy days. The old man who ran it had an oil heater that always smelled of burned clothes, but it made the place nice and cosy with misted-up windows. If he was in a good mood, he would let you try on the racks of vintage clothes that smelled of mothballs and damp, but if he was in a bad mood, then you would need to be quick about finding what you wanted before he threw you out.

It was unusual to find someone my age in the store, but on that particular day I noticed a small, thick-set girl, with a fierce look of concentration on her face, lifting old records up to the light to read the labels. I recognized her from school but our paths had no reason to cross. She was a year younger than me, and we took none of the same classes.

I was happily rummaging around for old magazines, either full of movie stars or women's magazines with problem pages. They were useful if you needed to know things about kissing boys, or wearing the right perfume – light and floral, but never too much. Being *too much* was a big thing; also wearing too much make-up, or clashing patterns. The rules were quite complicated for girls.

I was very focused on Rita, and how she managed her level of perfection, when the sound of Viola exclaiming when she came across a treasure made me look up and start watching her. When she slipped a record out of its sleeve, and found one without scratches across the vinyl, she would make such a funny screwed-up face and look so pleased with herself that I laughed out loud. At one point, Viola found something that made her do a hop-skip dance in the middle of the store. She caught my eye as I grinned at her antics.

'You need something?' The look was fierce, but the voice held a lilt of amusement.

'Sorry, I didn't mean to stare but you seemed excited.'

'And you ain't never seen a person excited before?' She gave me a look that made me feel whatever I said next would be the wrong thing, but in a beat Viola burst out laughing, and gestured to the small pile of 78s under her arm.

'You like jazz?'

I hadn't really paid much attention to jazz songs although my mother had some songs she used to love to play before she got sick.

'I don't know.'

I felt stupid, as if I was being tested in some way, but Viola didn't hold it against me, and she patiently explained each one of the records, and why she was excited about them.

She learned all this stuff from her father, who played trumpet for a local jazz band, mostly weddings and parties, but sometimes he got a gig in Jazzland, a tiny club on East 7th, where all the greats started out.

Viola and I became friends, hanging out in school breaks and meeting at our junk store on a Saturday afternoon, sometimes grabbing a soda, or sitting on other people's front steps, and shooting the breeze until we ran out of things to say. We were kind of shy about introducing our friendship to our families, and it was fair to say that my parents were surprised when Viola showed up with me after school one day, but they were at least polite.

I'd never known my parents to invite any black people to our house, but they never said anything bad, either, unlike some people. Sometimes other grown-ups made remarks around Viola and me, but she never once commented on it. In Viola's family I was always ushered to a seat at the table and fed until I begged for mercy. I loved her house; it was full of noise and music, and I guess love. Sure, they had their problems, but I always felt safe and welcome there, which was more than I did in my own home at times. Viola's mom occasionally took me to one side and casually asked me how things were at home, but I could never bring myself to say anything other than, 'Everything's fine,' and then smile as if I believed it. Over the years our friendship grew, but I had yet to learn to love jazz.

I pulled up the window and leaned right out so Viola could see me from the street. She waved at me with a record she was carrying.

'There you are. Your buzzer's broken. Let me in!'

I ran down the stairs as fast as I could and arrived panting at the front door just in time to see Viola giggling and pointing across the street where Cal was walking along with his kid brother. He raised his hand as if he wanted to wave but was put off by Viola acting the fool. I hushed her and watched him walk away, pretty sure that he was watching me too. I felt a flip of hope bubbling away inside and prayed that our neighbour-hood pool party would be the moment I could talk to him properly.

Viola breezed past me as soon as Cal was out of sight and started to climb the stairs to our apartment. I knew she was headed straight to our stereo record player. My dad had bought it brand new not long before he met Candy, and it was still there in the apartment. Viola purred like a happy kitten at milk time when she laid eyes on it; she only had a battered old Decca at home.

Viola was already on her knees in front of the stereo, ready to worship. She was babbling away about her record but all I kept seeing was my mom with her soiled nightgown and blood running down her wrists.

'Are you OK?' Viola didn't miss much.

'Yeah.'

'I mean . . . generally, is everything . . . y'know what I mean?'

I did, and I didn't want to talk about it. I nodded and Viola knew me well enough to let me be. She slipped a record out of the paper sleeve and reached for the arm to place the needle carefully in the groove. The record hissed and scratched a little but then a trumpet started blowing out a sad refrain.

'Man, it's hot in here. What happened to your cool-air? Why is it making that horrible noise? Listen to this. "Chet Baker in Paris". I was born at the wrong time.'

The air conditioner was gurgling and churning out tepid air that lay hot and heavy on our skin. Viola played a couple of tracks and we chatted for a while about the finer points of a trumpet sound that seemed like any other trumpet to me, before Viola came to her point.

'My brother's girlfriend . . . y'know Celeste? She got a new job at the precinct, cleaning for them. She means well . . . but she got a big mouth; anyway she told me they arrested your mom?'

I sighed. I might have guessed that Viola already knew what was going on with us.

'They didn't arrest her . . . I'm not supposed to talk about it. How did she know it was my mom?'

'Because your dad came to get her and brought that Candy girl with him. Celeste used to clean for old Mrs Zerilli in the mornings, and I might have mentioned about her and your dad once.'

'Viola, can you stop talking about my family business to your brother's girlfriends?'

Viola's brother drove a broken-down old junk heap of a car, but it made him popular with girls, and they seemed to change with alarming speed. Just last year there was Janice, Gloriana, Pixie (although we were never sure that was her real name) and now Celeste.

'I'm sorry. I was making conversation and it just came out of my mouth when she mentioned Zerilli's. I'm conversational . . . what can I say?'

'Great . . . Everything's fine. People just like to gossip.' I pulled a face at her, but it seemed everyone in this city had already told someone who told someone about my mom being carted away in her nightgown.

'My mom was asking after you.' Viola pinched my arm in a gesture of what passed for caring between us.

'I'm OK. My dad will be back soon.' I had no idea if that was true but I couldn't bear to tell anyone what was happening, not even Viola.

'Oh – for good? Or is he still doing the hoochie-coochie with Candy girl?' Viola shook her head and screwed up her face as though she could taste something nasty. I laughed. It was a relief to have someone to share it with.

'I guess.'

'Speaking of hoochie-coochie, what are you wearing to the pool party?'

'My navy one-piece.'

'Can I borrow your blue shirt? I love that shirt.'

'I want it straight back this time. Last time you kept it for weeks.'

'Laundering things takes time. I took care of it.'

I smiled at Viola but she was already on her way to my bedroom to collect her prize. It was nice to talk about normal stuff again and I wished I could tell her about my mom but I didn't have the right words to describe the past few days. I felt a deep burning shame inside.

Viola knew exactly which drawer to find my blue shirt in and she was quick to extract it, folding it on to her lap. Before I could say another word, she was stripping off her shirt and sliding her arms through the sleeves of my blue T-shirt. After admiring herself for a minute in my mirror, Viola was heading back out of my bedroom when she spotted the box and its contents spread over the floor where I'd left them.

'What's all this stuff?'

'Someone sent this box all the way from Paris. It's not addressed to anyone, and so far I can't find anything that says who it belongs to.'

'Say what? From Paris . . . as in France?'

'Yeah.'

'Well, let's see what you got!'

Viola dropped to her knees and started rummaging through the stuff on the floor one piece at a time.

'We need to find out who this stuff belongs to,' she said softly as she flipped through the photo albums.

'Look at this.' I offered Viola the picture of Dovie with 'LIAR' scrawled on it as evidence.

'Wow, somebody was really mad at her,' said Viola, staring at the photo.

'Yeah, but I don't know who. There's another woman in the photographs.'

Viola looked up at me with a firm resolve. 'We need to track them down.'

I frowned. 'But how? There's no note or anything.'

'Well, maybe someone is missing this stuff or it's for you. You know the girlfriend before Celeste? She got left an old house in New Orleans, by a relative she didn't even know. It was only a kind of shack that was pretty much falling down, and not worth the trouble to fix it up, but people leave strangers stuff all the time.'

'I don't think it's for us.'

'Could be, though. Someone could've left you her apartment in Paris, and we could go and live there, and walk around speaking French and looking cool.'

Viola was off on a flight of fancy that if left unattended would lead to a detailed description of the apartment, right down to the colour of the bedding. She had a point though; we should find out who the stuff belonged to. I worried about why it had turned up now after all this time. I wasn't sure why anyone would send a photograph with 'LIAR' scrawled on it and all the unfinished letters bothered me.

'Hey, is that new?' Viola pointed to my throat and I realized I was still wearing the butterfly necklace.

'No, it was in the box. I was just trying it on.'

'It's pretty.'

She started laying out the loose photographs just as I had done, stopping at a picture of the fair-haired woman that I'd seen in the other photographs, but here she was younger, maybe only nineteen or twenty years old. She was leaning against a tree and shielding her eyes from the sun with one hand; around her neck hung the same butterfly necklace.

'Who's this?' Viola asked.

'I don't know. See if there's anything written on the back. Some of the photographs have dates and stuff.'

Viola flipped the photograph over, and someone had written in pencil that was faded with time: 'Gillian, 1946.'

'So . . . this is Gillian's necklace.'

Viola was right; it was pretty and I ran my fingers over

the wing tips of the little butterflies before perching on the rug to show her the unfinished 'Dear Gillian' letters.

'These women were like . . . *in love* with each other?' Viola said.

'I guess so. Dovie and Gillian . . . D & G . . . they carved their initials on our fire escape. They must have lived right here in this apartment.'

'I've never met anyone who was . . . like that. Maybe we can find them; solve the mystery and get the reward money.'

Viola was big on reward money in all circumstances, but I felt I needed to point something out to her.

'There isn't any reward money, Vi. It's just an old box of junk. They haven't lived here for years so I don't know why anyone would send all this stuff here.' All the same it was gnawing at me and I couldn't stop wondering about the woman in the picture. What did she do?

'Girl, you have no sense of adventure. We need to search for clues.'

She started pulling out the photographs and reading the back of them for anything that might help us. I had no idea where we would even begin to look for two women called Dovie and Gillian. That was all we had to go on.

'Wait . . . here's something.' Viola shuffled over to where I was sitting and held out a photograph of three women outside a fancy stone building.

'That's Gray's School. See, right there in the background.' Viola pointed at the columns of the white stone building.

'I've never heard of it.'

'Yeah, it's right by Central Park on the Upper East Side, big fancy building. My mom went there for a job once. She didn't get it, but I remember walking by there one time with her and she said they were very polite about the way they turned her down. She said it was a sign of good manners.'

'So?'

Viola gave me a look. 'Ava, schools keep records. They might know who these women are. We should call them or maybe go over there.'

Viola was just getting started on her plans to solve the mystery when I heard the front door open and my father's voice calling me.

'I'm in here, Dad. You better go, Vi.'

'But what about Gray's?'

I shook my head.

'I'll call you. I don't know what I'll be doing.'

'You going to tell me what's going on? You know I'm your friend, right?'

'I know. Thanks.'

I playfully punched her arm and she did it back to me. It was our way of saying things were good between us.

My dad gave Viola a not unfriendly nod as she left, but I could tell he had something on his mind and I had a very bad feeling about what was coming next.

'Come sit down, honey.'

He patted the space beside him on the couch and I

obeyed. He cleared his throat . . . then there was silence. And then he cleared it again.

'Sweetie, you know your mom might be gone for a little while?'

I nodded. Fear crept right up my spine and wrapped itself around my chest so I couldn't catch my breath properly. My throat got tight and my mouth dry. My dad didn't really live here any more, and we both knew why. He leaned over and nervously patted me as though I was a small dog he was trying to comfort.

'You should pack some things for a couple of days while we work stuff out.'

'I want to stay here.'

'Ava, you can't stay here on your own at night. We need to fix the window and . . . look, you're not a kid any more. It's only until we see how your mom is, and then we can figure things out from there. Can you do that . . . for me?'

I nodded but I felt sick and miserable at the thought of it. My dad waited impatiently by the front door, occasionally calling out to me to hurry, as I threw nightclothes into my schoolbag and collected up my toothbrush. I stowed the box safely in the corner, before reluctantly closing my bedroom door, dreading the thought of a night playing third wheel with my dad and Candy Jackson.

I 2

New York City, 1955

Another lazy Saturday morning with Ella singing softly and thick pads of newspapers, served with hot coffee and cinnamon toast. Some of the tension had lifted, or maybe we'd just got used to it, but the three of us were sharing a peaceful interlude when the telephone rang. We all stared at it. It was unusual for anyone to call us so early in the morning, particularly on a weekend, and our minds inevitably turned to death and disaster. Gillian was the first of us to move, cradling the black receiver into her neck and answering with her customary tentative:

'Hello . . . ?'

Gillian always answered the telephone, but she hated talking to people on it. It was one of the many things I teased her about. I watched her as the tentative hello brought a shy smile, and her customary frown lines disappeared.

'Really . . . How are you? . . . I know, it's been so long . . . In New York? You're kidding me . . . Well, of course . . .'

I knew instantly who it was, and the knot of tension

in my stomach clenched into a tight ball of fury. She saw me watching her and quickly turned her back so she was facing the window, her fingers grasping the telephone wire and curling it back and forth between her thumb and forefinger. Her voice dropped so low that I could no longer hear the conversation, just the occasional soft laugh and hastily whispered words:

'Yes, I know it. All right then. See you later.'

Eventually she dropped the receiver back into its cradle and reached for a cigarette. Judith was chattering on about nothing in particular as usual, but for once I was grateful for it. Her chatter filled the air as Gillian exhaled a cloud of smoke, and I sat there waiting for the words that would be casually thrown into conversation . . . too casually, as if it was nothing at all. I stared at her but she wouldn't look at me.

'That was Paul. He's here in the city for a few days.'

I took a breath, struggling to find the right words. Our fragile truce could be broken with the wrong response now, so I didn't want to play tit for tat over Paul. Too much water had flowed under that particular bridge and I tried to keep it light.

'That's a surprise! I didn't know he had our number.'

I regretted it the moment I said it. It was the wrong tone: accusatory. Gillian stared at me, stubborn and a little petulant.

'I didn't give him our number. He got it from someone at home, I guess.'

Of course he did. I could just imagine him.

Hello. I was thinking about heading up to the city. You wouldn't happen to have . . . Oh, you do . . . That's great . . .

Gillian shot me a look and I tried to make amends.

'So, how is he?' I tried to keep my tone friendly, as if it was just a casual enquiry.

'He's great actually. He got a big promotion.'

'That's nice!'

'He's invited me to supper so we can catch up.'

Her voice caught a little as she spoke. By this time even Judith had picked up on the tension between us, and she wandered off into the kitchen, where I could hear the sounds of dishes being washed and stacked. Ella stopped singing and the needle was stuck in the groove at the end of the record, a crackling urgent repeat which we ignored.

'When?' I said.

'This evening.' She crushed her cigarette out in the ashtray rather than meet my gaze and then nervously lit another.

'Is he coming here?'

'Of course not. He has tickets for a Broadway show and we'll grab some supper after that.' I longed to be bright and breezy, to be the kind of woman who could laugh and say, *That sounds like fun. Have a wonderful time.* But I've never been that kind of woman; I tried to smile but my mouth merely grimaced in her general direction.

'I need to fix my hair if I'm going out. We can talk about this later.' She smiled at me. Pleading a little, I thought; she was trying, and I so wanted to reward her . . . but I couldn't. She paused for a beat, her smile fading, and she opened her mouth to speak just as Judith appeared in the doorway.

'More coffee, anyone? I've made a fresh pot.'

Gillian thought better of whatever she was about to say.

'Not for me, thanks. I've things to do.'

The living-room door slapped shut behind her and I got up to change the record. Charlie Parker now, loud and hard in my ears, drowning out my feelings. Judith was going out for the evening to say goodbye to her cousin Peggy, and so I would be alone; waiting for Gillian to return home, imagining Paul pulling out a chair for her to sit down, offering her a cocktail, showing her to the best seats in the house for a show he was sure she would love, and then a quiet supper while they reminisced about old times.

The first time I met Paul, he was carrying boxes of Gillian's books into the college room that would be our shared home for the next year. We disliked each other on sight. He shook my hand in a fairly perfunctory manner and barely raised a smile.

The moment Paul had driven away from our college building, Gillian and I fell into an easy routine as roommates. I'd always been an early riser while Gillian was a late-night person. I would bring her coffee to help her face the world and she would laugh at me, yawning as I chattered on and on about my plans for the future.

One Sunday evening, Gillian took her regular telephone call from Paul, sitting on the floor of the hallway and stretching the coiled wire down to meet her. Paul was tetchy because she wouldn't agree to something he wanted. There were hissed whispers and sighs. Gillian hung up the telephone without saying goodbye.

I scurried back to my place on the floor, trying to look as if I hadn't been eavesdropping. She came back into our room and flung herself somewhat dramatically on to the floor where I was pretending to sketch out a lesson plan for a poetry class. Gillian reached over and took the cigarette out of my mouth; she helped herself to a deep lungful before placing it delicately between my lips again. I smiled at her, turned back to my lesson plan, but she pulled the patchwork quilt over her legs and snuggled closer to me. She was trying to keep warm, and probably wanted to let off steam about Paul but I wasn't really in the mood to hear about it. The mention of his name made my stomach clench and my jaw tighten.

I could feel Gillian's warm breath on my neck, and she leaned into me, childlike, wanting comfort.

'What are you doing?' she asked.

'Robert Frost for seniors. "The Road Not Taken".'

'I've always liked that poem . . . Fancy a nightcap?'

A nightcap meant the end of work and the beginning of late-night chatting. I really wanted to get my lesson plan finished before morning, but the weight of her head on my shoulder persuaded me to down tools and reach for the whiskey bottle.

'Just one then,' I said.

'Just one.' She laughed. It was never just one; one led to 3 a.m. talks of the soul, as Gillian liked to put it. I poured while she held the glasses steady.

'To the road not taken . . .' Gillian said and offered her whiskey glass up for a toast.

I laughed softly.

'We haven't taken any roads yet. We're just starting out.'

'Then to all the roads ahead of us . . .'

We clinked glasses and the whiskey warmed my mouth. Gillian was staring into space and I could see something was really bothering her. I sighed.

'OK, what's up?' It was hopeless to resist Gillian. I threw the lesson plan on to the floor and gave up the idea of it for the evening.

'Oh, it's nothing. Paul's being an idiot. He wants us to go away for a weekend.'

'And this is bad?'

'He wants us to go away just the two of us to . . . you know?'

Gillian screwed her face up and shook her head. I stared at her for a few seconds before it dawned on me what she meant.

'Oh, I see.'

A sudden burst of jealousy shot through me. The thought of Paul with his enormous hands and farm-boy face being naked with Gillian made me feel ill. I took a breath.

'And you . . . don't want to?' I could barely speak the words.

'I don't know. I mean, I suppose I should want to, shouldn't I? We're getting married, so . . .'

Her voice trailed off, pitiful and sad.

'You should only go if you want to.' I kept my tone light and sisterly, but my heart was beating so hard I was sure she could hear it.

'That's the thing, Dovie, I don't know if I want to. I mean, I like Paul, of course. I mean, I love Paul, obviously, but I've never thought about that side of things. I like him being part of my family and me being part of his. I should want to though . . . if we're getting married. Don't you think I should?'

'*Do* you love him, Gill? I mean really love him?'

'Of course I love him.'

'I'm sorry. It's just you never seem that happy about it.'

Gillian pulled the patchwork quilt up to her neck and sighed.

'I hadn't thought about it like that . . . but I guess you're right. I can't remember the last time I felt we had fun together, not like *we* have fun . . . but that's different.'

'Is it?'

Gillian sat up straight and stared at me for the longest time. I leaned towards her, a little unsure of what to say next. I had gone too far. I shook my head slightly.

'I'm sorry,' I whispered softly into the cold air between us.

She got up and stood by the window and I remember

the sound of my breath as I watched her. Nothing was said but something in the air between us shifted.

'I won't be late but don't wait up.' She was dazzling, standing in the doorway with a nervous smile on her face. I was so used to looking at the Gillian I loved, with her hair hastily dumped into a messy bun on top of her head, wearing her favourite khakis and sweaters, but this woman was someone I didn't know. She was wearing her best pale blue evening dress, simple and fitted. She'd curled her hair and pinned a small white feather hat to one side of her head. It matched her white sling-backs. She hated fussy, uncomfortable clothes. Her lips were slashed with a deep red lipstick; simple gold hoops nestled into her ear lobes, and her yellow butterfly necklace lay at her throat. I wanted to tell her she looked beautiful, but the words wouldn't come. We looked at each other and I struggled to speak. Judith chose that moment to walk into the living room.

'Well, don't you look fancy? All dressed up. Going somewhere nice?'

'I'm meeting an old friend from back home.'

'Are we going to meet her?'

Gillian shook her head.

'I shouldn't think so. Paul won't be in the city that long.'

'Paul? Your friend who telephoned earlier? Well, of course.' Judith digested this piece of information and smiled her spiteful little smile. 'I'm going out myself tonight so poor Dovie will be all alone.'

'I'll be fine. I'm going to have a long soak in the tub and I have to call Franny. I keep meaning to get around to it, but it's been so busy. Be nice to catch up with all the family news. You should both run along and enjoy yourselves.'

Gillian looked embarrassed for a split second, but Judith carried on talking.

'I guess we all have our evenings set then.'

'Have a lovely time,' I said but my tone was icy.

Gillian turned to look at me. She paused, trying to think of the right words and then she smiled.

'Thank you. I'm really looking forward to it. It's good to catch up with home, you know how it is?'

The apartment door snapped shut behind her, and when I turned away my face fell into the disappointment and sadness that I no longer needed to hide.

It was eleven thirty before I heard footsteps on the stairs running up towards our apartment. A key in the door and then I was no longer alone. Judith had returned from visiting Peggy. Her face was flushed with excitement, her sharp little eyes filled with glee as she breezed into the living room.

'Waiting up?' she said.

'No point settling down when you're all going to come home and wake me up again.'

'Have a good evening?'

She gave me a sly look and I bit my lip. It wouldn't do to antagonize her.

'Yes, I did as a matter of fact. I had a good chat with my sister and then took a long hot bath. Did you have a nice time with Peggy?'

Judith settled into Gillian's armchair and plumped up the cushion behind her back. She was toying with me and I could feel her hesitation, waiting for her to say whatever it was that was making her so excited.

'It was lovely actually. We went to that new cocktail bar – you know, just past the theatre on St Marks? Anyway, we stopped in for one drink because it was already ten o'clock, and you know Peggy hates to stay out too late. So, we find ourselves a table close to the bar, but not too close if you know what I mean, we get two vodka gimlets . . . and the nicest thing, they serve them with a bowl of salted peanuts and those little cheese crackers, and I think that's elegant, don't you?'

I stifled a yawn with the back of my hand and thought about making an excuse to go to bed but Judith carried on:

'So we were having a perfectly nice time, and Peggy sees a gentleman standing at the bar and she thinks he's handsome – well, he was kind of handsome, I suppose, but not my type. Anyway, this man orders a couple of drinks, and we watch him carry them back to his table, and, well, you could have knocked me down with a feather . . . there was Gillian. I don't want to speak out of turn, of course, Dovie, but they looked pretty friendly to me . . . if you know what I'm saying.'

I swallowed hard. 'I don't know what you're saying, Judith. Gillian and Paul are old friends.'

'You mustn't mind me. They seemed . . . well, close, if you know what I mean. Oh, me and my big mouth. Now I've gone and upset you.'

I shrugged as innocently as I could manage. 'You haven't upset me, Judith, because there is nothing to be upset about. Anyway, if you'll excuse me, I think I'll turn in now.'

'Is that midnight striking already? I guess Gillian is our Cinderella tonight.'

I stood up and started to fuss with the cushions and stacks of exam papers that needed grading. The room felt stuffy and I threw open a window. Judith reluctantly got to her feet.

'I've said too much. I didn't mean to speak out of turn. I'm sure Gillian will be home any minute . . . I don't want to see you get hurt, Dovie. You do know I'm your friend, don't you?'

Her expression was a mixture of strange pity and glee. I felt a wave of anger and it was all I could do not to lash out at her. She was enjoying this.

'Goodnight.'

'If you wanted to talk . . . you know I'm a good listener?'

'You take first turn in the bathroom.'

I didn't care if she felt dismissed because I wanted to dismiss her. She hesitated but must have thought better of it.

'Goodnight then. Sleep tight.'

'Goodnight, Judith.'

I sat curled up on the couch listening to the noises of Judith retiring for the evening. The glass of warm milk. Doors opening and closing, water pipes gurgling, and then the final soft click of her bedroom door closing. I waited until the light vanished from the gap underneath the door, and I flicked off the living-room lamps so she would think I'd gone to bed.

I lit a cigarette and walked over to the window, where I sat blowing smoke out into the night sky and watching the people below in the street, walking home or getting in or out of taxis. There was no sign of Gillian. I felt a physical pain in my chest where jealousy ripped through me, and I tried to breathe through it. When I closed my eyes, I could see Gillian with her red lipstick and white sling-backs, kissing Paul under a streetlamp.

For all the years we'd been together there was part of Gillian I worried was never quite *all in*, as I was. I would do anything to protect her, and us. I was doing it by indulging Judith when every part of me wanted her out of here.

I was willing to take it all for Gillian: the shame of being found out, the humiliation that would follow and whatever awful things came our way. They could lock me away but as long as I knew she was waiting for me somewhere, then, for me, it was a price worth paying. In my loneliest hours, I wasn't sure Gillian would do the same. Tonight, I found myself wondering if maybe Paul was an easier option. After all, they had been engaged. We can put things away when we need to, but sometimes we never learn to fill the space they leave behind.

I closed the window and crushed out my cigarette. I was being perfectly ridiculous. I was torturing myself for no good reason. She wouldn't do that to me. We just had to stay calm and wait this out.

I yawned out loud this time and decided to sleep in our room, so at least when she did come home, we could talk without disturbing Judith. I got myself ready for bed, my ears straining at every car door or creak on the stairs. I crawled between the soft white sheets and laid my body down with a sigh. Crazy thoughts raced around my mind but tiredness eventually got the better of me, and I drifted off to sleep.

My dreams were filled with chasing something or somebody through a wood, and I woke at first light with my heart racing, feeling I'd lost something in the night. I reached my fingers out to touch the part of the bed where there was usually a mess of fair hair and a warm indentation. But it was cold, and there was no sign of Gillian at all.

13

New York City, 1975

The hospital, with its pale green walls, smelled of stale vegetables and urine. There was a long corridor with a dark navy tiled floor, lined with white metal doors that were all locked. At the end of the corridor was a patients' lounge with dozens of dull blue padded armchairs with tan wooden arms. They were old and worn, with sagging cushions and slight stains that nobody mentioned. The smell of cabbage and pee was only interrupted by a vague antiseptic aroma. My sneakers squeaked along the tiled floor as I walked. I was wearing a denim skirt and my favourite white T-shirt with a yellow smiley face on it. As we passed one or two patients in the corridor, they pointed at it and laughed but in a strange and quite horrible way. Feeling awkward and embarrassed I crossed my arms across my chest and wished I'd worn another shirt.

My dad was walking two paces ahead of me. He had been doing this since we left Candy in Clancy's diner across the street from the hospital. They must have had words while I was using the bathroom. By the time I came out, there was that sort of polite conversation which only happens when people are really mad at each other. Candy was chewing gum and twirling a piece of her hair into a large curl before releasing it and starting over while my dad was staring out of the window, his lips tightly pursed. He smiled when he saw me and since then he had marched two paces ahead of me, on a mission to get this over with.

Candy had stayed in the diner, lingering over a black coffee. My dad had said we would all get lunch there after the visit, and I could choose whatever I wanted on the menu. Candy had looked bored and I really didn't want to, but there was no arguing with my dad.

As we reached the patients' lounge a large metal trolley rolled up behind us. There were dozens of pale green cups and saucers, a large metal urn with boiling water, a jug of suspiciously glowing orange juice, and a plate of sad yellow cookies half-heartedly covered in a white cloth to keep the flies off them. The faded blue chairs started to fill up with patients. Some were wearing loose-fitting yellow gowns, others their normal clothes. They all had one thing in common: their blank faces. Some of the patients were crying but not with any emotion; their faces didn't move at all, but their eyes leaked silent streams of tears as if they couldn't stop.

A small red-haired nurse spotted us in the doorway as we paused to let the trolley push past us and made a beeline for my dad.

'Name?'

'Err . . . Tom,' he stuttered.

'Not *your* name.'

She sighed and waved a hand towards the patients, who were all slumped in the chairs while the orderlies poured hot drinks or cups of juice for them and offered the sad yellow cookies.

'Oh, right . . . I'm looking for Mary-Lyn Winters.'

'New patient? New intake in the far room. We like to keep people separate until we get their medication under control.' She had moved on to the next lot of visitors before she finished her sentence.

The far room turned out to be a small white annexe at the back of the patients' lounge. A fierce-looking nurse stood guard by the door taking our names yet again before she would let us in. My dad went first and I followed behind, trying not to make eye contact with anyone. When we reached the annexe, I could see my mother walking towards a chair; she was wearing a blue shapeless gown and hospital slippers that made her shuffle along in a strange way. She didn't look left or right but even I could see her lips were slowly mouthing words.

Dad hung back, suddenly shy, and shoved me forward.

'I'll be right here if you need me, but I don't want to upset her. You go and say hello.'

I wanted to say it was a bit late for that, but I bit my lip and took a deep breath. I took a tentative step into the room and then a familiar hand grabbed my shoulder.

'Don't mention Candy, OK?'

I nodded and Dad released his grip on me as I walked

over to where Mom was sitting. Her eyes searched my face, as if she was trying to recognize an old friend but couldn't find a name in her mind.

I moved forward and perched on the edge of a small footstool, not wanting to get too close to her. She reached out a hand and touched my hair, picking it up and letting it fall. Then she laughed and it was so loud that the people next to us turned to stare. I could see my dad's worried face poke around the door and then retreat again.

'Hi, Mom. How are you?'

She leaned back in her chair, less agitated now. Her eyes closed and her lips carried on in silent chatter. The same red-haired nurse who'd greeted us at the door appeared by my side, rattling tablets in a plastic dispenser.

'Mary-Lyn, time to wake up now, honey. You have visitors. Isn't that nice? Here you go. Open wide.'

Before my mother could say a word, the nurse jerked her awake and fed her two large white pills with a cup of water and then moved swiftly on to the next patient. My mother swallowed them down, but her eyes closed again and the silent chatter continued. I tried again.

'Mom? It's me, Ava.'

I patted her hand, but she didn't move. Somewhere along the sad row of chairs a woman started crying. She sounded like a child sobbing and before long it started to ripple out from her chair, making the other patients squirm and wriggle. It was uncomfortable to listen to so much hurt. I thought she might never stop. Eventually, the sobbing woman was led away by two orderlies and the room filled with a weird silence that wasn't really silent at all.

My mother's lips were still moving; they never stopped muttering all the time I sat there. From time to time I thought I caught a whisper of her lips forming the words 'Don't leave me' but whether she was talking to me I couldn't be sure. Whoever she was talking to, it was clear she had a lot to say to them. Eventually a bell clanged and that was the end of visiting hours. I wondered whether I should lean in and kiss her goodbye, but, honestly, I couldn't bear to get that close to her, and also I doubted she would have noticed.

Dad was in the corridor and pacing up and down. We were waiting to talk to the doctor in charge of my mom's case, but he was busy, so there was nothing to do but try not to get in the way of hospital business. I wanted to get out of that place so badly. It made my skin itch to smell the air and every sound was off, wrong and out of tune with the rest of us. I chewed on my fingernails and watched my dad tap his foot anxiously and keep glancing at his watch. I wasn't sure whether he was more worried about my mother's health or keeping Candy waiting any longer. I wasn't going to ask.

Eventually, a tall grey-haired man in a white coat walked towards us, his shoes clipping along the tiles and his eyes fixed firmly on the clipboard of notes he held in his right hand. He brushed the pages over the top of the clipboard as he finished reading and, when he was satisfied that he understood, he frowned a little and held out his hand to my father.

'Mr . . . Winters, right?'

'Right! Tom Winters.' My father shook his hand as though it was a normal business meeting and he was selling whatever it was that he sold to people.

'Bailey,' the doctor said in return, moving across to the window, where he leaned against the wall and started to speak as if he didn't really have the time to be there. 'Is this the first time your wife has had these problems?'

'Yeah . . . as far as I know. We've been married . . . umm . . . well, a long time.'

'Family history?' Dr Bailey didn't even look up from his clipboard as he scrawled notes down on a page.

'I don't think so . . . I don't really know.' My dad was staring at his shoes as if they might help him out here.

'Yeah . . . well, it's not down here. We can check with patient record archives. It can take a while to get the paperwork. As for now, your wife needs a course of ECT. We will start tomorrow and see how that goes.'

'What exactly is ECT?' my dad said. I was hoping he would ask but I was already pretty sure it wasn't anything good.

'Electroconvulsive Therapy. We restart the brain through a series of electric shocks.'

'Electric shocks? Is that dangerous?' Dad sounded worried.

'No, it's routine . . . Doesn't hurt a bit . . . We do this

all the time. You know it's pretty common for women to get this way ... We see a lot of it. Nothing to worry about ... Anyway, if that's all, I have other patients to see.'

'Yeah ... sure, doc. So, we can visit in a couple of days?'

'Yeah ... couple of days. Takes a while to see results but patients are usually a lot quieter after the first few treatments. It's very calming for them.'

I wasn't sure what would be calming about having electric shocks zapping your brain but I could tell nobody wanted to hear my thoughts on it.

'She'll get better though, right?' my dad asked.

'It's a very effective treatment. Nothing to worry about . . .' The doctor was already starting to walk away. 'Like I say, we'll get any records up from patient archives in a week or so ... though that makes no difference to her treatment. We'll start tomorrow . . .' and with that he left before we could say another word.

I was still reeling from the sadness of all the people in the lounge and the awful heavy smell that smothered everything. My dad slung his arm around my shoulder as we walked out of the doors and back into the heat and stench of the city and I could tell we were both relieved to be back on the outside of those doors.

Our apartment was west-facing and got the full glare of the afternoon sun, which was occasionally great in winter, but not so great in summer. Dad had not got around to calling someone to come out and fix the cool-air system, and nothing moved the hot air from room to room. I threw open all the windows but the smell of the garbage burning in the street, combined with the overflowing trash cans in the back alley, made the air sour, and my stomach churn a little. I went out on to the fire escape and stood outside in a shady spot for a few minutes, begging for some kind of a breeze but nothing was moving, except a fat brown rat I could see down in the alley. I tried to imagine Dovie and Gillian sitting out on the fire escape carving their initials. I could see them in our apartment, eating meals in our kitchen, and maybe even dancing around our living room like my mom and I used to do, her singing along to her favourite songs as we spun around to the music.

I thought about what Viola had said about Gray's School and wondered whether it was worth a shot. I had nothing else to do except hang out in the apartment on my own and my restlessness felt like an itch under my skin. Viola couldn't come over until tomorrow, and there wasn't anyone else to call. I couldn't stop thinking about all the people locked away in that hospital and their awful blank faces. The apartment felt desperately sad and empty but anything was better than being around Candy Jackson all day long.

The box was bothering me. The photographs, the carved initials, all those letters telling Gillian she loved her over and over again. I wanted to know who these women were and why someone sent that box of old stuff to our door. I felt a churning anxious feeling in the pit of my stomach every time I looked at the photograph of Dovie with 'LIAR' written across her face. It felt as if somebody had wanted to hurt her, and I needed to find out why.

I took a deep breath and flipped open the telephone directory. I hated talking to strangers on the telephone, but as I dialled the number, I tried to rehearse what I was going to say. I imagined Viola issuing instructions in my ear. She always knew what to do. The telephone rang out a couple of times, and I was about to give up and shove the phone back into its cradle when a voice said:

'Good morning, you've reached Gray's School, how may I help you?'

14

New York City, 1955

It was too early to call anyone, except maybe the hospitals, but as I sat clutching a mug of coffee and staring out of the window, I couldn't help but let my mind go to the darkest places. Gillian hadn't come home all night and the possible reasons for that were flooding my mind. I weighed up the risk of calling the police but I couldn't bring myself to. To invite questions about why I should care so much that my room-mate had stayed out with her former fiancé was unthinkable, and I certainly wouldn't want a police officer visiting the apartment while Judith was here. My stomach churned with fear and fury in equal measure. How could Gillian do this to me?

Outside in the street it was morning fresh and filled with people going about their early-morning business, off to push metal grilles roughly out of the way and open up their stores, or to go to their churches or temples. People were strolling with fat wads of newspapers tucked under their arms and women were checking their hair in store windows or stopping to rescue a heel caught in a cracked sidewalk. None of them was Gillian.

The pictures in my mind played out on a loop. Gillian naked in some hotel room being fed breakfast by Paul while they made plans for a future without me. My hands made little clenched fists, and I tried to unclench them but every part of me was rigid with fear and jealousy. I couldn't stop thinking about the times we had been happy together, and wondering if it was enough to bring her home again.

The day before the first semester ended and we were all about to go home for Christmas, I unwrapped a bottle of whiskey for the two of us. We lay around giggling and sharing those silly confidences that don't matter until you start sharing the ones that do. The whiskey danced around my head and I felt content. I was humming a record I loved and I really wasn't thinking anything except how happy I was right then.

I reached out my hand and caught a strand of Gillian's hair; the curl wrapped around my finger, and I gently tugged on it and moved my face nearer to hers. Our faces were so close I could feel the shudder of her breath and smell the soft flowery odour of her perfume. I let go of her hair, suddenly remembering where I was and what I could lose.

'I'm sorry.'

'Are you . . . ?'

'No.'

'Then what . . . ?' Gillian hesitated and I felt a rush of love for her. My voice was garbled and stupid.

'I'm not sorry. I'll never be sorry for the way I feel about you.'

'Dovie, we can't say these things.' Gillian moved away slightly, and I imagined her getting up and walking out of our room, maybe knocking on Lindy and Meg's door, and telling them about the awful thing that happened. I would be disgraced and humiliated, thrown out of college, but I carried on sitting there feeling a chill on my skin, and the warmth of the quilt where Gillian's body had been lying.

I busied myself with cleaning up the living room and pretended not to think about Gillian trying on her best dress and spraying perfume that only he would smell before she went out. The extra time she had taken to curl her hair and get herself ready. She had been trying not to smile too much, but I could tell she was excited to see him and desperate to escape. Maybe it was fair enough. It had been nearly ten years since Gillian had broken off her engagement, and sure, we were happy, but only behind closed doors.

We pretend the hiding is nothing but it's everything. We can't touch or kiss or stand too close to each other. We can't look lovingly at the other person or talk too much about them to a friend. We have to rehearse and monitor and check, always check on what we say or how we say it. We can't make friends because they might guess, and that would be the end of our lives together. We have to put on a face the minute we step out of our front door and keep it on until the minute we are safely behind a turned key. It's hard and it exacts a price. The price is to tarnish what we have, to make it seem difficult to love someone. We watch couples of men and women, hugging and kissing whenever they want to, casually reaching for an arm or a hand, stroking a cheek in public, and nothing happens to them at all. I feel Gillian's resentment. Some days I think she blames me for this life we keep under lock and key. Draw the blinds, dim the lights, lock the door and love. Little by little we love less.

To persuade myself that Gillian wouldn't have gone back to Paul, I tried inventing reasons for her being out all night with him, but I couldn't think of one. If there was a problem she would have called, and the fact that the telephone was just sitting there dumb and lifeless seemed insulting. After an hour or so of waiting, I heard the familiar sound of Judith stirring and her usual morning routine, feet padding down the hallway, her bathroom noises, and then the sight of her in her blue robe with its tasselled belt, and her spiteful smile when she saw my anguished face.

'Morning, Dovie, my . . . you look like you've been there all night.'

'Not quite.' I had no wish to make conversation with Judith this morning. There was nothing I regretted more than having ever agreed to her coming to live here. I scowled at her and turned away, hoping she would take the hint and go about her business without bothering me.

'Gillian not up yet? Must have been a late night.' Judith paused on her way to the kitchen. I could tell by her tone that she knew Gillian wasn't in her bedroom, and I realized with some annoyance that I'd left the bedroom door ajar.

I said nothing, busying myself with yesterday's crossword puzzle and my stone-cold coffee. I wouldn't give Judith the satisfaction.

She made a fresh pot of coffee and helped herself to her strange little cereal boxes. She loved children's breakfast cereals and snowed them with sugar. I couldn't bear to watch her eat for one more day or listen to the raspy sound of her mouth breathing. Everything about her irritated me, and what bothered me most of all was the fact she was here, an unwelcome visitor. I realized then that I hated her.

Judith stood in the kitchen doorway and smirked as she shovelled cereal into her mouth.

'You look pale, Dovie. Are you feeling ill?' She was quite gleeful as she spoke, her thin reedy voice warbling away, and I found myself staring at her, quite violently thinking that I would like nothing better than to see her suffer as she was making us suffer.

'I'm fine,' I muttered.

My thoughts were briefly interrupted by the sound of the front door opening and feet racing up the stairs. Gillian appeared in the doorway. She looked tired and dishevelled, her hair uncombed and her make-up faded, leaving her looking washed out and strained. I wanted to yell at her and shake her by the shoulders for scaring me, but in the end, I managed a weak smile. Judith with her mouth full of cereal was the first to comment.

'Have you been gone all night with that handsome man I saw you flirting with in the bar?'

I said nothing. Gillian rolled her eyes at me the minute Judith looked away but I wasn't in the mood to diminish the impact of Judith's spite. I glared at her, my stare demanding an explanation. She seemed anxious and fidgety, unable to keep still.

'Paul is in the emergency room. I've been at the hospital all night . . . I'm so tired that I can't think straight.'

Gillian sank down into her favourite armchair and rested her head against the back of it, closing her eyes. Judith came bustling towards her with a hot cup of coffee, which was of course the right thing to do, but also gave me something else to resent her for, because it should have been me doing it.

Gillian gave Judith a weary smile and took the coffee, taking hot gulps and then lighting up a cigarette, inhaling while she gathered her thoughts.

'What happened?' My voice was a whisper, filled with relief. I steadied myself to be normal, to pretend to care about Paul and whatever had happened to him. All I really cared about was the fact that Gillian was home and safe, and we were together again. Judith curled herself up on the couch with a fresh cup of coffee and settled back to hear what Gillian had to say. I wanted her to go, to make an excuse to leave us alone together so that Gillian could talk to me and I could comfort her, but Judith clearly had no intention of moving and she made little sympathetic coaxing noises until eventually Gillian started to explain what had happened to them.

'Paul and I went for drinks after the show . . . you know that new place that's opened right on St Marks? We drank a couple of cocktails and we were on our way to supper. We were a little giggly and having fun, teasing each other, and gossiping about people we know. I wasn't thinking, I guess.'

She lit up another cigarette and blew a thin trail of smoke out of her mouth. I could feel my mouth rigid with anger. I couldn't move my lips to smile at her or look sympathetically, ready for whatever was coming. She was describing her night out as if it was a date and she hadn't even realized it. I swallowed hard and tried not to show my jealousy.

'It was such a silly thing but, like I say, we were so busy talking and laughing that I wasn't really looking around us, and then some heavy-set guy walks up to us, and he gets annoyed because we were a little drunk, and he couldn't get through because we were walking arm in arm. It was such a stupid thing because there was plenty of room on the sidewalk for him to go around us. Anyway, this guy is angry . . . really angry. He squares up to Paul and says, "Hey, buddy, how much of this sidewalk do you and your girlfriend want?"

'Well, Paul didn't want any trouble but also he's not

the type of guy to just let someone be rude like that. Then the red-faced guy turns to me and he mutters something. I swear I didn't even hear what he said, but Paul must have heard him, and he yelled at him, "What is your problem?" and the next thing I know this man pushed Paul right into the traffic.

'Lucky for us the driver slammed on his brakes, but he caught Paul on his hip, and then he fell over and hit his head. There was blood and oh my God . . . I swear for one awful moment I thought he was dead, and the other guy ran off down the street. Well, of course Paul had to go to the hospital and the police were called. I couldn't leave him there all alone.'

'Oh my goodness, that's horrible. Why, Paul could easily have been killed by that awful man.' Judith was squeezing every drop of life out of this drama, but Gillian didn't notice. 'You need some breakfast and then get some sleep before you go back to the hospital. Is there anything I can do? I don't mind a bit if you want me to take some things to the hospital for Paul,' she continued.

She was in her element now and, far from her usual annoyance, Gillian seemed ridiculously grateful. She was beaming her tired smile at Judith. I on the other hand was sitting stone-like, unable to say a word. I felt a boiling rage and it was directed right at Gillian. She could have called me so I didn't worry but her main priority was obviously Paul.

Judith set about making breakfast for Gillian, feeding her and clucking around her like a mother hen, while I sat there in silence, unable to bridge the chasm between us. Eventually I couldn't keep quiet for one minute longer.

'Why didn't you call?' Even as I spoke, I knew the words sounded harsh and accusatory.

Gillian stared at me, confused. 'I didn't think about it. Besides, what could you have done?'

I wanted to say that I would have run to her in the middle of the night, no matter what time it was, but instead I nodded sullenly.

'Nothing, I guess.'

Judith appeared with a tray set out with a plate of eggs. She'd taken care to dress the tray with a linen napkin and a glass of water. I felt like smashing something. Instead, I sat and watched as Gillian wolfed down the eggs that Judith had made for her and then sank back in her chair with her eyes closed until it was clear that this time, she was fast asleep. The crossword puzzle was still in my hand.

When we got to the hospital, Paul was dressed and waiting in a chair next to the front desk. Some agreeable nurse found him a clean white shirt from somewhere and he carried his bloodied shirt and jacket rolled up under his arm. His hair was slicked back and he looked like a young boy waiting for his mother to collect him. His face lit up when Gillian walked through the double doors but fell again when he saw me tagging along behind her.

'You remember Dovie, don't you, Paul? I was meeting her today to go over some work stuff, and she kindly offered to come along in case she could help out in any way. Isn't that good of her?'

Paul nodded sullenly in my direction and I presumed he didn't think it was all that good of me at all. I don't know if he'd ever suspected that Gillian and I were together, but I wasn't about to ask.

Gillian was only the second girl I'd ever kissed. I touched her lips with mine for the briefest second. They were winter-dry, but there was something else too, a small flicker of warmth and then the heat of her mouth on mine. Her hand reaching into my hair. I waited for her to push me away, but she pulled me closer.

I don't know exactly what she said to Paul when she broke off their engagement. I didn't ask and she didn't want to talk about it. As far as I knew he and Gillian had not set eyes on each other since his father's funeral many years ago. I knew Gillian loved me, but beyond that I couldn't say that she no longer loved Paul, for she spoke of him often and fondly, or maybe it was the life that she had left behind, and those summer evenings with their mothers hatching plots on a back porch that she missed so much.

I busied myself as a friend would and tried to avoid talking to him other than a polite 'How are you feeling?' There was paperwork to sign, and I tasked myself with finding the necessary pieces of paper which allowed Gillian to sit quietly and ask Paul how he was doing. They sat so close to each other that their knees were practically touching, and all the time I was standing waiting for a Dr Keyser at the front desk to get the papers signed, I watched them out of the corner of my eye. Gillian seemed genuinely concerned about Paul and even I could see the large, bloody gash at the back of his head and how pale and serious his face was.

Eventually I got what I needed and waved the papers to show them we were free to leave. Paul got up and walked towards the door; he seemed a little unsteady on his feet and Gillian quickly took his arm, linking it with her own, and leaving me walking behind the two of them. We tried to flag down a cab and after a couple of near misses, one eventually crawled to a stop and we piled in and instructed him to take us to the police station.

Detective Geary was expecting us. A middle-aged Irishman who'd seen it all twice. He didn't bother with small talk, waving us into some hard, wooden chairs next to his desk while he tapped out on an old typewriter with two fingers. He only spoke when he needed information, barking out commands:

'Name . . . Address . . .'

It seemed to annoy Detective Geary that Paul didn't live in the city, as that meant extra paperwork, and he started complaining about tourists filing reports every day and then disappearing back home, meaning they never turned up for court, and making the whole process pointless. He was the kind of guy who was always thinking about a glazed doughnut hiding in his desk drawer, or maybe wandering down to Giovanni's for some meatballs.

Paul answered as best he could and then it was Gillian's turn to give her statement. He kept referring to her as Mrs Stewart which made my face flush red with anger and the worst part was that Gillian didn't notice at first and so didn't correct him. Eventually, he pulled the report out of the typewriter and clicked twice on his ballpoint pen, handing it over so Paul and Gillian could each sign their statements. I felt sick with nerves until we were safely outside the police station but at least Detective Geary showed no interest in Gillian's living arrangements and seemed focused only on the inconvenience of Paul living in another jurisdiction.

Once we were outside in the heat of the midday sun, Gillian quickly took charge, telling me she would take Paul back to his hotel room.

'See you at home. I won't be late,' she whispered to reassure me, but I wasn't reassured. This was my cue to leave them but I hesitated until Gillian guided Paul into a taxi and slammed the door, leaving me standing on the sidewalk watching them speed away towards midtown.

Part of me wanted to follow them back to Paul's hotel and set up camp outside his room, until I could be satisfied that nothing was going on between them. Instead, I took myself back to the apartment where I ran a bath and used the last of my good bath oil. As I sank down into warm rose-scented water all I kept thinking about was Gillian and what she might be doing.

At one point I must have fallen asleep because I woke up with a start to find the water stone-cold, and Judith standing over me calling my name.

The sight of her leaning over me made me panic and I put an arm across my body to cover my nakedness, but Judith made no move to leave the room, and instead carried on standing there with a peculiar little giggle:

'Oh, don't be so shy, Dovie. We're all girls together, aren't we?' she said. I wanted her to leave, but she stood there as if it was the most natural thing in the world.

'I need to get out now.'

'Don't mind me. I only came to get you because Gillian rang, and I thought you would want the message straight away, but obviously I should have waited.'

'No, it's fine, really. What did she say?'

Judith perched on the side of the bathtub, trapping me and making sure that I couldn't get out easily. My body recoiled and I forced myself up, trailing water in my wake and soaking Judith as I did so. She squealed and jumped to her feet. I grabbed the towel from its rack and wrapped it around me like armour.

'I'm so sorry,' I said without meaning a word of it.

Judith scowled but brushed herself down and moved away from me.

'So, what was the message?' I asked.

She fixed me with a stern look and said, 'Oh, only that she would call back when you were out of the tub. I'm sure it was nothing important.' And with that Judith gave me her sly little smile and walked out of the bathroom.

I read the same page of my library book over and over without taking in one word of it. Judith was knitting a scarf out of red wool and the click clack of her knitting needles was the only sound between us. The black telephone remained silent on the table. Outside I could hear the usual city sounds of sirens and car doors slamming, engines revving or people calling out to each other. New York is a loud city and everyone wants to be heard. I was glad of it this evening, because I had no wish at all to make conversation with anyone. When it turned midnight, Judith wound up her ball of wool and pierced it with her knitting needles, which she then placed in her wool basket. She yawned and quietly got out of her chair.

'I'm turning in now. Goodnight, Dovie.'

'Goodnight,' I murmured in return, but I didn't look up from my book.

Surprisingly, Judith went to her room without a final barb about Gillian not being home. This time I decided I wouldn't go to bed until she returned. I was frozen into silence, but beneath the stony silence I was boiling mad. It was one thing to have an emergency but quite another to make me worry, and not to call when she said she would. It didn't take long before my anger cooled just enough to feel a pang of regret and then sadness. How had it come to this? Just weeks ago we'd been so happy. Memories floated up to the surface of the two of us cooking dinner in our little kitchen, falling over each other to get into cupboards or to open more wine, with music playing and laughing all the time. Yes, it was hard sometimes not being able to hold hands on the street or tell people we were together but once we were safely behind our apartment door it was so different. We spent our evenings and weekends like any other couple. We were happy in our little home. We felt safe there, as if nobody could ever hurt us, and we loved each other so much. We could touch and hold each other in a way that wasn't possible outside our apartment. They were such happy times and thinking about them made me sad. I wiped a tear from the corner of my eye. The past seemed like a distant land we had lost our way back to.

15

New York City, 1975

Gray's School was empty at this time of the year. There was nobody around except for an old janitor sweeping up as though it pained him to do it. The halls were filled with polished wood and every wall was covered in framed photographs of past pupils, mostly in sports teams hoisting silver cups high in the air. There were three trophy cabinets past the entrance, each crammed with large cups tied with the purple ribbons of winners. It was different in every way from my own school. I took a minute to study the pictures on the walls, fascinated by this other world. Every girl was smiling, fresh-faced, and seemed so confident, although surely they couldn't all be.

I was staring at the photographs to try and find some mention of someone called Dovie or Gillian, but so far it was all pupils, past and present. I'd spoken to a Mrs MacDougal over the telephone but only to make the briefest enquiry about the school, and I was hoping that I wouldn't need to actually see her. I dreaded this part as I could think of all the things that I should say but they never came out right when I opened my mouth, and so for that reason I mostly kept my mouth shut.

There was a small waiting room off the entrance to the school with a front desk and a back office where I could see someone moving around, so I headed there. I took a deep breath and wished that Viola had come with me, but she was busy with chores and anyway she said that fancy schools probably wouldn't help us if she was with me. I guessed she was right because, for all the pictures hanging on their fancy walls, I didn't see anyone who looked like Viola, except the old janitor.

The front desk was empty but there was a shadow on the frosted glass wall that separated the desk from the back office. I cleared my throat nervously and called out:

'Hello?'

My voice sounded strangled and there was no response. I could hear a radio playing softly in the background and I guessed that whoever was in there was listening to a show. I rapped my knuckles on the front desk and tried again, but louder:

'Excuse me . . . hello?'

This time whoever was back there heard me and the radio got shut off abruptly and a woman wearing thick glasses and a yellow sweater, even though it was eighty degrees outside, appeared in the office doorway.

'Oh, hello, dear. I'm afraid they aren't out yet,' she said.

'I'm sorry?'

She peered at me over the top of her glasses.

'Exam results are next week.'

'No . . . I'm not a pupil. I mean, I have results to collect but from my own school . . .' I was making no sense, not even to myself, and I could see her waiting for me to get to the point and wanting to get back to her radio show.

'So, what can I do for you?'

'I was wondering if you could help me find somebody who used to work here.'

The woman seemed curious and moved forward towards the front desk; she leaned both elbows on it and whispered to me:

'Is it your mother?'

'No, nothing like that. I telephoned earlier ... It's complicated.'

Obviously, I didn't want to explain where my mother was, as that wasn't going to help. I opened up my purse and pulled out the photograph of Dovie, Gillian and the other woman and laid it carefully on the desk facing her:

'I'm trying to find out who these women are. I have something that might belong to them but all I know is their names are Dovie and Gillian. They might have worked here a long time ago?'

'Well, that certainly sounds very mysterious. Are you playing detective, young lady? You know I once heard a radio play about a man who was trying to find someone because they inherited a million dollars. Imagine that? It's not a million dollars, is it?' She laughed and raised the gate in the front desk so I could step through. 'Come on through to the back office. You can tell me all about this mystery you're trying to solve.'

*

Mrs MacDougal was widowed, with a grown-up daughter who lived in Wisconsin and rarely came home. She had been the school secretary for ten years now, and before that was a medical secretary, which she didn't like so much because the doctors were a little rude to her. She liked to talk, especially to young girls at the school; she kept a box of candy in her desk drawer in case any of them felt faint, and a tin of homemade cookies on a shelf next to the coffee pot, in case anyone needed to have a chat. Once she started to talk, Mrs MacDougal kept on going and it was obvious that she didn't like the school holidays where her days were spent mostly alone with only her radio for company, or the occasional teacher popping in to pick up their mail.

I had come at the right time.

Within five minutes I was seated on a stool with a squishy leather top and little wheels on the bottom, so you needed to be careful not to glide away. Mrs Mac-Dougal popped the lid off the dark blue tin. There were a few crumbling cookies left and I took one to be polite.

She settled herself down in her thick leather chair behind her office desk.

'So, what's your name? I like to know the company I'm keeping.' She smiled.

'Ava . . . Ava Winters.'

'Pretty name. So, Miss Ava, let's see how I can help.'

'Thank you . . . Mrs MacDougal.'

'You can call me Mac. All the girls call me Mac or Mrs Mac. Now, let's have a look at this picture.'

She flipped it over, read the date and then flipped it back and held it up to the light so she could get a good look at the faces.

'It's before my time so I don't recognize them at all, but if we have some information then maybe we could track them down. Wouldn't that be exciting?' She beamed at me and helped herself to a cookie.

'I have a name, Dovie, which is kind of unusual. I'm trying to track her down or a woman called Gillian who might have worked with her and I think is also in that picture.'

'What's this all about? I need to know why you want this information before I go looking at people's files. Can't give that information out to just anyone, you know, even if it was a long time ago.'

'Someone sent a box to our apartment and it came all the way from Paris ... in France,' I added for extra emphasis. 'I'm trying to find out who it belongs to and what happened to these two women.'

'Oh my, isn't that just like a movie? I saw a movie once like that, or maybe it was on the radio. Anyway, it sounds like a mystery we need to solve. Mmm: 1955? That has got to be in the basement, I would think. We keep staff records here, but we had a burst water pipe last winter and some boxes got flooded. We can look down there ... if you want to. Here you go ... do you like hard candy? I always keep some for visitors.'

Mrs MacDougal opened a tin that was crammed to the top with every kind of hard candy you could imagine. I took a small red piece and popped it in my mouth. She took a green piece and started to suck on it, slurping slightly as she did so. She seemed nice but in an overgrown kid kind of a way. Maybe she was lonely. I wondered whether the girls at Gray's actually liked Mrs MacDougal, or whether they made fun of her behind her back, with her tins of candy and butter cookies, because she seemed to be trying way too hard.

She picked up a large jangling bunch of keys off a hook by the door and gestured to me to follow her. We took a door off the hallway and then another one, which led to a spiral staircase that went down for a flight or so, until we reached the basement door, which was locked. Mrs MacDougal tried the first key but it was the wrong one, then another key, which was also wrong. She lifted up her glasses and squinted, eventually settling on a small brass key and the lock sprang open.

The basement was large and smelled musty and damp. She flicked on the light switch and there was a strange buzzing noise before a gloomy yellow light sparked into life. There was a whole corner filled with old sports equipment, most of which looked rusty, and in the far corner were piles of stacked cardboard boxes with some old metal filing cabinets pushed against the wall. Mrs MacDougal headed towards the cabinets, muttering under her breath, and then swerved to the right and started lifting up boxes.

I stood slightly to her left, watching as she lifted a box and checked the dates that were written in thick black ink on the top. She was only on 1965, so there was a way to go yet. She pulled a face.

'I was hoping they wouldn't be in that corner because if that's the 1950s, they may have got damaged in that flood. I told them we needed to move things from down here, but nobody listens until it's too late. Hand me that box, would you, Ava?'

I picked up one of the boxes from the far corner and handed it to her. Sure enough, it had 1957 written on the top of it and she grimaced.

'Are we going to be lucky or not?'

She pulled aside a couple more boxes and that left two at the bottom, the very last one was marked 1954/5.

'It got a little wet. Can you see right here?' She pointed to the left-hand side of the box, which was covered in a large damp stain.

'Let's take it back upstairs. I can't leave the desk for too long and the light is better up there.'

'Sure. Do you want me to carry the box?'

'Oh, you have lovely manners. Thank you. Girls with lovely manners get an extra piece of candy.'

I didn't want an extra piece of candy, but I could see that Mrs MacDougal really wanted to make me happy, and it was worth eating the candy if I could get the information I needed.

'Thanks, Mrs MacDougal.'

'Mac, please. I told you there's no need to be so formal. I prefer Mac.'

I nodded.

'Mrs Mac.'

Mrs Mac set the box down on her desk and we both took our seats with our mouths full of candy. I took the green one this time for variety and she took the red. She slid the lid off the top of the box and started to lift bunches of papers.

For several minutes, she pulled out sheaves of paper and set them down on her desk. She didn't speak but made disapproving tutting noises from time to time and shook her head. Eventually she looked across the desk at me and said:

'You know, dear, someone has stuffed papers in here and put a lid on the box. No filing system at all. That is sloppy work, in my opinion. I don't like to speak ill of people but I wonder how someone in my position could do such a poor job.'

She bundled the papers together, sorted them roughly and organized them. Then she sat back and flipped through them carefully, licking her thumb to peel the pages away from each other and peering at them through her reading glasses.

It was several more minutes before she said anything and I sat there watching her work and occasionally glancing around the office when I got a little bored, wondering if Dovie or Gillian had ever sat in this very spot waiting on some school paperwork. I didn't want to work in any sort of office, I'd decided, but this one was actually kind of cosy, and she had her little radio on the windowsill, and a pot plant with bright green leaves: a life of keeping tins of candy or cookies for visitors. I was right in the middle of imagining a whole life for myself when Mrs Mac said:

'Here we are, we have a McNichol, Gillian. Is that her?' She held out a piece of paper and I got off the squishy stool to go and look at it. She ran her finger across the line where it had printed Gillian's name in black ink. 'She was the art teacher. We don't teach art these days, which is a shame, I always think.'

'Are you sure that's the right Gillian? There was only the one?' I needed to be certain.

'Mmm, well, isn't that a good question? Let me see if I can't find a full staff rota for that year.'

She carried on thumbing through the papers, while I wondered how on earth I would find Gillian McNichol. All I knew was that she once taught art and lived in New York. I didn't have much to go on. I needed an address.

Mrs Mac was nearly at the end of the bunch of papers on her desk. I was starting to lose hope and had no idea where to go next if we didn't find something soon.

'Here we are. Staffing rota for academic year 1954/55. That's what we need.'

She started to run her fingers down the list of names. I watched as her hand got closer to the bottom of the page and then the final name and nothing.

'Well, there isn't any Gillian or Dovie on that list. There must be another page on the staffing rota. Let me see now.'

She licked her right thumb and tried to separate the pages but they were glued together.

'Oh dear . . . I worried this would happen. It's the water damage. They're stuck together. This is a very delicate operation, very delicate indeed. I don't really know . . . Maybe I could use the steam from a kettle? I saw a movie once where they did that. I think it was Lana Turner or maybe I'm thinking of someone else. We could certainly give that a try. I might be able to peel them apart that way. There's a kettle in the teachers' lounge.'

'Will it work?'

'I couldn't say but if I try to peel them apart like this, they will tear and we won't be able to read the names anyway.'

Mrs Mac took a piece of fresh white paper and wrote 'BACK SOON' in large letters with a thick black pen. She beckoned to me to follow her and she left the note on the front desk in case anyone should call while we were away, although the hallways were quite empty. We headed past all the photographs of the fresh-faced girls again until we reached the door marked 'Staff Only'. After a minute waiting for Mrs Mac to go through her jangly bunch of keys again, this time selecting a long silver key, we were inside the room that smelled of coffee and stale cigarette smoke.

It was a large room with desks against the walls and a selection of comfortable armchairs in the centre. Most of them looked as if they'd seen better days, and they all had indentations in the seats from years of use. To one side, under the window, was a tray table, an old stove and a kettle. Mrs Mac lifted the kettle and went to a back room, which I presumed was some kind of a bathroom or kitchenette as I could hear water running, and she returned with the kettle filled. We lit the stove and waited.

'Now this is the tricky part. I don't want burned hands.' She held the papers gently over the kettle as it steamed away. Whenever it boiled for too long, we emptied it out and filled it again. It was hard to hold the papers over the steam otherwise. The room was cool enough when we started but after several attempts to boil a steaming kettle it was hot and sticky and our faces glistened with the heat of the steam. Mrs Mac was as careful as she could be and started to gently peel the papers apart from each other. There was a sharp intake of breath as she watched it tear a little, but with a bit more steam, she managed to prise them apart.

She held one in each hand looking very pleased with herself.

'Will you look at that?' She beamed.

The papers needed to dry a little before we could try and read them and so we headed back down to the office. I locked up the teachers' lounge and carried the keys while Mrs Mac wafted the pieces of paper all the way down the hallway until we got back to her desk.

She laid both pieces of paper out and grinned at me again. I smiled back at her, feeling a sudden burst of gratitude towards this strange woman who loved to feed people candy and help them out. She was kind and I'd been missing kindness lately. She started to trace her finger down the page as I chewed on my fingernails and waited.

'Here we are, Dovie Carmichael, and look . . . there is our Gillian McNichol. You can see there is nobody else called Gillian on this list. I do believe we've solved the mystery.'

She handed me the piece of paper and I skimmed down through the names. There was Dovie near the top of the page, and then right near the bottom was Gillian McNichol. I'd found their names. All I needed to do was find an address now. I looked up at Mrs Mac and we were both beaming at each other.

She xeroxed the piece of paper for me and I held the warm fresh copy in my hand. It was my cue to leave, and one glance at the clock told me I'd taken up a lot of her time already.

'I really need an address for them, maybe from when they applied for their jobs here?'

'I'll need to go through more of those boxes. It would be in the personnel files. Can you leave that with me? Here . . . you write down your telephone number and I'll call you the second I find anything?'

'Sure. Thank you so much, Mrs Mac. You've been really helpful.'

'My pleasure. I love a good mystery. Here . . . take a piece of candy for the journey home.'

I took a piece of yellow candy this time and then I

picked up my photograph of the three women from her desk, putting it carefully back into my pocket.

The downtown bus was slick with heat, someone was playing music at the back and a mosquito was buzzing its wings furiously against a damp window. A crowd of people were trying to get off, and another crowd of people were trying to get on, and we all ended up shoving past each other. I saw a seat that was free about halfway back and aimed for that, getting there ahead of the crowd. As I leaned back, my elbow gently bumped against the person in the next seat and I turned to say sorry and looked straight at Cal.

He nodded to acknowledge me, but turned to stare out of the window so he didn't have to talk. I stared at the back of the seat, straight ahead and focused on breathing in and out. It was all I could manage. Our elbows grazed each other every time the bus jerked to a stop in traffic which was pretty much every few seconds. I could feel the tender warm patch of his skin against mine and the solid muscle of his shoulder from time to time. I scrabbled around in my brain for something to say, anything, just a small fragment of conversation. My mind was blank, stupid with longing for him and without any words. I tried to count the stops and wondered if he was going home, which could mean getting off at the same stop as me, or if he had other plans.

Think of something to say was the only thing going through my mind, but nothing came. A crushing blankness. The bus jerked to a stop at the lights and our arms lightly bumped together again. He shuffled around in his seat a little and moved his head from side to side as though he was stretching out a tension.

A thought flashed into my mind and I drew in a deep breath:

'So . . . are you going to the pool party next week?'

He looked at me with his full attention as if trying to work out who I was and what I was doing there.

'Yeah, maybe. You?'

He'd responded and we were making conversation, terrible, awkward, stilted conversation, but it was happening. I tried to remain calm and casual in my response.

'I was thinking about it. I guess you have a lot of plans for the summer, huh?'

My voice sounded as if it didn't belong to me but to a much older girl, the kind who dated boys like Cal.

'Not really. Just hanging out in the city.'

He hadn't asked me what my plans were but I found myself babbling an incoherent stream of words back towards him. Later, I couldn't even remember what I'd said. They were just words rushing out of my mouth to get to him.

'Oh . . . me too . . . just hanging out. Waiting on exam results and then the pool party.'

Cal nodded and stared out of the window. He seemed nervous. I fell silent but somehow thought our strange conversation gave me permission to look at him, tracing the slightly uneven line of his jaw with my eyes. Then I told myself not to stare and fixed my eyes on the back of the seat in front of me, but from time to time my eyes shifted right to take another peek at Cal.

'I saw you the other day with your family.'

The words took me by surprise as I'd imagined our conversation to be over, and I was firmly embedded in the staring part of the journey. I tried to frame a response where I didn't have to mention my mother or the purpose of our visit to Benny's, or Candy.

'Yeah, with my dad. We do that sometimes.'

My heart raced a little and I wanted us to carry on talking, but also I specifically did not want him to ask anything else about that day. I wondered if he'd heard about my mother and this was a pity conversation, but there was no way to know without asking and I wasn't about to do that.

Someone at the back of the bus rang the stop bell and we crawled to a halt. The doors hissed open like steam releasing and a bunch of people got off. Only one person got on, an elderly man with a walking stick. The doors hissed to a close again and we jerked away from the stop. The old man needed to sit down but the seats in front of us were also full of old people or mothers with small babies tucked on to their laps. I realized this too late and prayed for someone to move. The old man tried to cling to the rail and hold on to his stick. I got to my feet and offered him my precious seat next to Cal. The old man didn't even say thank you. He grumbled his way into the seat but before he could sit down, Cal leaped up and offered the old man the window seat.

'You sit, it's OK. I don't mind standing. I'm getting off soon anyway.'

'I'm OK. I'm getting off too.'

We stood trying to keep our balance while the old man tried to find his handkerchief, eventually pulling out a grey-looking piece of cloth and proceeding to blow his nose loudly and then inspect the contents of the cloth. Cal and I looked at him and then at each other. The old man kept on snuffling into his handkerchief and we stared at the floor to stop ourselves laughing at the strange noises he was making. It felt so natural now, all the awkwardness replaced by a shy familiarity.

A stray piece of hair was sticking out a little just by Cal's ear and without thinking I reached up a hand and smoothed it down. Cal looked surprised at this sudden intrusion but he didn't flinch or move away. He let me smooth his hair down and leaned closer to me. For a few seconds I could feel his warm breath on my face and his lips were so close to mine that I felt sure he was going to kiss me. I gazed up at him, wishing hard, and he gave me a sloppy grin in return. The bus jerked suddenly and I put my hand on his chest to steady myself and he held out his arm to stop me from falling. We both grinned at each other and I could feel the warmth of his fingers on my bare arm.

The stop bell rang again and this time it was our stop. The doors hissed open, releasing us into the heat of the sidewalk and the bustle of the avenue. It seemed natural that we fall into stride, heading in the same direction, and we walked along peacefully like that, me dreaming about holding his hand, and him staring at the boys outside the fried chicken store to see if he recognized them. He did. A skinny Latino kid they called Pedro, although his real name was Jesús. Pedro yelled out a greeting. Cal suddenly realized I was walking along beside him and slowed down so it looked as if we weren't together. I kept on walking. I could hear Pedro laughing and Cal saying:

'Cut it out, man.'

Pedro said something rapid fire in return that I couldn't catch, and they both started snickering in that nasty way boys do sometimes. I walked on with the sound of their laughter ringing in my ears and my heart breaking a little. By the time I reached our building the tears had started to fall, a sad, pathetic, disappointed trickle. I wiped them away with the back of my hand and let myself in, scurrying past Miss Schnagl's door and heading for the sanctuary of our apartment.

I was trying to put off going back to Candy's place for as long as possible. I needed to pick up a change of clothes, and I wanted to put the list I got from Mrs Mac and the photograph safely back in the box. I didn't want to risk losing anything. Not now I had a lead. It wasn't much, but at least I had two names now: Dovie Carmichael and Gillian McNichol.

I wondered what had happened to them. Maybe they

were still in New York? The 'LIAR' picture worried me, and I wondered if it was meant to be a threat. If I tracked them down, should I warn them?

I pulled out the photograph and the list that Mrs Mac found, and held it up to the light.

16

New York City, 1955

I'd been so lost in thoughts of happier times that I hadn't heard the front door open, and suddenly Gillian appeared in front of me, as if I'd conjured her there.

'Hi.' I dropped the library book into my lap and tried to sound welcoming.

'Hey ... Where's ... ?' Gillian gestured towards Judith's room.

'In bed,' I whispered.

She nodded and flopped on to the couch and lay down.

'She said you called and I waited.'

'Sorry, it's been crazy. Paul didn't seem well enough to be left alone so I stayed for a while to make sure he was OK. I called to tell you that.'

'Is he OK now?'

'I think so but he hit his head pretty hard.'

'Yes, but the doctor gave him the all clear.'

'I know but I'm worried about him. He doesn't seem quite himself and he has a long journey tomorrow. I suggested he stay in the city for a few more days just to make certain he's well enough to travel but he has to get back to work.'

'I'm sure he's fine if the doctor discharged him.'

'Yeah, I guess.'

I knew what Gillian was like when she got to fretting about something. I was glad to hear that Paul was going home tomorrow, and at least that part of our lives would return to normal. All we needed to do was get rid of Judith.

'Come on, let's get some sleep.' I stood up and offered my hand to Gillian.

'No, I'm going to take the couch tonight in case Paul rings.'

'Why would he call?'

'I told him to call if he didn't feel well.'

'Wouldn't it be better if he rang a doctor if he didn't feel well?' The words sounded bitter even to me. She flinched.

'You should get some sleep, Dovie. I'll be fine here. You take our bed. It's more comfortable than the nook.'

She was mad at me and I was mad at myself for allowing us to disintegrate into cross words again. I wished that I'd kept quiet. She was just worried about someone she'd known a long time and I was making too much of it . . . except somewhere deep inside a small voice was whispering a faint truth I didn't want to hear.

I couldn't sleep, spending the hours staring into the darkness, lying there with my body aching for Gillian, and for us to be alone and peaceful in that way we used to be. I wanted to hold on to her so tightly that all the fear I felt would subside.

I sighed and rolled out of bed, rubbing my eyes awake, and grabbed my robe from the hook on the back of the door where it hung. As I stumbled to the bathroom, I was trying to keep as quiet as possible, so as not to disturb Judith, avoiding the creaking floorboards as I walked. I used the toilet and then splashed cold water on my face. I was exhausted, and I couldn't remember the last time I'd looked in the mirror and a happy smiling face stared back at me. A frown furrowed between my eyes and my lips had a pinched look to them. I couldn't go on being pulled in so many different directions, and the thought of losing Gillian over this stupid situation was more than I could bear. I wished we could rewind to when it was just the two of us. More than anything I wished I hadn't lied to her about Judith. It was eating away at me.

Gillian was fast asleep and looked so peaceful I didn't want to disturb her. Her fair hair was spread out all over the cushion, and I stood in the doorway for several minutes watching the soft rise and fall of her breathing. In the early dawn light, the beauty of it took me by surprise, and I wanted to stand there watching over her as she slept. This is what I was trying to protect and it was all worth it, but it made me more determined than ever to resolve the situation with Judith.

Gillian stirred and I crept into the kitchen and put on a pot of coffee; the gas flame made a popping noise as I lit the match and the coffee pot burbled into life. The sound of it must have woken Gillian because the next minute I felt a familiar arm around my waist, and the heavy weight of her body behind me. I leaned back into her warmth and let her nestle into my neck. For a split second it was as if the past few weeks had never happened. I breathed in the scent of her and wished we would stay like this forever. We stood there together watching the coffee pot boil, saying nothing but at the same time making our peace with every breath.

I poured the coffee and set the cups down at the kitchen table. Gillian opened the window, and we sat side by side, sipping coffee and feeling the soft warm air on our faces. I leaned across and kissed her softly on her lips.

'I'm so sorry.'

'Me too.'

We kissed again and I stroked Gillian's hair, moving it away from her face. She kissed my fingers and we grinned at each other, suddenly remembering what it was we liked in the other person. The strain of the past few weeks seemed a million miles away. Suddenly a creaking noise from the living room reminded us that we didn't live alone any more.

Judith came into the kitchen, looking surprised to see us both sitting at the kitchen table.

'My . . . Well, aren't you two the early birds this morning?'

I ignored her and carried on drinking my coffee but Gillian responded.

'You're up early, Judith?'

'I just couldn't sleep. I was tossing and turning most of the night . . .'

'Maybe you need to drop an extra sleeping pill.'

'Oh, I stopped taking those pills weeks ago. I didn't want to rely on them. Trouble is I seem to wake up at all hours of the night, and you'd be surprised how much noise there is . . .'

She smiled sweetly but something underneath her words was steely and mean. Gillian's eyes opened wide and she stared at me; her mouth fell open with horror and fear crawled up my spine. I couldn't understand what Judith was playing at. We sat staring at each other, me desperately trying to reassure Gillian with my eyes while she shook her head from side to side, unable to believe what she'd heard. I prayed she wouldn't start crying in front of Judith but I could already see her eyes filling with tears. Judith flitted about filling her coffee cup and helped herself to cereal as if nothing had been said. When her cup and bowl were loaded up with her breakfast, she put them on a small wooden tray and headed towards her bedroom. She hesitated in the doorway for a moment and smiled at us.

'I'll leave you two girls to chat. I think I might have breakfast in bed this morning. I'm still feeling quite tired.'

Gillian leaned across the kitchen table and gripped my arm tightly.

'Did you hear what she said? She hasn't been taking those stupid sleeping pills. She's been listening to us. She knows something. We've been so stupid, creeping about, and all the time she's been awake listening.'

Gillian's voice was rising and I tried to hush her but I could see she wasn't going to calm down.

I took a deep breath and cleared my throat. My heart started to race a little and I felt a wave of fear crawl over me as I started to speak. There was only one way out of this situation now and it was long overdue.

'Gill, there's something I need to tell you and I don't want you to be mad at me. I've done a really stupid thing . . .'

Gillian's eyes narrowed and her mouth grew tight. She leaned back in her chair and stared at me.

'You're scaring me, Dovie. What is it? What have you done?'

She sounded frightened and I immediately regretted starting this conversation. But it was too late to turn back now, even if I wanted to. I bit on my bottom lip, raking it over and over with my teeth.

'Judith *knows* about us. She's always known.' I whispered the words, unable to meet her eye.

'*What?*' Gillian's face was a mask of fear. Her mouth snapped shut and then her hand slipped away from my knee where it was resting.

'I lied to you. She saw us kissing that night.' I felt relief at getting the words out but it was short-lived.

'How long have you known?' Gillian's voice didn't

sound like hers any more. It was blunt and harsh as if we were strangers.

'Since that first day at school after the dinner party. She promised me she wouldn't tell a soul if I agreed to let her move in here. She insisted it would only be for a few weeks. You heard her talking about that apartment she loved on 23rd Street and the key money. You heard her? I believed her and what choice did I have? I couldn't say no. She might have told on us. I did it for you . . . I did it for us, Gill.'

Gillian shook her head from side to side slowly and rubbed her hands across her face. She rocked slightly in her chair.

'No, this can't be happening.'

I reached for her but she stood up and picked up her cigarettes from the shelf by the window. Her hands were shaking so much she couldn't light the match and I took the strip of matches from her and lit her cigarette. She inhaled and then blew out a cloud of smoke as she ran her fingers through her hair. I could see her searching for a plan, some answer to this, but there wasn't one. She took another drag on her Pall Mall and then crushed it out in the ashtray and leaned her head back against the kitchen wall. She made little balls out of her fists and held them to her eyes. For a moment I thought she was crying, but then she turned to face me and I could see her white-hot anger.

'You did this and you didn't even tell me? You risked

everything in my life and you never said a word. How could you?'

I couldn't meet her gaze. I was so overcome with shame. 'I'm sorry.'

'It's too late to be sorry. Look what you've done. Everyone will find out. We will lose everything. Have you thought about that? What will we do? What will I say to my family? Oh my God, what if they find out?'

Gillian turned away from me and her hands made furious slapping movements on the kitchen wall. I reached out my fingers and tried to turn her face to look at me.

'They won't find out. It won't happen. It's going to be OK. She won't tell on us.'

She slapped my hand away and turned to face me. She put out a hand to stop me coming any closer and I could see the fear in her eyes.

'Of course she'll *tell* someone. Don't you see? She's blackmailing us and when we can't give her what she wants, she'll tell somebody.'

'Not if we help her get an apartment. I've got my savings; we could use them.'

I tried to hold her by grabbing on to her shoulders, pulling her towards me, but her body was rigid and unforgiving. I was desperate to make this OK again but Gillian wouldn't be pacified.

'Don't be so damn stupid. Don't you see nothing will ever be enough?'

Even as I denied it, I recognized that Gillian was absolutely right. Judith would keep on taking everything.

'We'll figure something out. We can think of a plan now that you know. We can sit down and work it out together.'

Gillian stared at me and slowly shook her head.

'This is all your fault. You've always been the same way. You did this because you couldn't stand that a woman neither of us even likes was upset with you. You should never have invited her over. You risked everything we have. Do you have any idea what will happen to us when she tells? Do you?'

I shook my head and tried to keep the tears from falling. My chest felt tight and I couldn't breathe for fear of what would happen next.

'They will fire us. They will take away our teaching licences so nobody will ever employ us again, and — worse — we could be prosecuted or locked up in a mental institution so they can try to make us "normal" again. You have ruined everything because you're a child, Dovie.'

Gillian's face was red with fury but the tears had started to trickle down her cheeks. She wiped under her nose with the back of her hand.

'We could leave right now. We could both go. We could go to Paris and live there. We've talked about doing that so many times and we could really do it. I've got enough savings for a few months if we're careful. We don't need much. Let's do it. She can't touch us there.'

'It's a *dream*, Dovie. Don't you see that? It's not real. People like us don't go and live in Paris. They don't pack up and leave and live happily ever after. There is no happy ever after for women like us. They will hound us until we stop.'

'Stop? Stop what? We can't stop being who we are. We can leave. We can make it real.'

'Shut up! I'm so sick of you dreaming all the time. Grow up, Dovie. I can't look at you. I don't want to lose everything. I don't want to be locked away. I'm not like you. You have your sister, but I don't have family who would understand this. I will lose everything and I can't do it.'

'There's nothing wrong with dreaming. People go and change their lives all the time. They move away. We could teach English in Paris . . . and women like us can make lives there. We've read about that. You just need to say yes and we could go right now. I could book two tickets for the boat and that would be that. You think you're the sensible one, the one with her feet on the ground here? Well, that doesn't keep you safe either. It only makes you miserable not to have dreams. There's nothing wrong with dreaming of a better future. It's all we have left now. Gilly, please listen to me—'

'NO! I can't do it . . . I need to get out of here.'

My face crumpled and the tears I'd been trying to hold back started to fall.

'You're leaving me?'

'I have to get out of here.'

179

Gillian pushed past me and went into the bedroom. I panicked and raced after her, not really caring what I had to do to stop her leaving. I followed her into our bedroom and stood in the doorway unsure of what to say or do next. Gillian was shoving arms and legs into her clothes as fast as she could. She grabbed her blue overnight case from the top of the closet and started emptying out drawers into it. She was making so much noise that I was afraid Judith would come in to see what was happening and that was the last thing we needed. I moved inside the room and closed the bedroom door, trying to muffle the sounds of our argument. Gillian carried on crushing her belongings into her suitcase. I tried to wedge myself between her and the suitcase to plead with her but Gillian shoved me to one side and struggled to close the lid.

'Wait . . . please wait . . . Let's talk . . . Come sit with me. Just sit and talk to me. Please . . .'

'I don't want to talk to you. I can't even look at you, and I can't think straight with her here. I'm so angry. You have no idea what you've done. You've *ruined* us, Dovie. You've fucking ruined us. We can never go back to being what we were. Never! Don't you understand that?'

I was silent, choking back the tears and willing her not to hate me forever. I needed so badly to fix things between us. If only I could find the right words, she would forgive me. She always forgave me. Yes, I was silly and a dreamer and spent too much time caring about what people thought about me, but I was other things too, good things. She had to think I was good deep down. She had to understand I would do anything to protect her.

'I love you, Gilly.'

It was her turn to be silent now. The tears had dried up and her beautiful face was pink and swollen. She was cried out and the storm had passed. I inched closer to her.

'I love you so much, Gill. I want to make this right, no matter what it takes.'

She nodded and I reached out a hand to stroke her hair but she flinched when I touched her. I took my hand away and sat down on the bed with both hands folded in my lap. My fate was up to her now.

'Please don't go, Gill. I'll do anything you say. Don't leave me like this.'

'Let me go home and clear my head. I can catch a ride with Paul and I'll call the school from there.'

The mention of Paul's name made me feel sick and I wanted to carry on begging her to stay, but there was nothing I could say that would change her mind and I knew it.

'Promise me you'll come back?' I felt so desperately needy that I couldn't see how she would want to return, and I hated myself for being so pathetic but I had to ask her.

'I need some time. Let me go. I have to get things straight in my head.'

'Can I call you?'

'It's best if you don't. If I have something to say then I'll call you.'

I'd tried to stay calm but now my voice grew shrill and I started to plead with her:

'Don't leave me, Gill. You can't leave me like this. Please . . . please . . . I'm begging you to stay, Gilly . . . I'm begging you. I'll do anything.'

I got to my knees and clung to her legs. I breathed in the smell of her skin, her perfume, and I clung on, desperate to make her stay. As she tried to free herself, I pressed myself closer to her body, unable to let go for fear of what would happen if I did. She leaned down and grabbed my shoulders and pulled me to my feet.

I couldn't say anything for the choking sobs as I clung to her. She put the palms of her hands either side of my face and pressed her lips to mine.

'Please don't do this. Please don't do this . . . Please . . .' I pleaded.

She released my face from between her hands and moved away from me.

'I didn't do this, Dovie. You did.'

She moved back towards me, wrapped her arms around me and crushed me to her. All I wanted was to hold on to her and never let her go. My heart was breaking at the thought that she might leave. I felt her stifle a sob as she embraced me and I tried in vain to think of something to say.

I was whispering 'Gilly . . . Gilly' like a prayer. My

arms were trapped by my sides and all I could do was wait and hope. Gillian was holding on to me so tightly that for a brief moment I actually thought she had changed her mind. But then she stepped away and was gone.

17

New York City, 1975

Viola was right on time and carrying a pile of old records under her arm, which meant she was headed for my dad's stereo again before we would get anything else done. As I opened the front door, she shoved a packet of Twinkies into my hands.

'I brought snacks.' Viola was big on snacks. She was still wearing my blue shirt, which in true Viola fashion had a plastic glittery belt tied around the middle of it. All my stuff looked better on Viola; she had that way with clothes. Today's record haul included Ray Charles and Betty Carter, and before long they were blasting through our apartment. I filled Viola in on what happened at Gray's.

Viola became busy inventing scenarios and I only made her stop when they started to get crazy. We got so hot in the living room that every few minutes we kept running out to the kitchen to open the refrigerator door, leaning our heads and arms against the icy shelves. We held a competition to see who could shove a whole Twinkie in her mouth, but I nearly choked and eventually Viola got bored and wanted to explore the box for more clues. I dutifully carried the box back into the living room so Vi didn't need to leave the stereo unattended and we spread everything out on the rug: first the plastic bag full of half-written letters, then the photograph albums, the loose photographs and the little pouch with the butterfly necklace, and finally the other stuff that looked less interesting, such as the pretty scarf and the whiskey tumbler.

Viola held up every item and we shook out all the papers and the photograph album until we were satisfied that we knew what everything was; then we sat back on our heels and looked at each other.

'So, we have these two women, Dovie Carmichael and Gillian McNichol.' Viola pointed out the two women in the photographs. 'And we know they used to live in your apartment. The letters are all written by Dovie, but we don't know why this stuff got sent to your apartment or what happened to either of them. We know they worked at Gray's School so here's what I think . . .'

I knew Viola was about to make yet another crazy plan for solving this mystery and given everything else that was going on in my life it seemed as if making sense of someone else's life was a much better option than making sense of my own. I was happy to follow her down that path for a little while at least, although I couldn't help but be worried about what had happened to Dovie and Gillian. Were they still around? Had they stayed together? Did somebody hurt them?

'Hey, are you listening?' Viola frowned at me.

'Go ahead, I'm listening.'

'It's hard enough to think with the heat in here, and where is that smell coming from?'

'The garbage in the back alley. They're burning it. It stinks out there.'

Viola wrinkled her nose and got back to her grand schemes. 'Do you think the box was meant for your mom or your dad?'

'It could be, but I doubt it, honestly. My dad said we didn't know anyone in Paris and, well, I haven't discussed it with my mother.' I really didn't want to go there and changed the subject so Viola would move on.

Viola sighed. 'It's a real shame I didn't get to talk to Mrs Mac. I'm good with people. I bet I could have got her to tell me everything.'

'Vi, you have a big opinion of your charm and Mrs Mac didn't know anything.'

Viola smiled.

'I'm charming, what can I tell you?'

I threw my mother's yellow cushion at her head and we collapsed in a heap of giggles. Viola tossed it right back at me and caught me on my jaw. It felt good to be silly for a while. I curled my lip back and made my cross-eyed face that always cracked Viola up. She laughed and flung herself back on the rug quite dramatically, stretching out her arms at right angles with her body and making 'snow angels' on the rug. Suddenly she stopped and started rolling towards the couch.

'What are you doing?' I asked.

'Wait a minute . . .' she said and flipped over so her face was touching the bottom of the couch and stretched her arm right out under it. After a few seconds of reaching out Viola rolled away on to her back and held her right arm in the air. She was holding a pale blue envelope in her hand. She sat back up on her heels and turned the envelope to face me. In dark blue ink the words 'La Famille Carmichael' was scrawled across the front of the envelope.

'It's a letter,' said Viola, stating the obvious.

'But how . . .' I stopped suddenly, remembering the box collapsing on to our rug. The letter must have fallen under the couch. I reached over and snatched the envelope from Viola's fingers.

'Hey . . .' She started to complain but before long we were both huddled against the armchair while I opened the envelope. I pulled out the pages and flattened them on my lap before starting to read. I tried to make out the words but I presumed they were French. It was signed, in a dashing black scribble, Christine LeGrand.

'It's in French.'

'I guess so.'

'We don't know anyone who speaks French?'

In our neighbourhood it was easy to find Italian, or Chinese, or Hebrew, but French not so much.

'We could go ask my dad. He's at Jazzland tonight. Musicians know everyone in this city.'

'I can't be out too late. My dad will be mad.' I didn't want to mention that I was supposed to be staying over at Candy Jackson's place although I was an unwelcome guest.

'My dad starts at nine o'clock but they always get there early to warm up. You'll be back home by ten at the latest. Come on, Ava, we've got to find out what this letter says.'

'OK, but as quick as we can. No staying to listen to jazz.'

Viola pulled a face at me but quickly nodded agreement. 'Straight there, and straight back.'

Jazzland was the kind of club that people played on the way up, and again on the way down. Viola's father liked to tell stories of playing with some greats back in the day, but he had gone from up and coming to never made it without much to speak of in between. There was a peeling poster half-heartedly stuck to the wall outside, announcing the acts for the coming week, and a black windowless door left over from the time it was a speakeasy, during prohibition. A hatch slid back at the very top of the door, so whoever was on the other side could see who wanted to come in, and decide if they were welcome without even opening the door. There was no need to do anything but leave the door open for people to walk in these days, but everyone liked that it was the same as the olden days so they kept it up.

Viola knocked and waited. The hatch slid back, and a pair of eyes was just visible. The bolt shifted, and the door opened a crack.

'Hey, honey, you looking for your dad?'

'Yeah, got a favour to ask.'

'OK, baby girl, but you gotta be quick now. I got a business to run after all.'

Cindy was old, really old. People said she started out as a singer before the war in this place, and some said she was even here during prohibition, when it was a speakeasy. Nobody knew for sure, but she always looked night-time even when you saw her around the neighbourhood during the day. Flame-red hair and bright red lips, long gold loops at her ears, and bangles that jangled when she moved her arms. She paused for breath halfway through a sentence, but it didn't stop her puffing away on a cigarette, often lighting a fresh one off the one she was about to crush out. She was nice though, always gave a smile and a wave if you saw her around town, and she usually let Viola in to watch her dad unless the club was full.

Once you walked past Cindy in her red chair at the top of the stairs, you went down into the darkness, and the smell of stale smoke and beer filled your nostrils, making you gag a little. The floor was linoleum but sticky underfoot, and the bar took up one whole wall. The bottles of liquor changed over often enough to always be clean and sparkling under the dim lights. A weary-looking black man was wiping glasses and arranging them on the shelf so when customers came he could work smoothly and without fuss. At the far end of the room were a few scattered tables and chairs, one booth against the wall and a stage so small it was barely big enough to fit a piano and drum kit on to it. Somehow, they did fit a band up there, and in a few hours this place would be heaving with glistening bodies dancing, with music so loud it would bounce off the walls and the ceilings and make your chest hurt. There was one guy tinkling some keys on the piano with a cigarette hanging out of his mouth, his eyes misty with drink or something that blurred him around the edges; a couple of women were smoothing down their hair and arranging their microphones, and Viola's father was standing front and centre, using his lazy smile on their good nature.

When he caught sight of Viola and me approaching, the lazy smile cracked into a wide grin and he moved away from the lady singers with their tight dresses and high heels.

'Hey, my two favourite girls. You too early to listen to us play. We ain't even got to tuning yet. What are you two up to this evening?'

Viola shrugged. 'We ain't up to nothing. It's OK, we can wait a bit; I need a favour though.'

'Is that the Benjamin Franklin kind of a favour?'

'No, I didn't come to ask you for money.'

'So what you need?'

Viola's father flipped a wooden chair around and sat astride it, leaning on the back of the chair and resting his trumpet lightly there as he teased Viola and pulled funny faces at her. It made my heart ache to watch them, and I wished my dad was a jazz trumpeter, and not running around town with Candy Jackson. Viola waited until he finished teasing her, and then I pulled out the letter and carefully unfolded it. Viola was quick to take it out of my hands and show her father.

'We found this letter – well, Ava found it – and the thing is it's all written in French so we need someone who can tell us what it says.'

'French? How did you girls end up with a letter all written in French?'

'Ava found it in some old books and it's a history project for school.'

Viola was the smoothest liar I knew. The words fell out perfectly composed and were always followed up by a beaming smile.

'I don't know no French people. Let me ask the guys. They always got people around from all over the place.'

He got to his feet and wandered back over towards the stage, where the singers and the piano guy had been joined by a drummer who couldn't keep his hands still; they were constantly moving, beating out a rhythm, his fingers brushing sticks over his drums faster and faster. It sounded good though, and the girls started to click their fingers, and murmur things like, 'That's right, baby.'

Viola and I knew the piano guy vaguely, as he did shifts at the laundromat when he wasn't playing piano. His name was Charles but everyone called him Button, although nobody could remember why. Button started to play along with the rapid drumbeat, and the girls were clapping their hands and snapping their fingers and making 'shoo' noises into their microphone. They did a funny little dance thing together, mirroring each other's movements, which Viola and I tried to copy sometimes, but we never could get the hang of it. Lois and Belle mostly worked the clubs together singing, but from time to time they went solo. There was nobody in the neighbourhood this gang didn't know. Viola's father picked up his trumpet and started to blow his way into the song. Viola loved to watch him work, and she settled down on the wooden chair right in front of the stage and listened to them play. The music shifted to a slower melody and Belle stepped up to the mic and started to sing. Her voice was like chocolate, and she poured her heart into a sad song that I'd never heard before.

'"All through my life they'll taunt me . . ."'

They worked the song up and down, each taking turns to show off a solo to the murmurs of approval from the others, and eventually they all gradually wound the song down until it fizzled into silence. This was their way of warming up for a night's work; sometimes they would do a couple of songs, but often it was just one, and then a break for a smoke or maybe a sandwich before the show. Viola waved the letter at her father to remind him, as his mind was full of music now and he was smiling at Lois, who seemed to be getting his attention that evening.

'Hey, any of you guys know any French people?' he asked.

'I do. You know her too, works at the Six Bars in

Harlem and sings real good. Marianne or some such name,' Lois said.

'Viola got a need of a French speaker. You reckon this Marianne can help her?'

'Why not? She don't live far from me. You want me to ask her?'

Viola's impatience cut in. She knew from previous experience that this favour could take a long road to get back to us.

'Do you have her address?'

Lois thought about it for a few seconds and smiled at Viola.

'Sure. You want me to write it down for you?'

'Yeah. You got a pencil?' Viola was all business.

Eventually someone tracked down a pencil and a scrappy piece of paper and Lois wrote down the address, pausing only to double underline it when she finished.

A noise at the other end of the bar interrupted us, and a gang of sailors in their bright white uniforms were lining up beers. A couple of local girls tagged along with them, and that was the sign for Viola and me to make ourselves scarce.

'OK, Lois, thanks. Bye, Dad, see you later.'

'Straight home now, you hear? Run and don't stop. Don't want you girls hanging around out there in the dark.'

'Yeah, OK.'

We raced past the sailors and back up the stairs where, Cindy shooed us out of the door. A line of people were waiting to get in and we squeezed past them. Viola didn't live far from the club but I had to make the trip all the way back to Candy's apartment on 23rd Street, or face the wrath of my father. We agreed to meet on Saturday to visit Marianne and I set off back to Candy's.

I headed past the fried-fish place and took a left past the laundromat, before having to choose to walk up the street where Cal lived, or continue on to Greenwich. I decided to take the chance and walk on the opposite side of the street to where Cal lived in an apartment with his mother and younger brother Benji, who had some kind of affliction that meant he swore at people all the time, and so he wasn't allowed to come to school. Cal's mother home-schooled Benji, but she usually got bored halfway through the day, and he was often left to sit out on their front stoop where he would launch a volley of cuss words at you if you walked past the house. This bothered me for several reasons: I didn't like being shouted at, and I was desperately trying not to be noticed. Once, I walked by on the opposite side of the street during my lunch break, and Benji let fly at the top of his voice, which meant his mother sent Cal to fetch him indoors, and I must have looked like I was spying on him, which I was, but still, it was embarrassing.

There was no sign of Benji, and I walked slowly along the opposite side of the street, casually glancing up at Cal's apartment windows from time to time. The lights were on and I was hoping for a sighting, but after our earlier encounter I didn't particularly want him to see me. I speeded up my walk a little, having changed my mind, but there was no sign of movement at his building anyway.

I was halfway along the street when I saw in the distance the boys who hung out on the corner all day and all night. They were a permanent fixture. I presumed they went home to eat or take a shower, but whenever I walked past, they were always there. There were about ten of them in various formations, all standing around, smoking or watching people come and go. They would whistle or growl, or shout obscene things at girls who walked by, telling them what they wanted to do to them, or commenting on their breasts or their backsides. When boys walked by, they would let fly with a cascade of insults, and see how many they could hit them with in the short time it took them to pass. I slowed my pace, waiting for a boy to walk along the street, hoping they would get the insults, and save me from the body commentary or worse. I hated to hear their words picking out the parts of me that I already hated in myself, and putting them on display for everyone in the street. It was the laughter that cut right through me, laughing at me, at my fat ass, or my lack of breasts, or they would suck their teeth and weigh up whether I was worth their trouble.

As luck would have it, a skinny young kid was sloping along behind me unaware of what was ahead of him, and I let him overtake me by stopping to adjust my shoe. As he got to the corner the insults started, calling into question his parentage, his manhood, and – always the final insult – his mother, and who she slept with. The boy got angry but there was nothing he could do to stop them, and I scurried along in his jet stream unnoticed, breathing a sigh of relief when I reached Greenwich and relative safety. I could still hear the kid shouting abuse back at them when I was a block away.

It was getting dark by the time I saw Candy's building in the distance and the streets were starting to turn over to night-time. I started to pick up the pace and walked briskly past shadowy doorways until I reached the front door. I didn't want to explain to my dad where I'd been or what had happened. I figured he'd go crazy if he knew I'd been out this late walking around in the city so I invented a cousin for Viola who'd dropped me off. By the time I turned the key I had named this cousin Alvin, and given him an occupation: cook. It would have to do. I was getting pretty good at this lying game.

As I let myself into the building, I could hear music coming from Candy's apartment. She was playing Marvin Gaye, but really loud, as if she was having a party. Candy's apartment was much smaller than ours. There was only one bedroom, a small living area with a pull-out that was my bed, a kitchenette, and a bathroom at the end of the hall. Everywhere you looked floaty coloured scarves were draped over lamps and there were drooping plants with yellowing leaves on each surface. A cloying smell of incense filled the air and the only chair was a faded orange beanbag.

By the time I got up the stairs I could see her front

door was slightly open and, when I pushed at it, there were a dozen people in there, all drinking beer and passing around a cigarette. It took a moment before I saw my own father take the cigarette and inhale a lungful, before softly blowing out the smoke, and then a big dopey grin spread all over his face. As I went through the door, which had been left ajar for visitors to come in and out, Candy spotted me first and leaped to her feet.

'Ava, we thought you weren't coming back tonight?'

The dopey grin disappeared from my dad's face and I could see him mentally cranking the gears to try and get back into father-mode, but it was way too late. He'd obviously forgotten all about me and was now struggling to get his tone right, but it came out angry and harsh.

'You should have called. I thought you were at the apartment. You're not supposed to disappear like that. This is someone's home, for Chrissakes. You can't treat it like a hotel.'

'I can go if it's a problem.' I started to back away. I'd reached the doorway when my father got to his feet. He was rubbing his face, trying to sober up, but he got his foot caught in the rug, and he stumbled a little before catching hold of the table to steady himself.

'Candy is having a few friends around.' He seemed stuck for what to do next, and kept glancing over at Candy for some help, but none was forthcoming.

I wasn't welcome. That much was clear.

18

New York City, 1955

It was three weeks to the day since Gillian had left New York and I must have picked up the telephone a dozen times to call her, but then I heard her voice in my head pleading with me to leave her alone. I put the telephone back down again and tried to find things to distract me from the pain of waiting.

I read books that I'd been putting off reading all year, long English novels full of manners and polite love affairs. I cleaned things, tidying and busying myself in meaningless tasks. I watched the sun rise and set from our window, sitting in Gillian's armchair and wondering if she was watching that same ball of fire coming and going. I felt desperate but there was nothing I could do except wait. The waiting hurt. I felt it in my bones, in every part of me. I ached from waiting.

Judith in the meantime brought home pot plants and cushions, making her presence felt in every corner of the home I loved. She didn't mention Gillian. It was as if she had never existed, and instead Judith was endlessly cheery, trying to persuade me to accompany her to summer concerts in the park, or picnics at the beach, all of which I declined. She made me soup to eat and brought me small packages of cookies or candies to comfort me. But I wanted to be alone. I circled vacant apartments in Judith's price range, looping large red circles around the classifieds and leaving them on the kitchen table for her to see. Whenever I did this, Judith would bring home another ornament, a china dog with a pink tongue hanging out or a colourful box for her herbal teas, and ignore my gesture. Little by little, she was taking over the space that was once a home for Gillian and me. She spoke of us as a pair, forever friends, and in my cowardice I said nothing.

The August heat soon grew too much and it seemed the whole city was unable to sleep. The electric fans only waved the air around and made no discernible difference to the temperature. Even a plain white sheet was too hot, and I tried sleeping with all the windows thrown open, but was kept awake by nightmares about masked strangers creeping in. The whole city was a swamp of heat and dust and noise. People were up half the night because it was too hot to sleep, and that meant music playing, or people talking out on fire escapes, or rooftops, until dawn. From sleeping too much I suddenly couldn't sleep at all. The small alarm clock glowed the minutes of my insomnia at me until eventually I gave up and went into the living room, hoping a whiskey would help encourage sleep to come.

I poured a glass, cracked a chunk of ice into it and made myself comfortable in the armchair by the window.

I liked to watch the apartment lights in the city at night, all those people living their lives, signalling to the rest of the world whether they were awake or asleep. I wanted to play some music, but I didn't want to risk waking Judith, so I curled up in my armchair, pressed the ice-cold glass against my cheeks, and thought about Gillian. I tried to remember Gillian's smile and what she was wearing the last time we were together. I could piece together fragments of her, a strand of fair hair, a fingertip, a glimpse of her breast, but I couldn't imagine the whole Gillian, or the way we were. I wondered how long I would have to wait before I heard from her. I worried it might be forever.

An hour must have passed, or maybe two. The whiskey glass was empty and the ice all melted. Sleep wouldn't come; nor was I fully awake, but trapped in some hinterland where nothing was quite real. At first, I thought I was dreaming as the living-room door opened quietly and my first thought was that Gillian had come creeping home in the middle of the night. My heart surged with hope, but it was Judith. She seemed startled at first to see me sitting there.

'Dovie? Oh goodness, I thought you were a ghost sitting there all in white. You gave me a fright.'

'Sorry, I couldn't sleep,' I muttered, trying to make it clear that I didn't want to talk to her.

'Me neither. We need a good storm to clear the humidity. It's too hot to breathe the air in here.' She stood in the middle of the living room looking awkward, clutching her robe closed and shifting from foot to foot, as if she wasn't sure whether to come in or stay away.

She moved closer to where I was sitting and I knew that she wouldn't go back to bed now. I wasn't much in the mood for chatter and particularly not with Judith, but I felt alone, more alone than I'd ever felt, and I didn't like the feeling one bit. I was so tired of being without Gillian and being lost in my own thoughts that even Judith seemed preferable to another round of dark brooding alone.

I gestured to my glass and she nodded. I got up and filled the two tumblers with whiskey and handed her one. She reached across and we clinked glasses in a strange, garbled toast that I didn't care about. Watching Judith's lips touching the glass made me feel as if I was betraying Gillian but I tried to push the thought to the back of my mind. I could feel her watching me as I stared out of the window, but the whiskey was making me too mellow to care very much about it.

'Dovie, can I ask you something?' Judith said.

'Sure.'

'What will you do if Gillian doesn't come back?'

Her voice was tentative, but the words stung me. Surely that wasn't even a possibility, and yet it was three weeks without a single word from her. She wasn't saying anything that I hadn't already thought myself, but I couldn't bear to hear it spoken out loud.

'She will come back.' I hoped it served as a warning to Judith, but she carried on.

'I really don't want to interfere, but I think of you as a close friend, and I would hate to see you get hurt.'

Her voice was slightly slurred from the whiskey and I wanted to make her stop talking.

'There's really no need for you to worry about this, Judith.'

'But I do worry. I feel responsible.'

Her voice was timid, searching for some response. She moved suddenly and knelt down next to the armchair, one arm leaning on the armrest and the other clutching her whiskey glass. Her face turned to gaze at me, her expression hopeful.

I wanted to scream at her that she *was* responsible, she had caused this, but deep down I knew that I was the one who had caused the rupture through my own stupidity. I wanted to slap the earnest look right off her face but instead I drained my whiskey glass for the third time.

'I don't want to talk about it,' I snapped at her. I didn't want to be reminded of the part I'd played in all of this. Even in the dim light from the street I could see her startled face crumple a little, and I felt a horrible guilt although I couldn't think why I should. Judith was good at that, making people feel sorry for her, issuing invitations they didn't want to make to her. If I could take it all back I would. I hated her and at the same time I was sorry for yelling. I was always saying sorry for something lately.

'I'm sorry I snapped at you, it's just . . .' Another day,

another apology, and I felt annoyed with myself for making it. Gillian was right about me. I was a child who couldn't bear other people to be angry with me.

'It's OK, Dovie. I know it's been very difficult for you, but I want you to know that I'm your friend and I would never try to hurt you.'

I was impatient for her to stop talking but she had something on her mind.

'Doesn't it bother you?'

'Doesn't what bother me?'

'All these lies you have to tell all the time?'

'What are you talking about?' I sighed, exasperated now and wanting her to go away.

'This *friendship* with Gillian . . . it's, well . . . it's built on lies. Don't you care about that?'

Judith raised herself up on to her knees and knelt in front of me, her head practically in my lap, and once again I had that awful feeling of being trapped by her. There was nowhere to go except to press myself against the back of the armchair as far away from her as I could get. Just as I couldn't move any further away from her, I felt her hands clutching at my hands. She managed to capture my left hand and pressed it tightly. Her hand felt clammy with sweat. She was so close now I could smell her freshly talcum-powdered skin – lily of the valley. It made me nauseous.

'You're a good person, Dovie. Please don't be angry with me. I know I shouldn't have forced you to let me live here. I feel bad about it, I really do, but I just wanted to be friends. I mean, I really did want to find a nice apartment that I could afford, and it's not so easy in the city these days, but honestly, I just wanted to feel part of something. Don't you ever feel lonely sometimes? I suppose you didn't because you had Gillian, but on your own in the city it can be hard. You don't hate me, do you? Please say you don't. I've never been any good at getting people to like me. I get so lonely and you've always been nice to me, always taking the time to stop and talk. You're not like the others. I know what the others say about me . . . I hear them laughing . . .'

Judith held my hand so tightly that I couldn't get it free without physically pushing her away. I felt sorry for her and hated myself for it. I would never learn. This pathetic, lonely, selfish woman had ruined the things I cared about – my relationship, my work and my life in the city – but I was sitting there feeling sorry for her. I was so stupid.

'You know, I think if you gave it a chance, we could become great friends. I'm happy to keep you company if you ever want to go out places . . .'

I started to laugh, a strained silly giggle, and I could feel the full effect of the whiskey flowing through me. Judith felt responsible. I couldn't stop myself laughing even though her face was hurt and a little bit angry; I carried on shaking my head from side to side in disbelief.

'Why are you laughing?'

'Because it's funny, Judith. Don't you see?' I pulled my hand away from hers.

'I don't see what's funny. I'm trying to be a good friend to you. That's all.'

'A good friend? I can't stand to be in the same room as you. You make me sick to my stomach.' The words kept falling out of my mouth, each one aimed at her heart, wanting to wound until she was bleeding. Her face was frozen in shock at the extent of my anger. She seemed frightened and put her hand to her mouth to cover it. She shook her head and for a second we were locked together staring at each other, waiting for the other one to say something.

'You don't mean that, Dovie. You're upset . . . that's all.'

There was the kind of silence that comes after a storm. Judith lurched to her feet, clutching her robe tightly to keep it closed, and she started to back away from me. She staggered a little and the whiskey tumbler she was holding fell and smashed into pieces on the floor.

I stared down at the shards. The glasses we used to toast our future from our college days were no longer a pair.

Another day without Gillian. The fragments of the whiskey glass lay splintered over the floor waiting for me to clean them up. Afterwards I ran a cool bath and washed the sticky city heat off my skin, before drying off and putting on my favourite summer blouse in pale blue cotton and a pair of black pants that were light and cool to wear. I curled my hair and added a dab of face powder and a slick of Max Factor Rose Red lipstick. It was the best I could do.

It was still early and the city felt slightly fresher, although it was still stubbornly hot, so I walked a block or two and then flagged down a cab to take me uptown. I had no idea where I was going, but I couldn't stand another day waiting in vain. I took morning coffee and an exotic-looking French pastry in an expensive café on the Upper East Side and then strolled through Central Park watching the dog walkers and newspaper readers sitting around on benches. The walking felt good; it grounded me and made all the problems with Gillian and Judith feel less significant in some way. My sturdy walking shoes hit the sidewalks with purpose and I felt stronger than I had in weeks.

After a stroll around an art gallery, I took a late lunch at a diner – an average chicken salad – tipping the waitress handsomely for being kind, and I started to walk again. Before I knew it, I'd walked all the way back down to the Village. I was hot now even though I kept to the shady side of the streets and my feet had less purpose to them, but my mind was clear. I dreaded the idea of returning to our apartment and facing Judith, or finding out that yet again there was no word from Gillian.

I passed a bar with some soft jazz playing and hesitated for a second before going inside and sitting down at a small wooden table with two comfortable leather chairs either side of it. I sat down in the one that faced the door, and a waiter in a starched white coat appeared from behind me.

'What can I get you, ma'am?'

'Could I get a whiskey sour?'

'Coming right up.'

It was early for drinking and the bar was empty apart from a couple of tables where lone men sat studying the bottoms of their glasses and ignoring everyone around them, which suited me. The waiter reappeared with a whiskey sour on a tray and a round silver dish of tiny crackers.

'Would you like the check now or are you waiting for somebody?'

The waiter's tone was friendly but the implication was clear. I needed a friend, even an imaginary one, to make him feel better.

'Oh, I'm waiting for a friend. Thank you so much.'

I oozed extra charm as I dismissed him. I finished my whiskey sour and gestured to the waiter for the check, making a poor excuse that I'd just remembered something. I kept it vague but he didn't care anyway. I paid in crumpled dollar bills and left a generous tip, although I gave myself a talking-to about it all the way down the street. I didn't want to go home and so I carried on walking, trying to find somewhere I could just sit for a while.

My feet started to ache and it was getting dark on the streets. I just wanted to go somewhere I could relax and not be bothered, but it seemed to be too much to ask. As

I turned the corner, I spotted the heavy black door to a club that I knew only by reputation. It had been a speakeasy during prohibition and changed hands several times since then. Gillian and I often walked past it and noted that it was mainly women who went in and out of the black door; it was the kind of place we knew about without ever having gone inside. The whiskey was buzzing around my brain searching for clues, but all it found was the loneliness I'd felt since Gillian left. I felt that lonely indigo mood which Sinatra sung about and the need to prove Gillian wrong. It wasn't a great combination.

I stood there in the street watching as two women knocked on the door, a hatch opened, and someone stared out and then shut it again. The door opened a crack and a woman in her late fifties with flaming red hair gestured to the women to come inside. As she was about to close the door again, she caught me staring and looked me up and down. I was fascinated and terrified by the sight of her. Part of me wanted to walk away but the other part of me was curious and too tired to do so. I longed to rest, to sit and nurse a drink and feel a little sorry for myself without being bothered. A couple of girls across the street waved and shouted:

'Hey, Cindy, you busy tonight?'

Cindy waved back.

'Busy every night, just the way I like it.'

She turned her attention back to me and the girls carried on walking up the street.

'Are you coming in, honey?' she asked softly.

I nodded and took a couple of steps inside, letting the black door clang shut behind me. A flight of stairs led down into darkness but I could hear jazz music playing below me. Cindy gestured with her hand that I should go down. And so I did.

19

New York City, 1975

Saturday morning washed away the heat of the city with a torrential thunderstorm. Lightning cracked across the sky and the deep rumbling woke me at first light. It felt like a relief to hear rain hitting the windows and bouncing like silver bullets off the sidewalk, and I hoped that maybe we could all breathe again, and life could get back to normal. For a moment when I woke up, I couldn't remember where I was, but when I opened my eyes fully I was alone in my bedroom. I'd spent the night here when it became obvious my dad and Candy didn't want me at their place. It was the first time I'd slept in our apartment on my own and I'd freaked out at the sound of every creak or gurgling pipe. My dad hadn't got around to fixing the window that my mom broke and so I slept with all the lights on. I couldn't sleep with my back to the bedroom door because I kept imagining someone coming in through the broken window, but I couldn't get comfortable on the other side.

In the middle of the night, I found myself holding imaginary conversations with Dovie in my mind as if she still lived here and I wasn't really alone. I could tell her all the things I didn't want to say to my mother. When I closed my eyes, I could see her smiling and hear music playing. Dovie curled up on our couch while Gillian did her crossword puzzle in her favourite armchair. From time to time they glanced up at each other and smiled or reached across to touch hands.

I wondered if they ever danced as my mom and I used to do. Somehow, they were still here, part of this apartment, part of my life. As the sky began to turn light outside, I made up a whole life for them full of tiny details. I hoped the letter would finally help me to find them and I rehearsed what I might say, and how happy they would be to meet me. I couldn't think of Dovie as a liar; she looked so friendly and nice in her picture. The kind of person who means well. I imagined Dovie reaching out her arms to me and drawing me in for a grateful hug as if I was part of her family now. Smiling with that bright smile of hers as though she was pleased to see me.

My mother was calm, slightly sleepy, but at least she wasn't yelling stuff at us this morning. Dressed in a loose blue gown, she sat in the armchair in the patients' lounge waiting for us. She slept OK and the medication was keeping her mellow, although they were going to monitor her, and there was some brief whispered talk that I probably wasn't meant to overhear about the side effects of the electric shock treatment as my dad talked to Dr Bailey.

'There is one thing . . . The nurses say Mary-Lyn seems to know her way around here. Could she have been here before?'

My dad frowned at Dr Bailey.

'Not that I know of.'

'Maybe to visit somebody?'

'I really don't know.'

The doctor shrugged and moved on to a family who were waiting anxiously to speak to him about their grandmother. We had been updated and that was all we were getting. The official report was they were giving her three sessions per week and she was already showing some 'improvements'.

The improvements were hard to spot. She didn't greet us or even make eye contact but kept on staring up at the ceiling, and she was definitely still talking to someone – I could tell, although her lips weren't moving.

'Hi, Mom, how are you feeling?' I asked.

She didn't look at me at all. There were no tears but no anger either. Her face was blank, her eyes unseeing. Nobody was home. The only signs of life were in one hand that was feverishly tapping on the arm of the chair. The fingers drumming away even when everything else was still. An orderly brought green cups filled with hot liquid which tasted neither of tea nor of coffee. It was grey with a slight skim of grease on top. There were cookies that were stale, and everything about the place was peeling and musty; even the walls seemed steeped in misery. I wanted to get out of there, but my dad was being dutiful, and so I was stuck. He sat down with my mother instead of hiding behind me as he usually did. She didn't take any notice of him either. He carried on talking to her, as if they were just another married couple sitting across from each other at breakfast. Her eyelids kept fluttering as if they wanted to close and shut out the world, but then she would stare at the ceiling again and her fingers continued drumming away. We didn't drink whatever was in the green cups, and eventually the signal was given for visiting hours to be over, and we gently patted my mother's hands and said our goodbyes. She didn't speak; nor did she seem perturbed by us going. She'd barely registered us arriving, and our departure was just another thing she didn't care about. When we got to the door, I turned around to look back at her, and noticed that her fingers had stopped drumming on the armrest, so I guess she'd known we were there after all.

There was no sign of Cal today in Benny's Luncheonette, and my father and Candy were on their best behaviour. Candy was doing a shift at Zerilli's in the afternoon, and I was determined to get out of there as quickly as possible to get to the junk store to meet Viola. I had no wish to get stuck in the middle of any argument between Candy and my father. She kept stealing nervous glances at me across the table, checking that I was OK with her. I wasn't OK with her, so I avoided meeting her gaze and kept staring down at my food. We ate quickly and managed a meal for the three of us with no drama at all, which I was thankful for. I picked at some fried chicken but refused the milkshake today. The pool party was still at the back of my mind along with my never-ending quest for perfection, so I drank iced water. I figured it wasn't going to make much difference but it was worth a shot.

The rain cleared up, leaving that freshly washed sheen over the city, and a weak sun started to push through the clouds, opening up tiny patches of blue in an otherwise surly sky. We said our goodbyes and I headed off towards East 13th Street, while my father and Candy walked towards Zerilli's, where he would deposit her at the door, and carry on back to her apartment to catch up with his own work in peace and quiet, before she came home again.

The junk store was full of girls trying on vintage evening gowns with feathery hats and laughing at themselves in the full-length mirror. One of them wrapped a musty old fox fur around her shoulders and its glassy little yellow eyes glared at us as she twirled and giggled. I found Viola searching through the old record box, as I knew she would be. She lost interest in them the moment she spotted me walking towards her. There was nothing new in the box of records since the last time she'd looked in there.

'You got the letter?' she asked.

'Yeah.' I patted my pocket where I'd carefully folded

the letter first thing that morning and had periodically checked to make sure it hadn't fallen out or got lost. I was trying my best to act normal but Viola searched my face for a minute.

'You OK?'

'Yeah, just tired.' I didn't want to tell anyone that my dad had left me all alone in the apartment. There was a long list of things I couldn't talk about now and I could feel the weight of it.

'You sure? You don't look so good.'

'I'm fine.'

'OK. Let's get going then. Marianne should be up by now.'

We headed east past the Jewish bakery and the store where they cash cheques without asking questions, and turned up past Quincy's dry-cleaning service. The oily puddles were drying up and we skipped around the worst of them, arriving eventually at Marianne's building. Viola searched the names on the buzzers before selecting the right one and leaving her finger on it for a second too long. The door buzzed open and we walked inside to a hallway filled with metal mailboxes, most of which hadn't been emptied in a while; there were newspapers stuffed in some of them, and leaflets scattered on the floor underneath the boxes: brightly coloured fliers for cleaning services or Chinese food or the local pawn shop.

Marianne lived on the top floor and we started to climb up the five flights of stairs. There was an elevator with an out-of-order sign on it that looked as if it had been there a long time. Our footsteps echoed all the way up the steps. By the time we got to the third floor both Viola and I were gasping for breath, and we paused to lean on the rail for a moment. A door opened behind us, and someone came out in a long red robe with glittery boots. We moved a little to get out of the way, and a man with a shaved head wearing full make-up and orange lip-stick squeezed past us. Viola and I stared a little but the man just smiled and said, 'Good morning, ladies,' and gave a funny little bow of his head.

Viola and I giggled a little shyly, not sure what to say in return, but then he was gone, and we carried on climbing those stairs until we got to Marianne's door. Viola gave a sharp rap on the wood, and after a minute or so Marianne opened it and Viola introduced us, explaining briefly what we needed.

She was wearing a coloured kaftan, with ropes of beads strung around her neck and hanging down to her waist. The sleeves came down to her wrists, but every so often she lifted an arm to smooth her hair down in a nervous habit, and I could see the thin line of tiny crusted pink scabs running down her forearms.

Marianne invited us to sit down at her kitchen table. In the centre of the table sat a small white statue of Buddha, and a burned-down candle with the ashy remains of an incense stick. The air was full of the heavy scent of patchouli oil and it made me feel a little sick, but once we were settled, I took out the letter, unfolded it carefully and handed it over to Marianne. Viola was carrying a notepad and pencil to write out an exact translated copy, if Marianne could concentrate long enough to get the job done. Her eyes seemed blurry and unfocused and from time to time she forgot what she was supposed to be looking at. She glanced at the letter but then went back to talking about some club she'd played with Lois back in the day, and the men they'd known there. Viola gently led her back to the matter in hand, but even so it was some time before Marianne was able to focus on the letter.

She ran her hands over the pages, flattening them out under the weight of her palms and then traced each line with her finger while reading them quietly to herself in French to get the gist of what was written there. Viola and I waited impatiently for her to get where she was going. I felt a prickle of excitement run down my spine and my pulse quickened. Every second that Marianne stared at the letter seemed like an eternity. I was about to find out where Dovie was and then I could make everything OK.

After a few minutes Marianne looked up at us and said:

'OK . . . you want I explain it to you, or write it down?'

'Can you do both?' Viola was quick to ask. She wanted to know now and get a translation to take away with us, and it wasn't a bad plan. Her tone made me frown a little at her, but Marianne nodded and didn't seem to mind.

'*D'accord.* The letter is from a woman called Christine LeGrand. She was a friend to this woman called Dovie, *oui*?'

We nodded at her, impatient for more.

'Oh . . . it's very sad . . .' Marianne put her hand to her heart and left it there. My own heart beat faster in my chest, and I stared at Marianne across the table.

'What does it say?'

'Dovie . . . she got very sick . . .'

'What happened to her?' Blood was rushing in my ears and I started to feel a little dizzy. I had a bad feeling about what Marianne was going to say next.

'I'm afraid . . . she died . . .' Marianne quickly crossed herself and looked at both of us, waiting for our reaction.

'*She's dead?*' My voice sounded strange, as if it didn't belong to me. The words felt like a crushing blow and my heart sank. Marianne was still talking, but I couldn't take in anything she was saying. All my hopes were gone. The dreams of Dovie smiling at me and hugging me in gratitude, as though we were family. I'd been sure that I could find Dovie and Gillian to give them back their photographs, and the butterfly necklace. They were going to be so happy when I took the box to them . . . I'd made up a whole story about these women, and now it was over. Dovie would never know me, or know that I had her box of mementoes. I felt raw and tender as if someone close to me had died, yet I'd never met this woman and now I never would.

'She died? Are you sure?' I asked, although as Marianne and Viola stared at me it was obvious that there hadn't been a mistake. I didn't know what else to say. I choked back tears I hadn't been expecting, and Viola squeezed my arm with concern.

'Are you OK?' she whispered, but I couldn't respond. Marianne carried on with the business of reading the letter.

'Yes, she died. Here . . .' She pointed to part of the text but as it was in French there was no way for me to read it. I nodded and Marianne carried on talking without stopping, to avoid further interruptions. I tried to follow what she was saying but all the while my mind was churning out the thought that I'd never get to meet Dovie, and the sadness felt unbearable.

'She left these possessions for her friend, Gillian. This woman . . . Christine, she doesn't know how to find Gillian, and Dovie died very . . . sudden . . . yes, quick . . . I don't know how you say this.'

'Suddenly?' Viola interrupted.

'Yes, she died suddenly from the sickness, before she could give the information to Christine. This address was the only one that Christine could find, so she has sent the collection to this address, to do her best in this circumstance. You understand me?'

'Yes,' I said. 'Gillian was her friend. I don't know what happened to her.'

I didn't want to say that I'd searched through Dovie's box of things in case Marianne thought badly of me, and I couldn't bring myself to explain about how Dovie and Gillian were lovers, as it felt strange to give away their secret. I was starting to feel protective towards these women I'd never met, and a crushing sense of loss that Dovie was dead. I thought of her as someone I knew. Someone who ate meals in our kitchen or read books in our living room. I felt as if I knew her and . . . as if she knew me. Now she was gone.

'So that's it?' Viola seemed disappointed.

'Yes. Christine wants the things to go to Gillian as Dovie wished, but she has no way to find her, because she doesn't know her last name or anything about her. She is taking a risk by sending the belongings but she says she has tried everything else and failed.'

Marianne waved a dismissive hand in the air and it was clear she was losing focus on the letter now it proved to be merely a friend lost over time, but Viola used all her charm to get a full translation of each word on the letter and she copied it out in her best handwriting.

Dear Carmichael Family,

I am sorry to write to you with such terrible news, but our sweet Dovie died on 21 February after a short illness. We gave her a beautiful service and burial here in Paris but it is a matter of regret that we could not meet her dying wish to find her close friend Gillian.

When Dovie knew she was dying, she asked me to look for a box of possessions that she had put aside in her apartment, and

to make sure Gillian got the things if she died before she could
send it herself.

She wanted very much to write a letter to Gillian to be
included in the box but she failed to finish it, or to give us a last
name or an address. I believe she thought there was time to
make the arrangements, but sadly there was not. I have included
all the things I could find and I hope that I have done as she
would have wanted me to.

While I was clearing out the apartment, I found this address
on an old lease agreement from when Dovie first moved to Paris,
and I am trying this in the hope that whoever receives this box
can make sure that Gillian gets these possessions.

This is my final act of love for a dear friend of mine, and I
am doing my best to honour her wishes even though I do not
know where Gillian is or how to find her; I do know she was
very important to Dovie, and on her mind until her last breath.
I would like to pass on these things if possible and have Dovie
rest in peace.

If you know Gillian or can find her then it is my dear wish
that you give her this box and this letter.

Again, I am sorry to be the bearer of such sad news but
please know she was very happy here and very much loved by
us all.

Yours,
Christine LeGrand

Once Viola was sure she had a correct translation,
we thanked Marianne and made our way back out on to
the street. We started to walk back home, both Viola

and I chewing over the contents of the letter and getting nowhere fast.

'So that's it?' said Viola ruefully. 'If she's dead then we should just toss the stuff in the trash.'

'No, we can't do that!' I protested furiously. 'I don't know what happened to them but they were in love. We should try and find Gillian. She needs to know that Dovie is dead and that she was thinking about her.' For some reason I felt myself thinking of my mom and it made my throat tighten and my voice became strained. 'That she *never* stopped thinking about her.'

Viola's eyes widened and she was silent for a moment. Then:

'Would you want to know if it was Cal the wonder kid, and his last dying wish was to send you a bunch of stuff? Gillian might be dead or with someone else. She might not want a box of stuff turning up out of the blue. We should let it be.'

But I shook my head, resolute.

'I *have* to find Gillian. There has to be a way to do it.'

'Ava,' said Viola gently, 'you're getting obsessed with this stuff.'

I frowned.

'You were the one who wanted me to go to Gray's and to get the letter translated.'

'Because it was a mystery and I thought there could be a reward.'

'We should do it because two people loved each other and you can't forget that like it never happened,' I snapped.

Viola raised her hands in a placating gesture.

'Hey, calm down, I'm just saying. Is everything OK with you? Because you're acting really strange since you got this box of junk.'

'It's not junk. It was important to Dovie.'

'She's dead, girl. You don't know her. Now let's focus on the pool party. What time do you want to meet? Are you dreaming about seeing Cal the wonder kid in his shorts?' Viola giggled and pinched my arm, but I shook her off. I wasn't in the mood.

'Don't call him that,' I protested in vain because I knew that Viola wouldn't give up. I was getting mad with her now.

'Aw, c'mon, Ava, I'm just kidding. You wanna go get a soda?'

'No, I'm gonna figure out how to find Gillian.'

'You know there are other things you could be doing with your time?'

'Like what? Hanging out in that junk store listening to old records? It's not like you're doing anything much with *your* time.'

It bothered me that Vi wasn't taking it seriously. Everyone in my life seemed to be missing in some way and finding out that Dovie was dead was the final straw. I didn't get mad with Viola often but I felt kind of bruised about Dovie and Gillian. It was the one thing I'd felt I could do something about.

'I need to try and find Gillian. I can't do much about my life but I can do that.'

The words came out angry and bitter and I saw them take Viola by surprise.

'Hey . . . what's up with you? You're really upset by this.'

I shook my head.

'It's nothing. I want to find Gillian and give her the box of stuff, that's all.'

My voice was cracking a little with emotion and I couldn't really explain why I felt so strongly about it. Viola knew me well enough to know that I was deadly serious and she hooked her arm through mine in a gesture of reconciliation.

'Maybe your dad would know? After all, he signed the lease on your apartment so he must have some paperwork on who was there before you?'

'Yeah, but he has other things on his mind.'

'Oh, right . . . sorry, I forgot. How's your mom?'

'She's OK.' I changed the subject as quickly as possible. Discussing my mother was not something I wanted to do with Viola or anyone else. Besides, as much as I thought of Viola as a sister to me, I knew she couldn't help blabbing to everyone, and it seemed enough people were gossiping about our family lately.

'Oh, shoot, I forgot, I promised my mom I'd get my dad his food when he wakes up. My mom's got a church thing going on. I need to run. Sorry, Ava. Here, you take the letter and I'll catch up with you when I can. Are you going home or back to . . . you know?'

Viola was loyal enough to avoid mentioning Candy's

name most of the time and she always pulled a face when she did it. I smiled at her. She drove me crazy at times but she was still my best friend.

'I'm at home. It's all good,' I lied.

'OK, I'll see ya.'

'I'll call you.'

'Sure.'

Viola started to run, all legs flailing out behind her and sharp elbows. I watched her get to the corner and then she was gone. I headed in the opposite direction towards our apartment and let myself in as quietly as I could manage. I wasn't in the mood for conversation with any neighbours today and managed to make it all the way up the stairs without being spotted by Miss Schnagl, or anyone else in the building. I felt crushed about the letter and I needed to be on my own for a while to think things over.

Dovie was dead. And yet it was important to her that she got the box to Gillian. It was on her mind right until the end of her life. I had no idea where Gillian might be, but there must be some way I could find her. And I was determined to do it.

20

New York City, 1955

The room was dimly lit and, to my surprise, it was full of
women. Everywhere I looked were girls, young and old,
sitting around in pairs, kissing or holding hands. Some
women were dancing with each other, shuffling slow
steps with their arms on each other's waists as though it
was the most natural thing in the world. I stood at the
bottom of the stairs and took it all in. The women
seemed different from all the women I saw outside on
the street. Some of them had slicked back their hair and
put on ties or vests. They wore shirts with sleeves rolled
up and one or two had cigars hanging out of their
mouths. Some wore dresses with layers of petticoats
and bright red lipstick. They flirted with the women with
slicked-back hair, giggling with baby laughs and coy
glances. Protective arms were slung over bare shoulders
and everyone seemed to have a role they were playing.
Nobody was taking any notice at all. Once the women
got through the black metal door it seemed they entered
a different world. Trays of drinks were carried above the
heads of the crowd, and set down at small round tables
with half-moon booths. The seats were red and crammed

with couples, leaning against each other and laughing. The bar ran along the full length of one wall, and there were a bunch of stools with metal legs and red leather seats. I slid on to one of them and tried to catch the eye of the girl who was pouring drinks out of bottles with great efficiency. She poured, she returned the bottle to the glass shelf and she moved on. Clink of glass, ring of the cash register and the next customer. I watched her work for a few minutes and then it was my turn. I ordered another whiskey sour but the girl frowned at me.

'Got no sour mix. You want a shot of whiskey or what? Rocks?'

'Double . . .'

'You sure about that?'

I nodded and the girl went into her dance again, glass, ice, bottle, liquid, cash. She nodded as she took my money. There was a jazz band at the back of the dance floor playing classics, and a trumpet player who was pretty good.

I gulped down the whiskey, enjoying my second drink of the evening more than the first. The heat at the back of my throat and the gentle chink of ice against the glass. I felt a little dizzy from drinking too quickly but in a good way. It was pretty loud in the club, the band competing with the chatter and flirtatious laughter. I tried not to stare at the women around me but I couldn't help myself. I'd never been in a place where women could do this. My eyes kept going to a couple at the table closest to the stage who were kissing quite passionately, and one of the women was fondling the breast of the other.

Nobody seemed to care at all. At another table were four or five women all seated together and drinking heavily, with rows of empty glasses piled up in a tower and more arriving regularly on a silver tray, carried by a waitress in a tuxedo with a pair of eyeglasses that were perched right on the end of her nose. I was fascinated by the scenes being played out at the different tables, their celebrations or flirtations, and the fact that the only men in the entire place were on the stage playing with the band. They didn't seem to take any notice of what was going on at the tables or on the dance floor; they were simply lost in making music.

I must have been staring at people a little too long because, as I was reaching the bottom of my glass, a woman appeared at the side of me. She was small and stockily built, with slicked-back dark hair, wearing a pair of grey pants and a white shirt with a grey vest over it. In the pocket of the vest was a gold chain and the kind of pocket watch I'd only seen old men and bankers wear. She saw me looking and frowned:

'Don't stare at people, it's rude.'

'I didn't realize I was. I'm sorry, I noticed your pocket watch.'

She nodded.

'That's as may be but you were staring. First time?'

I didn't get the chance to reply before she launched into a tirade of angry words all directed at me.

'Here's the thing: we don't like tourists coming down here staring at us, OK?'

'What do you mean, a tourist?'

'Jeez! Look at you, neither one thing nor the other. Just another kiki girl.'

'But—'

She interrupted me brusquely, completely uninterested in any explanation I might have.

'Girls like you bring bad luck, and a police raid usually arrives right on time when we get a kiki visit. Find another place to do your drinking, sister, before people get annoyed about it.'

'Hey, Kominsky, will you stop ragging on the clients? What did I tell you?' The bartender leaned across the bar and scowled at the woman. She glared back.

'Oh, sure . . . whatever you say, princess.'

With that she picked up her drink and disappeared back into the crowd, linking arms with a skinny girl with big eyes, who was wearing an old-fashioned sequined flapper dress and smoking a cigar. I was shocked by how angry she'd been with me. I didn't fit in here or anywhere in this city. The only place I truly felt that I belonged was with Gillian, but she was gone.

'This one's on the house. Don't take any notice of her. You drink your drink, honey.'

The bartender topped up my whiskey and managed a supportive grimace. I drank it down, enjoying the sensation of not caring about anything. It was strong and it hit me hard. She lit a cigarette and offered me one from her pack. I leaned in to catch the flame.

'So, what's your name? You don't have to give me your

real name. We use different names inside from outside. What can I call you?'

'Gillian,' I said without thinking.

She held out her hand. 'You can call me Maudie. Everyone calls me that.'

Her hand felt solid and warm in mine. She was staring at me, wondering about me. The whiskey made me brave and I didn't let go.

'Maudie? It's a nice name. I'm drunk, Maudie, so, you know . . .'

'It's a bar, honey. Everyone's drunk.'

'You're not drunk.' I giggled. It didn't suit me.

'I'm working.'

'You're working at getting people drunk.' The giggling turned into silly laughter. She didn't look so amused. Everything seemed funny to me now: the women, the music, the dancing and her.

'I am that.' She crushed out her cigarette into a small brass plate that served as an ashtray on the bar.

'Bartender, I need a drink.' I was slurring my words now. It embarrassed me, or it would have done if I was sober. I could tell by the look on Maudie's face that she was bored with drunken women. I tried to straighten up but my mouth felt swollen and stupid.

'You've had enough, honey.'

'I've had enough of everything, Maudie.'

'Gillian, you need to sleep this off.'

The sound of Gillian's name pierced my heart. I wished I hadn't given it to this stranger to use as she pleased. I started to say something but Maudie cleared away my empty glass and walked to the other end of the bar to serve someone else. I watched her talking with an older blonde woman who was much more sober than I was. Maudie looked pretty when she laughed. I didn't know what to do with myself, until it occurred to me that I needed to find the bathroom.

I looked around and saw a sign in the far corner to the side of the bar. Maybe if I took a few minutes to calm down and sober up a little then things might be different. I'd drunk all that whiskey way too quickly and as I got up off my stool, I steadied myself by holding on to the bar. I saw Maudie glance over to check I was OK and I tried to put one foot in front of the other without making a fool of myself.

The bathroom had seen better days. There was a cracked mirror over a sink that needed cleaning and two stalls with the doors tightly shut. The only lightbulb was yellowing and dim, with a buzz of black flies that circled it. From the noises coming from inside the stalls, I was pretty sure the occupants weren't alone. To the side of the sink was a window with thick dirty glass, the kind you couldn't see through. It was half open to let in some air and I put my face close to it. Outside was a small slab of concrete that led to a metal staircase going up to street level. Outside the window were the remnants of all the cigarettes that had been smoked out there. I could hear a woman's voice in one of the stalls issuing instructions to her partner. The instructions must have worked out for her because the next minute she let out a high-pitched squeal and then it went quiet.

The door opened and a blonde walked in. She was wearing an emerald-green evening gown that looked way too fancy for this place and carrying a glass that was almost empty except for a slice of orange. She took one look at the stall doors and then grinned at me before balancing her glass carefully on the edge of the sink.

'Busy, huh?' she said and took out a silver powder compact to inspect her face. She pushed back her blonde hair a little and ran her fingers around the outline of her mouth where her red lipstick had smeared. She waited for another few seconds and then started hammering with her fist on the stall doors.

'Hey, people out here need the toilet. Take it somewhere else.'

There were shouts of 'Fuck you' and the girl sighed and started to laugh. I couldn't raise a smile in return.

'Are you OK?'

I nodded dumbly and waited for her to leave but she didn't. She settled in to wait with me.

'I haven't seen you here before.'

'No . . . it's my first time.'

She pulled a pack of Chesterfields out of her purse and offered me one. I took it and waited for her to light it. As we leaned against the sinks, smoking, the girl rapped on the stall doors with the side of her fist one more time, but nobody was moving.

I tried to focus on where I was and what I was doing

by checking my face in the cracked mirror. My lipstick had also smeared a little, and I looked lop-sided. I hoped it was just the mirror but I couldn't be sure. Suddenly one of the stall doors flew open and two women shuffled out, fastening up zippers and buttons as they left. They didn't even notice us.

'About time too,' the blonde girl said but she laughed so softly that it didn't come out as nasty. She gestured to me to use the stalls but I shook my head.

'Oh . . . I wasn't waiting . . .'

'You hiding out in here? Me too.' She carried on smoking and didn't seem in any hurry to leave.

I shrugged, unsure of how to explain what I was doing there. The other stall door opened and another couple of women strolled out holding on to each other. One of them recognized the blonde and smiled at her. Then it was just the two of us alone again.

The blonde finished her smoke, before scraping the window open further and tossing the now dead cigarette through the opening. She stood there, feeling the light breeze and running her hands up through her hair.

'Man, this city is too damn hot in summer. I'd like to live on the beach, wouldn't you? I'd run straight out from my bed and jump in that cold salty water. Must be nice, huh?'

'I guess . . .'

She turned to check her look in the mirror again, frowning as she pinched at her cheeks and fluffed out her hair a little.

233

'I'd better get back out there,' she said and started to move towards the door.

'Sure.' I crushed my cigarette under my foot and nodded at her.

'You're not going to hide away in here all night, are you? It's not so bad.'

'No . . . I guess not.' I felt sick from the booze but the breeze from the window was helping to sober me up. The girl seemed kind.

'What's your name anyway?' She smiled so softly that I forgot all about my lies.

'Dovie.' The moment I spoke my name out loud I grimaced, knowing that I'd broken the rule.

She paused for a moment and moved back towards me.

'That's your *real* name, isn't it? It's OK, I won't tell,' she whispered.

I nodded, feeling stupid that I'd forgotten to use a false name, but the girl just grinned at me.

'Pretty name.' She held out a sweaty palm towards me and then giggled and wiped it on her emerald-green evening dress. 'I'm Mary-Lyn,' she said softly.

'Is that *your* real name?'

'That's me. So now we're properly introduced to each other we can be friends.' Mary-Lyn giggled and gave a mock curtsy.

I clasped her hand in mine and we nodded at each other.

'If you wanna stop hiding out I'll dance with you? I love to dance . . .' She grinned at me again and I found my face forming a smile. The door swung open and she was gone.

I don't know how long I stood there slumped against the wall as women came and went in ones and twos but, suddenly, I heard the sound of a siren from out in the street, so I went to the bathroom door and stepped out into the bar.

I could hear screaming and shouting and the bar seemed different somehow. It took me a while to realize it was because the lights were on and the music had stopped playing. There was a clamour as women were shrieking and running towards the entrance. I stood in the doorway, watching and trying to work out what was going on. Then the screams grew louder and the people started rushing back the other way towards a fire exit at the far end next to the stage. I was still drunk and swaying slightly but then, out of the corner of my eye, I saw men running down the stairs and into the club. In a split second, I realized they were police officers, and I could hear their whistles blowing and gruff voices shouting orders to women.

'Don't move!'

'Stay where you are!'

I was frozen. Fear pounded at my brain to do something, but my senses were all dulled by the whiskey I'd drunk. I didn't know what to do and I couldn't seem to move from the spot. I saw women being manhandled back up the stairs, their arms twisted behind their backs in handcuffs. One girl who had been dancing on a table top earlier and smoking a cigar without a care in the world was sobbing 'Please let me go', but the cop just laughed, and as he cuffed her he made sure to rub his hands all over her breasts and between her legs; then he marched her out.

It must have been just a few seconds but it felt as if everything was happening in slow motion. The next thing I knew, I saw a cop heading right towards where I was standing, but then Mary-Lyn was in front of me and pushed me back into the bathroom.

'Hurry!' she yelled at me.

I snapped out of my trance and backed into the bathroom, but she shoved her way past to get to the window. She forced it right up and then stuck her head out to check the coast was clear. I watched her moving urgently and yet my legs felt frozen to the spot. She was about to climb up out of the window when she stopped and turned around.

'Come on, this way. Quick, Dovie, I'll help you and then you pull me up. OK?'

She held out her hand to help me climb up on the window ledge and I grabbed it and pulled myself up. I landed awkwardly on the concrete slab on the other side of the window but at least I was out. I held out my hand to Mary-Lyn to pull her through, but the door burst open and I could see two cops racing towards her.

'Pull me up,' she yelled but all I could think about was the cops grabbing hold of me. Her pale green eyes stared at me, pleading. Her face was wild with fear and shock. I tried to pull her up but her hand kept slipping away from mine. I could see the police getting closer and closer.

Mary-Lyn gripped tightly to my hand. She started crying out to me, imploring:

'Help me! Jesus . . . Don't leave me!'

My body started to shake and I couldn't control my limbs. I felt as though I might pass out and I could hear blood rushing in my ears. When I looked into Mary-Lyn's eyes all I could see was my own fear reflected back at me. One of the policemen yelled at us to 'Stay right there', and Mary-Lyn's fingers started to claw desperately at my hands. I cried out in pain and my hand began to slip away. She screamed out as she realized what was about to happen and then quietly whispered, 'No . . .'

I shook my head and muttered, 'I'm sorry,' and then I let go of her hands.

I could still feel the pressure of her ghost prints long after I'd let go. Mary-Lyn slumped back on to the bathroom floor, sobbing and begging, and I scrambled up the metal staircase, terrified that an army of blue uniforms would be waiting at the top of the stairs. I didn't turn around but I could hear her yelling after me, her faint voice screaming, 'Don't leave me,' over and over again.

At the top of the metal stairs, I raised my head slowly to check for cops but they were all around the front entrance of the club. I checked up and down to make sure that nobody had seen me come out. The street was clear apart from a couple of drunks who weren't looking in my direction. I scrambled to the top of the steps and ran down the street as fast as I could.

As I passed the corner, I could see at least one hundred women being lined up on the sidewalk waiting for more wagons to arrive. I saw Kominsky trying to resist as they shoved her into a wagon. One of the cops smacked her hard on her back with his truncheon and yelled, 'Hey, if you wanna be the tough guy we can do this right here.' When she didn't move, he hit her again. 'You wanna be the guy? You wanna show me your dick? No, now you wanna be the lady? You shoulda thought about that. Get in there.' He whacked her once more, on her shoulder, and she stumbled forwards into the wagon. He gave her one last shove and she landed face down on the floor of the vehicle. That was the last I saw of her.

As I turned away, I caught a glimpse of an emerald-green evening gown sandwiched between two cops. Mary-Lyn was sobbing so hard I thought I could hear her over the noise of the raid. Her face was screwed up in pain and both her arms were twisted behind her back. I guessed she was handcuffed. One of the police officers picked her up and placed her on the last seat in the wagon. She looked like a broken doll being put away in a toy box.

21

New York City, 1975

My father sat at the kitchen table in my mother's usual spot, chain-smoking and staring at the wall. He was taking deep lungfuls of his cigarette and blowing tiny smoke rings into the air. He hadn't spoken a word for at least an hour and he was starting to remind me of my mother. I tried to imagine what it must be like for other kids having parents who fixed nice dinners and cheered them on at swim meets. I was never likely to find out. I sometimes caught *The Waltons* on television and thought it must be nice to have parents who were always ready for a deep and thoughtful talk about life. My life was filled with adults who thought parenting was chain-smoking and staring into space.

The telephone had been ringing on and off through the night, but I wasn't allowed to answer it because he picked it up once yesterday morning and it was Candy yelling at him. He didn't want to talk to her, he said. They were having one of their fights. It wasn't what he signed up for, he said. I felt like saying he'd signed up for a wife and daughter, but that hadn't bothered him when he was picking cherry-vanilla ice-cream with Candy. I sighed and put the radio on. I couldn't shake off the sadness I felt about Dovie, and wondered how she'd ended up in Paris and what had happened to Gillian. I was running out of ideas for how to track her down. I'd already checked the phone book and there wasn't a Gillian McNichol listed. There were several G. McNichols listed with just an initial, and I'd rung them all, but no luck.

We planned to visit my mother later on that day. She'd had more electric shock treatment and all I could think about were the old Frankenstein movies that we watched at Halloween, black and white bolts of electricity shooting through the monster. Dad said it wasn't like that. They'd told us all about the electroconvulsive therapy on our last visit; at first the doctors hadn't wanted to speak in front of me, but after a while they got used to me and so they pretty much talked about everything now. For some reason, Dad asked about it and so they told him. They lay her out on a special bed and then attach the electrical parts to her head; then they put a wooden bit in her mouth so she doesn't bite through her tongue; then they zap her with volts. Whatever they said, I couldn't get the image of the Frankenstein movie out of my head. It's funny they call it therapy, because to me it seemed just the same as electrocuting somebody. Either way, they were happy with her progress.

Dad sighed loudly and lit another cigarette. I didn't know how much longer this was going to go on, but I was really hoping they would sort it out soon. The silence was unbearable; we wandered around the apartment like strangers. I kept mostly to my room and Dad behaved as if he didn't really live here, which I guess was true. I switched the radio off and stood by the kitchen window eating Saltines straight from the box. Visiting days made me feel sick. My stomach churned with fear every time I set foot inside the hospital gates, and I'd started to have nightmares about being trapped in there, and not being allowed to leave when visiting time was over. Every time I heard one of the white steel doors clang shut, I wanted to run out of there as fast as I could.

I finished my crackers. I was wearing my only summer dress and my favourite pair of wedge heels. I watched my father for a few minutes, his hand going back and forth to his mouth, the trail of smoke rising and falling.

The silence was shattered by a familiar voice yelling out my father's name from the street.

'Tom? Tom, are you there? TOM! I know you're in there!'

Our street buzzer was still broken, and Candy was standing in the middle of the sidewalk screaming up at our apartment. At the sound of her voice my father leaped into action, quickly crushing out his cigarette and running to open the kitchen window. At the sight of his head appearing at the window, Candy stopped screaming and was now glaring up at us both indignantly.

'I don't want to fight with you,' he yelled down at her.

'Then talk to me.' She was angry, but I knew it wouldn't last.

'If you've come here to argue then—'

'We have to talk about this.' Candy cut him off, but I could tell that her voice had a sob buried in it.

I wanted to run down and let her in. It felt wrong to leave her standing out there, and it felt strange that I had pity for Candy Jackson after everything that had happened between us.

'Dad, let her in,' I said softly.

My father nodded and the next thing I knew he was running out of the front door and down two flights of stairs. I was watching out of our kitchen window, not wanting to miss out on what would happen next. My father appeared on the sidewalk and walked up to Candy, shaking his head. I could see her hands gesticulating as she spoke, and he went on shaking his head from side to side. This continued for several minutes, and then, just when it seemed she was about to walk away, he opened his arms and she ran into them. There they stood, his arms wrapped around Candy, and they were doing that make-up kissing you see in the movies. I could only imagine what Miss Schnagl was thinking, given he was still very much married to my mother. The kissing eventually slowed and ended in embarrassed grins at each other; then Candy waved up at me from the sidewalk, and they both started to walk back up to our apartment, arm in arm. I didn't know if Candy was back for good and I wasn't going to ask, but she didn't seem to find it a problem to be inside my mother's home again. She made herself comfortable and even asked for a glass of cold water at one point, which I fetched for her.

The brown crocodile suitcase was repacked while Candy sat on our old couch waiting patiently. She gave me a weak smile, both embarrassed and delighted at getting what she came for. Dad shoved his things back inside the suitcase, not caring whether they creased or not. Clearly, he just wanted to get out of our apartment and back to where he belonged. I hung around in the kitchen waiting for him to finish packing, and not particularly in the mood to make polite conversation with Candy today. He appeared in the doorway, kissed me on top of my head, tousled my hair – which I hated – and told me to meet him later at the hospital for visiting hours. He promised to take me out to eat after the hospital visit, just the two of us, but until then he and Candy needed some alone time to figure stuff out. He left, carrying the brown crocodile suitcase, with his other arm slung around Candy's shoulders. She clung around his waist with both arms, not wanting to let him go. I put the radio on for some company and the DJ played another sad song. I turned it off. I was tired of sad songs and other people's love affairs.

The hospital had its usual sad atmosphere. I was starting to recognize some of the patients now. There was a girl, Judy, not much older than I was, who was brought in because she kept cutting her arms until they poured with blood; she usually sat next to Dora, who was very old and thought she was some kind of prisoner, which I guess was right. My mother had stopped repeating her strange little chant since the third or fourth electric shock treatment, which was progress. She was kind of blank, so they gave her therapy so she had something to do with her hands. She was making a rag doll and it was pretty. It had a body made out of old stockings and wool for hair. She had a square of emerald-green silk that she was using for a dress. They all sat around a big wooden table, with baskets of leftover balls of wool that somebody had donated to the centre and large blunt needles so they didn't hurt themselves or anyone else.

My mother was obedient and did what was asked of her, and I watched her from the window in the door for several minutes as we were early for visiting hours. All the nurses recognized us now, so they let us wait in the corridor. We were regulars at the funny farm. My mom looked up and spotted me outside; she looked puzzled, as if I was familiar but she couldn't quite place me. This happened a lot and then someone would say, 'Oh, look, it's your daughter come to visit you. Isn't that nice?' and then usually she would search what was left of her mind for how to behave and find a smile and a mother mask for her face. I swear if nobody had told her she wouldn't have known who I was at all. Sometimes she got emotional and kept calling me her baby, but then she would ignore me for the rest of the visit, so it was hard to tell whether she was really seeing me or not.

Eventually, the occupational therapy class was over, and my mother appeared in her sloppy blue gown clutching a partially finished rag doll. Her eyes were glassy and unknowing but she managed a half-smile, as if somebody had told her she should do this whenever she saw a stranger. She shuffled like an old woman but at the same time was strangely child-like. I was afraid to look at her too closely in case it set her off, so I returned her half-smile and stared at the floor until we were settled in the patients' lounge. The routine trolley with coffee, juice and the sad yellow cookies appeared, dispensed by an orderly in a green uniform with a wide Afro and enormous gold hooped earrings. She was loud and cheerful, urging drinks and cookies on sad faces.

'How's my favourite girl today?' She smiled and I wondered how she kept her spirits up surrounded by the broken people all day long.

My father was his usual distracted self, staring around the room and trying to make polite conversation when the silence became overwhelming. He wanted to get back to making up with Candy and I knew it. I didn't know what to say to my mother. There wasn't really an easy conversation about how someone's stay in a mental hospital was going. I tried my best.

'How are you, Mom?'

No answer, just the same half-smile, some vague nodding.

'Do you want some juice?'

No answer. Slightly bewildered look.

'A cookie? Do you want a cookie, Mom?'

No answer. Blank face staring at me.

'You're my baby girl.' She knew me, and then she started to cry quiet, apologetic tears.

'It's OK, Mom.' I reached out for her hand and patted it gently. She pulled it away and started a rocking motion, back and forth.

Silence. Dad cleared his throat.

'It's hot in here.'

Great, we were going to talk about the weather again.

My mother stopped crying and held out the unfinished rag doll towards me.

'It's for my baby,' she said confidently.

My father gave me a hard stare, a warning not to say anything. Neither of us were sure she was talking about me. She started to hit the edge of the trolley with the rag doll until a nurse gently stopped her. I pulled on a strand of my hair and twisted it around my fingers until it hurt.

A bell clanged and visiting hours were over. It was all going to plan, my dad said. She was so much better. I wondered about his definition of better. She could be as crazy as they come, but as long as she didn't start talking to imaginary people and could make a rag doll, I guessed they would let her out eventually. I stopped to tie up the laces of my sneakers as we left the patients' lounge and by the time I reached the corridor, my father was already deep in discussion with Dr Bailey and as I approached I could hear snatches of their conversation.

'. . . like I said, this is a pretty unusual situation.'

'Unusual in what way?' Sounded like he didn't really

want to hear the answer, but felt he should ask the question anyway.

'Patient Records found this in the archive and sent it over. See here . . . it's right there in her notes. Winters is her married name? You told us her maiden name was Bergman, right? We have a Mary-Lyn Bergman, same birth date, who had a course of ECT during the summer of 1955. It's unusual to have to repeat it like this with such a long gap in between, that's all. That's your wife, right?'

'Mary-Lyn Bergman . . . um, yeah, that's her. We didn't meet until '57, I guess. I used to work with her old man, Mikey. Great guy . . . She used to bring him a hot lunch over most days . . . Pretty little thing she was too. We married in '58. Are you *sure* she's been here before?'

'Looks like it. She never mentioned it?'

My dad shook his head.

'So, her family brought her in last time . . . ?' My father's voice tailed off as he saw me walking towards them but the doctor carried on talking in his matter-of-fact voice.

'Yes, that's right . . . It's a little delicate as you can see right here . . .'

Both of them were staring at my mother's notes and Dad did that 'trying to get rid of me thing' where he pretends he isn't but really he just wants me to walk away, so I walked away a little . . . but slowly.

'Are you *sure* that's the reason she was brought in here?' I heard him ask. His voice sounded strained as if he was trying not to yell at the doctor.

'It's right there in black and white. "Unnatural activities." July 1955.'

I couldn't even pretend that I wasn't listening any more, as my mouth had dropped open and I was standing there staring at both of them. My dad caught my eye and started clearing his throat in an awkward way and trying to stop the conversation. The doctor was done talking anyway and flipped his notes back over his clipboard and walked away. My dad grimaced and gestured for us to leave. The words rang around my mind: *unnatural activities*. What did that even mean? I swallowed hard and headed for the door to the street.

Outside on the sidewalk, baking in the mid-afternoon heat, my father shuffled about awkwardly like a man who has stuff he doesn't want to say. It was OK, because there was stuff that I didn't want to ask.

'Sweetie, you know you're my world, don't you?'

I recognized the signs that I was about to get dumped on again and raked my teeth along my bottom lip to stop myself from having a row about it.

I shuffled my own feet, stepping on and off the cracks in the paving stones and scraping the soles of my wedges along the concrete. I didn't look at him. He stuck his hands in his pockets and his head to one side; it was a look I'd seen many times before. It meant: *Don't be mad with me*. I guess it was supposed to be endearing, and my dad *was* endearing, but this was not one of those times.

'Ava, don't be mad at me. Look, Candy and I have

some things to think about, serious things. We could use some alone time today so I was wondering if it was OK with you . . . the thing is . . . just for tonight . . .'

'You want me to stay at our apartment so you and Candy can be alone?' I rolled my eyes as I said it, as I had no intention of making this easy for him. He sighed, and squirmed a little, which I was pleased about.

'Just for tonight, baby, I promise you. I know I've been leaving you alone a lot lately but I'll make it up to you.'

I nodded, sullen and clearly irritated. I wanted to make him sorry, but I could also see there was nothing I could do or say that would change his plans.

Dad grabbed my shoulders and pulled me towards him, hugging me tight and kissing the top of my head.

'You're a good kid, Ava. Go straight home now, OK?'

'I thought we were getting dinner? You promised it would be just the two of us.'

'We can absolutely get dinner . . . but not tonight. Hey . . . you're not going to sulk with me? We're good then?' He tousled my hair until I put my hand up to stop him.

I nodded.

I watched him walk away, that familiar jaunty little walk he did when there was something that he was particularly happy about. Brisk steps towards wherever he'd arranged to meet Candy. By the time he'd got to the corner, he had forgotten all about me.

*

By the time I got to 10th Street I was a hot sweaty mess. I wanted to get home as quickly as I could, but it was hard to make progress when I had to bypass the garbage that was stacked up all over the sidewalk. A fat brown rat scurried from one pile to another and I squealed slightly and held my breath as I walked past each rotting pile, until I came to the Pit.

We called it that because the sign fell off so long ago that nobody remembered the name of the café with black-painted walls, strange music playing at all hours, and Russian coffee cake that everyone said was the best thing. It was the place where the *popular girls* hung out. They sat at a table in the window drinking black coffee and posing. They did nothing except watch people walk past and make catty comments about them. I knew this because I had often been the subject of those remarks.

The *popular girls* were five in number. All blonde, except for Barbara Mulkenny, who was a redhead. Apart from Barbara, there was Andrea Edwards, Pearl Groves, and the Freds. The 'Freds' were Georgia and Eileen Fredericks. They were not related in any way but they'd called themselves the 'Freds' back in second grade and it stuck. These five girls were the most popular girls in our school. They'd cemented their reputation at one school dance where they arrived wearing white pant suits with different coloured paper roses on their lapels. They danced in a formation line with actual dance steps they knew by heart. It was the coolest thing any of us had ever seen and I'd watched them enviously from the corner of the room, stuffed into brown corduroy with zero dance steps to offer anybody.

Walking past the Pit when the girls were in session was an ordeal I tried to avoid. It was a form of torture because, even if you missed the actual observation of your figure, or clothes, or very being, you would certainly hear the laughter and know that you'd failed to meet the required standards once again. Sure enough, one of the Freds spotted me approaching and my heart sank. I tried to suck in my stomach, straighten my shoulders and walk tall, but nothing helped.

It took fewer than ten steps to walk past the Pit. By the third step they'd lined me up, by the sixth step the target was identified, by the eighth step I heard Eileen Fredericks say:

'Oh my God, did you hear about her mother?'

I didn't catch what was said next but I heard the inevitable laughter, and made the mistake of turning around to look at them before I got to the tenth step. Eileen slapped a hand across her mouth and collapsed into embarrassed giggles. The others thought this was *too funny*, and the laughter got so loud that other people turned to look at them. I quickened my stride, desperate to get away from their taunts. It seemed the whole neighbourhood knew my mom was crazy and I couldn't bear it.

As I turned into our street and headed down the block, I was still reeling from the shock of what Dr Bailey had told my dad and the fact that everyone knew my mom was in the hospital. I was fighting to hold back the tears that I could feel prickling behind my eyes when in the distance I saw Cal coming out of Zerilli's on his own. I stood there gasping slightly, trying to recover enough to say something. I wondered if he knew about my mom and flushed crimson with shame. I barely had time to pull myself together because he was walking right towards me.

'Hey, Ava.' He smiled as he spoke and the sound of my name on his lips made my heart sing.

'Hey, Cal.' I smiled in a pretty OK way, I thought. At least I imagined my face looked normal compared to the silly commotion my heart was making.

We stood in the middle of the sidewalk, smiling at each other but with no real conversation happening until Cal said:

'Are you going to the pool party tomorrow?'

'Yeah.' All I could think was that he'd remembered my name. 'Are you going?'

'Sure.' He seemed to be looking over my shoulder but I couldn't turn around to see what he was staring at.

'Should be fun . . .' I couldn't think of another thing to say and stood there awkwardly staring up at him.

'I guess I'll see you tomorrow then . . .' He smiled at me, a shy grin, and shrugged his shoulders.

'Um . . . yeah, I'll see you there . . .' I grinned back at him.

He knew my name. And, unless I was going crazy, he was looking forward to seeing me at the pool party. Was this a *date*? I couldn't bring myself to ask so I tried to be cool and kind of shrugged in a casual way. My voice sounded calm but the rest of me was yearning to be sure of him.

'I'll see ya then,' he said.

'Yeah . . . see ya, Cal.' I could barely push the words out for the squeeze of excitement that rushed through me. I stood there watching the back of his faded denim jacket getting further away from me and felt a wave of desperate hope fizzing inside.

Cal was all I could think about as I opened our front door and ran up the stairs to our apartment. I had a date – well, as good as . . . and now all I had to do was find Gillian. I grabbed the crackers and a jar of peanut butter and headed to my room where I spread the contents of the box out over the faded old blue rug that covered the floor. I picked up every photograph and piece of paper, going over and over them. There had to be something I was missing. I lay back against the wall and stared at the old yellow water stain on the ceiling, searching for clues until, suddenly, an image flashed through my mind. Scrambling to my knees, I started to flip through the photographs until I found the one that I was looking for: the picture of the three smiling women outside Gray's School. There was nothing but the date scribbled on the back of it.

I stared at the three women. Something was gnawing at me, but I couldn't pin it down. I wondered where I'd seen the woman who was standing right between Dovie and Gillian with a sly smile on her face. I was sure that her face was familiar.

Suddenly my heart started racing. Her hair was a different colour, and her face younger, but it was definitely her. I laid the staffing list that Mrs Mac gave me flat out on my bed and started to read it again from top to bottom, tracing my finger along each line to make sure. It couldn't be her . . . it just couldn't be . . . Then I found it.

Sitting at the very bottom of the page, in faded black ink, was one more name that I hadn't noticed the first time around . . .

Judith Schnagl.

22

New York City, 1955

I plumped up a pillow behind my back and poured a couple of fingers of whiskey into the glass. I wanted to carry on getting drunk, to be so drunk that thoughts were no longer possible, and I wasn't sure how many drinks would make that happen so I kept pouring. Each drink made my head woozy and my body clumsy, but I kept pouring until I couldn't stand another drop. I couldn't get Mary-Lyn's voice out of my mind. Sobbing and begging as I ran away.

I tried to imagine what might happen to her and to all those women. I couldn't change what I'd done so I just kept telling myself that Mary-Lyn would be all right, but somewhere deep inside I didn't really believe it. I kept rubbing at the palms of my hands as if she was still clutching at them. To drown out the sound of her voice in my mind, I kept on swallowing whiskey until she faded away and instead it was Gillian standing there smiling at me, whispering that she missed me.

The whiskey was soothing, and the mist that had been covering my thoughts seemed to lift and I was suddenly clear about exactly what needed to be done. I could give

Judith her marching orders, let her do her worst. We would leave New York and go travelling where nobody would know anything about us. Well, I couldn't work out all the details but the way ahead was clear. I wasn't a dreamer. I was a realist.

The idea caught hold of my mind and wouldn't let it go. I needed to speak to Gillian and tell her all about it. I had so many ideas: they were pouring out of me. It was simple. Once I thought of one possibility then a host of others opened up; paths we could take branched off each other until there were so many choices ahead of us, I wondered why we'd ever considered we had a problem. We were saved, and I'd saved us. I couldn't wait to tell Gillian. It was going to be all right.

It was probably really late but maybe Gillian would still be up; maybe she couldn't sleep either, knowing what a mess we were in. Somewhere in my whiskey-fuddled brain I saw her sitting in the dark all alone thinking about us and wondering what to do. Of course she would welcome hearing from me now that I had a solution to all our problems.

I jumped up off the bed too quickly and felt instantly dizzy. My mind was clear but my body was stupid drunk and unable to obey. Taking a deep breath, I steadied myself before opening the bedroom door and heading into the living room. I didn't bother to put on a light but staggered slightly towards the armchair and the side table with the telephone. Slumping into the chair and picking up the receiver, I slowly dialled the number for the operator.

A sharp, bored voice answered and within a few seconds I could hear the telephone ringing somewhere far away. I cradled the receiver with both hands, praying for Gillian to pick up and hoping that it wouldn't be her mother who answered. The ringing carried on for several more seconds and then a sleepy voice said:

'Hello . . .'

It wasn't Gillian.

'I'm sorry to bother you. I know it's awfully late but I was wondering if Gillian was there?'

'Gillian? What time is it? Why, it's after eleven. Hold on, dear, I'll check.'

The telephone receiver made a dull clunking sound as Mrs McNichol placed it on to the table, and I could hear the swish of a door opening as her footsteps shuffled away. I held my breath and rehearsed exactly what I would say to Gillian. It was now or never.

I could hear the soft pad of feet approaching, and the gentle swish of the door again. The telephone receiver was picked up and the same sleepy voice said:

'I'm sorry, dear, but Gillian hasn't come home yet. Can I take a message?'

'Do you expect her soon?' I didn't want to leave my name and a message. My bright plans were fading in my mind and a sick feeling was starting to rise from my stomach.

'Oh, I really couldn't say what time she'll be home. She's probably out with Paul again and they could be out until all hours.'

All I could hear was *again*. She was out with Paul again. For three weeks I'd punished myself for ruining everything, while all the time she was out with Paul. I imagined them dancing, eating dinner, raising a glass and gently clinking it in a toast, *to us*. I took a sharp breath and tried to make my whiskey-soaked brain think of something to say.

'Any message? Who shall I say called?' Mrs McNichol sounded tired, and slightly peeved at being dragged out of her comfortable bed and made to account for Gillian's whereabouts.

'She'll know who it is. I'm sorry to have disturbed you so late.'

Mrs McNichol started to say something, but I put the telephone down before she could question me further. My mouth flooded with a hot metallic taste, and I ran to the kitchen sink and vomited up whiskey until my stomach wrung itself out.

I sipped some water and then sat in the armchair, brooding and watching Judith's tightly closed bedroom door, until a lilac dawn light crept into the room, when I dragged myself to bed.

I woke with my head pounding, and my stomach feeling bruised. I spent a few seconds just lying there, blinking up at the yellow water stain on the ceiling. Eventually I crawled out of bed and grabbed my robe from the back of the closet door. My foot caught in the blue rug that covered our bedroom floor and I stumbled, catching hold of the dresser to steady myself. I caught a glimpse of myself in the mirror and my face was white and hollow-eyed. I recoiled from my own reflection and stripped off my nightgown, shoving it deep inside the laundry hamper. Pulling my robe around me, I ran my hands through my hair to put it back into place and made my way to the bathroom where I splashed cold water on my face until I could remember precisely what I'd done the night before.

The memory of Mrs McNichol sounding tired and slightly grumpy came back to me and I put my head in my hands to try and get rid of it. I flushed hot with shame. I shouldn't have called. All I could hope was that Mrs McNichol hadn't realized I was drunk and that Gillian would call today so we could make up.

All the clarity the whiskey brought last night disappeared with the bright mid-morning light. I needed coffee and to get my thoughts in order quickly. Last night I was ready to sell everything I owned and get on a boat to Europe; today I felt sick and fragile, and desperate for some comfort. Images from the police raid at the club kept coming back to me. Mary-Lyn's face pleading with me not to let go of her. The shock of seeing women groped and beaten for being who they were. I knew right then that I couldn't live a life in this city without Gillian. I couldn't fit in anywhere except with her. I hadn't wanted to listen to Gillian when she'd spoken of her fears about what could happen to us but now I'd seen it for myself. I'd been such a fool, risking everything, and I had no idea what to do now. There wasn't anyone else in the city I could turn to. I'd never felt so completely alone.

I could smell fresh coffee, so I knew that Judith was up. Although I was in no fit state to talk to her, I was hoping she might shove a mug of coffee in my hand until I could decide what to do with my day. I walked barefoot down the hallway and opened the living-room door. She was curled up in the armchair, carefully sipping from her favourite cup. The minute I entered the room she leaped up like a guilty child and started babbling. She disappeared into the kitchen and reappeared carrying my usual grey mug, which was filled to the brim with hot dark brown liquid. I gulped at it greedily and flopped down on to the couch. My head was splitting, as if some kind of machinery was crashing against the sides of my skull. I finished the coffee and, without saying anything, Judith took the cup from me, refilled it and set it down beside me on the table. She held out her hand and in the centre of her palm lay two white aspirin which I swallowed, washing them down with hot coffee and burning my throat a little in the process. I couldn't say a word to her.

An hour later, I felt no better and stumbled back to my bed too weak to protest when Judith closed the blinds for me, and then fetched a cold cloth for my head, and a glass of water that she set down on the bedside table. The aspirin had kicked in but my head still felt fuzzy, and I was good for nothing except sleep. Judith's voice was faraway and soothing as she hushed me, dabbing at my clammy forehead with the ice-cold cloth. Even though I didn't want her anywhere near me, the cold cloth felt delicious, and the warm air meeting my cool skin lulled me into a sleep filled with dreams.

I dreamed of Gillian: I could see her so clearly that I wanted to reach out my hand and brush a strand of hair from her face, but she seemed angry with me, although she wouldn't tell me why. I kept pleading but no matter how many times I begged her; she couldn't hear me. Her face remained the same, a strange little smile on her lips as if she felt sorry for me, but it was Judith's little smile not Gillian's. Then I was pulling Mary-Lyn up and through the window. She was crying and pleading with me. No matter how hard I struggled our hands kept slipping apart, but this time I was left trapped on the floor of the bathroom while Mary-Lyn vanished into the air.

I woke exhausted, the room dark thanks to the blind, except for a sharp glimmer of sunlight from one corner that was caught on the windowsill, indicating it was late afternoon. I'd been asleep for hours. I stirred and rubbed the sleep from my eyes, swept the hair off my face and sat up. I was completely alone and yet I'd felt there was somebody there when I woke. I let out a strangled yawn and reached over to throw back the bedcovers. A soft dint on the eiderdown was still warm from the weight of another body and for one minute my heart leaped at the idea that Gillian had come back. It took a few seconds before I realized it must have been Judith watching over me as I slept and the thought disturbed me.

'You're awake? I thought I heard you.'

Judith was standing in the doorway, holding a fresh glass of water and smiling at me as if I was a patient who couldn't understand her treatment. She walked over to the bedside table and replaced the empty glass with the full one.

'Thought you could use this, sleepyhead.'

She bustled around the bedroom that wasn't hers, smoothing down bedcovers and pulling open the blinds, filling the room with blinding sunshine. I shielded my eyes and turned to gulp down some water. I needed to be fully awake but at least my head felt much better for the sleep.

I sat, leaning against a plumped-up pillow and considered having a cool shower to wake me up properly.

'Did anyone call while I was asleep?' I asked in between mouthfuls of water.

'Oh, you poor thing, you mean did Gillian call you? I wish you wouldn't get your hopes up, Dovie. She's gone, and I don't think she's coming back. I don't want to be mean or say things to hurt your feelings, but there comes a time when we have to see what's going on. I wouldn't be a very good friend to you if I allowed you to carry on thinking that this was somehow all going to work out. I saw the way she looked at Paul in that bar, and I'm sorry to be the one to tell you but I've never seen her look at you that way since I've been living here. I know it's none of my business but—'

'Shut up!'

Her mouth was still forming the words when I yelled at her and it stayed that way, hanging open, her eyes popping slightly, staring at me as if I'd gone mad.

'There's no need to be rude, Dovie. I'm your friend. A good friend. And someone needs to tell you the truth about things.'

'I said shut up!'

I slammed the water glass down on the bedside table and got to my feet. I raised myself to my full height so I could look down on Judith and got as close to her face as I felt able. My heart was racing but I couldn't stop the rage pouring out of me, no matter what the consequences might be.

'Stop talking about Gillian! Do you hear me?'

Her mouth clamped shut, and she looked slightly frightened at my tone and took a step backwards. I took a pace towards her because I wasn't going to let her do this to me, and we ended up in a peculiar dance, with her retreating and me following her, until she nudged up against the wall. I lunged forward, trapping her between the closet and the bed.

'I don't know what you want, Judith, and I don't care. I want you out of here, and I want you out by the end of the week. Do you hear me?'

I had no idea what I was about to say but the words

kept coming out of my mouth and the truth tasted like freedom.

'I was nice to you. I was taken in by your sad little act, but not any more. You are a vicious little sneak. I'm certain you could have got Gillian a ticket for that concert, but you wanted her to feel left out. You should never have lied about those sleeping pills. You should never have blackmailed your way into our home at all. You've tried to ruin things for me with Gillian, and I'm not going to let you.'

'I don't know what you mean, I'm sure. I've done nothing but care for you, Dovie. Why, I even spent the last few hours right next to you to make sure you didn't vomit in your sleep. You don't know what you're saying. I know you don't feel so good today and you're just upset, that's all.'

'Upset? You have some nerve. I don't want you here. I'm going to have my shower, and then I'm going to pack a bag and go to my sister's place for a few days. When I get back, I want you gone. Do you understand?'

Judith nodded, the shock evident on her face. She couldn't think quickly enough to talk her way out of it, and for one minute I'd quite forgotten that she could tell people about Gillian and me. I didn't care what happened to me. I felt brave and free but the feeling lasted mere seconds. Judith pushed past me and moved towards the doorway. She hesitated for a moment and then turned to look at me, her face perfectly in control now. Her eyes hard and staring.

'You need to stop before you really make me angry. I think you are forgetting who you're talking to. You really don't want me to tell everything I know about you and your girlfriend, do you? You might not care but what about her? I've heard such terrible stories about what happens to girls like you. You wouldn't want to cross me, Dovie. That would be a mistake.'

The words hung there in the air and then I ran towards her, screaming. Rage like a hot-red mist descended and I wanted to hurt her. I shook her until her face lost its smug little expression and I could see the fear in her eyes. I must have grabbed her by the collar because the next thing I knew she was struggling to get free. I didn't want to stop and the words kept pouring out of me.

'I don't care! You can do your worst. I won't be black-mailed by you for one minute longer. They can lock me up for who I am but I might decide to take you with me. I could admit everything but I'll say it was you and not Gillian. I'll tell them we were lovers and that's why I moved you in here. I'll tell them Gillian was my lodger and knew nothing about it. I'm going to be free of you whatever it takes. Look at you! You're pathetic. It's over. I want you out of here!'

Judith's face turned white and she was wriggling to get free of my grip. Gradually I relaxed my fist, watching as she collapsed against the wall with relief. She didn't say another word. All her bravado disappeared and she was coughing and trying to straighten her dress where I'd gathered her collar in my fist. She edged her body along the wall to get away from me, and then disappeared out of the bedroom door and fled to her own room down the hallway. I heard the key turn in her lock and felt nothing but relief.

I grabbed a towel from the hamper and went to the bathroom, locking the door because I didn't want her suddenly appearing while I was naked in the shower. I took my time lathering shampoo into my hair and rinsing it out again, standing under the beating water for ages until my temper cooled and my anger hardened into sheer determination. Drying myself quickly, I smoothed cold cream on to my face, set my hair into pin curls and tied a headscarf over the top of them.

Then I grabbed my khakis and a shirt, a pair of stout walking shoes, and my small black suitcase. Filling the suitcase with underwear and enough clothes for a few days, I stuffed my small vanity case with toiletries, added a few snacks and a book to read before clicking the locks shut on both. Finally, I grabbed a cream sweater from the closet in case I got chilly on the bus and draped it over my arm. Then I picked up the cases and tucked my purse in between them. I was a little weighed down but not terribly so. If Gillian called, well *she* would have to track *me* down for a change. I was tired of other people, tired of waiting and tired of this whole situation. My case bumped against the front door, but I turned the lock, and inched it open with my foot. Once I was out in the hallway, I put down the suitcase and slammed the door shut behind me. It was louder than I'd intended, and the sound echoed through the building. Being on the other side of the door from Judith filled me with instant relief as I picked up my suitcases and headed out of the front door to hail a cab to the bus station.

I felt better than I'd done in weeks. Telling Judith what I thought of her and ending her vile blackmail made me feel hopeful again. By the time I came home this would finally be over. Judith would be gone, and then I could see what the future held for Gillian and me.

23

New York City, 1975

I approached Miss Schnagl's apartment door with its little polished brass door knocker right in the centre. I stood there for a few seconds, listening, trying to make sure that I couldn't hear any voices, because I only wanted to do this once if I could help it. Knowing Miss Schnagl, she liked to talk and talk, and I really didn't want to have to explain the comings and goings in our apartment to her if I could avoid it. I could hear the sound of a radio playing, but there were no voices. I assumed that, as usual, she was alone, so I gently raised the door knocker and let it fall.

It took a few minutes, but Miss Schnagl eventually peered out through a crack in the door; the security chain was still on. Her sharp little eyes flitted above my head before they rested on me and I heard her say:

'Oh, it's you. Just a second.'

The door closed and I could hear the chain being lifted, and then the door opened again and there she was. Miss Schnagl was in her usual dull summer dress, the kind that looked as if it had been worn every summer since the war. It was a cross between a red and a pink, but so faded it was hard to tell what it started out as originally. She had an identical one in pale blue. She wore her house slippers and stockings, even though it was ninety degrees outside. There were two electric fans whirring away and a chill of cool air hit my face as the door opened and made me want to go inside very badly.

'Hi, Miss Schnagl, I'm sorry to bother you but I'm doing some research about the building, and I was wondering if you could help?'

The lie came out of my mouth so smoothly I surprised myself. I straightened my shoulders, gazed at her all wide-eyed and smiled my best smile. She looked me up and down for a second and then opened the door just enough for me to walk inside.

'Come on in. You want some tea? I only have herbal. I don't keep soda.'

'Tea is good.'

'Sit down. I'll be right back.'

She switched the radio off and went into the kitchen, where I could hear the kettle being filled and the chink of cups as they collided with the saucers. Her room was smaller than our living room and wallpapered with some strange bird pattern. The couch sagged and was covered with those cloths people put on to stop the arms from getting worn or greasy. There was an armchair also sagging from years of use, and a heavy wooden sideboard with a glass fruit bowl on top of it. It was empty. Behind the fruit bowl were three china dogs with their pink tongues hanging out of their mouths. There were pictures of landscapes on the walls: ocean scenes and country gardens. The room was very neat but also muddled as if things were acquired and then thrown into any corner, or put up on a wall without any thought at all.

Miss Schnagl appeared in the kitchen doorway with a tray set out with a teapot and two china cups; squeezed in next to them was a small plate containing black and white cookies. They looked home baked and good, unlike the sad ones at the hospital. I took one of the china cups and balanced a cookie on the saucer.

'I'm sorry to bother you but I didn't know who else to ask.'

'It's no bother. I'm glad of the company. I'm rattling around on my own here.'

Miss Schnagl sat herself down in the armchair with her cup and we stared at each other, both smiling in that weird, polite way people do when they want the other person to say something.

After several seconds of this, I realized that I was the one who should be saying something. I took a nervous breath; the room was silent, apart from the sound of my cup rattling in the saucer as I tried to put it down on an occasional table next to the couch.

'So I'm trying to find out some information about anyone who lived in this building. You know, over the years?'

'What's it for? A school project?'

'Yes, local history, you know the kind of thing?'

'So how far back are you going in history? Because I'm not that old, you know?'

She laughed, so I laughed.

'Oh, not that far. Maybe since the war.'

'Let me see. Well, I've been here since 1955. I took over this lease when Mr Prince left. I'm not sure that was his real name. He was some kind of performer and really spent very little time here as he was travelling so much. It might have been his stage name. It was lucky as it turned out because I needed somewhere to live and this place came up out of the blue. He got a job out west I think, maybe a B-movie or some such thing. He was gone very quickly and really gave me a good deal on the lease, because if I hadn't taken it, he would have been quite stuck.' She fixed me with a stern look. 'Are you going to write this down?'

I'd forgotten about my notepad lying idle on my knees, but I could think on my feet and quickly said:

'Oh, I've got a good memory.'

'Anyway, that was September or October 1955. I have no idea who was living here before Mr Prince, and you know I can't even remember his first name now. It was an unusual name, Brigg, or Brick, or something like that. Like I said, that could be his stage name. I can't say I really knew him. We had one conversation about the lease and that was that.'

I nibbled on my cookie, which tasted as good as it looked.

'How about our apartment? Do you know who lived there?'

Her eyes never left mine and a strange look came over her face.

'Well, now, before your father and mother moved in here, there was a young married couple who worked in the university, but they were only here for a year or two. I think they moved to Chicago, as I remember.'

I held my breath a little and then asked the question I really wanted the answer to:

'And before them?'

'It's so long ago. Let me see . . . I'm not sure I can remember.' Her voice was thin and strained.

'Are you sure? Maybe two women were living there?'

'I really couldn't say.'

She sipped at her tea and so did I, letting the silence fill the room. I thought of how I might push the conversation back towards Dovie and Gillian without giving too much away. My eyes glanced around the apartment. It was cluttered but at the same time I noticed there was only one photograph on display. I squinted up my eyes to try and see what it was, but it was too far away. There were none of the usual family pictures at all. I was curious about Miss Schnagl and unsure of how much I could ask her.

'Do you have family in the city, Miss Schnagl?'

'They're all gone now. I had a sister but she took sick and died young. I'm the only one left. Couple of cousins but they moved away. I was about your age when my

272

mother died . . . her lungs . . . That reminds me, how is your mother?' She had a strange unblinking way of staring at you that made me feel uneasy. She shifted the conversation away from her family so quickly that I felt a little sorry for her. She seemed so lonely and I'd never seen her have a visitor. I tried to steer the conversation back around to Dovie as gently as I could.

'She's fine.' I gulped at the tea and it scalded my throat a little, which made me cough. 'That box you brought up to us . . . it came all the way from Paris.' I spoke as softly as I could manage. Her eyes went flinty and hard.

'Paris? Now that's a long way to send a box.' She was waiting for something and I felt a stab of fear.

'Yes, it belonged to someone called Dovie Carmichael. I wondered if you knew her?'

The air around us seemed too still, as if we were both holding our breath. I watched her lips move slightly and a flash of anger cross her face. Then it was gone and she smiled her strange little smile.

'Oh yes, now I remember. I knew her many years ago.' She hesitated and I felt my stomach flip over.

'Do you remember the woman she lived with?' I asked nervously.

'She was nasty. I didn't like her. Some people you just don't take to at all and it was that way with us. The type who was cruel to people who weren't like her. She got what she deserved anyway.' Her voice faded away.

'What was that?'

Suddenly Miss Schnagl realized what she was saying and her mouth snapped shut. She eyed me suspiciously.

'I didn't know them, really. They moved out. I thought this was a school project?'

'Umm . . . I . . .' I was stuttering, trying to find a way to explain.

Miss Schnagl put down her teacup and stood up.

'Anyway, if that's all, dear, I have to get ready to go out. I volunteer at the Y one afternoon a week and I don't like to be late. I'm sorry I wasn't more help.'

She got up and so did I, rattling my teacup in the saucer as I did so.

'Thanks for your time, Miss Schnagl. If you remember anything else maybe you could let me know?'

I walked slowly towards the front door with her leading the way. As she opened the door, I made a point of trying to look at the small black and white photograph in a silver frame on the wall. There it was, three young women side by side outside of Gray's School. It was her with Dovie and Gillian, the exact same photograph I had upstairs. I stopped dead.

'Is this you?'

'Oh, that . . . yes, a long time ago.'

'You look so young.'

'I was.'

I took a gulp of air into my lungs and braced myself.

'But isn't one of those women Dovie Carmichael?'

Her eyes grew wide with fear and her mouth hung slightly open as she took a deep breath.

'Why do you want to know that?'

Miss Schnagl backed away from me and started to close the front door, leaving me on the wrong side of it. I put out my hand to stop her and managed to catch hold of the door just in time.

'Wait!' I shouted.

She was startled and hesitated long enough for me to put a foot forward to block the door.

'Please, Miss Schnagl, it's important.'

'I don't know anything. I don't know what you're talking about.'

'That box you brought upstairs – it's her things. Dovie's things. I'm trying to find Gillian. Do you know where she went?'

'I told you I don't know. Leave me alone.'

Her voice started to rise, flooded with panic. She put her hand across her chest as if trying to keep her heart steady.

'I'm sorry, it's OK. Really, it's OK.' I lowered my voice, trying to calm the situation, but her eyes were wild and terrified. She seemed like a frightened old woman to me and I was scared I'd upset her. The way her hand kept fluttering over her heart made me worry she was going to have a heart attack right there in front of me.

'I don't remember. I don't know . . . please.' I thought that she was going to cry but her eyes remained dry and flinty.

'That photograph, it was in the box.' I pointed to the little frame on the wall and Miss Schnagl glared at me.

The fear was gone but she was furious now and started to push at the door to get rid of me.

'Wait, Miss Schnagl! I just wanted to ask . . .'

I took a step backwards as the pushing and shoving seemed to be over. Miss Schnagl took a deep gulp of air and moved to close the door again. I jammed my foot in the way again to stop her.

'Wait a minute! I have something to tell you.'

'I told you I don't remember. I don't want to talk to you. Leave me alone.'

'She's dead, Miss Schnagl. Dovie Carmichael died.'

The pushing stopped and the door opened wide once more; Miss Schnagl stood there in the doorway and this time her eyes were filling up with tears.

'Dovie's dead?'

I nodded and took my foot out of the gap in the doorway. She stared at me for several seconds unable to speak, and then the door slammed in my face and I was left standing in the hallway on my own.

24

New York City, 1955

The bus jerked around the last corner before my stop. I was aching from the long journey and eager to wash the dust off my face. I'd managed to pull the pins out of my hair and run a comb through it during a bathroom break, so at least I wasn't turning up looking as if I'd run away from home, although in a sense I guess I had.

The woman in the seat across the aisle was still asleep; nothing had disturbed her the entire journey, no matter who got on or off the bus, she leaned against the window with her mouth hanging open. I watched a small trail of drool make its way down her chin for part of the ride, but eventually I lost interest, and gazed into the darkness on the other side of the glass until the sun peeked out from the farthest part of the horizon. A new dawn but the same old problems.

I could see the signs for Buffalo in the distance, and the familiar road that would eventually lead to the old farmhouse. The driver yelled the stop and I staggered to my feet, snatching my vanity case and purse from the rack above my seat. The driver was already out of the door unlocking the luggage flap and stacking my case in the dirt, along with a number of boxes that didn't appear to belong to anybody. The fresh wind blew across the farmland, which was all you could see for miles around. It was so familiar to me and I'd probably run across every inch of it as a kid.

The bus stop itself was out front of Rose's diner, which served passing truckers all day long. It was a good living, they said, although whenever I visited, there only ever seemed to be one lone trucker eating a bowl of soup or a plate of pie at the counter, and I never understood how that kept them in business, but somehow it did.

The other people who got off at my stop were a middle-aged couple who disappeared into a waiting car. I watched their tail-lights all the way up the road, and then the bus followed them the same way. Eventually there was just me and I headed for the pay phone to call my sister Franny from the diner, so she could come and get me. I was neither expected nor was I particularly unexpected. That was the deal with Franny and me.

The thing with an older sister is they never get over the fact that when they could stand up, you kept falling over. It stays with them for life, and they always treat you as if you are slightly lacking in ability. I'd always felt that way around Franny, as though I was the idiot kid sister who didn't quite measure up, but I loved her dearly.

She was the kind of woman that other women liked. She baked pies at the farm shop all day long, she would help at the local church, and she organized a thousand bake sales for charity. If people wanted a favour, they called my sister Franny. She was good with people in a way that I wasn't able to grasp; she'd married her childhood sweetheart, Bill, and raised two children, a boy called Jack and a girl, Eleanor, that everyone called Lola. They were both robustly healthy fair-haired kids who grew up drinking milk fresh from the cow and running through fields. Franny was the most practical, organized person I'd ever met, and I couldn't stand to be in a room with her for more than five minutes. She didn't read books because she believed in doing things. I liked to read books so I could read about other people doing things. I was looking forward to seeing her, but also dreading my visit in equal measure. The only thing that kept me going was the fact that Judith would be gone, and at least one of my problems would be solved by the time my visit was over. I inserted the coins into the slot, dialled Franny's number and waited.

The battered red pick-up truck spun its wheels a little as it ground to a halt. I was smoking a cigarette outside the diner and watching the road when I saw it kicking up dust. Franny was driving, and she didn't look pleased about it.

'Hey, sling your bags in the back. Come on. I need to get breakfast on the table for the kids.'

I obeyed and climbed into the passenger seat.

'Sorry to be a nuisance. I needed to get out of the city for a few days.'

She took a beat, studied my face and then slammed

the truck into gear and off we went, tyres throwing up gravel. We drove a way down the deserted road in silence and then Franny said:

'So, what's so terrible about the city that you need to run away?'

'I'm not running away. I wanted to get away. There's a difference. I can go if it's a problem?'

'I didn't say it was a problem. I was just asking. The kids haven't seen you in ages, so they are pretty happy about your visit. It's just a busy time for us.'

'It's only a couple of days, Franny. I can help out with the kids. I am a teacher, you know?'

'School's out for summer break. They're done with books for a bit. They have chores to do.'

I sighed and lit another cigarette. The five minutes we were able to tolerate each other was already up. I was always in the wrong with Franny, and it stung. No matter how hard I tried to please her, it always seemed as if I messed up somehow.

The farm lay at the next crossroads, off a dirt track that got flooded in winter and baked dry in summer. It was not enough acres to make money, but too many acres to make life simple. Franny had a constant stream of things to do. Bill took on men to help out at harvest, or occasionally during winter if there were complicated repairs that needed doing, but mostly he and Franny did it all between them. It was hard, grinding physical work, up at first light and asleep shortly after dark.

I could see the twinkle of early sunshine lighting up

the farmhouse across the next bend. Inside the farmhouse kitchen, two sleepy kids were sitting at the long wooden table with their heads resting on their arms. Bill had already gone to the top pasture to rescue a heifer that had got stuck. Franny parked up, grabbed my suitcase and hurried into the house. I followed along somewhat reluctantly behind her.

'Hey, kids, look who's here. Your Aunt Dovie has come to see you.'

The kids raised their sleepy heads and looked happy to see me, although they were probably happier to see breakfast arrive shortly afterwards.

We chatted away about nothing important as Jack and Lola packed away porridge made with thick yellow cream and drank their apple juice. After an hour or so of polite enquiries about their schoolwork or general interests, we ran out of easy conversation and they were glad to be dispatched to the top pasture to take their father his breakfast in his billycan.

Franny cleared away the plates, shushing me as I offered to help her, and then eventually, as the sun grew into a fireball outside the kitchen window, she sat down, sipping a lukewarm cup of coffee and stealing one of my cigarettes.

'So, how are you?' she said, blowing smoke out through her nostrils.

'I'm OK.'

'What's going on, Dovie? You don't just arrive out of the blue like this?'

Franny had a way of talking to me that reminded me of being a child and getting punished for something. Our parents were strict Baptists, and there was always some transgression or other that I was guilty of. My mom had sat in that same spot, asking me questions about my life. Franny had the look of her, not so much in her features exactly, but more like an impression that was imprinted over whoever she might have been in a different life. The way her lips curled up impatiently when I was talking; the way her eyes shifted to the furniture if I said something she didn't approve of: it was like being five years old all over again.

'Gillian and I broke up.'

As I spoke the words, I felt them inside me, solid and real. We had broken up. Gillian had left me.

Franny knew everything and nothing at all about Gillian. She didn't want to know too much so she couldn't be accused of lying about anything. I was careful only to mention Gillian by her first name and keep details of her to a minimum. All Franny knew was that I loved her and we lived together. She had kept my secrets for years and this was just one more. When I was sixteen and had never had a boyfriend, she teased me for being a bookworm, but by the time I was nineteen I couldn't keep the truth from her any longer. Franny, to her credit, would invent dates I'd been on, boyfriends she'd met and was glad I was no longer seeing. My too-perfect, hard-nosed sister covered for me and lied her ass off. We drove each other crazy but she'd never let me down.

'For good?' She put her coffee cup down on the table and stared at me.

'I don't know. She won't talk to me.'

'What happened?'

I started to tell her the whole sorry tale, managing it without tears, and only finishing it when I heard the yells of the children running back across the field with their father's empty billycan. She nodded and squeezed my shoulder gently as she stood up.

'You'll be OK. I need to bake pies.'

Pies are what Franny did best. Golden discs of buttery pastry over sweet fruit, served with thick cream on the side. My sister churned out dozens of pies every day, all different flavours according to the season: apple, plum, peach, blueberry, raspberry, banana cream, chocolate cream, pecan and maple, and cherry. In the little farm shop that was attached to the side of the house where people would drive up to make their purchases, Franny would run through the whole list without stopping for breath. By the time she arrived at *and cherry*, people had forgotten most of the other choices, and she'd have to start again. As the choices rarely changed and neither did the customers, it was surprising that more of them didn't actually know the list off by heart, as I surely did.

I wandered up to the farm shop, my arms loaded down with the freshly baked pies. A tantalizing smell of baked sugar and butter filled the air; I watched Jack and Lola having a race to see who could get to the shop first, and not for the first time I envied Franny. This was solid and real. The city was an illusion filled with dream-chasers, and people who thought more buildings meant more reality. Out here, with the fresh breeze blowing the tall grass in the distance, and the smell of freshly baked pies, you could see what you got for your work. I had no idea if any of the girls I taught cared a damn thing for the manners of unmarried ladies in English novels. Franny never stopped moving all day long. She baked the pies and arranged them on wooden shelves out of the sunlight. She scrubbed the cabinets and mopped the floor and told me to sit and stay right there when I tried to help her.

The hours were spent serving those pies to neighbours who knew what time to call of a morning to have first pick. Every transaction was preceded by a long conversation about someone's sick relative, or new baby, or wedding preparations. Franny knew everybody, and they all knew her. Of course, most of them knew me too. Our family had lived here for generations, but for most of them I was a stranger now: the girl who wasn't Franny, the one who read too many books and moved away. I was greeted with polite nods and an occasional enquiry as to my wellbeing, but my sister was queen of all she surveyed.

When the last pie was sold, we cleaned down the shelves and mopped the floor again, finally locking the door and carrying the little bag of dollar bills back up to the farmhouse. In the distance I could see the familiar outline of Bill traipsing back across the pasture in time for his dinner. Another day was done for them.

Dinner was pork chops and, of course, pie (a pecan and maple that Franny kept back); Bill, a man of few words at the best of times, decided to turn in early, leaving, as he put it, 'you girls to catch up'. The kids listened to their radio show, and then they too were sent off to clean their teeth and get themselves off to their beds without fighting, or too much in the way of giggling.

Franny pulled down a whiskey bottle from her hiding spot, behind the enormous steel tin that held the flour. She picked up a pair of glasses and filled them generously, handing me one and settling herself across the table from me. We clinked glasses in a toast and sipped at the whiskey.

'Can I ask you something?' she said.

'Sure.'

'What do you want from life?'

I couldn't think of an answer for a long time. What did I want? I wanted Gillian, that was true, but what else?

'I want to be happy, I guess. I want a life that makes me happy, like you have.'

Franny took a slug of her whiskey and started to laugh a little bitterly.

'Like I have? What the hell would you know about my life? When was the last time you even asked me how I was doing?'

'Aren't you happy, Fran? I thought all this was what you wanted. I always thought I was the one who was desperate to get away from the farm, not you.'

'It's not the farm. I wanted to stay here, and it suits me. It's . . .' She didn't look at me and I could see her mind churning over whether to say whatever it was that she wanted to say. She took a long sip from her whiskey glass.

'You can tell me anything, Fran. God knows you've kept enough of my secrets over the years.'

Franny took another sip of her whiskey and traced her finger across the scratches on the old wooden table.

'It was a long time ago. It doesn't matter now.'

'It matters to you.'

She sighed and reached over to take one of my cigarettes out of the packet. I lit one for her and then one for myself, and we both sat across from each other, exhaling smoke.

'Do you remember before we got married when Bill had his accident and mashed up his leg real bad?'

'Sure.'

'We took on a young man called Joel to do Bill's work on the farm. Dad was too old to manage the physical stuff while Bill was recovering. I took care of everything else and went over to Bill's place to visit him when I could. He was frustrated being stuck indoors all day, and I guess he got kind of cranky with me and I got cranky back at him. I was worn out with it all . . . Joel was kind and funny and I . . .'

Franny went quiet and her cheeks flushed a little. She stared down at her whiskey glass, gently swirling the liquid around and around. I waited for her to carry on but there was silence.

'Did you fall in love with Joel? I had no idea . . . I thought it was always you and Bill.'

'It was always Bill . . . and then it wasn't. It was only three months, and then Bill was up and about again and we let Joel go.'

'Did you keep in touch with him?'

'He wrote once or twice, but I'd made my choice and I couldn't be with him.'

'But you loved him?'

'Yes, I loved him.' Franny's voice was soft as air.

'But you married Bill?'

'And there hasn't been a day that I haven't regretted it. He's a good man and I do love him of course and I love my kids so much, but I keep busy because if I stop, I can't get Joel out of my mind. We fitted together like we belonged. It was like finding a missing piece of something. I regret letting him go more than I can say.'

Solid, practical Franny, my sister who seemed to exist only to care for children or bake pies or scurry around the farm organizing everyone, was carrying a painful secret, and had carried it for so many years. I felt a wave of pity rush over me.

'But if you truly loved him . . . I mean, you weren't married then, why didn't you choose him?'

Franny sighed and then looked me straight in the eye.

'Because Joel was a black man, Dovie.'

My mouth fell open and I stared at Franny. She took a sip of her whiskey and nodded.

'Can you imagine what would have happened? I couldn't . . . I had to let him go. People around here . . . well . . . you know how they are. Where would we go? Nowhere that would give us peace. I knew it was too hard. Turns out it was hard either way so the joke's on me.'

I reached across and put my hand over the top of hers and squeezed it. I had no idea what to say to make it better.

'Oh, Franny, why didn't you tell me?' I murmured.

'Wasn't any point. He was gone by then.'

I blinked, slowly taking this all in.

'Why are you telling me this now?'

'Because I see you about to give up on your dreams. I've listened to you over the years. You talk all the time about Gillian and about Paris, and I hear you get excited, but you never *do* anything, Dovie. You've got yourself in a mess with secrets, and if you let them those secrets will make you live a half-life, and I don't want that for you. It's too late for me now. Don't feel sorry for me, it's not as if it's a terrible life, but it's not the one I wanted and I didn't know it until it was too late.'

'It's not too late, Franny. Don't say that.'

'Sometimes it is . . .' Franny was biting on her bottom lip and trying not to look at me.

'What happened to Joel?'

'He joined the military . . . after I called it off. Told

him it wasn't possible. He knew it. He left without saying goodbye. He wrote me and I wrote back but then the letters stopped. I never heard from him again. Then last week a couple of the neighbours were waiting on pies. Just gossiping . . . and one of them said, "Do you remember that boy used to help out around here?" and I thought my heart would stop beating. Turns out he used to help out at one of their farms too, and I guess they knew his folks. "Killed in Korea. Ain't that a shame? Hardworking boy too." Turns out he was killed two years ago but nobody knew until they saw his mother in Buffalo one day. They stood there and carried right on choosing their pies and I couldn't say a word.'

'Oh, Franny . . . I'm so sorry.'

I wanted to walk around the table and hug Franny until she cried the tears that she needed to cry, but I knew my sister better than to do that. She gave me a fierce nod. She put the whiskey glass to one side and pulled a face.

'I shouldn't be drinking this. Makes me nauseous.'

She held my gaze and then nodded. I felt myself sink back in my chair with recognition.

'You're pregnant again? I thought you were done,' I said quietly.

'Oh, I was done but here we are. Due at Easter.' She pulled a face. 'We don't make it easy for ourselves. I love you, Dovie, you're my only sister, and I'm happy to have you visit, but when you've had some time with me and the kids, I want you to leave and go be happy however that looks for you, because life is short. It's so short and we make so many mistakes. Promise me you will choose the life that makes you happy?'

She reached across the table and gripped my hand tightly, her eyes pleading with me.

'I will . . . I promise.'

I meant the promise, but I couldn't help but wonder what kind of a life I would be able to make out of the mess I'd created. They say you can only shame a woman once, and after that maybe you can never shame a woman again. I wondered if I was brave enough to find out.

Franny got to her feet and collected up the whiskey glasses to wash them. She rinsed them out and then dried them carefully with a cloth, putting them back on the shelf where they lived. I put my hand on her shoulder and let it sit there, warm and comforting. Franny reached a hand across and patted it. Then she moved away and our conversation was over.

Later that evening as I lay under the eaves, my mind raced through the possibilities: things I could say to Gillian and lives that we could live together. There had to be a way forward, and I was determined to find it.

At first light, I could hear a rooster crowing in the distance, and the usual early-morning farm activity of cows that needed milking and eggs that needed collecting for breakfast. It was time to make my way back home to New York. I felt clearer in my mind after a few days away, and I leaped out of bed to start getting ready. I splashed cold water on my face and cleaned my teeth, before dressing for my journey home. I folded up my things and packed them away and left the suitcase and my vanity in the hallway ready to go.

Franny was already at the stove, coffee made and eggs in the skillet. She gestured to me to sit down and filled my cup with strong black coffee, and then heaped a plate full of eggs and bacon for me. When I was finished, I wouldn't need to eat again until I reached New York, but it would be another long day travelling. Franny handed me a brown paper bag.

'I cut you a slice of pie for the journey.'

'Thank you . . . for everything.'

She looked at me and smiled softly. We hugged each other and I held on to her for the longest time.

'You better get going. I'll drop you at the bus stop. Hey, kids, your Aunt Dovie is leaving, come say goodbye.'

Jack and Lola shouted their goodbyes from the door and sped off to have some adventure away from the farmhouse. Bill had already gone off to milk the cows, and I was glad about it, as I couldn't look at him quite the same way after what Franny had told me. I gathered up my bags and headed out to the truck. Franny jumped in the driver's seat and the engine flared into life. We rolled away down the dirt track and back towards the bus stop. Franny didn't speak much on the drive but she did put the radio on, and we sang along for a bit with a song we both liked. It felt good, and for the first time I wasn't itching to get away from my sister. We smiled at each other from time to time, and when she set me down opposite the diner to wait for the bus, she leaned across from the driver's side and shouted:

'Be happy, Dovie. That's an order.'

'Bye, Franny . . . and thank you.'

'No need to thank me. You know what to do.'

I leaned in and held her tight. I wasn't sure when I would see her again and I wanted her to know that I loved her. She patted me awkwardly on my shoulder before I pulled away and said:

'You take care now.'

And with that she slammed the truck door shut and sped off back to her life with Bill and her kids.

The bus was late, but I was glad to see it all the same. I couldn't wait to get back to my home and start making plans. I wasn't going to hide away any longer, and neither was I going to let Judith ruin my life. Gillian and I would work it out. I didn't know how but I would think of something.

The bus creaked to a halt and was almost full. I took the last seat available, right at the back of the bus, squeezed in between a bunch of full-bodied farmers' wives going to the nearest town for supplies. Their muscular bodies pushed me into a corner, until I was pressed right up against the window on the left-hand side. Eventually they got off, and I could stretch out for the rest of the trip, as I was one of only three people making the full journey to New York. I reached for my little paper bag and took out the slice of pie. It was apple and it tasted of home. I finished it quickly and brushed the crumbs off my lap. I took out my compact mirror and ran a comb through my hair, and fixed my face a little, pinching my cheeks to make them look a little healthier and putting on a faint smear of lipstick. In the distance I could see the tall buildings of New York City, and I felt my heart rise to greet them. I watched the familiar buildings pass by my window and the people, city people, all crowded together with no fresh breeze to cool them, and felt glad to be back.

The cab stopped right outside my building and the driver brought my cases up to the front door. I turned my key in the lock and carried my bags upstairs to our apartment. I reached for my door key to get inside but paused. I could hear music playing, and it was coming from inside our apartment. I felt a thrill of excitement bubble up inside me. Gillian had come home. I was so happy that my hand shook a little as I opened the door and I just abandoned my cases in the hall, as I was in such a hurry to get to her. I ran into the living room and stopped dead in my tracks.

Sitting in the armchair by the window was Judith.

'What are you doing here? I told you to get out!'

I was so angry I could barely stop myself screaming at her. She seemed strangely calm, considering our last meeting, and sat back in the armchair smirking at me.

'Don't get mad, Dovie. I waited for you to come back

because I thought it was for the best . . . all things considered.'

'What are you talking about?'

'I only stayed on because I didn't want you to come home and be on your own.'

'What are you *doing* here? I told you what would happen if you didn't leave and I meant it.'

'Dovie, I know you're upset with me and I'm sorry, I truly am. I was going to leave because I don't want to be here if that's how you feel about it. You've got it all wrong about me. I figured it would be cruel to leave you when . . . Look, there's not an easy way to tell you this but Gillian was here yesterday.'

Her voice was oozing with sympathy, but I wasn't fooled. Her words had landed soft and wheedled their way into my mind. I tried to make sense of what she was trying to tell me and then I knew.

'Gillian was *here*? Where is she? What happened?'

I glanced around the room and suddenly noticed some things were missing. Gillian's clock and the lamp she liked to read by were gone. Panic flooded my mind and I couldn't catch my breath properly. My fingernails were scraping against the inside of my palms. Judith was still curled up in the armchair, watching me trying to understand.

'Dovie, I'm sorry, I really am. Gillian came here with Paul and well . . . they were together . . . if you know what I mean. That was plain to see. She's gone for good and she doesn't want to talk to you.'

'No! She wouldn't do that,' I yelled as I hurried into our bedroom, throwing open the closet doors and rifling through the drawers in our old chest. They were all empty. Gillian had packed all of her things. She was gone.

I threw myself down on the bed unable to believe what was happening. She'd left me. I looked for a note of some kind, an explanation, but there was nothing. Then I noticed something out of the corner of my eye, a small glint of yellow. Puzzled, I got up and moved towards the door, pushing it closed. Pinned on the back of the bedroom door was the yellow butterfly necklace. It hung loosely from the pin, swaying slightly from the movement of the door. Underneath the necklace, and stabbed through with the same pin, was the photograph of me that Gillian loved to carry around in her purse. The word 'LIAR' was scrawled right across my face.

I felt numb as I pulled clothes from drawers and closets and folded them neatly. Everything I'd hoped for was gone. All I could think about was what Franny had said to me about being happy. I didn't believe I could ever be happy without Gillian, but I couldn't stay in the apartment and carry on as normal. I felt perfectly calm, as if I wasn't really there, standing in our bedroom emptying out all my belongings into suitcases. I pulled out the stack of photo albums from under the bed and shoved them into a case. The air in the apartment felt heavy with silence. I didn't know what I would do with all the sadness when it came, but I knew exactly where I would be when that happened. The suitcases bulged at their tops, filled with a life that was over. I clicked the locks shut and tucked my passport into my purse. I would stay in a hotel tonight, and tomorrow I would start to book tickets. I wanted a long journey, one that exhausted me and let me drift away in my mind. I would go by boat with nothing to do but watch the waves build and sweep across the bow and maybe at the end of it I would have thought of how to begin again.

Judith sat in the armchair watching me as I stacked my suitcases in the hallway. As I closed the bedroom door, the yellow wings of the butterfly necklace glinted in the light. I grabbed the necklace, and the photograph of me with 'LIAR' scrawled across my face, shoving them deep into my purse. I didn't want to take them, but I couldn't bear to leave them hanging there for anyone to look at.

I laid my keys carefully next to the telephone and glanced back to take a last look around. Judith didn't say a word. Her strange little smile was missing and her face was flushed and tear-stained. For once, I didn't care. I snapped the front door shut behind me without saying goodbye.

25

New York City, 1975

I'd waited as long as I could but there was no sign of my dad the next morning and I presumed he'd forgotten all about me. I would need to rely on Viola being able to stand me the price of the entrance ticket to the pool party, otherwise I'd have to miss out and the thought of that was unbearable. For all the bad things happening at home Cal was a glimmer of hope for a future where somebody cared about me. I replayed our last few encounters over and over: his smile, his casual invitation . . . was it an invitation? I couldn't be sure but the hope welled up inside me until I couldn't stand it. All I could think about was him holding my hand or putting his arm around me and pulling me in close to him. The navy one-piece was still horrible, but I took extra time over my hair and did what I could.

Viola was standing at the entrance gates to the pool waiting for me. A loose cotton bag was slung across her shoulder, and a strange-looking bucket hat with huge pink roses was hiding most of her face. She grinned as she saw me walking up the street towards her, and I waved.

'I'm glad you're early. We can get a good spot.'

'A good spot?' I asked.

'Yes, where we can see everyone but without getting stared at.'

The pool party was an annual event and, truth be told, I'd been dreading this day since school broke up. It was a regular thing that the outdoor pools in the city opened once school was out, and they would hold a pool party, which everyone in the neighbourhood would attend. The popular girls would sit around in their beautiful costumes being popular, and the good-looking boys would crash in and out of the water making thunderous dives, and shouting 'Hey, watch this!' a lot. At the exact time my mother was talking to her imaginary friend, I'd been fretting about how I could go swimming without having to be seen in a bathing suit. It was my worst nightmare.

My biggest fear in life was being caught in possession of some flaw that I was not yet aware of. The thought of being seen in my old navy one-piece tortured me, and I'd seriously considered crying off with some serious (but not too serious) sickness, but then I didn't want to miss out on seeing Cal. I couldn't wait to see him. I was going to make a move, say something, maybe even ask if he wanted to get a coffee sometime. I'd definitely fallen for him, so much so that I couldn't breathe around him, and I fully intended to tell him how I felt, just not yet. I dreamed of holding hands with Cal as we walked down the street so that everyone would know I was someone's girl. My heart felt full at the thought of it and my lips formed themselves into a secret smile.

Viola was happy to pay for our tickets, and as we walked through the gates I could see the pool was already pretty full. Everyone had the same idea to come early and get the best spots. To the right of the sparkling blue water most of the girls who really wanted to be seen laid out their beach towels and were lying around in tiny bikinis. They smothered their pristine bodies with coconut oil and from time to time they would look up on the pretext of turning over and ask one of the other girls to rub more oil on to their backs. They occasionally wandered off to sit on the edge of the pool, dangling their tanned legs into the water to cool off, but not once did they ever plunge in. Getting wet was not the point of their pool party. The entire point of their pool party was to be seen and, of course, to see. They would spy the boy they wanted to notice them and fix him with a shy smile; when they were sure they had his attention, they would flip themselves over on their towels like little hotdogs on a barbecue. The entire row of girls would lie in a line and they would mostly co-ordinate from position one – the lying on their backs with one knee slightly raised – to position two: lying on their bellies and resting their heads on their arms like a pillow.

On the other side of the pool, boys were spread around in groups according to their friends, and often their clan: Latinos hung with other Latinos, and blacks with blacks; the preppy guys stuck together; but for the most part each group of boys had a loud mix of characters.

There was a set of changing rooms with brightly coloured stable doors; every door was a different pastel colour and resembled the counter at Zerilli's. At the far end of the pool was a set of ancient wooden diving boards, reaching higher and higher, until the top board was so high you could barely hear the laughter from down below. I knew this because I'd once climbed up there with Viola, but chickened out of diving as my legs were shaking so badly.

I was a pretty good swimmer but I hated to be stared at. At the far end of the pool was a concrete sunbathing platform at the top of some thick stone steps, and that was the best spot if you liked to watch but not be seen.

'So what's new? Did you solve the mystery yet?' Viola was asking out of politeness now and I could tell her heart wasn't in it, the way her eyes kept looking past me to check for a prime spot where we could situate ourselves.

'No.' I was still mad with Vi and didn't want to share my news about Miss Schnagl.

'That's sad,' said Viola perfunctorily. 'Quick, grab those spots over there!'

There was just enough space in the corner and we scurried over to spread out our towels before anyone else could lay claim. I didn't say another word about Dovie . . . and Viola didn't ask.

Then came the worst part. I'd already struggled into my navy one-piece that morning and slipped my denim skirt and white cheesecloth shirt over the top, so now I could step out of my skirt and arrange myself on my towel before slipping off my shirt. If I lay down flat, I was already half-hidden behind the small wall that stopped people falling off the platform and I felt relatively safe from ridicule. My skin was pale and seemed even more so lying next to Viola, who was wearing her bright pink one-piece. It was the brightest pink I'd ever seen, but Viola wasn't all that bothered about what other people thought about her. She loved what she loved, and never worried that other people wouldn't love her for it. I wished I could be more like her.

I rubbed suntan lotion over every inch of me and lay back on my towel. I didn't have any sunglasses, so I rested one arm across my eyes, and started to enjoy the feeling of my skin tingling under the sun, and the slight breeze. Beneath us I could hear the sound of people in the pool splashing and yelling at each other, and I raised myself up on one elbow to see what was happening.

One boy I didn't recognize was filling balloons with water and running around the side of the pool where the popular girls were all tanning in a row. He crept up behind one of the Freds, and then popped the water balloon right over her head. The ice-cold water drenched her and Eileen screamed. Eileen was a sprint champion at our school, and she started to chase the boy around the pool which got everybody shouting and laughing. She was stronger than she looked and for a while they grappled with each other, and had their play fight, until everyone else lost interest, and they ended up, the two of them, sitting together and sharing a Coke, before Eileen got bored and went back to join the other girls in their tanning routine.

I casually glanced around searching for Cal until eventually I spotted him with a gang of his friends under the diving boards. He was wearing bright green trunks, and he must have just arrived because his shirt was open, and he was carrying a towel tucked under his arm. I studied him for several seconds, until I noticed him watching the popular girls all flipped over on their bellies. I must have stared for a beat too long, because he looked up suddenly and I ducked back down behind the wall to carry on sunbathing. I was building up my courage to go down there and say hello but I didn't feel brave enough to do it yet.

Viola had brought her radio and we placed it carefully at the top of our towels, right by our heads so we could listen to the music as we lay there. Frankie Valli was blasting out 'My Eyes Adored You', and I was feeling it. Viola was singing along and doing a strange kind of shoulder dance as she lay on her towel. I was laughing at her and it felt good being outside and away from everything, and I soon forgave Viola and started to feel as if it was going to be a good day.

Viola had quickly lost interest in the contents of the box, now it was not going to lead to buried treasure or a lost inheritance. She was practical like that. She didn't have a romantic bone in her body, and her view on Dovie and Gillian was that as one of them was certainly dead, then it didn't matter if the other one got the box or not.

I really wanted to make it right though. I didn't know exactly what had happened between them, but I felt the need to try and find Gillian if I could. It felt important to me. Every time I read those unfinished letters or looked at one of the old photographs, I felt as though I understood how desperate she was to be loved. I found it hard to explain that to Viola because she would think I was crazy, and maybe I was.

As the music faded into a commercial break, I saw Barbara Mulkenny wander over and stand next to Cal. I hadn't noticed her earlier with the other girls, which in itself was unusual because they were normally inseparable, but she looked like some kind of movie star today. She was wearing a yellow gingham bikini, and her red hair was loose and flowing around her shoulders. She was all smiles as she reached Cal and I couldn't help but stare at her. She'd been dating a freshman in college, but that fizzled out before the school year ended. My heart started to speed up as I watched her chatting to Cal and his friends.

Cal couldn't take his eyes off her and her yellow gingham bikini. My palms became clammy and a wave of panic broke somewhere deep inside me, and I whispered to myself, 'Oh no.'

Barbara Mulkenny had walked right up to Cal and stood so close to him that you couldn't get air between them. I was holding my breath, waiting . . . and then the worst thing happened: Cal draped one arm around her shoulders and pulled her close to him.

I couldn't get my breath properly and there was a horrible ringing in my ears. This couldn't be happening. But, somehow, it was. She leaned into him, putting one hand on his bare chest and giggled. He whispered something in her ear and they strolled off towards the cart with the red umbrella that dished out ice-cold Cokes and ice-creams all day long. He was holding her hand and delicately leading her around the pool so that everyone could see them. Eventually they reached the cart, where Barbara Mulkenny simpered and giggled for a full minute before deciding on a Coke. Cal had the same and they carried their bottles to a shady spot in one corner where a concrete ledge made an impromptu seating area. Barbara stretched out her legs and sipped at her bottle of Coke; from time to time she put the ice-cold bottle against her forehead, and laughed about how hot she was. Cal couldn't take his eyes off her. Even when he sipped his Coke, his eyes never left her face. When she spoke to him, his face lit up and before long he was twirling a piece of long red hair around his fingers, and gently stroking her shoulder. I wanted to die. I felt as if everyone knew, but of course only Viola knew, and she was right next to me watching them with me.

'Mulkenny? Wow, I thought she only liked college boys?' Viola was trying to cheer me up.

'It's fine,' I lied. My insides felt as if they were being shredded with pieces of glass. The pain was so sharp I couldn't breathe.

'Do you wanna leave?' she asked.

'Nah . . . it's OK.' I couldn't bear it but I couldn't look away either.

We lay back down on our towels and Viola turned the transistor radio up. The DJ segued in from a commercial break with 10cc's 'I'm Not in Love'. It was the last thing I wanted to hear and I sat up abruptly.

'Let's go swim. I'm too hot.'

Viola raised an eyebrow.

'You sure you wanna go down there?'

'Sure, why not? I'm not a kid. I'm nearly sixteen years old, and so what if Cal is getting it on with Mulkenny. I don't care.'

My not caring sounded very much like someone's heart breaking into a million pieces, but Viola knew better than to argue with me. If I wanted to swim, then we would swim.

'Come on, let's race. Loser buys the Cokes.' Viola was a terrible swimmer, and she knew I would probably leave her for dead by the second or third stroke, but she was desperately trying to take my mind off Cal and Barbara.

We turned off the music and tucked the radio away under a pile of our clothes, before heading back down the concrete steps to the blue tiles of the pool. We eased our way into the shallow end, and stood there for a while getting our breath back. The water was freezing cold and my skin filled with goosebumps. I gently splashed a little water over my shoulders to get them used to the temperature, but nothing worked except to plunge myself under. Viola was still shivering when I emerged.

'You ready?'

'If I haven't frozen to death by the time you say go.'

We eyed each other and then I plunged forward, shouting, 'Go!'

The next minute was filled with the smell of chlorine and the swell of the water as my arms reached through it. I prided myself on my crawl: it was something I could do well, and it made me feel powerful to slice through the water leaving everyone in my wake. My feet kicked up a lot of water behind me and I tried not to spray Viola, but every time I took a breath, I could see her fading and starting to splutter. I eased off, slowed my pace and let her catch up a little before I stretched out for the final few yards. I touched the blue tiles at the end of the pool and declared myself the winner. Viola stopped right where she was and started floating on her back.

'I didn't want to win anyway. I prefer to float away.' She stuck out her tongue at me and looked so funny with her toes sticking up and the rest of her barely floating at all. Eventually she reached out a hand and I dragged her towards the side of the pool, so she could cling on to the edge. She pulled herself over towards the metal ladder. I followed closely behind her. I placed my hands carefully on the tiles and hauled myself up. All my ease and ability flowed away from my body the minute it hit dry land. My arms hurt a little from pulling myself out of the water and I made an inelegant landing on the concrete, lying there like a landed fish.

As we straightened our costumes and checked each

other for stray fallout – breast, hair, ass – I caught a glimpse of Cal and Barbara Mulkenny out of the corner of my eye. The Coke bottles were discarded at their feet, and they were kissing. She had placed one hand at the back of his hair, and their faces seemed to be moving in slow circles. Her eyes were closed and I couldn't see his face, but his hand was placed very deliberately and firmly on her bare waist.

'We could take the Cokes to go?' Viola was watching me carefully. I nodded. I couldn't speak or I would start to cry, and that was the last thing I wanted in front of everyone. I rubbed my hands over my face as if I was wiping away the pool water, but in reality, tears had started to trickle down my cheeks. The sun burned hot on our skin once we were out of the water, drying up the droplets left on our arms. Viola looped her arm through mine and walked me briskly to the cart, where she bought us two Cokes.

We walked away from the pool party with towels slung around our shoulders, weighed down by our bags and guzzling cold Coke to wash the swimming pool out of our mouths. We didn't speak for several minutes and then Viola said:

'You OK?'

I shook my head:

'I really thought he liked me. I'm so stupid. Why does he prefer Mulkenny?'

'I don't know. She's not that interesting to talk to.'

I knew she was trying to make it better, but I didn't want to feel better this way. I'd failed some test I hadn't even known I was sitting.

'Well, Cal certainly thinks so.'

'Well, maybe Cal isn't that interesting either.' Viola sucked in her breath as soon as she said it. 'OK, I'm sorry. I know he's your boy and all.'

I shook my head. We walked on not speaking. I was annoyed with Viola for what she'd said about Cal, but I got that she was on my side, and then for no reason that I could understand I started to laugh.

'What are you laughing at?'

'Everything,' and then the laughter turned to great choking sobs.

Viola took my arm and steered me into a doorway where we could talk.

'Ava, I don't know what's going on with you, but you can come back home with me if you want to. My mom won't mind.'

'No, I want to be on my own.'

Viola was getting frustrated with me but I couldn't tell her how I felt. I wiped my face with the back of my hand and turned to face her.

'C'mon, Ava, what's gotten into you these days?'

'Nothing's gotten into me . . .'

'You're acting crazy. Where are you going?'

'Leave me alone . . .'

I couldn't explain and I wasn't in the mood for Viola's wisecracking or concern. I just wanted to get away.

'Ava, come on. Don't be like that! Come back here . . . Ava!'

I heard Viola calling after me, but I was already walking away.

As I turned the key in the front door and let myself in, the building was eerily quiet, and there was no sign of Miss Schnagl behind her curtains. I went up to our apartment and set about stripping off my wet swimsuit and slightly damp clothes. I wrapped myself up in a dry towel and lay back on my bed, staring up at the ceiling. I fully intended to get dressed but once I was lying down I couldn't seem to get up again. I lay there staring at the ceiling, not wanting to move. The same old yellow water stain staring back at me. There didn't seem any point. There was no sign that my father had turned up, my mother was probably being zapped with electric volts, and Cal was sticking his mouth all over Mulkenny. I felt so miserable. I knew that Viola meant well but she didn't get it. I had nobody who cared what happened to me. I'd counted on that someone being Cal and all the time it was Mulkenny he wanted. I felt so stupid and hopeless. For the first time in my life, I could understand why my mother spent her days just staring at the walls.

I flipped on to my side and curled up into a tight ball. I felt a cramping sensation which reminded me that I hadn't eaten, and a wave of unbearable sadness washed over me as I clutched my knees to my chest. I was so tired of being alone. The tears started as a trickle, sad little drops that fell on to the pillow, but the trickle soon became a stream. Just when I thought I would stop crying, another wave would hit me and off I would go again. With every new wave of sobbing it all came out: how scared I was watching my mother go crazy; how angry I was at my dad; how miserable I felt . . . and most of all how heartbroken I felt over Cal. I cried so hard that I couldn't stop; I cried until my eyes were red and swollen up like little bee stings; I cried until I was empty, and then I stopped and gave myself a talking-to.

I set about hanging my wet swimsuit over the fire escape to dry off and took a long cool shower. I couldn't stop thinking about Cal and Mulkenny, and I cried a fresh batch of tears in the shower as I imagined them doing all the things together that I'd imagined us doing. I wanted somebody to comfort me, but there wasn't anyone and that made me cry harder. I was beginning to think I would never be able to stop sobbing, but eventually I managed to break off long enough to get out of the shower and dry myself off.

I felt another cramping pain in my lower belly and headed to the bathroom where I noticed a tiny spot of blood staining my underwear.

Suddenly, my crazy crying jag made perfect sense, and I rushed into my mother's bedroom to search the drawer where she kept the sanitary pads. I pulled it open to find that it was empty. I tried the other drawers, in case she'd put them somewhere else by mistake, but there was no sign of them.

I checked my bedroom in case I'd tucked away a spare Kotex, although I knew that I hadn't. Since I'd first got my period aged thirteen, we always had the same system of keeping the pads in my mother's closet drawer, tucked under her petticoats so nobody except us would see them. My underwear felt quite damp by this point, and I looked around for something to use as a makeshift pad, finding an old white flannel and folding it neatly into a long strip before tucking it into my panties. It moved slightly as I walked and felt anything but secure, but it was the best I could do, and I set about searching the kitchen for any loose change that I could use to buy some Kotex.

The coin jar we kept in the cupboard was empty. I would have to track down my father and make him come over as soon as possible. I reached for the telephone and dialled Candy's number. It rang a bunch of times and I let it ring as long as I could, but there was no answer, and I had no idea where he might be. I leaned my face against the wall as I listened to the telephone ringing, but I knew it was hopeless. Nobody cared and nobody was coming to help me. Deep choking sobs gathered at the back of my throat and my fingers slapped at the wall helplessly. My face felt raw from crying and I blew desperate little breaths until I finally hung up the telephone.

Almost as soon as I hung up, the receiver started to vibrate against its cradle and a loud ringing filled the air. I scooped up the receiver as quickly as I could, trying to speak between jagged breaths.

'Dad?'

I heard a vaguely familiar woman's voice on the line.

'Hello . . . is that Ava?'

'Yes, this is Ava. Who's this?'

'Hello, dear . . . it's Mrs Mac . . . I've *found* her!'

'What?'

For a moment I didn't register what she'd said but then Mrs Mac carried on chattering away down the line at me.

'Gillian McNichol. I went through all the boxes, every single one of them . . . and I found her in 1960 . . . where she should not have been.'

'Oh . . .' I felt weird and kind of numb inside. My thoughts felt scrambled like a puzzle that's got messed up but Mrs Mac kept on talking into my ear.

'Well, here's where it gets interesting, and I needed to do a little detective work. I found her old address, and I tracked down the telephone number from an old directory. It was an adventure, let me tell you, and I had to get a very kind telephone operator to do me a favour.

'Turns out we are distantly related . . . the operator that is, not Gillian McNichol. She's not Gillian McNichol these days. She married and her name is Stewart. It was quite the adventure and it took me most of the afternoon but . . . well, to cut a long story short, I have her current address and her telephone number. I haven't contacted her because I thought you would want to do that yourself?'

Mrs Mac sounded pretty pleased with herself, and I couldn't hold that against her for one minute, but at the

312

same time I couldn't find it in me to care about what she was saying. I just wanted to crawl into my bed and sleep. I'd lost too much and none of this mattered to me any more. It seemed to me that nobody cared about anybody for very long. I was certainly done caring. I was pretty sure that Gillian wouldn't care either about some old girlfriend from twenty years ago. It was all a stupid dream and I was finished with it.

The voice carried on happily jabbering away but I cut across her:

'I'm sorry to have wasted your time, Mrs Mac, but there's no point me talking to Gillian. It was a dumb idea.' My tone was sharper than I'd intended but I just wanted her to go away.

'Are you sure about that? I thought you were keen to pass on that mysterious box of yours?'

'Turns out it was just a pile of junk so there's no need . . .'

'Oh . . . well . . . that's certainly disappointing to hear. Are you sure you don't want the address in case you change your mind?'

'I'm sure, Mrs Mac. There's really no point.'

'Is everything OK, Ava? You don't seem—'

She was still talking when I hung up. The moment the phone hit the cradle, I sank down to the floor with my back against the wall, put my head in my hands and wept.

26

Paris, 1955

I set off for Paris at the beginning of September. I'd arranged to stay my first few nights in a small hotel on the Left Bank, and then to take lodgings somewhere more permanent when I settled in a bit. I had no firm plans and I wasn't particularly interested in making any. My ticket was open-ended and my savings were enough to live on for a while if I was careful. After that, I really didn't care.

From the outside, the small hotel was pleasing, a sort of grand sand-coloured building with beautiful ornate windows and black metal Juliet balconies. I imagined them in summer bursting with window boxes crammed with red geraniums, and I couldn't wait to see my room.

I was instantly disappointed. The lobby was dark with a strange musty aroma. The woman sitting behind the front desk spoke little English, and appeared sombre with her black dress and white cuffs. She didn't smile, nor was she at all friendly. She was reasonably polite and called me 'madame', but she reeled off the list of rules in a mixture of French and the little English that she knew.

'No visitors . . . *Comprenez, madame?*'

I presumed she expected a single American to be inviting back a long line of Parisian men to share the long winter nights, given the stern tone of her voice. She rattled off instructions about hot water, which appeared to involve not using it if at all possible. She then handed me a large brass key with a red fringe attached to it, rather like the kind of thing you see on heavy drapes, and pointed to the smallest elevator I'd ever seen. It was nothing more than a tiny metal cage. The elevator held precisely one decent-sized person and seemed reluctant, to say the least.

My room was small with a poky little window looking over the back alley and the orange-red rooftops beyond. I reminded myself they were at least Parisian rooftops but it seemed little consolation. The whole thing was desolate and grey, and not at all how I'd imagined it. It was perfectly light outside, but my room was already filled with shadows, and barely enough light to read a newspaper by.

I flicked a switch and a dim yellow bulb glowed briefly; then it flickered twice and died. Everything felt cold and slightly damp, although in one corner stood a small fireplace. I searched the surrounding closets hopefully but there was nothing to burn. I laid my bags out on the floor and sank on to the single bed. It felt lumpy in strange places, as if moulded to unfamiliar bodies over the years. The sheets were starched and white but the quilt was thin and worn; it had been patched many times by the look of it. It too smelled of damp. I hung my coat and headscarf on a hook on the back of the door, and went down the hall to investigate the shower. Behind a dark wooden door marked with a picture of a bathtub lay a strange-looking contraption with a metal bar and a hose strung across the top of a tub, with one rusty-looking faucet attached to it. It was unlike anything that I'd ever seen before, and I dreaded to think how it would work, or whether there would be hot water.

It was nearly dinner time and, after freshening up my face and hands, I made my way downstairs to the hotel dining room, which was bare and austere-looking, with two or three small wooden tables and chairs, and a lop-sided portrait of a stern-featured elderly woman on the far wall. A young woman also dressed in a black dress with white cuffs and a white apron brought in a bowl of onion soup and good French bread. I broke off large chunks and stuffed them greedily into my mouth. After the soup came stringy pork chops swimming in a greasy sauce, and then some sort of milky pudding that tasted of nothing in particular. The meal was followed by undrinkable coffee that tasted of chicory. There was nobody else dining and the only sounds were the soft pad of the waitress's shoes and my breathing. I ached for home.

When I finally turned in for the night the room was so dark, I felt quite frightened by its strangeness, and I deliberately left the thick dusty drapes open a crack, so the moonlight could comfort me a little. I tossed and turned on the lumpy old mattress and wished Gillian were with me so we could laugh about it. I was finally in Paris, but I felt so tired and lonely that I couldn't say I was happy to be there. My fingers clutched at the butterfly necklace at my throat.

The morning after I first kissed Gillian, I'd woken up to find she was gone. There was a scribbled note telling me she needed to see Paul. I waited for two hours hoping she would telephone, but there was nothing. I was in a desperate panic about things, and I started to cry, fearful little tears which I furiously wiped away. I gave myself a good talking-to and made some coffee to calm myself down.

Sometime later, having wiped my face dry and examined my red and now slightly puffy eyes in my compact mirror, I tried to hide the worst of it by dabbing face powder over my nose and under my eyes, but it was clear that nothing much was going to help. I buttoned my coat tightly at the throat and, shoving my hands deep into my pockets, I slipped out of the college grounds and past the large iron gates. I decided against returning to our room after I'd finished my errands and carried on past the turn that led up to the college campus, and kept on walking.

I must have walked around for hours and hours, because I heard a clock chime, and as I walked briskly up the street past the bookstore, I noticed that it was already packing away for the night, and a restaurant had started to light candles for the evening crowd.

At the top of the street, I turned left and found myself

in front of a small second-hand jewellery store that I'd never noticed before. Its window was full of slightly tarnished pearls and ropes of jet beads in flapper style; in one corner stood a jewelled headdress with inky-blue ostrich feathers and a large black stone at the centre. Everything seemed dulled with age and I could see many of the shabby strings were frayed, so the creamy pearls might all tumble on to the floor if you tried to fasten them at the neck. I wondered who had owned them; imagined their lives, the dinners those pearls went to, a wedding day.

I was about to walk away when I spotted a necklace on a fine silver chain comprising three bright yellow enamel butterflies, one large and two smaller butterflies on either side. It gleamed in the dimly lit shop window, and something about it made me want to run my fingers over the delicate wings. It was far too bright for me to wear and it wouldn't match my uniform of khaki slacks or black wool skirts at all, but for some reason I couldn't walk away. I wasn't the kind of woman who would wear a bright necklace of yellow butterflies, or run away to sit at a Parisian café, or break the rules in any way. I was never very special or able, and hiding away in an English classroom playing it safe seemed the extent of my abilities. Certainly, I was lonely and sad and hungry, with feet that ached from walking over the town all day, but I felt more alive than ever, and I'd found my way here. I hesitated and then pressed the door handle, and it opened with the sound of a bell clanging.

A man wearing a grey suit stood behind a glass counter and seemed surprised to see me.

'Are you still open?' I offered timidly.

'We have just closed.' He pointed to a sign that I hadn't noticed on the front door that said so. I sighed but I didn't move.

'I'm very sorry to keep you but I would like to look at the butterfly necklace in your window. I'll be very quick, I promise.'

The man shrugged as if it made no difference to him what I did and walked towards the window. I felt brave for not having walked away from something that I wanted, and it felt good. He returned with the delicate butterflies dangling from his fingers into the palm of his hand.

'Here you are. It's a very nice piece and we only got it in last week.'

I reached for the butterfly necklace and ran my fingers over the wings, touching the delicate wire tips, and then fumbled a little with the tiny silver catch.

'Allow me, miss.'

The man swiftly unhooked the clasp and I turned for him to fasten the necklace around my neck, patting the butterflies gently as they lay below my throat.

'Here – you can see.' The man held up a mirror and I took it from his hand and admired the gleaming butterflies. They seemed to take flight with every movement of my neck and I smiled.

'I'll take it.'

And just like that I knew I wanted the necklace no matter what the price, which as it turned out was not all that much. As the door to the jewellery store clicked shut behind me, I felt lighter somehow, and for the first time since I'd woken up that day, I felt capable of doing something other than walking the streets feeling in low spirits.

When I got back to the campus, there was a light at my window and I raced up the steps and down the corridor. As I fumbled with the door, it opened, causing me to almost fall into our room, and there was Gillian, smiling.

'I decided to stay,' she said.

'I bought you something.' I was rambling, unable to think straight, but I pulled out the little blue velvet bag. 'I want you to have this.'

Gillian carefully opened the velvet bag and tipped the butterfly necklace into the palm of her hand.

'It's beautiful.'

She leaned across and kissed me. There was no need for words.

A chink of grey light peeped through the crack in the dusty drapes and the pitter-pat of steady drizzle beat against the window, as every so often a gust of wind rattled the glass pane. A thick mist of condensation clung to the inside of the glass and the room felt cold. I felt so lonely and the memories of the early days with Gillian made me ache for the feel of her.

Wrapping my winter coat over my pyjamas, I tiptoed down the hallway to use the bathroom, not wishing to run into whoever my neighbours might be. A tepid shower later, I dressed in a thick pair of pants, a red sweater, and laced up my stout walking shoes. I fastened the yellow butterfly necklace and tucked it under my sweater. I liked to wear it so other people couldn't see it, but I knew it was there.

I decided to avoid the bleak dining room and whatever was on offer for breakfast, and tied my headscarf firmly under my chin and headed out into the rain. Now it was daylight, albeit somewhat grey and wet, I took a few seconds outside the hotel to inspect the street. There was an old church directly opposite the hotel with gargoyles grinning down at me; next to that was a pretty bookstore with boxes of old books set outside on a wooden table and covered by a green tarpaulin to keep the rain off. I took a left turn and kept on walking briskly, my hands shoved deep into my pockets to keep out the chill as I'd forgotten my gloves.

I marvelled at the windows of cheese shops, and bakeries with the most delicate jewels of cakes all laid out on silver trays, and stopped to watch butchers slamming carcasses down on to chopping blocks and wiping their hands on their bloody aprons. It was thrilling to hear French spoken all around me, greetings of '*Bonjour*' and the chatter of shopkeepers as they pulled down their awnings to keep out the rain.

Parisian women strolled around with little wicker

baskets nestled in the crook of their arms and a brightly coloured scarf casually thrown around their necks. Occasionally a *grande dame* would stroll along the boulevard with a small dog on a lead, and a beautiful hat, or an extravagant cape in forest green, or navy blue. They had an elegance that I would never possess if I lived here a hundred years, but walking along the same streets as them made me stand a little taller.

At the end of the street the road draped down towards the Café de Flore and I headed towards it. I hesitated at the door, unsure and slightly afraid to go inside on my own. I wished for the millionth time since I'd left New York that Gillian was here. The windows were slightly steamed up with the heat of chattering crowds and hot drinks. I put my hand on the door, but I couldn't bring myself to go inside on my own. I felt foolish, and ashamed to be so alone.

I must have been walking for hours, and possibly going in circles, as I was sure I'd passed some buildings at least once before. My feet were starting to ache and a wave of tiredness overtook me. The greyish light of day was starting to become the purple dusk of evening and the cafés and restaurants were starting to fill up with diners. Little orange lights glowed with welcome but everywhere I looked there were couples or families all together, drinking wine or eating delicious plates of food. Nobody seemed to be alone, except in one or two places where some gentleman sat with a brandy or reading a newspaper.

I wanted to be brave and slide into a small pavement table, resting my aching feet and sipping on a *pastis*, but I couldn't find the courage to do it. I couldn't face steeling myself to go inside, and suffer the stares or being made to feel stupid and childish by the waiters, and so I limped on for a while, before turning into a narrow, cobbled street and finding myself in front of the church opposite my hotel. I'd no idea that I was even close to where I started out that morning, as I must have walked in a complete circle.

I stood in front of the church, looking up at the gargoyles. The exotic stone beasts on the side of the church were craning their devilish necks, and I could see their snarling mouths far above me. The church doors were flung open, and I walked inside, finding it empty and all the better for that. It was so empty I could hear my footsteps echo a little, and the beauty of the votive candles flickering in front of the altar were an invitation.

There was a high vaulted ceiling and brightly coloured glass in the windows; the wooden pews were set inbetween thick, mountainous pillars, and I walked slowly down the aisle towards a white stone figure of the Madonna at the very front of the altar. I slipped into the front pew glad to rest my body and aching feet.

A feeling of loneliness crept over me and I couldn't shake it off any longer. I'd dreamed of visiting Paris my whole life but now I was here all I felt was alone and miserable, and a little homesick. Nothing brought me comfort and I couldn't help wondering where Gillian was, and what she was doing.

I sat back against the wooden pew, which creaked a little, and looked up towards the white stone Madonna, her face so full of kindness and her arms thrown open, and for the first time since Gillian and I parted, I started to cry. Somehow the loss of Gillian felt more real sitting in an empty church, thousands of miles from home. Tears ran down my cheeks and dripped on to my coat. I wiped them away but more came. Something that had been frozen deep inside me unlocked and I couldn't stop. I ached with loneliness; my heart was so broken it would never mend, and for the first time in my life I felt hopeless. Tears poured out and there was nothing I could do to prevent them falling. I cried for the loss of Gillian but also for my disappointment, for the Paris I'd dreamed about and now couldn't find. I cried because I was lonely, and because nobody would ever love me again. I cried for all the hopes I'd had, and the secrets we'd struggled to keep. I felt as if I would never be able to stop.

I couldn't imagine one day where I might be happy, or even sad in an ordinary way. I'd run away, but I couldn't seem to forget.

27

New York City, 1975

It was over a month since the pool party and my mind felt as though it was wrapped in grey clouds.

I lay around on my bed all day long listening to sad songs. I couldn't seem to get motivated to do anything much. I couldn't even say that I felt sad about things, because, honestly, I didn't feel much of anything. I got up in the morning, took a shower and put on some clothes, but apart from that my life was one long blank space. My dad and Candy turned up from time to time but mostly I liked being alone. Staring at walls was the one thing I was getting good at. I'd shoved the box under my bed so I didn't have to look at it. I thought every day about stuffing it in the trash.

It was my last visit to see my mother in the patients' lounge. She'd finished her electric shock treatments and would start coming home for weekends so we could see how that went. If it all went well, she would come home for good. I wasn't sure how that was going to work out as there was the small problem of Candy to solve, but there was a way to go before we faced that.

There was an end-of-summer storm brewing and the strip lights were all on in the patients' lounge owing to the dark clouds that had sucked all the light out of the city. It made everyone's skin look slightly jaundiced and unwell. My mom smiled when she saw me coming. She did this when I arrived, and it was a good sign that she recognized me and was reasonably pleased to see me. I smiled in return, a forced, polite offering, because I'd grown to hate this place. It made my skin crawl every time I walked the corridors and heard the cries of someone who was out of their mind, or smelled the stale, antiseptic odour of the rooms. I had to force myself to walk through the gates and sit down with my mother to make small talk.

'Hi, how are you?'

'I'm OK.'

Silence. Then more pointless questions.

'Yes, I'm fine . . . Yeah I'm going back to school soon.'

We shuffled our feet and stared at the floor, both lost in our own thoughts.

We went through our usual routine of the drinking of the awful coffee, and the eating of the sad cookies.

My mother wanted to show me the rag doll she'd made in therapy. It was finished, like the electric shock treatments, and she was proud of both, I guess. It was good, just as good as the ones you see in stores. The doll wore her little emerald-green dress and felt booties on her chunky little feet, her hair was all yellow wool tied in two braids, and her eyes were huge and saucer-like. It made me smile, and the really odd thing was I wanted it. I was way too old for dolls and wouldn't have wanted anyone from school to know about it, but I *really* wanted it.

I felt distracted and kind of numb, sitting there watching all the sad people eating their cookies. It occurred to me I might be that sad too, and the thought made me fidgety. I kept glancing up at the clock every few minutes, although my mother didn't seem to notice. She seemed calm enough but she didn't say much, and every time I asked her a question she said, 'Oh, I don't remember that.' They'd said the shock treatment might affect her memory, but it seemed to me that there were things that she didn't want to remember.

I set my cup back down on the trolley that was abandoned right next to where we were sitting. I was about to make my excuses and leave, but my mother started rambling on about a friend she'd made on the ward. Jeannette had tried to commit suicide by putting her head in the gas oven but she was much better now, my mother said. Jeannette also had visitors, her mother and her daughter, a stern-faced child with a furrowed brow and flame-red hair. The kid must have been around five or six years old, and she sat moodily in one corner, and from time to time eyed the plate of sad cookies on the tray next to me.

My mother waved and smiled her strange blank little smile. It was the kind of smile that was meant to make everyone think she was OK when it was quite clear that she wasn't. I couldn't stop looking at her and wondering about how she'd ended up here back in the summer of 1955. The words *unnatural activities* kept rolling through my mind.

'Hello there,' she called over to the little girl, who didn't reply, but instead eyed her warily and drummed her little feet against the edge of her chair. She reached across and clung to her mother's knee, but Jeannette was busy clinging to *her* mother's knee, and begging her to get her out of there, so nobody was taking much notice of the kid.

'Hello, what's your name?' My mother tried again and this time the child responded.

'Bernice,' she lisped.

'Bernice is a pretty name. Aren't you lucky?'

The child kept her eyes on my mother, as Jeannette was busy crying on her mother's shoulder, and not interested in her at that point. Then my mom leaned forward out of the sagging blue armchair and held out the rag doll towards the child.

'Do you like dolls, Bernice?'

Bernice was instantly in love. She shuffled her little bottom off the chair with some effort and walked over to my mother to take hold of the doll.

'Here, you take her home and look after her. You might as well have her. I don't have a little girl to give her to. Would you like that, Bernice?'

Bernice liked it. She grabbed the doll by her yellow wool braids and tucked her under one arm. She wandered back towards her own mother and climbed on to her chair, where she proceeded to bend the arms and legs of the rag doll into violent poses.

My mother carried on smiling with her weird, medicated smile, while I sat there sullen and raging inside. I was so angry with her for being sick and for not caring about me. It was as though I didn't exist as a child in her mind, let alone her own child. Even at nearly sixteen years old I was hurt by it, but as usual I said nothing. After a few more minutes we were all released by the sound of the bell that signified the end of visitors' hours, and I got to my feet and headed out of the door in double quick time.

I was glad to be outside even as the rain skittered off the sidewalk. I never wanted to walk through those hospital gates again for any reason, and I vowed that I would never go back, no matter what.

My dad needed to go see about some work so I made my own way home. It was raining so hard that I decided to get the bus downtown, and I tucked myself into the doorway of a liquor store to wait. There was a drunk homeless guy taking up the entire bus shelter, and he was casually waving a knife around, and yelling a lot, so I didn't want to get too close. Next door to the bus stop was Clancy's, which was doing good business with the rain, and it looked as though every table was full of coffee-drinkers and sandwich-eaters. I got lucky with the bus: one turned up within five minutes. The doors gasped open and I got on. It was crowded and I stood in the aisle clinging on to the strap and swaying from side to side as we crawled along the street. The windows were misted up with condensation and occasional circles where someone wiped their fist to clear it. You couldn't see much even then for all the rain outside.

I was relieved to be on my own and to get back to lying around on my bed playing music. I watched the rain hitting the window for a long time; I then stared at the ceiling and wondered what I was going to do with myself. The sound of the street-door buzzer split the air and I didn't move. I wasn't in the mood to talk to anyone and I wasn't expecting visitors. I was starting to wish my dad hadn't got it fixed.

BUZZZZZZ.

Whoever it was had their finger on the buzzer and they were not taking no for an answer. I sighed; there was only one person in my life that it could be.

I hadn't spoken to Viola since the day of the pool party. It wasn't so much that I was still mad with her, but more that I didn't have much to say to anyone right now. I rolled over on my bed and hoped she would go away, but the buzzing noise kept on going. I was going to have to answer the damn door or she would keep on going all day.

'I brought your T-shirt back. I laundered it and everything.' Viola smiled and offered my blue shirt to me as a peace offering. I dropped it on to my bed and sat down, leaving Viola standing there.

'You didn't bring your records?' I didn't really care but I was making conversation.

'I came to talk to you. I tried calling but nobody answered except one time when your dad picked up and said you weren't feeling well.'

'Yeah, I've been sick.' I was lying, and we both knew it.

We stared at the rug for a bit and the silence felt worse for it being Viola. Normally you couldn't keep her quiet and we spent most of our time laughing or play fighting with each other, but I didn't have the energy to try.

Viola sat down awkwardly on the edge of the bed and pinched my arm in that playful way we used to do. I shrugged my shoulders and looked away. Everything felt hard; talking was too much effort and it took all my energy just to get out of bed these days. I felt as though I was behind a curtain that separated me from the rest of the world.

'Ava, I'm sorry I upset you. You know me – I always have a smart mouth at the wrong time. I was trying to help but . . .'

I nodded but couldn't look at her. I wanted to pull the covers over my head and be left alone.

'OK . . . well, now that's out of the way I want you to tell me what's going on?'

'Nuthin's going on.' I really didn't feel like talking. I preferred the blankness to the uncomfortable feelings that were starting to emerge under the weight of Viola's gaze.

'We've been friends a long time, and you're not OK.

I've been trying to keep out of your business because sometimes people need a minute, but you've had your minute, and now I'm going to sit here until you tell me what's going on with you.'

Viola had that stubborn look on her face and I knew she wouldn't go until I started talking.

'I can't tell you.'

'Hey, I'm your friend,' Viola said softly and gave my hand a squeeze to let me know she meant it.

'C'mon, talk to me. I won't tell anyone, I swear.'

She crossed her heart with her fingers and sat there waiting.

I could feel the blankness inside me start to dissolve, and I didn't like it. If there wasn't the blank space then there were all the feelings I didn't want to feel right now. My bottom lip started to quiver and I focused on the raindrops racing each other down the window. Viola pressed my hand tightly.

'Hey, it's going to be OK.'

'Why do people *say* that?' I felt a flash of anger burst through the grey clouds of my mind.

'Because I don't know what's going on with you so I don't know what else to tell you.'

'There's nothing to talk about. You can't fix it.'

'Maybe nobody can fix things for us. But I'm your friend and I care about you so it's not about fixing stuff . . .'

She was still squeezing my hand and staring at me, as though she was waiting. My eyes prickled with tears and I couldn't hold out.

'My mom went crazy . . . They locked her up and gave her those electric shock treatments.'

Viola's mouth opened as if she wanted to say something but thought better of it.

'I think she's been sick for a long time. My dad doesn't care . . . and I've got nobody.' The tears started to trickle down my face and I wiped them away with the back of my hand.

'You should've told me.'

'I couldn't. It's so awful, Vi. That place they put her in is like the most hopeless place in the world, and every time I go in there, I worry I won't be able to find my way out. I'm so ashamed of having to go there. I didn't want anyone to know.'

'It's not your fault your mom's sick.'

'But it might be. I think there's something wrong with me.' The sobs came from somewhere down deep inside and I couldn't hold them back.

'Are you sick?' Viola looked scared.

'Not sick like that.'

'Then what do you mean?'

'Nobody cares what happens to me.'

'I care.'

Suddenly the dam broke and all the words came rushing out in one go.

'There must be something wrong with me. You don't know what it's been like . . . I was trying to look after her for so long on my own but I couldn't do it. I tried so hard to stop her going to pieces but now I don't know if she's ever going to get well and my dad doesn't even live here any more. He's shacked up with Candy Jackson . . .'

'Oh, man!' Viola gave a half-whistle under her breath.

'When she's around he barely notices I'm there.'

Viola's eyes widened.

'Wow, that's not good.'

'It doesn't matter. None of it matters. The problem is me. Don't you see?' I could feel my throat getting tight and my voice was starting to crack. My cheeks were wet with tears.

'None of this is your fault. You should've told me. I didn't know that things had got that bad for you.'

'I think I *did* this to them. I see the way your mom and dad are with you: the way they fuss around you and are always checking how you are.'

'That's mainly annoying, you know?'

'I can't remember the last time my mom and dad looked pleased to see me when I walked in the room. I'm always in the way. I see your mom and dad looking at you like it's Christmas when you arrive. You're so used to it that you don't even notice. I see it. Nobody looks at me that way, Vi.'

'D'you ever think maybe it's their fault? We're kids, Ava. We're not supposed to be taking care of people and fussing about them. That's their job.'

'But suppose it is my fault? I've tried so hard. I'm so tired all the time because I can't ever be me. I don't know what else to do . . . because I'm *never* enough.'

'But who else can you be? You're my best friend. You're funny . . . and smart . . . and kind.'

'And I really thought Cal liked me . . . but it was Mulkenny he was after. I feel so stupid and I'm so . . . *lonely*. I'm lonely like a big ache all the time.'

My face crumpled and the tears streamed down my cheeks and dripped off the end of my chin on to my shirt. Viola leaned across and squeezed my arm.

'You got me. You've been keeping this all wrapped up like it was a big dirty old secret. Your family is going through a tough time . . . and yeah, it didn't work out with Cal, but a lot of people are going to love you in your life and you *have* to believe that.'

I wiped my tears away and looked up at Viola. For once she was being deadly serious and I knew she meant every word and I so wanted to believe her.

'How do you know?' I whispered.

'Because I *know*.' She nodded, jutting out her little chin, determined and stubborn.

I exhaled and noticed, for the first time in a long time, that my breath wasn't jagged and caught up in my throat. Viola grinned at me and I managed a weak smile despite my tears.

'Thanks, Vi.'

'You don't need to thank me. I'm looking out for you, like you would do for me. So, if you ever feel like this again you tell me. Promise?'

I nodded meekly.

'Say you promise.'

'I promise. You're so bossy, Vi,' I said, giving her a watery grin.

'I know it. It's another talent I have.'

I smiled back at her. Viola curled up next to me on my bed and we lay there for a while staring at the ceiling.

'So, catch me up with your news. Did you find anything out about Gillian?'

I shook my head.

'Mrs Mac called after the pool party. She found Gillian's address. She changed her name so I guess she got married.'

'You *found* her? Wow! What did she say?' Viola sat up, her legs under her, and made herself comfortable on the end of the bed.

'I didn't write to her. I didn't take the address down.' I felt silly admitting it after the big fuss I'd made after the pool party.

'What are you waiting for? You seemed so obsessed with finding her. Damn, I can't believe you didn't run right over there.'

'I felt sad, I guess, and I dunno . . . I just . . . gave up. I wouldn't know what to say to her. I know you think I'm crazy for caring so much about these women but . . . it's hard to explain.'

'Well, try me, because I want to understand so we won't have to fall out again.'

I hesitated, my fingers picking at a thread on my sheet.

'I thought . . . I thought Gillian needed to know that she was *really loved* by somebody.'

Viola thought about it and then she turned to look at me.

'Ava, I think you're the one who needs to know that.'

I paused, thinking over what Viola said, and all the pieces started to fall into place.

'I hadn't thought about it like that.'

'You still got the box?'

'Yeah, it's right here.'

'If you like we could write a letter to Gillian? You want me to help . . . ?'

Viola was about to spring into action solving all the problems in her way and I loved her for it but it wasn't necessary. The grey clouds were gone and I felt a flicker of hope rushing through me. I took a deep breath and sat up straight.

'No, thanks, Vi. I'm going to call Mrs Mac and finish what I started.' I felt more determined than I had in weeks.

'You sure?'

I nodded, catching Viola's arm in a playful squeeze.

'I think I'd like to do this on my own. Gillian needs to know that Dovie was thinking about her right until the end. She deserves that. If she doesn't care . . . then fine, but I need to find her and tell her the box is here. After that it's her call. I need to do this for me.'

'You gonna be OK now?' Viola patted my arm.

'Yeah, I think so.' I smiled at her and her face broke out in to the widest grin.

'Great! Would it be OK if I hung on to our blue T-shirt until the Labor Day party?'

'OUR blue T-shirt?'

'Oh . . . did I say *our*?'

I picked up the blue shirt from the corner of the bed where I'd flung it down and threw it at Viola. She clutched it and headed towards the door, laughing as she went.

'You call me if you need to talk. You got that, right?'

'I got it. I'll call you tomorrow.'

'My mom's cooking mac and cheese. You wanna come over later? She's always happy to see you.'

I considered the prospect of mac and cheese with Viola's family all talking over each other and telling their crazy stories.

'I'm going to write the letter and then I'll come by. Vi . . . thanks for everything.'

Viola waved my blue shirt at me and was out of the door before I could say another word.

28

Paris, 1955

Le Conti on Rue de Buci was already crowded. Christine's friends were spread out over two or three tables at the back of the bar. Their winter coats were stacked high on a spindly wooden chair and the table tops were covered with small glasses of a pale amber-coloured liquid that I didn't recognize. They were a noisy group, all chattering over each other so much that it was impossible to understand what was going on. They held their cigarettes in elegant poses, although they rarely appeared to actually smoke them. Everyone seemed so much more sophisticated than anyone I'd known in New York. It was one month exactly since I had first laid eyes on Christine LeGrand, but my stay in Paris had already been transformed by her.

After a week of feeling pretty miserable in my gloomy little hotel, and a series of lonely meals in the awful dining room, I had decided that I would try to find a room that suited me. I wasn't ready to admit defeat and go back home, although every day I edged closer to it.

On the Monday morning as I walked along to a café to get some breakfast, I noticed a card had been placed in the window of the bookstore across the street from my hotel. It was all in French but I picked up one word – *chambre* – and hoped it was a room to let. I checked my appearance in the window of the bookstore, straightened my hair and rang the bell.

Christine opened her apartment door with a bright smile, and within minutes offered me her spare bedroom and I was overwhelmed with gratitude to be out of my dismal hotel room.

'American . . . yes?' She smiled.

'Yes.' I smiled back. She spoke little English and I spoke no French at all, but we managed through smiles and gestures to communicate, and the painstaking pace of our interactions somehow made it better. I felt less likely to say the wrong thing or speak too hastily; everything was measured and careful, and I liked it that way.

Standing awkwardly in the middle of her apartment, I spied a gramophone and then familiar faces: Charlie Parker and Miles Davies, Billie Holliday, and the Blue Stars – dozens of records in thin paper covers. My face lit up with pleasure, and we grinned at each other with the sheer delight of finding another person who loves as we do. From then on Christine practically adopted me, escorting me around Paris and taking me from one smoky dive to another.

We arranged to meet that evening in Le Conti, as Christine wanted to introduce me to her friends for the first time, and then she promised me a special surprise.

As Christine approached her group of friends, they all got to their feet and there was a lot of cheek-kissing that included me. I was still not used to this custom, and couldn't help but flinch slightly when a stranger firmly planted two kisses, one on each cheek, as if we'd known each other forever. A tall boy with a fringe that flopped over one eye soon found us a couple of chairs, and we squeezed around the table. The chattering and laughing rose and fell like waves, and I couldn't understand a word of it. My face ached a little from constantly smiling, because if I didn't smile it felt as if I was being unfriendly. It was a constant reminder that I was a stranger, and could expect nothing to be easy.

The boy with the floppy fringe liked Christine very much. I could tell by the way he sat very close to her, and hung on every word she said. If she drew out a cigarette from her pack, he leaned in close to light it, and I watched him trying too hard to impress her. What or who Christine liked was a mystery to me. We didn't have the language between us to discuss complicated subjects like relationships. Her apartment held few clues.

It consisted of one small space with two armchairs, a range of cushions scattered over the floor to sit on if extra chairs were needed; and what passed for a kitchenette. There was Christine's bedroom which was all white, and held her bed and small bedside table, a lamp with a lopsided shade on top of it, and a tiny closet that held Christine's very beautiful clothes, which she made herself.

As part of her job in a fancy dressmaker's, she was occasionally allowed to take home old season bolts of fabric, and one corner of her bedroom was taken up with a sewing machine and an enormous tin filled with all manner of coloured buttons. My room was smaller, with enough room for a single bed, and to make it seem welcoming Christine had set up a lamp perched high above the bed on the small windowsill. It gave the room a cosy light but meant I had to get out of bed to turn it on and off. There was a hook on the back of the door for some of my clothes, and Christine kindly offered me half her closet. It was clearly only going to be a temporary measure but until I made up my mind what I was going to do it felt like the closest thing to a home that I'd had in weeks.

There was a black and white photograph of a young man in uniform on the table by Christine's bed. When she caught me looking at it, Christine said softly, '*Il est mort.*' Other than that I knew very little about her.

Christine quickly introduced me to the crowd sitting around the tables: there were seven of them in all. The floppy-haired young man was called Luc; there were three girls: Béatrice, Marie and Éloïse; then three young men who were obviously partnered with them in some way: Bertrand, Jean-Paul and Claude.

More drinks were fetched from the bar and the aniseed drink made me feel a little sick. From time to time, Christine glanced up at me and smiled. She asked 'OK?'

342

and took a moment to check that I was. I felt like a child in a room of adults. I couldn't understand how things worked, and could only pick out the simplest of words, like *merci* or *oui*. I focused on the room and the chatter, the strangeness of it and the very fact that I was here, at long last, in Paris. That quickly led to thoughts of Gillian, but that was another life.

They talked over each other with constant interruptions and loud bursts of laughter until eventually the chatter subsided, drinks were finished, and coats and scarves fastened tightly to go back out into the cold night. It was dry but there was a distinct chill in the air and the possibility of an overnight frost. I slipped on my winter coat and fastened it, remembering to pick up my gloves from the table. Christine leaned over and whispered to me:

'We go to Le Tabou.'

'Where?' I asked although I was sure I wouldn't understand the answer.

'Le Tabou is . . . er . . .' Christine made a gesture. I pulled a face, and Christine obviously gauged my reaction and realized that I didn't understand, so she squeezed my arm affectionately and said, 'Jazz . . .'

I was cheered by the word straight away. *Jazz* meant loud music and the ability to lose myself in that, and not have to smile and nod at conversations I couldn't understand.

As it turned out, the club Le Tabou was only a few yards away, and we linked arms as we spread across the road, annoying passers-by and giggling so much that for the first time I felt a small sense of belonging. Christine grabbed my right arm and Béatrice was on my left. She had been a nurse during the war and spoke much better English than the others, and for the few minutes that it took to wander down the street towards Le Tabou, I felt the ease of being able to speak freely again.

'Are you enjoying Paris?' she asked in that dutiful way that people do when they feel that they have to say something to you.

'Yes, I think so, but it's all very strange to me.'

'Of course . . . Christine is a very good person, you know?'

I thought it was an odd thing to say and I was quick to respond.

'Oh yes. She's been a great help.'

'It's nice for her to have company too. She is alone too much, I think.'

I didn't quite know how to respond to that so I just nodded. Béatrice smiled.

'You will like Le Tabou. It is very good fun.'

I could see a large crowd gathered outside a doorway, and a neon sign with 'Le Tabou' set out in lights. As we got closer, a black and white chequered car drove up with horns blasting and people jumped out of every door; and before long there was a crush of people trying to get in to one small wooden doorway.

Above the wooden door were large windows covered in muslins, which made it look as if an ordinary family were living there. Downstairs were two wooden doors side by side, and two glowing orange lamps on either side of them. Claude and Éloïse started to run and, because our arms were all joined together, we were dragged along behind them. At one point I almost lost my footing but was saved by Christine steadying me on the other side, and we joined the back of the crowd to get in.

I held on to Christine for dear life as the crowd jerked forward, spilling through the doorway, and then found myself at the top of some rather steep-looking steps. A long dark rail fixed down the side of the stairs gave some support at least, and over the top of the stairs were some strange-looking drawings of a cat-like face or some kind of hieroglyphs. The stairs were filled with people trying to get down to where the music was blasting out from a small stage at the far end, and another line of people who were desperately trying to get back up.

Standing right in the centre of the stairs was a man in a sharp-looking suit who was trying to chat to one of the women on her way to the bathroom, with a predictable result. There was a lot of exclaiming and shouting until the man moved on, and, like a cork being released from a bottle, we all stumbled down the stairs and into the main room of Le Tabou.

I'd never seen anything like it in my life. It was obviously no more than an old cellar with a vaulted ceiling; half of it was exposed brick, and much of the old brickwork had been painted on or written over. It was a sprawling mass of coloured figures and strange patterns. Tucked away at the farthest part of the club was the smallest stage I'd ever seen. There was room for a piano and a bass, but other than that musicians fought with each other for enough room to hold their instruments aloft, which somehow miraculously they found. There were two large stone steps that led up to the stage, and it was on these that musicians played, and the girls who wanted to get close to them perched awkwardly.

The noise was incredible, the music sharp and piercing, the chatter matching it, and the air hung thick with smoke, mingling with the spilled drinks and the sweat of hardworking musicians. Right in front of the stage was a small area for dancing. Tables and chairs were shoved back against the walls, and a young man threw a girl high up into the air, and then spun her wildly.

The crowd was a mixture of black and white faces. If the players were good, they stopped chatting to each other; if the players were average, they carried on talking. There were girls but all escorted by boys. I couldn't see any woman on her own or even with other girls. The whole place had an aroma of maleness, of sweat and smoke accompanied by the sound of brass instruments blown sweetly into the night. In dark corners men held their girls close and nestled into them, their fingers working a spine along with the double bass.

At the opposite end from the stage was a bar with overworked staff who worked at a breakneck pace, gathering dirty glasses to wash them just in time to fill them up again and again. There was a never-ending parade of dark-suited young men lining up in front of them.

Claude and Éloïse shoved their way through the crowd, clearing a space for the rest of us to follow behind them. They got to the edge of the dance floor and found a small space with one table and one chair. We occupied the space swiftly, and then set out to find other chairs to overwhelm those next to us and make them move. It was an effective tactic if not a particularly friendly one.

It took a little while but eventually we all squeezed in, even if Béatrice and Marie had to sit on Bertrand and Jean-Paul's laps. Luc offered Christine a lap as the spare chair was ceremoniously given over to me as a guest. She declined and squeezed on to half the chair next to me.

Opposite us another crowd of people were wearing funny paper hats, and one of their party was standing on top of a beer barrel pretending to be a rabbit. On the stage a young man in a grey jacket was bent over the piano, his face indicating he was blissfully unaware of anything except the sound his fingertips made on the keys. His eyes were closed. Christine squeezed my arm and pointed to the side of the stage and I gasped with delight.

A young man stepped up to the stage and put a gleaming golden trumpet to his lips; the crowd went wild, shouting, cheering and slapping their table tops as he started to play. His shirt was dark, the cuffs fastened neatly around his slim wrists; the spotlight caught the sharp angles of his face and his slick black hair.

'Hi . . . um . . . *Bonjour* . . . hey . . . It's good to be here. Anyway, this is a new song called "Rondette". Hope you like it.' He paused to acknowledge the crowd, and then nodded to the piano player and off they went. I couldn't believe my eyes, and for a split second I thought there was some mistake, but Christine whispered into my ear:

'Surprise, *oui*?'

I grinned back at her. A surprise was not the word for sitting so close to Chet Baker and Dick Twardzik that I could see the beads of perspiration building on their skin. The trumpet notes shot through the crowded cellar, and then there was silence, and we all let the sharp notes linger and fall. Cigarettes were offered and lit, drinks refilled, but I stared in wonder at the stage as one song bled into another. Applause came and went, and the music flowed, frenzied at first, and then soft and gentle as they were spent. On and on they played, lulling the crowd, finishing with a beautiful version of 'Summertime', and the crowd went wild, cheering and clapping.

'Thanks, and we'll be seeing ya,' Chet said as he clipped his trumpet back into its black case.

They disappeared into the crowd and all I could see was a wave of hands slapping their backs as they left.

Some new players took the stage and Luc asked Christine to dance but she didn't want to, so he asked Éloïse and for a time ended up dancing with both her and Claude; they twirled her round and round until she was dizzy. Béatrice and Bertrand were kissing in the farthest corner and Jean-Paul and Marie had disappeared to the bar. For a few minutes I sat watching Luc and Claude spinning Éloïse into more frenzied shapes; Christine and I were alone, but she didn't move from the seat we were sharing even though there was more space now that the evening was coming to a close. She stayed right by my side.

Eventually Éloïse got bored being twirled around the dance floor and collapsed into a heap on the seat next to us. Christine finished her drink and gestured to the others that we were leaving. We rescued our coats from the corner where we'd thrown them. They were crumpled and smelled of smoke, but we shook them out and fastened them up. We gently pushed our way towards the back of the room and up the steep steps once again. There were fewer people gathered on the stairs on the way out, but we did have to duck under the arm of a man determined not to let one poor girl get by on her way to the cloakroom, until with a determined shove she freed herself and he almost toppled down the stairs. They both seemed to find it all funny though, and we could hear them laughing as we tumbled out on to the sidewalk.

The cold night air hit us but to be able to breathe something other than smoke was refreshing. Luc walked steadily by Christine's side, insisting on escorting us home. He planted his hand across Christine's arm in a proprietorial manner, trapping her arm through his, but she didn't seem to mind. We walked along streets that I didn't recognize, but then I saw the *boulangerie* with the bread basket made out of clay in the window, and I knew that we were very nearly home. I felt awkward suddenly, as if I was in the way. I wasn't sure whether Christine wanted to be alone with Luc but when we reached the front door she didn't hesitate at all.

'*Bonne nuit*, Luc,' she whispered and kissed him on both cheeks. I didn't step forward to kiss him but nodded in his general direction.

He laughed, clutched at his chest, and gave an exaggerated bow in the middle of the street; then he wandered off back in the direction of the *boulangerie*, whistling, with his hands shoved deep into his coat pockets. Christine fumbled around for her keys, and then we were inside scraping back the old iron gate of the elevator, which creaked and groaned its way to the top floor. Christine closed her eyes and held her hands together in a mock prayer until the metal cage finally arrived at its destination.

Once safely inside her apartment she busied herself turning on the lamps in the living room. They threw out a dim yellow glow, and she threw herself down in one of the chairs without taking off her coat. Her eyes closed, her arms thrown over the sides of the chair and her legs splayed, she looked like a strange rag-doll-like creature, and then she opened her eyes and smiled up at me.

'You enjoyed?' she asked.

'Yes, of course, it was wonderful to see Chet Baker.'

Christine nodded.

'You've been so kind to me. I really can't thank you enough.' I wanted to speak her language so I could explain myself, but we made do with smiles and gestures. Christine leaped from the chair and went into the kitchen. She returned with two small glasses which she filled with a finger of brandy each. She handed me one and I held on to it with both hands, cradling it between my palms and trying to think of some way to tell Christine what I was doing in Paris.

When I looked up, I realized Christine was watching me. She smiled and drank a little of her brandy. I shrugged, unable to find the words.

'I think . . . we are . . . the same,' she said.

Then she touched her heart and mimed a breaking of it into two pieces. I bit my bottom lip because I could feel tears welling in my eyes. I could only nod.

'The same. *Tu comprends?*

'Yes,' I whispered. My throat felt so tight that I could barely speak. 'Luc likes you.' I don't know why I said it because it was none of my business.

'Luc is my friend. He waits . . . There is someone . . . ?'

I nodded because I didn't have the words to explain about Gillian, and I didn't even know what I would explain, or even if I should. Christine looked at me for the longest time.

'In America . . . yes?'

'No, there was, but there's nothing left for me in America.'

Christine leaned towards me and raised her glass.

'Then you can stay.'

29

New York City, 1975

I'd been back at school for a few months now, a year older and maybe a little bit wiser in some things. I'd turned sixteen, although it wasn't much of a birthday. Viola and I were still making our own way through the tribes of cool and uncool, popular and unpopular, fitting in nowhere except with each other. But, honestly, I didn't even mind any more.

I could see a familiar young couple sitting together at the back of the bus, their faces serious and grim. Cal was still with Barbara Mulkenny, and gossip flooded the school lunch breaks that they had 'done it' over the summer. Rumours were rife that Barbara had recently gotten an abortion in some upstate clinic that her father paid for. I had no idea if the gossip was true or not, but her reputation was trashed and she looked different now. I thought back to the day of the pool party when she'd shone with a glow about her, with her perfect long red hair and her perfect yellow gingham bikini. She and Cal had both seemed kind of golden that day, touched by something extraordinary, and I had envied it and studied it but to no avail. It couldn't be replicated. You either had it or you didn't.

This was the first time I'd seen her for a while. She was late starting the semester, which didn't help the rumours of what she'd been up to over the summer. The girls who had been her friends sniggered as she walked by. She was always with Cal, their arms wrapped around each other. I couldn't help but look at her while the bus jerked to a stop and people got on and off. Her beautiful red hair was cut short and her face was pale, greasy, with a few pimples scattered across her forehead. Cal leaned over her as though he wanted to protect her. I couldn't even be jealous about it because she seemed so unhappy. I carried on with my furtive glances all the way to my stop, making sure I got off one stop earlier than I knew they would. I had no wish for an awkward conversation, but I couldn't take my eyes off them the entire journey.

By the time I reached our apartment, the rain had eased a little, but the threat of more was ever present. The apartment felt damp and cold. The old green radiator felt warm to touch but it wasn't doing much for the actual temperature of the room. I lit the gas and opened the oven door to let the heat out. On many cold nights Viola and I drew up the kitchen chairs and sat toasting our feet in front of the open oven door as we drank mugs of hot chocolate and gossiped about the state of our lives. It would take a while to warm the place up and

I pulled a navy sweater from the drying rack. It didn't look the best but at least I was warm. I let the oven do its work and headed off to my bedroom, where I sat in front of my mirror fixing my damp hair into a ponytail, because I didn't want to think about my meeting.

It had taken weeks to get Gillian to agree to talk to me. I wrote three letters in all, and it was only after the final letter that she wrote back and agreed to collect Dovie's things. We spoke briefly in an awkward phone call to confirm what time she might come around.

I didn't want to look like I was dressed up for the occasion, but on the other hand I was worried about looking like a crazy person who stalked people. I decided that jeans coupled with the sweater were serious but casual, and that was the look I was trying to convey. I rubbed some balm across my chapped lips and headed back into the kitchen, which felt considerably warmer with the oven blasting out heat.

Outside, a howling gust of wind rattled the windowpanes. A couple of street kids were pretending to be Ali v Frazier, throwing knuckly fists and jumping around in the puddles to try and avoid each other. I watched them for a while and fidgeted while I waited.

Eventually, out of a need to distract myself, I cleared the coffee table of its usual mess: unread newspapers and back copies of *Seventeen*, which Viola and I pored over for hints and tips on how to be like other girls. Wandering between the kitchen and the living room, I picked up the telephone receiver to check the dial tone was working, in case Gillian was trying to call me for some reason. Unable to settle, I kept checking out of the window, watching for her to arrive.

As I fiddled about with my ponytail, constantly tightening it until my scalp ached, I wondered what Gillian might say. I felt nervous, as if this was a date, and I might be found wanting in some way. I didn't know what I would say to her or how she might act.

I filled the coffee pot and laid out Dovie's box on the floor beside the table as I waited for the doorbell to ring. Then I straightened the yellow cushion and paced around the living room.

Glancing out of the window again, I saw a dirty yellow Pontiac crawl up the kerb and make a stop right outside our building. The cups were trembling in their saucers as I set them out on a wooden tray and I heard a car door slam shut. A moment later the buzzer sounded. I kicked the oven door shut with my foot and ran down the stairs to make sure I got there before she could change her mind.

I opened the door and there stood Gillian McNichol. It was strange to see the face that I recognized from the photographs in Dovie's box, slightly worn and creased around the eyes. She was wearing a trench coat belted at the waist and a pair of long black boots. A wool beret was placed at a strange angle on her head, so it kept her ears warm, but it made her look slightly eccentric.

'Hi . . . Ava? I'm Gillian. We spoke on the telephone.' Her voice shook a little and it occurred to me that she might have rehearsed this part.

'Please, come on up.' I kept my voice deliberately low in case Miss Schnagl had skipped her regular committee meeting and might suddenly appear in front of us. I moved quickly past the neat line of green mailboxes and up the stairs, leaving Gillian to follow on behind me. I was halfway up the stairs when I foolishly said, 'It's not that much further,' before realizing how dumb I was. 'Oh, of course you know that. I'm sorry,' I added ruefully.

'It still looks the same after all this time.' Gillian sounded wistful. 'You're so young. I thought you would be older.' She stood in the doorway to our living room, hesitating, as if she'd been trapped somehow.

'I'm sixteen . . .' I felt shy suddenly, as if I'd failed a test.

'I don't understand. What made you want to find me?'

It seemed as if she might run away at any moment and I did the only thing I could think of.

'I can make some coffee if you'd like some? I can explain everything, I promise.' I sounded more confident than I felt and for a moment I sensed Gillian soften; she moved towards our old couch and sat down awkwardly with her coat still buttoned all the way to her throat and her knees tightly pressed together.

The coffee pot made its little spitting noises to tell me it was ready. I opened the oven door while I was there, feeling embarrassed at how cold the apartment was. I wondered if it looked better or worse than when Gillian lived here and what she might think of it now, but I didn't ask.

I carried the tray of coffee and set it down in front of Gillian. As I poured her a cup, she watched me, carefully. I was a kid as far as she was concerned.

'Can I ask you something?' I said softly.

She looked surprised, as if I couldn't possibly have questions, but she nodded reluctantly.

'What was she like?' I asked.

'Dovie?' Gillian stared into her coffee cup for several seconds and then she smiled to herself. 'I haven't talked about her in a long time. She was kind but a bit too much, y'know? Used to drive me crazy that she couldn't say no to people in case they got upset with her. She always needed to be loved by everyone in the room. She liked to laugh, and she could make so many plans for the future, you wanted to believe her.' Gillian chuckled to herself and I could tell she was back there with Dovie, sitting under the same yellowing ceiling and making plans for a future that never came.

'I wondered about her for so long. What happened to her. And to you, of course.'

'It was a terrible time and it ended badly. She lied to me and I felt such a terrible fool. I was heartbroken for a long time. Things were different in those days. I couldn't stand it. We were always afraid of getting caught. At least I was . . .'

Gillian paused and for a moment stared around the room. She shook her head and smiled.

'So she got to Paris after all . . . We always talked about it. We used to play this game where we would make believe that we lived there . . . and she did it. Dovie was always much braver than me.'

'If you'd been caught, what would've happened to you?' I couldn't bear to hear the answer but I needed to know.

'It depended on who you were, but mostly women like us got fired from our jobs and prosecuted. Sometimes women were sent away to those awful mental hospitals for treatment. They tried to *cure* us. That was the idea that frightened me the most. They locked women away and gave them those electric shock treatments until they were cured. Some women never got released and others . . . well, they were broken, I guess. It could have happened to me. I came close to being caught and if I hadn't married Paul then . . . who knows?'

My face must have looked pained because Gillian put down her coffee cup and stared at me.

'Why do you ask?'

'No reason . . .'

She nodded, not believing a word of it, and waited.

I didn't want to say any more but I had to know. Ever since the day at the hospital when I'd overheard the doctor telling my dad about my mom's *unnatural activities* I'd known the truth somewhere deep inside me.

'It's just that . . . my mom's been in the hospital having that treatment and I heard . . . I heard the doctor tell my dad that she'd been there before, in the summer of

1955, for "unnatural activities" and I don't know . . . I mean I wondered . . . if . . .'

'Oh!' Gillian gnawed on her bottom lip trying to think of something to say.

'Do you think she was like you and Dovie?' The question just came out, garbled and rushed as if I hadn't expected it. I took a deep breath, needing to know the answer now.

'I can't tell you that. Women got locked away for lots of reasons. That's between you and your family but I'll tell you this much . . . if she was, then she couldn't help what happened to her. It was a horrible time. The government got it into their heads that we were the enemy and they did everything they could to hurt us.'

'I don't want to ask her about it,' I whispered.

'Oh, sweetie, she's your mom and nothing will change that. How's she doing?'

'She's getting better. They're letting her come home for weekends, but I don't know . . .'

I must have looked upset because Gillian leaned over and patted my arm in such a tender way that I felt tears well up and I cleared my throat to stop myself crying.

'What about your dad?'

I shook my head.

'I think it's just going to be me and my mom . . .'

Gillian nodded and looked at me with such kindness that I struggled to hold the tears back. She spoke softly.

'You should talk to her . . . when she's up to it.'

There are some questions that can't be answered and

some wounds that never heal. If my mother was like Dovie and Gillian I wondered if she might not be able to love me because I reminded her of a life she never wanted.

'I will . . . when it's the right time.' Even as I spoke the words, I wasn't sure that I would ever really do it.

For the first time since she arrived, Gillian seemed to relax a little, and she smiled at me.

I reached into the box and handed her the letter and the copy Viola had written out so carefully.

'This is the letter that came with the box. We got it translated and, well, you can read it for yourself.'

I pushed both copies of the letter into her hands and she reached into her purse and pulled out a red case with a pair of brown eyeglasses inside. Once she could read the letters clearly Gillian sat running her fingers across the paper until she understood every word on the page. When she had fully digested the contents, she nodded but didn't speak. She folded the letters up and slipped them inside her pocket. I didn't know what to say and so I watched as she held the warm coffee cup between her palms, occasionally sipping. She sat quite still with her coat all buttoned up, and the only sign of her discomfort was the way her eyes kept glancing up to look at me real quick, and then sweeping back down to stare at the floor again. She seemed to be searching for something to say, and I had no way to help her be comfortable with it, so I held my coffee cup between my palms to mirror her and waited.

'It's funny. You know, after you wrote to me, I tried to

track down Dovie's sister Franny. We've never met but I wanted to . . . I don't know . . . say something. Her youngest son Joel has started college, here at NYU. Anyway, he dropped me off right outside here . . . I wonder what Dovie would think if she knew that? Sorry, I'm rambling . . .'

Gillian shifted awkwardly in her seat, her voice cracking with emotion, and I chewed the inside of my cheek and said nothing. She unfastened her coat and pulled nervously at the sleeves.

I offered the coffee pot and refilled her cup while she settled in and carried on talking.

'I cried so hard when I read your letter. She got away and went to Paris. That was our dream for a long time. I don't know why she hated me so much in the end . . .'

Gillian gulped at her coffee and exhaled a long deep breath as if she'd been holding on to it for too long.

'What makes you think she hated you? I think she must have loved you very much to have kept all these things for so many years. She never forgot you.'

'But what she did to me . . .' Gillian's voice finally cracked under the strain and she stopped talking.

I couldn't put together the puzzle that was forming in my mind.

'But look at these letters.' I reached into the box and pulled out the crumpled sheets of paper. I smoothed them out and handed them over to Gillian: the half-written apologies and the declarations of love drawn out in ink.

Gillian went back to reading Dovie's words and then looked up at me, puzzled.

'I don't understand. Judith told me . . .'

'Judith told you what?'

Gillian stared around the room as if she was walking right into the past. Her face clouded over and she started to tell me what happened.

'From the minute I stepped inside our apartment it was clear to me that I was no longer welcome. There was no sign of Dovie, but Judith was standing guard by the door. She followed me from room to room, staring at me as I filled cardboard boxes with my belongings. Paul had driven me to the city in a truck he borrowed. We drove in silence all of the way. I told him I'd decided to move back home. What I didn't say, could never say, was her name . . .

'Oh, he busied himself carrying boxes down the stairs out to the truck. I carried on filling them up and eyeing Judith to check where she was and what she was doing. Then we were done. There was only one more box to fill. A small life had been packed away and I asked Paul to wait for me outside because there were things I needed to say to Judith, and I didn't want him to hear.'

Gillian paused and shook her head, took a deep breath and then carried on.

'I was biting my lip to stop myself crying. I would not cry in front of that woman. I hadn't slept at all since I'd spoken to Judith on the telephone and she'd told me Dovie wanted me to move out. My mother told me that Dovie had called me late one night but when I rang the apartment, I got Judith. I could scarcely believe the words coming out of her mouth.

'"I want you to know that I'm just passing on the message so . . . I don't want you to think badly of me," she said. I could hear the victory in her voice and it broke my heart.'

Gillian exhaled softly. I nodded encouragement at her and she got to her feet and walked over to the window.

'Well, Judith seemed nervous and kept trying to hurry me along but I wouldn't be hurried. ·

'"If that's everything . . ." Her voice sounded anxious and I wondered why this was bothering her so much.

'"I'll go when I'm good and ready," I snapped.

'"You should leave your keys with me." Judith's voice was calm but I could tell she was angry.

'"You're enjoying this, aren't you?" I turned out the contents of my closet drawer into the box and in the process knocked my purse off the bed and on to the floor.

'"There's no need to take that tone with me," she snapped back. Her eyes were flashing with anger. Really nasty . . .

'"You've been trying to come between Dovie and me since the day you blackmailed your way in here . . ." I said to her.

'The contents of my purse had spilled over the rug and I knelt down to collect them. Judith took a step towards me and I found myself on my knees staring up at her and then . . .'

Gillian put her hands to her face as if it was too painful to continue.

'What did she say?' I whispered.

'She looked straight at me in that angry, mean way of hers and said:

'"Oh no, Gillian, you've got it all wrong. Dovie wanted me to move in here. I didn't blackmail anyone. She was quite happy about it. We've been friends for a long time. She just couldn't bring herself to tell you about it. You know how she hates to upset people? Lately, though, she's come to see she really would be better off without you. I told her you wouldn't react well. You've always been *nasty*. You're no good for her. Dovie and I have become *very* close since you left. She's very dear to me." She stood there smirking at me.

'I laughed in her face as she said it because I didn't want to believe it was true.

'"As if Dovie would be interested in you," I yelled at her.

'Judith shook her head. "Oh dear, Gillian, you really are quite the fool."

'She practically spat the words out and then turned on her heel and walked back towards the doorway.

'I leaped to my feet, throwing my purse and its contents into the cardboard box on the bed.

'"What are you talking about? You're crazy!" I carried on yelling after her.

'Then she paused and stood in the doorway looking

at me with her spiteful little smile playing on her lips, like she'd won.

'"I don't know what game you're playing here but you're crazy if you think I'm going to listen to anything you have to say," I said.

'"You think you're so clever, Gillian. You should be very careful in this day and age. It only takes one phone call and you might end up tied to a bed at night. I hear they have quite the range of treatments these days."

'She knew just how to wound me but I carried on trying not to show she'd hit her mark. I staggered towards her, furious now, screaming:

'"Shut your mouth!"

'I was so close that flecks of my spit hit her face. She didn't move an inch. She raised an eyebrow and stared straight at me.

'"I wonder you're not relieved to get out of here. I wouldn't want to stay where I wasn't wanted. Look on the bright side, at least you will be away from that awful lumpy bed. It's so uncomfortable I'm sure I don't know how you've managed. I think Dovie and I will have to buy a new mattress. Dovie's moved on . . . and it's time you left."

'The words felt like a slap and I couldn't move or speak. I stared at her, trying to understand what she'd said. How could she possibly know that? Unless . . .

'I saw another glimmer of her spiteful little smile and then she picked up my apartment keys from the top of the dresser and slid them into her pocket before turning her back to me. I had no idea what was going on or what to do next and so I slammed the bedroom door shut as hard as I could. I could still hear her laughing as she walked away.

'I was determined not to cry but I could feel a hot rage boiling over me. Then I caught a glimpse in the mirror of the little yellow butterfly necklace at my throat so I grabbed the clasp and unhooked it. The photograph I'd always carried in my purse was lying there on the rug and I couldn't stand to look at it: Dovie's face smiling up at me. Her eyes, that lying mouth that kissed me goodnight.

'I felt such a stupid fool. I thought back to all those times Dovie told me off for mocking Judith; she said I was being cruel. Then there was the night out they'd had without me. Things began to add up. Somewhere deep inside, I began to wonder.

'I knew Dovie hated conflict with anyone and I thought this was just like her, to run off and leave me to find out what had really been going on from Judith Schnagl. I couldn't understand why she'd lied about Judith blackmailing us but I guessed she was just biding her time before she told me the truth. I couldn't bear to think of them lying in our bed but they must have been.

'I couldn't think straight. I wanted to run down the hall and pound on Judith's face with my fists. I couldn't keep still: my feet kept spinning me around in a circle; and then I placed my butterfly necklace right there on the dresser with the photograph. I didn't want any mementoes of Dovie . . . and I wanted her to know that I knew everything and I would never forgive her.'

'And then you left?'

Gillian nodded dumbly and picked at the hem of her coat. She caught a glimpse of the small blue velvet bag that I'd placed on top of the box and her face lit up. She sat back down on the couch looking exhausted and tearful.

'Is that . . . ?' She plucked it out of the box and slid her fingers delicately inside the bag. She spread the butterfly necklace on to the palm of her hand and ran her fingers over the wing tips. 'She bought this for me not long after we met. I never took it off until . . . I did.'

'And you were so mad at Dovie that you wrote on the photograph?' I asked.

'What do you mean?'

I pulled out the picture of Dovie with 'LIAR' scrawled across it and passed it to Gillian, who held out the photograph, her face shocked and her eyes searching mine for answers.

'I didn't *do* this.'

Somewhere in the back of my mind I could hear Miss Schnagl's voice saying, 'She got what she deserved.' *She got what she deserved*? I gasped at the thought of it.

'None of this makes sense. What Judith told me, and these letters . . . all these years later. I don't understand. Who did this?' Gillian was clutching the butterfly necklace and trying to piece together what had happened.

I couldn't believe that Dovie had left Gillian for Miss Schnagl. It didn't make any sense that she would do that and then go to the trouble of keeping all the things that reminded her of Gillian.

'I think maybe Miss Schnagl lied to you. I think she did this and she blamed you,' I whispered. As I said the words, I knew it was true. Everything about Miss Schnagl suggested it was she who hated Gillian and not Dovie. That she wrote on the photograph, and blamed Gillian for it.

I knew I would have to tell Gillian the whole truth, and I wasn't looking forward to it.

'She lied to me? No! I wouldn't . . .' Gillian stopped and stared at me.

The full horror of exactly what Miss Schnagl had done to these women hit me, and I couldn't begin to imagine how Gillian was feeling. She stared around the room as if she was searching for someone or something.

'Why would you say that?' she said.

I gulped at a lungful of air and looked straight at her.

'I spoke to her. Judith Schnagl still lives here,' I said.

'Here in this apartment? What the hell is going on?' Gillian scrambled to her feet, looking around her as if she had been trapped.

'No, she lives downstairs. She's not here now. I wouldn't do that to you. It's just that I spoke to her and she didn't say much but she did say . . .' I wasn't sure whether to tell her exactly what Judith said.

'What did she say?' Gillian was angry now.

'She said you got what you deserved.'

'What I deserved? I don't understand.'

'I don't know for sure but she seems such a sad and

lonely woman. She didn't like you. That's all I know really. I'm pretty sure she lied to you and Dovie.'

'It was *all* a lie?'

I nodded, wary, but I thought it was pretty likely that Miss Schnagl wasn't involved with Dovie given how she'd reacted.

'But if it wasn't true then . . .' Gillian looked puzzled and then her face crumpled.

Her mouth opened but no words came out. Her lips parted in a silent scream. She couldn't speak or even take a good clean breath. She collapsed on to the couch. Her head fell backwards and her face grew flushed. Then the tears came, sliding in ones and twos down her cheeks and dripping off the end of her chin, on to her freshly ironed white blouse. They made tiny damp circles where they fell and she didn't wipe them away. Her mouth was stretched open and her teeth clenched. She looked as if she was in terrible pain and I didn't know what to say or do to make it better.

Eventually Gillian's face relaxed and her shoulders seemed to sag from the weight of holding her up, and then the sounds came, awful gasping sobs, and the trickle of tears turned into a flood. She buried her face in her hands and cried until there was nothing left, her heart breaking right there in front of me.

When Gillian eventually stopped crying, she made little blowing noises out of her mouth as if she was trying to calm herself. She wiped at her face with a frayed handkerchief and then she stood up and walked over to the window. She looked out at the view which must have been so familiar but the effort of it seemed almost too much for her to bear, and she ended up hunched over with her face pressed against the glass of the window-pane. She was still mumbling apologies to me as she wept.

'How could I have believed Judith? Oh my God. What have I done? Poor Dovie . . .'

'She wanted you to know that she loved you. That's why she sent you the box. I'm so sorry.'

Gillian's face was red and tear-stained, and I felt awful that I'd been the cause of her finding out. I could feel my own tears welling up.

'No, I'm sorry . . . what must you be thinking?'

She slumped back down on to our old couch and rubbed her hands over her face. Her breathing slowed but she was clearly still agonizing over all the things she had failed to do and say.

'I think part of me took Judith at her word because if Dovie wanted to break up then that was a decision I didn't need to make. I've spent twenty years telling myself I didn't have a choice because Dovie made it for me, but now . . .' Her voice tailed off.

'But she loved you right until the end.'

Gillian nodded and twisted the handkerchief between her fingers.

'I miss her so much. Every day . . .'

*

The box weighed heavily on my arms, and I couldn't see the steps properly to walk, but I managed to get downstairs without falling over. In the hallway, Gillian turned and took one last lingering look around, running a finger over the line of green mailboxes, tracing their outline. Staring at her face in the old hall mirror, the reflection telling her how many years had passed since the last time. When she'd finished remembering, Gillian pulled open the front door – and came face to face with Judith Schnagl.

I felt the air being sucked out of my lungs. I wasn't sure whether to put the box down or carry on standing there with it in my arms. It took Judith Schnagl a few seconds to recognize Gillian but then, when she finally realized who was standing in front of her, I saw the colour drain from her face.

Gillian's face didn't change apart from a slight flush to her cheeks. She stared right at Judith and took a deep gulp of air.

'Hello, Judith. I presume you weren't expecting to see me again?'

Her tone was icy and Judith stood rooted to the spot with her mouth flapping open, unable to move or speak.

'Well, aren't you going to say anything?' Gillian's face was stone-like but her eyes were piercing as she stared Judith down.

'I . . .' Judith stammered, trying to press herself against the wall away from Gillian's terrible stare.

'Why did you do it?' Gillian's voice was calm.

'I didn't do anything. I don't know . . .' Judith tried to squeeze past Gillian but she couldn't get all the way to her apartment door because I was blocking her path and I wasn't about to move.

'Tell the truth. It was *you* who wrote on Dovie's photograph. You *lied* to me and to her, didn't you?' Gillian raised her voice just enough to frighten Judith into speaking. Her mouth flapped open and closed again and she searched around for a means to escape but there was none.

She was trapped by her own lies after all these years. Her face folded into misery.

'You *left* her! You were the one who walked out on her. You didn't deserve Dovie. You're a liar. I would never have done anything to hurt her. You didn't see what she was like when you took off. I looked after her. I was her only true friend . . . I never meant for her to go . . .'

Her voice became strangled with emotion and her mouth hung open. She looked frightened and broken, just a sad, lonely woman cowering in the hallway. I watched Gillian look her up and down. I thought she was going to hit her. Her jaw clenched tight and her hands balled into small fists, but then she thought better of it. She unclenched her fists and sighed. When she spoke it was in a furious cold voice.

'You've ruined so many lives – you're a spiteful, miserable woman. At least I know I was loved, even if I didn't deserve her.'

Judith reared back and then in a slash of fury she hurled her next words like stones. Any pretence at sorrow was gone and her face was a mask of rage and malice.

'You make me sick. You think I didn't hear you all those years ago, always mocking me? Dovie was always kind . . . but you . . . you were mean and cruel. Pulling faces when you thought I couldn't see you. You *left* her. She could have depended on me to be a true friend but oh no . . . she was still moping around after you. *You* drove her away, not me. You have nobody to blame but yourself.'

Gillian gave a pitiful laugh.

'Yes, I left her, because I was stupid and cowardly. Dovie was nothing but kind to you, yet you tried to hurt her by breaking us apart – and I let you do it. I will be sorry for the rest of my life. But for all my faults, she never forgot about me. She forgot about you the minute she left this building, and so will I. It's all you deserve.'

'Oh, is that so? I'm an honest woman, not like you. You were nasty and deceitful. You made Dovie dishonest and she wasn't like that. She was a kind person. I saved her from you and a life of lies. You're so full of yourself . . . but you got what you deserved.' Judith stopped in mid flow as if she'd said too much and she bit down on her bottom lip so hard I could see it turning white.

There was a strange silence as Gillian watched Judith flinch at the mistake she'd made.

'It was *you*!' Gillian took a step backwards and stared

at Judith as if she'd been slapped. Her mouth opened and then closed as she tried to make sense of what Judith had said. 'You reported me . . . *You* did that?'

'I don't know—'

I had no idea what she was talking about, but Gillian suddenly launched herself at Judith and forced her backwards with such strength that Judith's head hit the wall. I dropped the box on to the hall floor and tried to come between them. Gillian was screaming at the top of her voice.

'You broke us up and that wasn't enough for you! You wicked, miserable woman. That's why the police came. I thought it was coincidence, just crazy rumours . . . but it was *you*!'

'You deserved it. Women like you *should* be locked up. Dovie would have been normal without you. She was a good person – or she could've been. You were the one who was wicked and unnatural. If it hadn't been for you, Dovie would have stayed here with me.' Judith was practically spitting the words at Gillian now, red-faced and spluttering her hatred.

I reached out an arm to try and stop Gillian from hurting Judith: she was gripping her so tightly her head was pressed back against the wall at a strange angle. Gillian brushed me off.

'They arrested me because of some rumours – that's what they said. I was back in Millersburg and it was months and months later. I had no reason to think it was deliberate. The police questioned me for hours on end.

Hours and hours . . .' Gillian's knuckles were turning white with the pressure of holding Judith against the wall.

Judith was wriggling to get away from Gillian but she kept pushing, her face staring upwards, gripping Judith tighter and tighter; and then, perhaps realizing she was going too far, she released her. She shoved Judith away from her, and bent over with her hands on her knees, panting and gasping.

'Paul rescued me. He stepped in and told them we were getting married . . .' She paused and shook her head sadly. '. . . and we did.' Her voice trailed away and for a moment there was just the sound of her jagged little breaths until Judith's voice cut through the silence.

'Dovie left me all alone and she went off to Paris. It was *your* fault she left. You filled her head with all this nonsense about love. She didn't want me to be her friend. You took her away from me.'

Gillian straightened up and turned to me; she shook her head. Judith was still rearranging the clothing that had got twisted and trying to compose herself, but I could see her hands shaking and her eyes darting around trying to find a way out. Gillian looked Judith straight in the eye.

'Yes, I mocked you and I wasn't always nice but what you did . . . I would never have tried to hurt you like that. I would never have told such spiteful lies about you. D'you have any idea what would have happened to me if they had believed you? If Paul hadn't stepped in? Do you know what you did? You call me unnatural . . . you stupid woman. Dovie *loved* me ... she *loved* me and I loved her. That's all it was.'

She took a deep shuddering breath and started to move towards the front door.

'I pity you, Judith. You're so full of hate and jealousy. You ruined everything and for what? You're all alone.'

The words landed like blows on Judith. She was silent now, strangely still, and Gillian's rage was spent.

Gillian swept past her without another word, and I scurried after her as fast as I could, given the weight of the box. Judith stared after Gillian, her mouth still hanging open with the shock of it all. I scowled at her on my way out of the door and she stared at the floor. She couldn't even look at me.

The dirty yellow Pontiac was parked at the kerb; a young guy who was maybe eighteen or nineteen years old leaped out to open the trunk and rescue the box from my arms. He was taller than I was and wearing a Lennon tee and paint-streaked jeans with sneakers. He had dark hair that was a little wild and curly, with deep brown eyes. He took the box and laid it carefully in the trunk before flashing me a smile.

'Hey.'

I smiled back at him.

'Hey.'

We stood there on the sidewalk in the spitting rain smiling at each other until Gillian introduced us. Then it was time for goodbyes and for them to hit the road.

Gillian turned and put her arms around me. She held me close for a few seconds and murmured:

'Thank you, Ava. You'll never know how grateful I am. You've given me back Dovie after all these years. I can't thank you enough for that. I hope everything works out for your family . . . I just . . . I wish I could have been with her at the end . . . There's so much I needed to say . . .'

She let go without finishing her sentence and her eyes were moist with tears. She mouthed 'Thank you' at me and then she got into the passenger seat, and Joel walked around to the driver's side. He hesitated for a moment and nodded at me, his mouth pulling back into a shy grin.

'See you around then.'

I nodded back at him and he got into the car, leaving me standing there on the sidewalk.

I waved them off, and I must have stood there for a solid ten minutes watching that car disappear into the distance, until there were only fumes left in the air.

30

Paris, February 1975

I can't sleep again. Another dawn and I'm standing at the apartment window watching the light change from inky black to damp grey, warming the palms of my hands on a cup of hot tea. I ache to see the sun again; the days of winter have been hard and cold. I wonder if I will live to see the spring flowers and I think of how strange life is when you are running out of time. Everything is the last time.

I've made all the arrangements so as not to be a bother to anyone. I would hate for my friends to feel burdened by my carelessness so it's all laid out in small blue envelopes. The funeral arrangements, the dividing up of my possessions, the financial arrangements, my love and final words. I've already posted a special word for Franny . . . I don't want her to have to worry about anything. There is just one more thing to make sure of.

I shiver slightly and pull my thick blanket around my shoulders. The fire is burning in the grate but I can't get warm. I sip at my tea and feel a cough rising and then another one. I'm so tired now and yet most of the time I feel strangely content as if I am leaving a job well done.

Fat raindrops land on the glass of my window and I look out at the empty window boxes of the street I've lived in for the past twenty years. The familiar sights of cafés and shops where I am known; the community I feel part of. It has been my home for a long time now but somewhere deep inside I always thought I would see New York again. I dream about it and how it was back then. Some nights I wake from frantic dreams of that green-eyed girl begging me not to leave her behind. Her voice echoing down the years, still pleading with me. On other nights I dream that I'm back in our old apartment with Gillian. We are dancing together. When I wake up, I can smell her perfume and the scent of her hair; I want to stay there in my dreams of Gillian . . . but I can't. It's gone and soon this little life will be over. Even to think about it doesn't seem quite real. I guess we are all the same. Vain enough to be unable to imagine a world without ourselves as the star of the show.

On the dining table I've put all the things I want to send to Gillian in the box. The photograph albums, the whiskey tumbler, the butterfly necklace and her beautiful scarf that I spoiled. I've tried to write a letter to say everything that has been in my heart for all this time but so far, I have failed. The remnants of my attempts to tell her how I feel lie scattered next to the box. I can't seem to find the words and yet I know that I have to do it before it's too late.

I wonder where she is, and what kind of a life she's had without me.

From the window I can see the café across the street blink into life. The warm yellow lights twinkling in the gloom as the pavement tables are unstacked and the chairs are wiped down for another day. If I can manage it, I will go out for my morning coffee. The fresh air may help to revive me and I can try one more time to write this letter.

I struggle to get dressed. Pulling on a thick sweater and a wool skirt, I have to keep sitting down because the effort makes me cough and the coughing makes me weary. I lean back in the chair and close my eyes for a second. Sorting through the things that remind me of Gillian has brought her back to life so vividly that I feel she's right here with me. As if I could reach out and touch her skin or feel her warm breath on my face. It's a horrible thing to have made such a mistake. I only hope it's not too late to tell her.

I thought there would be more time to reach out to her. One day . . . I thought. One day I will pick up a pen, or find her number and call her. Birthdays came and went. Anniversaries we used to celebrate. But as the years went by, I became strangely shy. The more time passed the more I felt too shy to bother her. We parted on such awful terms and yet I never stopped hoping.

My throat tightens and I feel a crushing despair rising up in my chest. It doesn't do to dwell on these things but when there is no future to plan for what else is there to do but dwell on what you've made of your time here?

I can hear the sounds of the first customers being greeted in the café. Neighbours wishing each other

'*Bonjour*' as they go on their way. I get my breath back and haul myself to my feet, using the edge of the table to steady myself. I must write the letter today. Once I do that I can find out where Gillian is and I've asked Christine to make sure that she gets these things, if I can't manage that myself.

I pull on my winter coat and boots and the coughing starts again, a wheezing deep cough that feels like the sands of an hourglass running out. I imagine my life that way but I don't know how much sand is left and I can't bear to think about it emptied out.

I'm happy to have a street-level apartment now for I cannot climb stairs. I remember running up our stairs in New York two at a time. I can't begin to imagine how that would feel now . . . to be able to do that, to be that young and strong.

The café is quiet and I love this time of day. The owner, Madame Arquette, is a petite bird-like woman who wears dresses with roses on them every day. She has silver-grey hair and she never smiles. She is pleasant but a most serious person. I like Madame Arquette but I often wonder how she has managed a life with so little smiling and yet she doesn't seem unhappy at all.

She greets me with a wave and a hearty '*Bonjour, madame. Un petit café?*' It's my usual order and I slide into a chair at my usual table. The coffee machine makes a hissing sound and then Madame Arquette appears by my side, carrying a small white cup and saucer.

I take my writing paper out of my purse and tap the end of my pen on the table in a rhythmic drumming. There aren't the right words for this moment and yet I don't have other moments to spare.

The air is fresh and chilly but I love to sit outside and watch people go past. This is the Paris that I've loved for twenty years. The small interactions; the sights that still surprise me even now. Fancy dogs being walked, enormous bouquets being delivered, white boxes of pâtisserie and baskets of fresh crusty loaves poking out of shopping bags. It still thrills me to be here.

I have to stop distracting myself and settle down to write but the past few months I have been unable to stop myself staring at these small things, as if I was trying to imprint them on my mind. I want to take each memory and run it through my fingers, hold it up to the light and appreciate the twists and turns, the gentle folds and dazzling colours. I sweep my pen across the page with a grand gesture:

Dear Gillian

I wonder if that's too formal, yet 'Darling Gillian' sounds pretentious and I don't feel that I have the right after all this time.

This letter is long overdue but that doesn't mean I haven't felt these words deeply every single day since we parted. You always said I was a dreamer and I dreamed my way to Paris but without you. I've made a happy life here over the years but deep inside I always thought we would be here together one day. I imagined calling you out of the blue and us putting the past behind us and picking up where we left off, back when we were so happy together.

We were happy, Gilly; at least I was. Oh yes, of course I was younger and stupid with love and dreams. I made you crazy because you were so careful and precise and wonderful. I'm so sorry that I broke us. It was all my fault, Gilly.

'I'm sorry' doesn't really do it justice. I don't have any time left. I can't be too proud, nor can I waste time imagining a future where you just appear right next to me as I sit in this pavement café sipping coffee and smelling warm, freshly baked croissants. Paris is everything we dreamed it would be, except for one thing: I don't have you.

I have made good friends and occasional lovers. I have twisted in warm sheets with strangers but my heart has always belonged to you. It's too late for regrets. I can't sacrifice whatever time I might have left to chew over what might have been and yet I cannot leave this world without telling you that I love you now as I loved you then. I never stopped loving you, not for a minute.

You were my reason for everything: all of my happiness and all of my pain. Nothing has mattered except the love I felt and feel for you. I'm sorry that it has taken me so long to write this letter and I pray there is enough time for you to receive it. I dream of you replying or even (forgive me for even now I can't stop indulging myself with that damn dreaming that drove you nuts) seeing you in person.

I had not thought of ever being able to hold you again in this life but, as I write this letter, I know that I have never stopped hoping for it. Should this letter find its way to you across the ocean I hope you will remember me with love and fondness. I couldn't bear to think that you still hated me after all this time. I wish I could

The pain is sharp and sudden. The pen drops on to the table and then rolls to the floor. I take one deep juddering breath and I know it will be the last one. As I fall to the floor, unable to move or cry out, a gust of wind picks up the pages of my letter and carries them away along the cobbled stones of the street.

On and on until the pages are scattered like leaves.

Epilogue

January feels fresh and clean like a blank page. It's a new year and my mom is coming home for good today. She's getting better all the time, but it's still early days.

On my walk home, I look up as thick snowflakes drift gently down from the black sky. My boots crack the icy ridges of the snow-bones on the sidewalk. It's already dark and the whole world seems to be hidden behind glass. Orange lights glow fiercely in the inky blue.

In my pocket is a thick envelope: another letter from Gillian. She writes to me every week, full of her news and eager for mine. Meeting her has made me think a lot about forgiveness and leaving things too late. I'll be seventeen this year and I hope there's still plenty of time to make mistakes and put them right.

The lights are all on in our apartment, and the warmth stings my cheeks as I clamber up the stairs two at a time. As I open our apartment door, I can hear music playing and I smile.

My mom is dancing, her arms thrown up in the air and her body twirling around and around. Her eyes are closed and she is singing to herself. I notice she has stuck the faded Coney Island poster on the living-room wall above the record player. The sea shines turquoise in the light.

Out on the street, a wild-haired boy in an old Lennon tee is muffled up against the cold. He is staring up at the lights of our building.

Inside, my mom opens her pale green eyes and sees me standing in the doorway. She smiles and reaches out her hand.

'Come dance with me,' she says. And I do.

Acknowledgements

I love acknowledgements. They are the Oscar speeches of authors, so here goes.

I'd like to thank the academy – in this case Faber Academy. My tutor Lee Weatherly for all her help and support during the early beginnings of this book, and my writing group, especially Ann Roberts, for the careful feedback. It was entirely due to the Faber Academy anthology that I found my incredible agent, Nelle Andrew.

There aren't enough acknowledgement pages in the world to describe the combination of absolute support and tough love that Nelle brings to my life on a daily basis. You are the best of the best. I am so lucky to have you as an agent. Thank you for everything!

Thank you to my wonderful team at Penguin Michael Joseph. To Lauren Wakefield for designing the gorgeous cover, Madeleine Woodfield for all her support and editorial work, Sophie Shaw and Olivia Thomas for their brilliant marketing and publicity work, and Nick Lowndes for making sure it got to print. Thank you all for giving your best to my work. I'm beyond grateful to each one of you.

What can I say about my brilliant editor, Clio Cornish? From our first telephone conversation I knew that you had the most incredible vision for this story. I have

LOVED editing with you and you have made it such a creative and joyful process. I raise a Negroni to you, Clio. You are Queen of the Edit.

Thanks also to my wonderful copy editor, Richenda, who has saved me from myself on multiple occasions. I am so grateful for your careful work.

Thanks to everyone I know who has supported me in this crazy quest to get published. You have kept me going.

People have shown me such enormous kindness in the wider writing community. Huge thanks to Dolly Alderton and Louise Hare for offering to be my first readers. Thank you both so much. It means such a lot to me and I won't forget your kindness.

My life has been hugely enriched by my Tweethearts. A community of smart and kind people who make me laugh and give me support every day. I told you I would put you in the acknowledgements and here you are. Thanks, everyone!

Thanks to Paul Burston, who pointed me in the direction of *Odd Girls and Twilight Lovers: A History of Lesbian Life in 20th-Century America* by Lilian Faderman, which was such a wonderful resource, and Professor Ian Hamerton for his knowledge of jazz.

Thanks to Bruce Springsteen, whom I like to think was supporting me at a distance (even though he doesn't know who I am). If his tour conflicts with my book launch in 2022 then make your own arrangements, guys, because I'll be singing 'Thunder Road' in a pit somewhere.

A special word also for gin manufacturers, who keep the world turning. I appreciate you greatly.

Thanks to my two cats, who did nothing except lie on my keyboard and demand food at awkward times.

When I was a kid growing up in a council house, I occasionally committed the awful crime of appearing to want more than we had. My family would often say to me, 'Who do you think you are?' and I wouldn't know what to say because I didn't understand why it was wrong to want more.

Anyway, turns out this is who I thought I was ... I just didn't know it then. It's OK to want things that other people don't understand.

This book is obviously a work of fiction and the characters are not based on real people, but behind the awful politics throughout history there are thousands of small stories of women locked away and tortured for being themselves, of lives ruined and of shame too hard to bear. This book is for them.

And last but not least, thanks to my husband, Sean, who always believed I could do this even when I wondered if I was crazy to try. If I should fall behind, wait for me. I love you.

If you have bought this book, or picked it up in a library, I want you to know that you have made my dreams come true so THANK YOU.

Julie x

Read on for an extract of
73 DOVE STREET

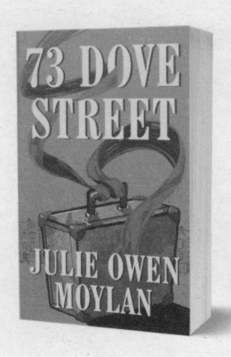

COMING SUMMER 2023

NURTURING WRITERS SINCE 1935

I

London, October 1958

Something was burning. A tall plume of black smoke curling high up into the air, accompanied by the crackling of bright orange flames.

Edie blinked twice, slowing her pace before finally coming to a halt next to a rusty garden gate. The fizz of sparks climbed upwards, and just to be sure she blinked again – but there it was . . .

Someone had set a bonfire right in the middle of the pavement.

It was one of those London streets that had become a canvas of tatty boarding houses: windows filled with crooked pieces of cardboard saying 'Room to Let'. The houses all looked the same: bay-fronted with scruffy front gardens filled with dustbins, and children loitering on doorsteps with their runny noses and scraped knees. In one front garden sat an abandoned pram still bearing the thick, dark traces of the coal it had recently carried, while a surly cat leapt from an open dustbin where it had been ferreting for scraps.

Up ahead, the flames crawled high into the air and the heavy black smoke turned to grey as it drifted over the upper part of the street, which was quite empty now, apart from a barefoot child playing hopscotch, the chalky-white squares of the game scratched over the grey stones of the pavement.

Edie watched as the girl tried to turn without putting her foot down. The sole was caked in grimy black dirt, and Edie couldn't help but stare. The child stuck out her defiant arms, wobbling violently but forcing herself to hop back to safety. Suddenly aware she had an audience, her head jerked upwards. Pushing her wild tangled hair out of her eyes, she glared at Edie, sticking her little pink tongue out.

'What *you* looking at?' the girl cried and Edie hurried on, embarrassed by her own curiosity.

She began to walk towards the strange bonfire up ahead of her, a furious blister forming on the back of her left heel. It was unseasonably warm for October and she felt hot and tired. A trickle of sweat ran down the channel between her breasts. In her arms, she clutched a small cardboard suitcase to her chest as the handles had broken. The suitcase was bound up with string because the lock didn't work either – a neat little knot holding it all together. An old leather handbag nestled softly in the crook of her elbow.

Edie was gripping a crumpled scrap of paper between her fingers; the skin around her fingernails was raw and broken where she'd been gnawing at them. From time to time she checked it anxiously, although she knew the words off by heart now: '73 Dove Street'.

Pressing on, she glanced nervously behind, but there was nobody following her. The smoke began to claw at her eyes and Edie didn't really want to go any further, but she couldn't go back either. It was too late.

'You've made your bed, Edie Budd . . .' she muttered to herself while mentally checking off the numbers of the houses one by one. There was number 65, with its sooty bushes either side of a bright green front door. The fire was getting closer now, and the smoke surrounded her. A few more steps, and Edie was standing outside number 69: the front garden a graveyard of wheels, most of them buckled, surrounded by the remains of broken prams and bicycles. A child's red scooter had been abandoned on the ground. She checked the piece of paper one last time, counting out loud – it must be . . . *that one*. Her mouth fell open as she gazed at the fierce blaze right there on the pavement outside her destination. Number 73, Dove Street.

The house was a dirty red brick with a mud-brown front door, a black iron gate creaking back and forth on its squeaky hinges every time the wind blew. The front garden contained only weeds and a path leading to a grey metal dustbin, its lid fastened by means of a house brick carefully placed on top of it. The surly cat strutted past, with its questioning tail, and jumped over the low wall that separated number 73 from the neighbouring house. Next to the dustbin was a dirty white step leading up to the mud-brown front door with a brass knocker in the shape of a lion's head. The brass lion was roaring and seemed to indicate that casual visitors should not bother knocking.

Edie hesitated, trying desperately to find some welcoming feature about the house, then turned back to the fierce blaze on the pavement in front of her. Underneath the dense smoke and leaping orange flames was a small mattress – which had seen better days even before someone had seen fit to set it on fire. On top of the single mattress lay the smouldering remains of a man's suit in navy blue, along with a funeral pyre of assorted belongings.

Vinyl records melted into the mattress, black and tarry. To the side of the flaming mattress was a blackened pan; clearly, blazing lard had been thrown over both these belongings and the bodily fluids of whoever had last laid down on that mattress.

Edie was about to turn around and walk away from number 73 when suddenly a stout middle-aged woman wearing a furious expression on her face appeared at the front door and shouted, 'If you've come about the room, best get inside . . .'

The two women eyed each other cautiously. After a long few seconds, Edie gulped down an anxious breath and slowly picked her way past the crackling whip of sparks in the air and a lone sock, whose mate was lost in the fire.

Five Years Earlier

The first time Edie laid eyes on Frank Budd, she was on the other side of the city: dancing on a table with a sailor in the Rivoli Ballroom. She hadn't intended to dance in front of everybody, but the music had carried her all the way up there, every drumbeat and trumpet blast giving her feet an energy they didn't normally possess. Her arms couldn't stop moving, and when a passing sailor grabbed hold of her, twisting her under his arm and back again, Edie could only laugh and throw her body into it. At some point the crowd parted a little as people watched them jive, then the sailor jumped up on a table to carry on dancing. For a moment, Edie stood there all alone in the middle of the dance floor being cheered on by strangers, not knowing quite what to do until two pairs of strong arms hoisted her up, and suddenly there she was: swinging her arms in time with the music and tapping her feet, while the sailor spun her around and around until she was dizzy.

Eventually the music stopped and everyone went wild, clapping and cheering. Another sailor put his arms around her waist and picked her up, showing her off to the crowd for their applause before placing her delicately back on to the dance floor. Edie laughed and turned her head to look for her friends but she couldn't see them. The thirsty sailors wandered off to the bar to fetch more drinks and she was left alone, her heart still racing and a sheen of sweat cooling on her forehead and arms.

There he was, standing in front of her, watching everything with those pale blue eyes. They were smiling, mischievous eyes and he nodded, staging a funny little bow to her.

'Quite the little dancer, aren't ya?' he said with a soft voice. It didn't sound entirely like a compliment.

'I like that song, that's all.'

He made her feel she had failed some kind of a test that she hadn't known she was sitting. Strangely, she found that she wanted to pass it. This handsome stranger with the pale blue eyes was watching her, and, unlike the other boys, he hadn't asked if he could get a dance, or if she'd like a gin and lime. He was older than the rest and there wasn't that feeling of desperation which sometimes poured off them, or that sense of it all being a game to see if they could get her to go outside for some 'fresh air', where they would demand kisses as the price to light her cigarette, or even to let her go back inside the dance hall again.

Frank just leaned back against the wall and watched her. Edie giggled nervously and then when he didn't join in the laughter; she stopped.

'I can't work you out,' she said.

'Ahh, you're not alone there. I've been trying to get to the bottom of me for years. If you get there before me, I'll be quite upset.' His eyes glinted and he grinned at her.

Edie laughed with him this time, moving closer to where he was standing. It was hot inside the dance hall and she could smell soap and sweat, cigarettes and the sour tang of Brylcreem on his hair. From the corner of her eye, she could see other girls eyeing him up but he carried on smiling softly at her.

'You're a funny one . . .' She moved closer, feeling as if he was pulling her to him.

'What's your name?' he asked.

'Edie.'

'Pretty name.'

'What's yours?'

'Frank.'

Edie stared up at him, her lips curling into a smile. Somewhere deep inside, part of her was already attaching her name to his: *Edie and Frank* . . . as if they belonged together.

'I'll walk you home, if you like?' He took her arm gently and she let him lead her towards the entrance. Edie hadn't even wanted to go home before that moment but once she felt his fingers pressing against the warm skin of her forearm, she didn't want to stay without him either.

As they reached the door Frank paused next to a

lanky dark-haired man who had trapped a small red-haired woman against the wall and seemed to be trying his best to persuade her to go outside with him. Frank tapped him on the shoulder,

'Pete, I'm off. Catch you tomorrow.'

Reluctantly, the man turned his attention away from the redhead, turning to look Edie up and down, before grinning at his friend. 'Don't do anything I wouldn't do . . .' Pete laughed at his own joke but Frank was already walking away, with Edie following behind him.

The streets were scattered with people coming and going from the dance hall. As they walked along, car headlights lit up couples tucked in doorways or alleyways, their mouths open and their hands inside each other's clothing. Frank made no attempt to pull Edie into one of the dark openings and do likewise with her. They just walked in silence; the only sound was the click-clack of her heels hitting the paving stones. She wasn't usually stuck for words, but for some reason this man made her want to choose what she said carefully.

'I haven't seen you there before,' she said eventually.

'I haven't seen *you* there before,' he said and took hold of her hand.

His fingers wrapped around hers, feeling warm and solid, as if he was something that she could hold on to. Edie liked the feeling of him touching her and to her surprise thought she wouldn't mind if he did pull her into one of those dark doorways to kiss her.

The pub on the corner was kicking out, and Edie could see her neighbours and her Uncle Bert wandering slowly back to their houses, shouting goodnights and sharing the last moment of the joke that had no doubt kept them chuckling for much of the evening. As their laughter faded away into the night air, Frank's pace slowed, as if he had no wish to get caught up in their chatter. On either side of the street, the little houses leaned one against the other, as if they'd all fall over if someone moved the pub on the corner. As they approached Edie's front door, the street was quiet again, with only the sounds of muffled arguments going on inside the little houses as drunken husbands were greeted by their wives.

Edie could hear the sound of her own breathing as she waited for Frank to kiss her goodnight. Instead, he just kissed the hand he had been holding, pressing the back of it to his lips. Soft, warm lips they were too. She gazed up at him, wanting to fall into those smiling blue eyes, but finding something steely and unrelenting about them. He wasn't smiling now. She snatched her hand away from his lips and stood there pouting with her chin jutting forward.

'Goodnight then. Thanks for walking me home.' She put her hand to the letterbox, pulling out the piece of red wool they kept the front-door key on. The key rattled up against the wood of the door until it was in her hand and she slotted it into the lock.

'I'll pick you up next Friday at seven o'clock,' he said. Edie turned to face him, puzzled now and a little annoyed. She didn't like the game he was playing, keeping her off balance and wanting her never to be sure of him.

'Oh, is that right? I think I'm washing my hair that night.' Edie regained her composure and stood there, staring him down. She wouldn't be taken for a fool.

'If you like . . . I'll be here though – seven o'clock.' And with that he started to walk away, whistling softly under his breath.

'Hang on a minute there. I haven't said I'll go out with you.'

'Then you won't answer the door when I call, will ya?' he shouted over his shoulder and raised his hand to wave as he walked away. Edie watched him go; the memory of his mouth still tracing the skin on her hand.

He just wanted a decent book to read ...

Not too much to ask, is it? It was in 1935 when Allen Lane, Managing Director of Bodley Head Publishers, stood on a platform at Exeter railway station looking for something good to read on his journey back to London. His choice was limited to popular magazines and poor-quality paperbacks – the same choice faced every day by the vast majority of readers, few of whom could afford hardbacks. Lane's disappointment and subsequent anger at the range of books generally available led him to found a company – and change the world.

'We believed in the existence in this country of a vast reading public for intelligent books at a low price, and staked everything on it'
Sir Allen Lane, 1902–1970, founder of Penguin Books

The quality paperback had arrived – and not just in bookshops. Lane was adamant that his Penguins should appear in chain stores and tobacconists, and should cost no more than a packet of cigarettes.

Reading habits (and cigarette prices) have changed since 1935, but Penguin still believes in publishing the best books for everybody to enjoy. We still believe that good design costs no more than bad design, and we still believe that quality books published passionately and responsibly make the world a better place.

So wherever you see the little bird – whether it's on a piece of prize-winning literary fiction or a celebrity autobiography, political tour de force or historical masterpiece, a serial-killer thriller, reference book, world classic or a piece of pure escapism – you can bet that it represents the very best that the genre has to offer.

Whatever you like to read – trust Penguin.